LORD ASPER HAD BEEN FORCED TO FLEE HIS ENEMIES!

Once again Safar looked at the small map of the world. And once again he traced the lines showing Asper's travels. His flight from Esmir to Hadin and back. Beneath the map was a tiny sketch of the island where Asper ended his days.

The island's name, scrawled in red ink, was Syrapis.

Musing, Safar said the name aloud—"Syrapis." Then, "I wonder what Asper sought there?"

Suddenly his fingers itched with a powerful desire to touch the drawing of the island—a need as strong as a thirsty man's obsession for water. His fingertips touched the paper and a surge of energy flowed up his arm. There was a boom! of distant thunder and a sharp crack! of lightning quite near.

Suddenly all was blackness and his hair rose up on prickling roots . . .

Other Cosmos Books

WOLVES OF THE GODS

THE
TIMURAS TRILOGY
BOOK 2

by

Allan Cole

COSMOS BOOKS

WOLVES OF THE GODS
January 2008

Published by

Dorchester Publishing Co., Inc.
200 Madison Avenue
New York, NY 10016

in collaboration with Wildside Press, LLC

Typeset by Swordsmith Productions

ISBN-10: 0-8439-5915-0
ISBN-13: 978-0-8439-5915-4

One moment in annihilation's waste,
One moment, of the well of life to taste—
The stars are setting and the caravan
Starts for the dawn of nothing—oh, make haste!

The Rubaiyat of Omar Khayyam
EDWARD FITZGERALD TRANSLATION

WOLVES OF THE GODS
THE
TIMURAS TRILOGY
BOOK 2

Part One
Wizard In Exile

1

TO DREAM OF WOLVES

Up, up in the mountains.

Up where Winter reigns eternal and her warriors bully earth and sky.

Then higher still. Climb to the reaches where even eagles are wary. Where the winds cut sharp, paring old snowfields of their surface to get at the black rock below. Where moody skies brood over a stark domain.

Yes, up. Up to the seven mountain peaks that make the Bride and Six Maids. And higher . . . still higher . . . to the highest point of all—the Bride's snowy crown where the High Caravans climb to meet clear horizons.

Where the Demon Moon waits, filling the northern heavens with its bloody shimmer.

It was at the cusp of a new day; the sun rising against the Demon Moon's assault, the True Moon giving up the fight and fading into nothingness. It was spring struggling with late winter. A time of desperation. A time of hunger.

Just below the Bride's crown a patch of green glowed in defiance of all that misery. The green was a trick of nature, a meadow blossoming from a bowl of granite and ice. The winds sheered off the bowl's peculiar formation making a small, warm safe harbor for life.

But safe is in the eye of the beholder. Safe is the false sanctuary of innocent imagination.

And in that time, the time that came to be known as the Age of the Wolf, safe was not to be trusted.

Three forces converged on that meadow.
And only one was innocent.

The wolf pack took him while he slept.

He was only a boy, a goat herder too young to be alone in the mountains. He'd spent a sleepless night huddled over a small fire, fearful of every sound and shadow. Exhausted, he fell asleep at first light and now he was helpless in his little rock shelter, oblivious to the hungry gray shapes ghosting across the meadow and the panicked bleating of his goats.

Then he jolted awake, sudden dread a cold knife in his bowels.

The pack leader hurtled forward—eyes burning, jaws reaching for his throat.

The boy screamed and threw up his hands.

But the ravaging shock never came and he suddenly found himself sitting bolt upright in his bedroll, striking at nothingness.

He gaped at the idyllic scene before him—the meadow glistening with dew under the early morning sun, his goats munching peacefully on tender shoots.

There wasn't a wolf in sight.

The boy laughed in huge relief. "It was only a dream!" he chortled. "What a stupid you are, Tio."

But speaking the words aloud did not entirely still Tio's thundering heart. Nor did it lessen his sense of dread. He stared about, searching for the smallest sign of danger. Finally his eyes lifted to the heights surrounding the small meadow. All he could see was icy rock glittering beneath cheery blue skies.

The boy laughed again and this time the laughter rang true. "You see, Tio," he said, seizing comfort from the sound of his own voice. "There's nothing to harm you. No wolves. No bears. No lions. Don't be such a child!"

Tio and his older brother, Renor—a big strapping lad who was almost a man and therefore, Tio believed, feared nothing—had brought the goats up from Kyrania a few days before. Then one of the animals had been badly injured and Renor had left the herd with Tio while he hurried down the mountainside for help with the goat strapped to his back.

"You only have to spend the one night alone," Renor had reassured him. "I'll be back by morning. You won't be afraid, will you?"

Tio's pride had been wounded by the question. "Don't be stupid. Of course I won't," he'd said. "What! Do you think I'm still a child?"

Tio's boldness had departed with his brother. Soon he was agonizing over the slightest unfamiliar stir. Then at dusk he'd had the sudden feeling he was being watched. His imagination had conjured all sorts of monsters intent on making a meal of a lonely boy. He knew this was foolish. Kyranian boys had been guiding the herds up into the Gods' Divide for centuries. The only harm any had ever suffered was from a bad fall and this had occured so rarely it wasn't worth thinking about. As for voracious animals—there weren't any. At least none who lusted for human flesh. So there was nothing at all to fear.

Tio had repeated these things to himself many times during the night, as if chanting a prayer in the warm company of his friends and family in the little temple by the holy lake of Felakia. It did no good. If anything, the dreadful feeling of being watched only intensified. Now, with the sun climbing above the peaks and flooding the meadow with light, Tio's boldness returned.

"Such a child," he said again, shaking his head and making his voice low in imitation of his brother's manly tones. "Didn't I say there was nothing to be afraid of? What did you think, stupid one? That the demons would come and get you?" He snorted. "As if Lord Timura would allow such a thing! Why, if a demon ever showed his ugly face in Kyrania, Lord Timura would snap his fingers and turn his nose into a . . . a . . . a turnip! Yes, that's what he'd do. Make his nose look like a turnip!"

He giggled, imagining the poor demon's plight. He held his own nose, making stuffed sinus noises: "Snark! Snark!" More giggling followed. "The demon couldn't even breathe! Snark! Snark!"

Then he had a sudden thought and his laughter broke off. Tio remembered his dream hadn't been about demons, but wolves. He glanced nervously about the meadow again, smiling when he saw it was peaceful as ever.

"Wolves don't eat people," he reassured himself. "Just goats. Sick goats. Or little goats. But never people." He picked up the thick cudgel by his side and shook it in his most threatening manner. "Wolves are afraid of this!" he said bravely. "Everybody says so."

Satisfied, he munched a little bread and cheese then settled back on his bedroll to await his brother's return—the stout cudgel gripped in his small fists.

A few moments later exhaustion took him once again. He fell into a deep sleep and the stick fell from his hands and rolled onto the grass.

Graymuzzle was anxious for her cubs. Her teats were aching and swollen with milk and she knew her pups would be whining for her in their cold den. Graymuzzle's hollow belly rumbled and it wasn't only in sympathy for her young. Weeks had passed since the pack had made a decent kill.

It had been a hard winter, the hardest and longest in Graymuzzle's memory. First disease and then fierce storms had wiped out the herds in her old hunting grounds. The wolf pack, with Graymuzzle leading them, had ranged for miles searching for food. They'd been reduced to digging deep into the snow to claw up maggoty roots. When winter had finally ended, spring brought scant relief. The weather remained treacherous, going from calm to storm with no warning. Vegetation was sparse and there was little meat on the bones of the few deer and goats they'd found.

Graymuzzle used all her skills, won over twelve hunting seasons, to feed her pack. She took them high into the mountains, looking for meadows with sweet grass and fat herds. None of her old tricks worked and by the time her cubs were born the pack had been reduced to six wolves so scrawny their faces seemed to consist entirely of muzzles and teeth. The rest had died on the trail—her mate of many years among them. Still, she'd managed to eat enough to make milk for her cubs. Her packmates had seen to that, checking their own hunger to share their food with her; thus assuring the pack's future.

They crouched in the heights above the meadow, bellies grumbling at the promised feast below. The wolves had spent most of the night in their hiding place, whining eagerly whenever they'd heard a goat bleat. To their surprise, however, each time they'd risen to move in for the kill Graymuzzle had leaped to block them. Snapping and nipping at their heels until they obeyed her and sank down onto the cold ground again.

Graymuzzle sensed a wrongness. She didn't know what it was—there was no smellsign in the air; no sound that couldn't be traced to an innocent source. Still, she felt as if something was watching. Not her. Not the pack. But the boy and the goats in the meadow below. Whenever she moved forward her hackles rose of their own accord in warning. Graymuzzle was an old wolf, a careful wolf, who had learned to trust her deepest instincts. So she waited and watched.

Now dawn was breaking. The morning was bright, the air without the slightest taint of strangeness. Whatever it was that had troubled her was gone. She could see the goats grazing in the meadow and the sleeping figure of the boy sprawled behind the low stone walls of the windbreak. There was nothing to fear. No reason to hesitate.

She yawned. It was a signal to the others and when she came to her feet they were waiting.

Graymuzzle slipped out of the hiding place and trotted down the rocky path—her packmates at her heels.

A moment later she felt the soft wet meadow grass under her pads. Heard the wind sing a hunter's song as she quickened her stride, smelled the strong goat smell as she rushed her first bleating victim.

Then lighting cracked—bursting from the ground in front of her, exploding rock and turf in every direction.

And all she'd feared during the long night of hunger howled out of nothingness to confront her.

Tio could hear the goats bleating. He was awake, but he couldn't open his eyes. He tried to move, but a heavy weight crushed down on him so hard he could barely breathe. He heard growling and bleats of pain.

You must get up, he thought. The wolves are coming, Tio! You must get your stick and drive them off. Get up, Tio! Get up! Don't be such a child! What will Renor think?

He forced his eyes open.

A nightmare shape rushed at him. All burning red eyes and slavering jaws.

Long fangs stretched out to take him.

Tio threw up his hands and screamed.

2

UNDER THE DEMON MOON

The wolf leaped for him and Safar shouted, scrabbling for his dagger.

He rolled out of bed, landing in a crouch; bare toes digging into the rough floor for balance, dagger coming up to strike.

He blinked out of sleep, then gaped about in amazement. He was standing in an empty room—his room! There was no wolf, there was no threat of any kind. Instead he was presented with the most peaceful of scenes—the morning sun streaming through the bedroom window, spilling across his writing desk where the cat was sprawled across his papers basking in the warmth. The window was open and he could hear birds singing and smell the fresh breeze coming off the lake.

Safar turned away from the strong light, dagger hand sagging in relief. He came out of the crouch and suddenly found himself shivering in his thin nightshirt.

Nothing but a damned dream, he thought. Safar padded over to his desk, set the dagger down and poured himself a goblet of brandy. He drank it off, shuddered at the sudden heat rising from his belly and started to pour another. The cat stared at him, an accusing look in her eyes. She was only irritated for being disturbed but the look make Safar feel guilty for entirely different reasons.

He glanced at the brandy jug and made a face, thinking,

you've certainly been doing a little too much of that of late, my friend. But the nightmare had been so realistic he only felt a little guilty when he gave in and poured himself "just a bit more" to calm his racing heart. Safar had dreamed he was a small boy, alone on the mountain, with a wolf pack closing in. He'd awakened just as they were attacking—the pack leader rising on its hind feet and its front legs turning into demon arms, reaching for him with razor-sharp talons.

At the last moment, as he hovered between dream and consciousness, the wolf's mask transformed into a human face. Long snout retreating into a strong human jaw, sharp brow broadening and rising into a human forehead, a human mouth with human lips parting to speak . . . and it was then that he'd awakened . . . just before the words were spoken.

Safar set the tumbler on its tray, wondering what the dream beast had been about to say. He snorted. Don't be ridiculous! The brandy's got you. It was a dream. Nothing more.

He glanced down at his notes, a scatter of linen pages peeping out from under the cat who had gone back to sleep. Yes, nothing but a dream. Brought on, no doubt, by the long fruitless night he'd spent poring over the Book of Asper. Trying to make some sense of the ancient demon wizard's musings.

And yes, he'd imbibed a bit too much and worked a bit too late. The last thing he'd read before he'd fallen asleep was another of Lord Asper's warnings, maddeningly couched in murky poetry.

What was it? How did it go? Oh, yes:

". . . *the Age of the Wolf will soon draw near*
When all is deceit and all is to fear.
Then ask who is hunter and who is prey?
And whose dark commands do we obey?
With the Heavens silent—the world forsaken—
Beware the Wolf, until the Gods awaken . . ."

Safar sighed. It was no wonder he'd dreamed of wolves. Too much brandy and Asper's poetry was a certain recipe for nightmares.

He put the jug down, found a robe, shrugged it on, then stuffed his feet into soft, hightopped slippers—a habit he'd formed during his years at the court of King Protarus. Felt-lined comfort on a chilly morn was only one very small luxury of many he'd enjoyed in his days as Grand Wazier to the late, unlamented by him, King of Kings.

Once Safar had possessed more palaces than there were cusps in the Heavenly Wheel. The finest food, wine, clothing, jewelry and women were his for the asking. Men and demons alike bowed when he passed, whispering his name for their children to hear and remember. Safar missed none of this. The rough, healthy life of Kyrania—the remote, high mountain valley of his birth—was all he'd ever really wanted. In the greater world he was Lord Timura, a wizard among wizards. A man to be to be feared. Here he was merely Safar Timura, son of a potter and now village priest and teacher to giggling school children. A man whose main faults were a citified taste for warm slippers on a chilly morning and possibly, just possibly, a bit more of a desire for strong spirits than was good for him. The only spoiler was that his fellow Kyranians called him by the title King Protarus had bestowed on him. So even here among the people he loved, the people he had known all his days, he was called Lord Timura.

As for women—Safar glanced at the tangled covers of his empty bed—well, he hadn't had much luck in that area. Oh, he supposed he could wed just about any maid in the village if he so desired. He was barely in his third decade of life, after all. Taller than any man in Kyrania and stronger than most. In the past women had called him handsome, although his blue eyes in a world of dark-eyed people made some nervous in his presence until they had been in his company for a time.

He was also quite rich. Thanks to Lieria he'd fled Zanzair with enough precious gems in his saddlebags to match even the greatest miser's measure of immense wealth.

Since he'd returned to Kyrania the young maids had buzzed about him like ardent bees, making it known they were available. A few had even made it plain that marriage wasn't necessary and they'd be satisfied just to share his bed. Scandalous offers indeed in puritanical Kyrania. In the early days, when Leiria still graced his bed, many an old Kyranian woman's tongue had been set clucking whenever she passed. In the moral double-standard favored in

Kyrania, Safar was not blamed. A man will do what a man can, was the motto. And it is a woman who must preserve respect for Dame Chastity.

Now that Leiria was gone, Safar's mother and sisters were constantly conspiring to get him betrothed to a "decent woman."

Safar had gently eluded their little traps. To tell the truth he thought it unlikely he'd ever marry. He had good reasons for this, although he didn't mention them to family and friends. It was his secret shame. A secret he'd mentioned only to Leiria, who'd told him he was insane. Insane or not, Safar was convinced he had caused the deaths of two women who had loved him and broken the heart of a third.

Safar frowned, remembering Leiria's final words on the subject . . .

. . . It was their last night together as bedmates. Neither had spoken of this, but it was understood between them. Leiria had come home that day after a long ride in the hills. She'd been in a reflective mood, but full of single-minded determination at the same time. Safar had watched in silence as she gathered her things, then whistled up a boy to get her horse and a pack animal ready for the morning.

Finally she'd hauled out the brandy and they'd both gotten gloriously drunk and had made love until they'd fallen asleep. But an hour so later they'd both awakened, made love again, slow and full of secrets and depths neither could decipher, much less plumb. Then they'd talked. Retold old stories about shared adventures. About the time the Demon King Manacia thought he had them cornered and they'd sprung a trap on him instead. And the trick they'd pulled on Kalasariz, who had seized Kyrania with a demon army. And then the even better trick they'd played on the demons to free the valley.

They talked until it was almost dawn.

And then Safar said: "I'm sorry, Leiria. I know I said that once before, but this time I have even more—"

"—Six years ago," Leiria interrupted.

"What?" Safar said, confused.

Leiria nodded. "Yes, it was six years ago almost to the day. I remember we were in the stable near the east gate of Zanzair. You didn't know if I was friend or foe and you were thinking about killing me. By the Gods, you were stupid! To ever think I'd ever hurt you!"

"Yes, and I'm sor—"

Leiria put a finger to his lips, silencing him.

"Let's not make it three times," she said. "Twice is once too many. I deserved the first 'sorry.' Back when we were in the stable and you were doubting me. But I don't want, much less deserve, the second.

"As always, my love, you reach too deep for guilt. Be sorry that you ever doubted me. I'll keep that. I'll put it away for some weepy hour when I need to drag it up, along with as many others as I can. There's nothing I like more than a good cry on the eve of battle. It loosens the sword arm wondrously.

"As for any other 'sorries,' I say camelshit! You didn't break my heart, Safar Timura. I broke my own heart. It was a good lesson for a naïve soldier. And it was also something every person needs for the future. Man or woman. If you're wounded early in life it gives you something to reminisce about when nobody thinks you are worth a tumble.

"So, camelshit! Safar Timura. You didn't break my heart, anymore than you killed Methydia or Nerisa!"

"You have to admit," Safar said, guarding the odd comfort of familiar guilts, "that if they hadn't met me they'd be alive today."

"That's ridiculous!" Leiria said. "They were on whatever road the Fates decided. Sometimes you're ambushed. Sometimes you turn it around and ambush your enemy instead. Either way, you're on the same road the General commanded you to take. So you do your job. March when they say march. Fight when they say fight. Rest when they say rest. And when you're resting you pray to all that is dreaded in the Hells they keep for soldiers that you meet somebody you can love. Methydia and Nerisa had that, Safar. And if they were alive today they'd both give you a piece of their minds for feeling sorry for them. They weren't the kind of women who could bear that sort of thing. If their ghosts were to speak they'd tell you exactly what I'm going to tell you now. Which is this:

"Almost no one ever really experiences love, Safar. You get

bedded. You get warm. Maybe you even get a sort of intimacy. I don't have much experience at such things, so I can't really describe what I mean. I've only been with two men in my life, after all—you and . . . Iraj. And yes, I loved him too . . . once. And that's my own 'sorry.' Hells! I have more sorries than I care to think about when it comes to Iraj.

"Sorry that I didn't see who he really was. Sorry that I gave him everything I had to give. Sorry that for a moment, however small, I really did think about betraying you. One thing I'm not sorry about. You killed him. And good riddance to Iraj Protarus. The world is a better place without him.

"So don't you feel guilty, Safar Timura. Especially not about the women who have loved you.

"I speak for all of them!"

That was the end of the conversation. They cuddled for awhile in silence. Then Leiria rose, bathed, and dressed in her light armor.

He didn't watch her leave. He stayed in his room, head bent over the Book of Asper. He heard her ride away. Heard the clatter of her armor. The creak of her soldier's harness. And just before the sounds faded from hearing he thought he caught a whiff of her perfume on the morning breeze.

In his whole life he'd never encountered a scent that lingered so long and lonely . . .

Safar shook himself back to the present, thinking, no matter what Leiria had said, his hesitation would remain. It would be a very long time—if ever—before he chanced being the cause of harm or sorrow to another woman. But guilt, large as it was, had only a supporting role to play in the drama that made up Safar Timura. To him it seemed whenever his emotions came into play it exposed him—and, more importantly, his purpose—to danger.

Take love, for instance. The last time Safar had declared himself to a woman . . . say her name, don't dodge the pain of that old wound . . . her name was Nerisa.

Nerisa was a former street urchin who grew to became a woman of beauty, wealth and power. These three things—but mostly it was his love for Nerisa—had brought him into conflict with the king. And Iraj Protarus had used that love to find a weakness to betray Safar. The incident had ended with Nerisa's death and Safar's bitter repayment. The epilogue of the tale saw Safar kill Protarus and bring down his empire.

He'd fled the glorious demon city of Zanzair, leaving palace and riches behind in the flames that had consumed the city— flames evoked by the great spell he'd cast to slay Iraj.

Six years had passed since that day. A little longer, actually, since it had been several months since the day Leiria had noted the tragic anniversary. Six years of relative peace—at least in Kyrania. In the outside world things were much different.

Safar went to his bedroom window and looked across the beautiful valley he called home. His house—a narrow, two-story cottage set on a hillside near the cherry orchard—overlooked the dazzling blue waters of Lake Felakia, named for the goddess whose temple was now in his care. On the lake he could see fishermen casting their nets. In the rich farmland surrounding the glistening waters men and women were tending the green shoots that were just now poking their heads from their warm blankets of soil to greet the spring sun. In the distance two boys were driving a herd of goats up into the mountains to the high meadows where the lush grasses made their milk sweet. The shouts of the boys and bleating of the goats drifted to him on the breeze flowing down the mountainside. It was an idyllic scene, which Safar doubted could be matched anywhere in the world.

Yet his thoughts were not on the beauties of his native valley that morning. Or even—after he'd stirred through the pot of guilt—were they permanently fixed on Leiria, Methydia or even Nerisa.

He was still troubled by the dream that had awakened him. It was no ordinary nightmare. It was so strong an experience he wondered if it might actually be a vision. But there was no magical scent lingering in the nightmare's aftermath, so he was fooled for a time, thinking that maybe it really was only a dream. So when Safar looked through the window he barely saw all the beauty that so beguiled the rare outsider who visited Kyrania. Instead he focused on all the troubles the beauty hid.

Three poor harvests in a row, followed by harsh winters, had sorely tested the people of Kyrania. They had lived in ease for so many generations they were ill prepared for the hard times that had descended on the world in recent years.

The income from the great caravans that had once crossed the Gods' Divide from Caspan to Walaria and back again each year had ceased. Kyrania suffered from this. Yet once again in the age-old Kyranian story, Safar's people didn't suffer nearly as much as everyone else.

In the outside world—the world beyond the foothills of the Gods' Divide—all was chaos.

Protarus' shattered empire had turned Esmir into a confusion of petty kingdoms, so weak they couldn't keep the bandits off their own roads, so unstable that any bold warrior prince with an army at his back could easily step into the gap left by the mighty Iraj. Kyrania was cut off from the rest of Esmir, so Safar couldn't be certain that such a prince hadn't risen.

In the past, news would have come through the great merchant princes who knew the route over the mountains to Kyrania. But they were either dead, or huddled at home praying the chaos would soon end.

Safar thought it unlikely their prayers would be answered any-time soon. If at all.

He looked north and saw the Demon Moon—a silver comet trailing in its wake—rising over a mountain peak. As long as that moon ruled the heavens, he thought, plague and war and hunger would ravage the land. From his studies he knew things were likely to get worse, not better. Someday the Demon Moon might reign over lifeless seas and plains and mountains. The world, Safar believed, was slowly poisoning itself—shedding humans and demons and animals and plants as if they were so many parasites, like lice or ticks or aphids.

Once Safar had thought he might find the answer—the means to end the abysmal reign of the Demon Moon. It had been this search that had brought him to Protarus' court and all the terrible things which followed. Now, after more than six years of study and magical experiment, Safar was starting to wonder if he had been a fool from the very beginning. And that there was no answer to the riddle.

That damned old demon, Lord Asper, claimed the gods were asleep in the heavens and didn't care a whit about the fate of human or demonkind.

Safar eyed the brandy jug, thinking, if Asper were right, why should he, Safar Timura, care?

He picked the jug up, thinking, why should I fight the natural course of things? The gods must hate us, he thought. From what Safar had seen in his three decades of life the gods had good reason to abandon this world to its fate. Humans as well as demons were masters of misery, striking out at themselves as much as at others.

He started to pour himself one more drink, thinking, to the Hells with them all! If that's what the gods want, who am I to say nay?

Then he heard a small voice in the other room:

"You show him!"

Another voice protested.

"No, no, you show him!"

"He'll get mad."

"No he won't."

"Yes, he will."

"All right, all right. I'll do it."

Listening, Safar smiled, thinking—There's your reason, my friend!

He heard his son call, "Come here, father! Come and see quick!"

Safar laughed and went into Palimak's room. He entered cautiously, not knowing what he'd find.

The smell hit him first.

It was like something had died, then risen from the dead just short of complete mortification. It was more redolent than flesh. It was more like . . . Then smell shock became vision shock and Safar jumped back as a huge creature lumbered toward him.

"Surprise!" Palimak shouted.

The creature confronting him was buttery yellow with holes running through it so huge you could see to the other side. One of those holes opened—Safar imagined it might be a mouth—and then he knew he was right when the creature spoke:

"Cheese!" it said in a deep bass voice. Or at least that's what

Safar thought it said. And then he was sure because it spoke again, saying: "Cheese!"

It waved clumsy arms at him, like an clockwork toy from a child prince's chest of pleasures.

Safar buried a smile, then made a motion and the creature froze in place.

Palimak clapped his hands, chortling, "What do you think, father? Isn't it good?"

He was a handsome boy, not quite eight, with curly brown hair and a slender body with long legs and arms splayed across the bed. He had a long elfish face, with rosy cheeks and skin so fine it was almost translucent. At the moment his normally hazel eyes were huge and golden—dancing with magical fire.

"Well? Say it!"

Safar put on a solemn face and examined the creature, trying not to laugh, which was difficult because behind Palimak was a small, green creature, doing its best to keep out of sight. It was an elegant little figure—about three hands high—dressed in fashionable tights, tunic, and feathered hat. It had the body of a man, but the face and talons of a demon. The creature was Gundara, Safar's Favorite. Gundara knew he was in a great deal of trouble with his master, ducking behind the boy, teeth chattering like a monkey's and giving him away.

Safar ignored Gundara for the moment and observed his son's creation. It wasn't yellow all over as he'd first thought. It also had brown, loaflike arms and legs that bore neither hands or feet. And it was indeed, shaped like a man—a stick figure with a big ball for a body and a smaller ball stacked upon that for a head.

Safar couldn't quite tell what the creature was made of. He sniffed the air. "What's that?" he asked.

"Guess!" Palimak demanded.

Safar looked past the boy to glare at Gundara. "Come out here," he said.

Gundara grumbled and hopped out onto the bed. "It wasn't my fault, Master!" he said. Suddenly his head swiveled around, little eyes fixed on a small stone turtle sitting next to Palimak.

The turtle had the mark of Hadin painted on its back: a green island, outlined in blue, and on that island was a red mountain with a monster's face spewing flames from its mouth.

Gundara's long delicate demon's tongue flickered out, and he said, "You just shut up, Gundaree. You hear me! Shut up!"

"That's not nice," the boy admonished Gundara. "You shouldn't say shut up!"

Gundara was hurt. "You used to say it all the time, Little Master," he said. "'Shut up,' were the very first words you spoke. Why, I remember when—"

"Never mind that!" Safar broke in. He pointed at the moldy, man-high thing. "What's this?" he asked Gundara.

Gundara hung his head. "Cheese, master," he muttered. "Just like it said." And he lowered his voice to match the creature's, intoning, "Cheese!'"

Despite himself, Safar laughed. For just as Gundara said, the magical creature Palimak had created really was made entirely of cheese—other than the legs and arms, which he now realized were made of bread.

"It's breakfast, father!" Palimak piped. "See. I made you breakfast!" He wrinkled his nose. "Although, maybe it doesn't smell too good."

"I told him not to use the stuff under his bed, master," Gundara said. "But he wouldn't listen. I said, 'that's somebody's old snack . . . some dirty little thing's old snack. Some dirty little thing who sneaked under the bed to eat." Gundara glared at the stone turtle. "I won't mention any names, but we all know who I mean."

Palimak clapped his hands. "Gundaree!" he shouted. He grinned at Safar. "Gundaree likes eating under the bed, father," he said. "And he likes his cheese, really, really old." The boy pinched his nostrils to show just how old Gundaree preferred his cheese to be.

Gundaree was Gundara's twin. The two of them had dwelt in the stone turtle for at least a millennium. A gift from Nerisa, the idol and the Favorites it contained had been created in Hadin—a world away from Esmir. Whoever owned the idol had the decidedly mixed blessing of the twin's magical assistance. They had a constant war going between them, making it quite disconcerting for whoever was their current master. The only consolation was that they couldn't appear at the same time before normal beings. Gundara serviced humans, Gundaree demons. Only little Palimak—who was part human and part demon—could see them both at the same time.

Mischievous as they were, their magic was very powerful and Safar had ordered them to protect Palimak. The boy kept the idol with him at all times, giving him a permanent set of child minders and magical playmates.

At the moment Gundara was doing his best to appear the innocent above all innocents.

"I warned Palimak, master," he said. "I told him, 'Oh, no, you shouldn't use that smelly old stuff to make a breakfast spell, Little Master. Your father will be angry.'"

"You never said that!" Palimak protested.

"Yes, I did!"

"You taught me the spell!"

"No, I—"

Safar clapped his hands twice. The first won him silence. The second commanded the collapse of the cheese beast. There was a pop! and it returned to its original, disgusting shape, which was a small mound of old cheese and bread piled on the floor. Safar swept the mess up and dumped it out the window, counting on Naya, the old goat who made her home in his yard, to make short work of it. Then he mumbled a cleansing smell, snapped his fingers and the air in Palimak's room was sweet again.

When he turned back Gundara had vanished—fleeing into the retreat of the little stone idol where he would, no doubt, continue his argument with Gundaree.

Palimak sighed. "I'm awfully tired," he said. "Making breakfast is hard work."

"I suppose it is," Safar said.

"The hard part was making the Breakfast Thing talk," Palimak said. "I thought that'd be a really, really Big, Big Surprise!" He spread his hands wide to indicate just how amazing the effort was.

"It said, 'Cheese!'" Safar said. "You can imagine how surprised I was. I've never had breakfast speak to me before."

Palimak hung his head. "I'm sorry it was so smelly, father," he said. "There's some good cheese in the kitchen, but Gundara said I couldn't get out of bed until you woke up." He shrugged his shoulders. "There sure are a lot of rules in this house," he said.

Safar aped the sigh, making it long and dramatic. "I guess there are," he said. Then he shrugged—again mimicking Palimak. "But what can we do? Rules are rules!"

"I suppose you're right, Father," Palimak said with weary resignation. "What can we do? But I'd sure like to know who makes up all those rules!" He yawned. "Well, maybe I'll go back to sleep for a little while."

Palimak made a magical motion and soft dreamy music floated out of the stone turtle. He hugged his pillow tight, yawning again. "Wake me up when it's time for breakfast, father," he said.

Then he closed his eyes and went to sleep. Lips trembling with his last words. The child went from wakefulness to sleep in less time than it took for a heart to beat. Safar smiled at the boy, watching how the sun streaming through the window lit up his milky skin. Palimak positively glowed and Safar could see, deep, deep, under the child's skin, the faint gleam of bluish green. Demon green. And his little hands, clasped together, had pointy little nails, so paper thin you could only tell they existed because of the darker blush of the pink skin beneath them. When Palimak became excited and forgot himself those pointy little nails could hook out like kitten claws and accidentally draw blood from an unwary adult.

Palimak possessed amazing magical powers for his age. Although he called Safar "father," the boy was a foundling, a child of the road, whom Nerisa—an orphan herself—had taken pity on and adopted. Safar had assumed responsibility for Palimak's care after Nerisa had died, raising him as if he were his own. How a demon and a human—bitter ancestral enemies—had come together in love to make the child was surely a tale of complexity and tragedy. Unfortunately, Nerisa had died before she could tell Safar much about what she knew of Palimak's origins and as the boy had grown older it had become increasingly difficult to explain that his all-wise father should be ignorant about something so important.

Safar tucked a blanket around the boy and returned to his rooms, purpose renewed. He washed, dressed—leaving on his soft

slippers—and ate a little yogurt and drank cold strong tea left
over from the day before. A village woman would bring breakfast
soon, so he had a little free time before Palimak would be thundering around.

He slipped behind his desk and retrieved the little book from
beneath his notes. It was an old book, curled and dry and quite
small—no bigger than a man's hand. It was a master wizard's
book of dreams. The musings of Lord Asper, who was perhaps
the greatest wizard in all history. Asper had lived long ago and in
his old age had started recording his thoughts and discoveries.
The old demon's writing was so small that Safar found it more
comfortable to use a glass to read. There was no order to the
book, making it even more difficult for the reader. A theoretical
phrase or two about the possibilities of mechanical flight might
find itself on the same page as an elaborate magical formula
whose only purpose was to keep moths away from a good wool
cloak.

Maddening as it was, all that was known about the world was
contained between its brittle covers. And all that wasn't cried for
recognition's ink.

Safar opened the book at random. On one page was a large
sketch of the world—showing the two halves of the globe in a
split ball. The four major land masses were inked in, but as actual
formations, rather than the usual stylized maps of Safar's time that
showed the turtle gods carrying the lands across the sea. The
names of the continents were inked below each drawing. Floating
in the Middle Sea was Esmir, the land where Safar lived. To the
north was Aroborus, to the south, Raptor. Last of all was Hadin,
on the other side of the world—directly opposite Esmir.

Hadin, land of the fires, the place where Safar believed the
great disaster that was slowly consuming the world had begun.

He had seen Hadin in a vision long ago—handsome people
dancing on an enchanted island under a threatening volcano. The
volcano erupting, hurling flame and death. The dancing people
were gone in the first few moments, but the volcano continued to
spew huge poisonous clouds charged with such magical power
that it had seared Safar through the vision. Since that time
nothing in the world had been the same.

And it was Safar's obsession and self-sworn duty to somehow unravel the mystery of Hadin and halt the disaster.

Asper had seen the same disaster, not as it was happening, but in a vision hundreds of years before the incident. The coming death of the world—no matter that it was far in the future—so disturbed the old demon that he had made an abrupt shift in all his thinking. It was as if a blindfold had been lifted from eyes, he wrote, and suddenly "Truth was lies/and lies were truth . . ."

It was then that Asper began the greatest work of his life. Old age sapping his strength, bitter realizations stalking his dreams, he raced against Death's imminent arrival in an ultimately futile effort to solve the riddle that was the coming end of the world.

Near the end, during a moment of great despair, he had written:

Wherein my heart abides
This dark-horsed destiny I ride?
Hooves of steel, breath of fire—
Soul's revenge, or heart's desire?

Not first for the first time, Safar wondered what particular incident had caused Asper to write such a thing. After long study it was plain that Asper faced much opposition at the end of his life. He was speaking heresy after all. Uncaring gods asleep in their heavenly bower. A world doomed. And the greatest heresy of all—that humans and demons were not so different. He even speculated that the two species, who were historic enemies, were originally twins—the opposite sides of a single connubial coin.

Safar was both a wizard and a potter. The wizardly side of him tended to question everything. The potter's side demanded practical proof as well. He still had many questions about Asper's theories. But as far as practical proof went, he only had to look at Palimak, a child of the two species. What greater proof could one need to show that demons and humans had once supped the milk of a common mother?

Like Safar, Lord Asper had been forced to flee his enemies. Unlike Safar he had no home to return to and had wandered the world for nearly twenty years. Before he died—Safar guessed he lived nearly three hundred years, ancient even for a demon—

Asper had visited all four continents and had made notes and drawings of his experiences and conclusions. In Aroborus, for instance, he spoke of trees that ate meat and could uproot themselves to chase down and trap their prey. On Raptor, Asper said, there was a strange birdlike creature that was nearly twelve feet high. It couldn't fly and hunted in packs, cornering its victims to hammer them down with huge, ax-shaped beaks. On Hadin Asper told of a once great civilization containing both humans and demons that had destroyed itself in a religious war so fierce only barbarians remained among the ruins.

It was at this point that the riddle of Asper truly began. The old wizard had suddenly, and without explanation, left Hadin. There was a great gap in months, possibly even in years, between the time of his flight—Safar guessed he was escaping something—and his arrival at a small island in the Caspan Sea about two hundred miles off the coast of Esmir. The island, Safar learned from his research, was the mythical birthplace of Alisarrian The Conqueror, who had welded demons and humans together under one rule many centuries before.

Safar eyed the brandy jug, sighed, then turned back to the book. Once again he looked at the small map of the world. And once again he traced the lines showing Asper's travels. His flight from Esmir to Hadin and back. Beneath the map was a tiny sketch of the island where Asper ended his days.

The island's name, scrawled in red ink, was Syrapis.

Musing, Safar said the name aloud—"Syrapis." Then, "I wonder what Asper sought there?"

Suddenly his fingers itched with a powerful desire to touch the drawing of the island—a need as strong as a thirsty man's obsession for water. His fingertips touched the paper and a surge of energy flowed up his arm.

There was a boom! of distant thunder and a sharp crack! of lightning quite near.

Suddenly all was blackness and his hair rose up on prickling roots.

3
THE WIZARD'S TOMB

Safar felt a great force seize him, lift him up, then hurl him away.

He flew through darkness—so far he lost all sense of motion and direction. Then he was falling, plunging, an eerie voice whispering in his ear, "Down and down and down. Down, and down and down . . ."

And then he just . . . stopped!

There was nothing between the two feelings of falling and stopping. One moment his insides were rising up and the next moment he felt hard ground under his feet and the comforting sensation of weight. Still, all remained blackness and he had no idea where he was. All he knew was that it was someplace hot and dank. Perspiration flooded from his pores, soaking his clothes. Under his feet, still shod in slippers, he could feel heat rising from the rocky floor. And then far off he thought he heard the sound of dripping water and he wondered if he might be underground.

He stayed quite still, trying to get his bearings. As he was about to probe the darkness with his wizard's senses he suddenly heard rustling all around him—like dry insect wings. He also heard whispering, or at least what he thought was whispering—he couldn't make out the words.

Then he heard, quite clearly: "Sisters! Sisters!"

The voice was like sand polishing glass. Keeping his head motionless, Safar forced his eyes toward the source of the sound. He saw two large red holes burning through the darkness—floating a good ten feet above the ground.

It spoke again—"Sisters! Awake, sisters!"

The voice came from just below the red holes. Safar's heart

quickened as he realized they were huge eyes and the voice was likely coming from an equally enormous mouth.

Then someone, or something, answered, "I hear, sister!"

The words had the same sand against glass sound to them. But harsher. And he realized the voice was coming from directly above him! It was all Safar could do not to look up.

Others answered: "I hear! I hear! I hear!"

The voices came from every direction and the darkness bloomed with a ghastly garden of many glowing red eyes.

Then the first voice said, "I smell a human!"

A harsh chorus answered, "Where? Where, sister, where?"

"Here with us!" was the reply.

Horrid shrieks filled the air: "Kill him, kill the human, kill him!"

Talons and scaly bodies scraped against stone, heavy wings flapped from above and there was a great gnashing of teeth. Burning eyes rushed about like huge fireflies fleeing an oncoming storm. Safar needed no magical help to keep absolutely still in that chaos of hatred. His blood turned to ice, his heart to stone and his breath fled from him like an escaping ghost.

Then he realized they couldn't see him. The realization was small comfort, especially when next he heard a shout:

"Silence, sisters!"

It was the first voice, the commanding voice. And it got the silence it demanded.

A pause, then, "Where are you human? Show yourself!"

Safar had the sudden hysterical desire to laugh. It hit him so quickly it was all he could do to bite it off. Show himself? Did she think he was insane?

She also must have thought he was deaf as well, because she said, "You have nothing to fear from us, human! We like humans, don't we sisters?"

"Yes, yes, yes," came the chorused reply. "We like humans. We like them all!"

"We would never hurt a human, would we sisters?"

"Never hurt, never, never!"

Silenced followed, as if the creatures were waiting for Safar's answer.

When it didn't come, the commanding voice said, "You are insulting us, human! You should speak and show us your trust. Speak now, or we will forget our love of all things human. You will suffer greatly for angering us."

Another long pause, then Safar heard: "Sisters! I think I smell him over here!"

The voice came from quite near. Safar heard heavy talons rattle on stone and a snuffling sound, like a large beast following a strong scent. He knew he had to do something quickly before he was found.

The idea jumped up at him and he knew he couldn't wait and think it through, because with thought would come fear and fear's hesitation would be the end of him. He made a spell and clapped his hands together and roared:

"Light!"

And light blasted in from all sides, nearly knocking him over with the sudden shock of it. He had been blinded by darkness before, now he was blinded by its white-hot opposite. There were awful screams of pain all around and then his vision cleared and the first thing he saw ripped his breath from his body.

The beast towered above him, enormous corpse-colored wings unfolded like a bat's. It had the stretched out torso of a woman with long thin arms and legs that ended in taloned claws. There was no hair on its skull-like head and instead of a nose there were only nostril holes on a flat face shaped like a shovel.

Safar nearly jumped away, but then he realized the creature was too busy screaming in pain and clawing at its eyes to be a threat.

He was in an enormous vaulted room, filled with blazing colors. Great columns, red and blue and green, climbed toward glaring light then disappeared beyond. The room was filled with hundreds of death-white creatures, some crouched on the floor howling pain, others hanging bat-like from long stanchions coming out of the columns. They twisted and screamed, horrid flags of misery blowing in a devil wind of conjured light.

Safar spotted the one he wanted. Again he shouted, his magically amplified voice thundering over the wails.

"SILENCE!"

The shrieks and screams cut off at his command, and now there was only moaning and harsh pleas for "Mercy, brother, mercy!"

Safar paced forward, moving through the writhing bodies until he came to the throne. It looked a great pile of bones—arms and legs and torsos and skulls stacked in the shape of an enormous winged chair. As he came closer he saw the bones were carved from white stone. The creature who commanded that grisly throne was like the others, except much larger. A red metal band encircled her bony skull to make a crown. Unlike the others, however, the creature was silent and although she was hunched over, claws covering her eyes, she made no outward show of pain.

Safar stopped at the throne and said loudly for all to hear: "Are you queen to this mewling lot?"

"Yes, I am queen. Queen Charize." As she answered she couldn't help but raise her royal head, carefully keeping her eyes shielded. "I command here."

"You command nothing," Safar replied, voice echoing throughout the chamber, "except what I, Lord Timura of Kyrania, might permit."

Queen Charize said nothing.

"Do you understand me?" Safar demanded.

He made a motion and the light became brighter still. The creatures shrieked as their pain intensified. Even the queen could not stop a low moan escaping through her clenched lips.

"Yes," she gasped, "I understand."

"Yes, Master," Safar corrected her. "You will address me as Master."

The queen gritted her fangs in protest, but she got it out: "Yes . . . Master!"

Safar motioned and the light diminished. There were gasps of relief as he dimmed it until the room was merely a soft glow. But no one rose or uncovered her eyes. Dim as the light was, it was still too painful for the sisters of darkness to bear. He could also smell the fear in them. They knew that if their new master was threatened, he could instantly retaliate.

To make certain, Safar said, "You may be queen here, but that doesn't mean you actually have wits to rule elsewhere." Queen Charize hissed indignation. Safar laughed to grind in the humiliation. "Hiss all you like," he said. "Just so long as we understand each other. I've already formed a spell that will turn you and all these filthy things you call subjects into dust. I only have to cast it. It would take a word, no more."

This was a lie. As far as Safar knew there was no such spell. But his days with Methydia's circus had taught him how to lie most convincingly.

"I will do as you say . . . Master," the queen answered. "On my word, no one will harm you."

"Fortunately," Safar said, "I don't need to test your word.

"Now, tell me, what is this place? And what do you do here?"

The queen answered simply. "We are the Protectors," she said.

"And what, pray tell, are you the protectors of?"

The queen's head jerked in surprise. If this human wizard, this Lord Timura, was so powerful, why didn't he know the answer? Safar didn't give her a chance to scratch his pose further.

"Well, answer me!" he demanded.

"Why, as all know on Syrapis," she said, "we are the Protectors of Lord Asper. And this is his tomb."

The answer so surprised Safar he nearly lost control of his spell. Syrapis? This great vault was in Syrapis? And what was this about Lord Asper? Protectors!? Protecting what? Asper had long been dead.

What happened next surprised him even more. The queen began chanting in a harsh whisper:

"We are the sisters of Asper,
Sweet Lady, Lady, Lady.
We guard his tomb, we guard his tomb,
Holy One . . ."

The other creatures joined her in a harsh chorus, as if coming from the grave. It seemed to be a prayer to some goddess, but coming from those throats of malice it made a mockery of all that was holy.

They sang:

"We take the sin, we take the sin,
Sweet Lady, Lady, Lady.
On our souls, on our souls,
Holy One."

Safar thought, if these creatures had souls he didn't want to meet the god who made them. Then he felt a dry, spidery web drifting over him and he realized they were trying to trap him in a spell.

His own spell was weakened and the light dimmed further. The creatures began to stir.

Safar saw the queen's great red eyes come up from the shield of her claws like twin suns rising over the sharp peaks of the Hells. But he only laughed and clapped his hands, bringing the light back to its most shocking brightness, nearly more than even he could bear.

The prayer song collapsed into shrieks of torment. He ignored their pain and turned his back on the queen, who was squirming on her throne in such agony he was confident he had little to fear from her.

He looked around the gaudy room, shielding his eyes against the glaring light, until he saw a raised dais not many paces away. The dais supported a large black coffin, shaped like a demon. Emblazoned on its lid in blood-red paint was a hauntingly familiar shape—a winged snake with two heads, poised to strike. The sign of Asper! This was the burial place of Lord Asper himself. The source of all the wisdom Safar sought.

But how had these evil beings come to infest the Master Wizard's tomb? Safar had no doubt that Queen Charize's claims of being Asper's Protector were lies. Just as the prayer song had been a lie.

Amazed as he was, Safar kept his wits about him. He wouldn't make the same mistake twice. Tightening his control on the spell of light, he went to the dais and climbed the steps, being extremely careful not to stumble and lose concentration. When he was a few feet away, he felt the buzz of magic.

The snake heads came alive and shot toward him, then stopped. Still buzzing, but more a buzz of recognition than warning.

Asper knew him!

An odd thought came—How strange! Why should he recognize me?

Then he saw another familiar symbol on the side of the coffin.

It was the outline of the island of Syrapis, exactly the same as the one in Asper's book—although much larger.

His fingers tingled with the sudden desire to touch the symbol. He mounted the dais steps, hand outstretched, so taken by the notion he forgot the warding spell. The light began to dim. He paid no attention, drawing closer and closer to the symbol of Syrapis. As the light dimmed still more, he heard Queen Charize mutter commands and her subjects rising up behind him, dry insect wings stirring old dust from the floor. Still he ignored them, climbing higher until the coffin was within his reach.

His fingers moved toward the symbol of Syrapis. He thought, I only have to touch it and all will be explained.

Words came to him, he didn't know from where, and he whispered, "Wherein my heart abides/This dark-horsed destiny I ride?"

And a whispered reply came back—"Khysmet!"

His journeying hand froze. What was this? Who was speaking? And what did he mean?

Was it Asper's ghost?

"How do you know me, Master?" Safar asked.

And the ghost whispered: "All wait for thee, Safar Timura. From Esmir to far Hadinland. Come to me, Timura. Come to Syrapis!"

"But how shall I come, Master?" Safar asked. "Syrapis is a long journey across the sea."

And the ghost said: "First to Naadan, then to Caluz. That is the way to Syrapis."

"But what if I fail, Master?" Safar asked. "What if by some accident I am killed?"

"Then send the Other," replied the ghost.

"Other?" Safar asked. "What Other?"

Just then he heard the queen shout: "Kill him!" And the creatures closed in on him.

But he didn't care. If only he could know the answer, it didn't matter . . . death didn't matter . . . nothing mattered but the knowledge he was certain was waiting to be revealed in one blinding flash, brighter even than the light he'd used to keep the Protectors at bay.

"Tell me, Master!" he shouted. "Who is the Other?"

His fingertips were scant inches away from the sign of Syrapis when he heard another voice shouting:

"Father! They're coming, father! They're coming!"

It was Palimak's voice.

A small hand plucked at his sleeve, dragging his fingers away.

"No!" Safar shouted. "Noooo!"

"Father!" Palimak's voice insisted. "They're coming! The men are coming!"

Asper's chamber vanished and Safar found himself in his bedroom again. He was clutching the edge of his desk, staring at the open page of Asper's book. The drawing of Syrapis still beckoning.

He turned, seeing Palimak next to him, tugging at his sleeve.

"Something awful has happened, father!" the boy said.

Palimak pointed out the bedroom window. "Look!"

Dazed, so sick to his stomach he wasn't sure he could hold its contents for more than a moment, Safar raised his head and looked.

Through the window he saw six men approaching his house, bearing a litter. And on that litter was a small, frighteningly small, human form. He didn't know who it was, because blood-soaked blankets covered the features.

"It's poor Tio, father," Palimak said. "I think the wolves got him!"

4

THE WOLF KING

The skies were somber, the lake ashen, when they sent little Tio to his watery grave. The village was draped in black and the winds came off the Bride's slopes cold and moaning, black bunting flapping like the tongues of so many ghosts.

All of Kyrania was in shock that one so young and innocent had met such a horrid fate. The mourning women wailed and tore their hair. And all the men got drunk and swore vengeance. Against whom, no one was certain.

Safar presided over the funeral ceremonies, casting cleansing spells and leading the village in traditional prayer.

And everyone sang:

"Where is our dream brother?
Gone to sweet-blossomed fields . . .
Our hearts yearn to follow . . ."

When the song was done, Safar and four temple lads fired the boat and pushed it away from the lakeshore. The mourners watched in silence as the funeral craft, festooned with yellow ribbons, was pulled this way and that by errant winds. Black smoke trailed through the curling ribbons and everyone wept in relief when the boat bearing Tio's remains finally halted in the middle of the lake. This was lucky for Tio's spirit. Everyone had worried the misfortune he'd suffered in this life would follow him to the next. The boat burned to the waterline and then wind-driven waves slopped over to hiss and steam in the flames. The boat sank slowly, smoke and steam columning up into heavy gray skies. Then it was gone.

Safar's heart sank with the boat. He thought of the dream he'd had only yesterday morning. The dream of wolves in which he'd witnessed Tio's death.

Suddenly his hackles rose and chill fingers of danger ran up his spine. Palimak suddenly clutched his hand.

"Somebody's watching, father," the boy whispered. "And he's not very nice!"

Safar felt eyes boring into him—eyes from nowhere and everywhere. He squeezed Palimak's hand. "I can feel it too," he said. He kept his voice easy, but with just a tinge of concern. "And you're right. He's not very nice."

"What should we do, father?" Palimak asked. "I don't like this! It isn't right! Watching people, and . . . and . . ." He shrugged. "You know . . . Looking at everything!"

Only Safar and Palimak were aware of what was happening.

Their fellow mourners were solemnly engaged in singing songs and beating their breasts to help speed Tio's ghost to the Heavens.

"I could use your help with this, Palimak," Safar said. The boy's face brightened, worry lines vanishing.

"Do you have a trick, father?" Palimak asked, flashing a sharp-toothed smile.

"I certainly do," Safar said. "But it won't work unless you help me."

He felt the remainder of the child's tension vanish. Now the ominous presence seemed only a game.

Palimak giggled. "We'll get him! Really, really get him!"

His gusto was alarming. Safar remembered his own blood-thirsty ways as a child and forced himself to stanch a sudden, unreasonable feeling of parental concern.

"Yes," he said, "we're going to surprise him. Maybe even hurt him . . . but just a little bit. Enough to make him sorry."

Palimak drew in a deep breath, gathering his concentration. And then, "I'm ready, father."

Safar nodded. "Here's what we'll do," he said. "Let's make ourselves really hot! Let's be so hot he feels like he's looking right at the sun. Can you imagine that?"

"That's easy," Palimak said.

"Not that easy," Safar warned. "I want you to think really, really hot. Hot as you possibly can."

Palimak chortled. "We'll burn him!" he said. "That'll teach him!"

Safar started to add a few more words of caution, but then Palimak's eyes started to glow and the air crackled with a surge of magical power. Hells, the child was strong! Safar leaped in to catch the surge and blend with it. Then he gained control, added his own power, and focused their combined strength like a magnifying glass intensifies the rays of the sun.

He smelled the stink of ozone and then the air became hot and heavy and it was difficult to breathe. He heard Palimak cough. And then from far away he heard a howl of surprised pain. Like a wolf who had just sprung a steel trap.

Then the eyes were gone—snatched away—and all was normal again.

"Will he come back?" Palimak asked.

"I don't know, son," Safar said. "But we'll have to be careful."

Then the crowd descended on him and he was shaking hands and commiserating with the family as if nothing had happened.

The following night he called an emergency meeting of the village elders.

First they heard from Renor, Tio's older brother. The men's eyes became moist as they listened.

"It was only for the night," Renor sobbed. "I didn't think there was any danger, or I wouldn't have left him there. I'd have taken him with me and made the herd fend for itself!"

Safar, a master of old guilts, said, "You had no reason to act differently, Renor. That is the way things are done in Kyrania. Boys have always taken the herds into the mountains to learn how to be on their own and act responsibly. That was what you were doing with Tio." He waved a hand at the others. "All of us have had that first time experience of a night alone on the mountains. It's a tradition—a necessary tradition."

The other men muttered agreement. "My brother did the same for me when I was a lad," said the headman, Foron, who was also the village smithy.

Renor wiped his eyes, trying to regain control.

Safar's father, Khadji, leaned in. "Tell us the rest, son," he urged. "Then you can go home to your family. They need your strength now."

Renor nodded. "On the way down the mountain," he said, "I didn't see anything to worry about. And I was looking, believe me. I mean, I had an injured goat on my back, didn't I? No sense giving some big cat ideas, or reason to think I was the goat. Tio has . . . had . . . a good imagination. I knew he'd be frightened. So I didn't even wait until morning to go back up the mountain. I just left the goat with my father and set off again."

The young man said he'd made good time on the return, but then it became too dark, the trail too treacherous, and he was forced to make a cold camp a few hours from the meadow.

"I couldn't sleep," he said. "I was worried about Tio the whole the time so I got up before first light—I didn't even eat—and set off to meet my brother."

Finally he came to the meadow. "It was like walking into a nightmare," he said.

The ground was torn up, barely a blade left untouched, and there was a huge smoking crater in the center. There was blood everywhere and the mangled remains of animals strewn about the field made it look like a giant's butcher shop. Renor ran for the shelter and there he found Tio's body, ripped so badly he barely recognized him. Next to him was a big gray she wolf, also torn to pieces.

"I couldn't figure out what happened," Renor sobbed. "I went mad for a bit. I rushed all around the valley and the hills calling him, 'Tio! Tio!' He didn't answer, of course. But I couldn't believe what had happened. I kept thinking of my mother and father. And of Tio, poor little Tio who never did a wrong to anyone. Then I became angry, stupidly angry, and I ran all over the meadow looking for something to kill. But everything was already dead. Goats and wolves . . . all dead."

"I don't understand," said another of the Elders. "How could they all be dead? Goats and wolves alike?" The man was Masura, who was second in command and no friend of the Timuras. A prissy fellow, Masura considered himself the ultimate word in village morality.

Renor shook his head. "I don't know," was all he said.

Safar remained silent during the discussion. He had an idea what was at the end of this bumpy trail of logic, but he thought it was important the Elders find it for themselves.

Foron scratched his grizzled chin. "If the wolves killed Tio and the goats," he said. "Tell me—who killed the wolves?"

"Maybe it was another pack," Masura suggested. "But stronger, much stronger."

"That doesn't make sense," Safar's father said, drawing a hot glare from Masura, who disliked being contradicted. "I've heard of such things, of course. Wolves attack other wolves all the time. But only when they come on the same prey. And then the weaker wolves run away as soon as they see all is lost. They don't stay around to be killed."

Foron agreed. "You're right, Khadji. Also, once the others took flight, the stronger pack wouldn't chase after them. After all, the object would be to eat goats, not to fight other wolves."

"There's another thing that was strange," Renor said, breaking in. Then he ducked his head and blushed, embarrassed by having interrupted the headman.

"Tell us what you saw," Safar said, gentle as he could. "We have to know everything."

"Well, it wasn't what was done," Renor said, "but what wasn't done that bothered me. I mean—nothing was eaten. All the bodies were ripped up, but they weren't gnawed on . . . or anything. They were just . . . I don't know . . . torn apart!"

"Sorcery!" Masura exclaimed. "Of the foulest kind." He glared at Safar as if he were responsible for all the foul magical deeds in the world.

All eyes turned to Safar. "I suspect you're right," he said. "In fact, if you think about it closely, you'll see there is no other reasonable explanation."

The house became so silent Safar could hear the ticking of the roof beams and the scuttle of insects hunting in the cold hearth. The men only looked at him with fearful eyes.

"What could it be, my son?" Safar's father asked. "And what have we done to deserve such a curse?"

"The whole world is cursed, father," Safar replied. "It isn't just us. Down on the flatlands people are suffering greatly, as you know. And there are all sorts of magical beasts plaguing them. I once dealt with a creature who had a whole region under its thrall." He was thinking of the Worm of Kyshaat, whom he had defeated some years before.

The Worm was just the first of many manifestations to infect the world.

Safar sighed, mourning the end of his people's innocence.

"What should we do about this . . . this . . . creature, Lord Timura?" Foron asked.

"Exorcise it," Safar said firmly. "That's what I did before." He turned to Foron. "If you'll provide me with a guard I'll go up into the mountains tomorrow and see what I can do."

As frightened as everyone was they were so angry at what had happened to Tio that Safar was deluged with volunteers to accompany him. He held them off, preferring to hand pick the party in the light of day.

Then he said, "If you will excuse us, Renor, I'm sure your family is anxious to see you."

The young man looked startled, then realized Safar was politely indicating he should leave. Safar turned back to the group when he was gone.

He hesitated. There was much he had to say, but his thoughts were disorganized. The emergency had left him little time to consider the vision of Asper's Tomb. Still, he knew one thing: he had to leave Kyrania. If there was any chance to stop the magical poisons blowing on the winds of Hadin, he would find it in Syrapis. Before he left, however, he had to protect them as best he could.

So absorbed was he in his musings, he forgot the others. His father's voice brought him back.

"What is it, son?" he asked. "You seem as if you wish to tell us something."

Safar started to speak, then shook his head.

"Let it wait," he said. "We can discuss it later."

There was heavy fog upon the mountain when Safar entered the meadow where Tio had been killed. The mist was so thick it was like a midnight garden; wet, heavy cobwebs breaking before him, then clinging and trailing behind. He was accompanied by five of Kyrania's best men, including Sergeant Dario, the village's elderly fighting master, as dangerous at seventy as when he'd fought on the Jasper Plains fifty years before. Guiding the group was Tio's brother, Renor.

"Better let us secure it first, me lord," Dario said. He tapped his sharp, beaked nose. "Don't smell nothin' amiss. And the old sniffer never failed me all these years. But like I always tell the lads—better a good professional look around than blind guessin'."

Safar stopped a grin and nodded solemnly. Dario was a proud little man—short, bowlegged and so skinny and wrinkled he looked like a whip made of snake hide. His only concession to age was a tendency to be a bit loquacious. Even so, he was no figure of fun as he motioned to his men and they fanned out. He gave another signal and they all disappeared at once—slipping through the fog like ghosts to investigate the meadow.

It was cold and Renor wrapped his arms about his heavy coat

and stamped his feet. He started to speak, but Safar shushed him.

He took a small pot from his cloak and set it on the ground. Then he withdrew a little silver tinder box, lit a wick and pulled the stopper from the pot. Oily, orange-tinged fumes coiled out, heavy smelling, like overripe fruit. Safar quickly inserted the smoldering wick into the fumes. Flames sheeted up and a great trumpet blared.

It was a great hammer of a sound, smashing against the foggy shield. Then there was the indrawn whop! of an implosion as all moisture was drained from the atmosphere and air rushed in from all sides to quarrel over the vacuum left behind. The fog vanished, showing Dario and the others creeping forward, looking a little foolish as they turned to gape at Safar and Renor.

Safar pointed past them. "Over there!" he said, indicating the blackened crater in the center of the meadow.

The men revolved to look and it was if the force of their eyes let loose nature's darkest side. With sight came smell, and the odor of the goat corpses drifted across the torn up ground and the men had to turn their faces away to gasp for sweeter air.

Safar made a magical gesture and a slight breeze blew through, infused with the smell of violets. Dario nodded at him, made his mouth into an "O" as he drew in fresh air, then shuffled forward to the crater. He peered inside.

"There's nothing here, me lord," he called back.

Safar concentrated, radiating a cautious "find and flee" spell across the meadow. It was a difficult exercise. The rocky encirclement forming the meadow also made a natural cup that urged spells to flow back to their source.

The group had returned to his side by the time he was done.

Safar shrugged. "As far as I can tell, sergeant," he said, "it's safe. Hells, there's barely a sign of the magic that was done here. Certainly nothing to exorcise. Whatever spirit visited this place has either gone or is in such deep hiding that I can't find him."

His words were hardly reassuring—nor were they meant to be. Dario and the others scanned the area, nervous. A few moments before they'd been full of fire, set on vengeance. Now they were wondering if anyone . . . or thing . . . was examining them, measuring them for the grave.

It was Renor who broke the mood. He drew himself up. "I'm ready for whatever they're after," he said.

His comment made no outward sense, but it resonated deep into the cavern of last resorts, where all threatened things retreat to make their final stand.

Dario nodded—a downward jerk of his sharp features, like an ax cutting through. "Sure we are," he said.

Warmth spread through them all like a comforting wine as the villagers, including Safar, drew on their common strength.

It was then that the first wolf howled.

This was a howl from the earth. A hunting howl, ululating across the glen, then turning sharper, higher, victorious, as the Hunter found its prey.

There was not a man standing on that bloody meadow who did not know in his heart the Great Wolf was calling, and that its hungry call was meant for him.

A moment later another wolf howled in reply; a huge creature from the sound of its baying, but not as large as the Great Wolf. Then another acolyte of the fang joined the first two. And then another, until the whole meadow rang with their ungodly song.

The howling stopped as suddenly as it began. Only a deathly silence remained, a void almost as frightening as the devil wolves.

Dario coughed—hard and harsh to choke up the phlegm of fear. "I was never the sort what opposed an orderly retreat, me lord," he said in a gruff voice. "Assumin' the circumstances called for it."

Dario jerked as the howling resumed—even closer than before. The old warrior forced himself to relax and then he smiled, carved wooden teeth making an old man's splintered grin.

"What I'm sayin', me lord," Dario continued, ignoring the howls as best he could, "is that right now appears to be one of them circumstances I was talkin' about. For retreatin', I mean."

Serious as the situation was Safar couldn't help but laugh. "I don't think you'll find anyone here who objects to such a strategy," he said.

The laughter calmed the other men. They all grinned and nodded. Safar gestured toward the trail they'd taken into the meadow.

"You can have the honor of leading the retreat, sergeant," he said. "But go as quickly as you can. Don't look back. Only forward. And don't pay any attention to anything that might confront you. Just charge on through. Do you understand?"

Dario licked his lips, then nodded. He formed up the group, young Renor in the center, and at Safar's signal he charged, moving at an amazing pace for one so old. The others had to strain to keep up.

Safar followed until he reached the meadow's edge. There he calmly halted and shed his pack. He unbuckled it, drawing out a half dozen small stoppered bottles. He waited, the howls growing louder and closer.

Then he saw them—gigantic wolf-like shapes bounding out of the rocks. There were four of them, twice the size of a man. They were a misty gray, like fog, but so lightly formed Safar could see through them.

Safar picked up one of the bottles, hefting it in his hand. It was filled with a silver liquid tinged with purple—wolf bane mixed with mercury. It was heavy for its small size. He tossed it from hand to hand like one of Methydia's circus juggling balls.

And he intoned:

"Wolf, wolf,
Trickster,
Shape changer—
Bane
Of our existence . . ."

He hurled the bottle.

It sailed through the air, falling a good twenty feet before the charging spectral pack. Safar turned away, shielding his eyes, just as the bottle struck. Great sheets of purple flame exploded. He heard satisfying howls of pain and rage. He scooped up the other bottles and ran after Dario and the others.

For fifteen paces or so the only sound was the ringing in his ears from the explosion and the terrified yowls from the ghostly wolf pack. Then he heard the eerie, commanding cry of the Great Wolf ordering the pack to follow. It echoed through the small meadow, was pinched in by the frozen rock, and then blasted forward to sear his back.

The ghost wolves, however, recovered almost immediately and he hadn't taken more than five paces before he heard the sound of their running feet just behind him.

They were so close he didn't have time to stop and aim. He hurled a bottle over his shoulder as hard as he could, digging his toes into the ground with such force that he practically levitated as he flew down the trail, sliding where it curved toward a cliff edge and sending a shower of ice and frozen pebbles over the side. He fought for balance, hearing the debris tumble down a frightening distance and the sound of his howling pursuers drawing near. Then the bottle struck and the explosion was so forceful he almost went over the edge himself. He recovered at the last moment, boot heels skittering at the cliff's edge as he hurled himself to the side and back onto the path.

Again he heard the yowls of pain. Again he heard the Great Wolf howl for his spectral pack to follow. But from the sound of the baying pack there was a more comfortable distance than before.

Safar caught up to the others as they entered a canyon, shrouded on all sides by a thick, clinging fog.

He heard a growl then a grinding and he shouted, "Faster!" And everyone threw caution away and ran as fast as they could. But it wasn't quite fast enough to avoid the huge boulders that rumbled into their midst. Safar heard someone scream and turned just in time to see one of his fellow Kyranians fall beneath a huge rock. It crushed his legs, then bounced away down the mountainside.

Dario shouted a halt and as the men hastily lifted up their moaning, badly wounded friend, Safar swept about and hurled two more jars into the surrounding fog. He aimed blindly, but he heard shrieks of pain and knew he'd struck his mark.

Then they were running again—on and on, until all their strength was gone and they could run no more.

Safar and Dario directed the group to a clump of snow-covered boulders, where they sat their injured friend down and turned to meet the pursuing horror.

To their immense relief there was only fog and silence. After a moment or two Safar probed the mist with his senses. He found nothing.

The Great Wolf and his ghost pack were gone.

They crouched in their camp all that night and set off at first light. It was a cheery day, with only the Demon Moon hanging on the northern horizon to remind them that this was not the most delightful place in the world to be. Birds were singing, fawn were dancing in the forest and small animals darted underfoot.

No one was fooled.

They could hear heavy bodies moving through the underbrush behind them and knew they were being trailed. Even so, they reached Kyrania by late afternoon with no further incidents.

Everyone was too tired to do more than report the barest details of what happened. Still, those details were harrowing enough to rouse the village into mounting a guard at all the main entrances to the valley.

Safar collected Palimak from his parents' house. The boy ran into his arms, sobbing as if he had undergone an unpleasant ordeal. When Safar asked what was wrong he didn't speak, but only clutched him tighter. Palimak was silent on the short walk home. He ate little of his dinner and went to bed without complaint.

Late that night Safar was awakened from a dreamless sleep. His limbs were heavy, yet his mind sang with urgency. He forced his eyes open and saw Gundara crouched on his chest.

The little Favorite was frantic, clawing at his nightshirt. "Hurry, Master!" he cried. "The boy! The boy!"

Safar groaned out of bed, fighting rolling waves of lethargy. He grabbed his little silver dagger and staggered to Palimak's room.

He paused at the door, fighting the strange weariness. Gundara was perched on his shoulder, fangs chattering in fear.

Safar looked inside.

A tall man stood over the sleeping child. Flanking him were gigantic wolves, reared up on their hind legs.

When the man saw him he smiled and said, "Hello, Safar."

The wolves growled menacingly.

"Silence!" the man commanded. "Can't you see I'm speaking to my friend?"

It was Iraj Protarus. Back from the dead.

5

THE RETURN OF IRAJ PROTARUS

She rode in from the north, keeping the Demon Moon at her back and staying well within its long shadows. Her horse's hooves were muffled, as were her weapons and armor. The night wind was up, moaning through trees and gullies so the only discernible sound was the occasional creak of her harness, or the faint rattle of pebbles when her horse misstepped.

Leiria drew up when she neared the bend where the first sentries should have been posted. She knew where they'd be because it was Leiria herself who had reformed Kyrania's methods of guarding the approaches. She'd not only drawn up the map but had trained the sentries. She'd also imposed an orderly system for challenges and knew what passwords the lead sentry would use when he demanded if she were friend or foe. The plan was that as the approaching party or parties considered the response, two other guardians of the trail would move in on opposite flanks. If she appeared threatening, they'd cut her down with their crossbows while she was still focusing on the lead sentry.

That was the plan—as foolproof as anyone could make it. She'd drilled her charges thoroughly, warning all the while that the fools she was attempting to guard them against were on their side.

"If the enemy presents himself," she'd told Rossthom, the man she'd schooled to take her place when she left, "it's safer to assume he isn't a dimwit. If he's to be worth anything at all as a potential enemy, he'll have scouted your defenses before the approach. He'll know very well who is the greatest dullard on your side. The one most likely to fall asleep. The one who favors a nip or three on the jug to keep off the chill. When you issue your challenge he'll pause to consider for an arse scratch or two, while his best men cut your laggard friend's throat. By the time you repeat the challenge his entire force will be on you."

Rossthom had heeded her well—and to a lesser degree, so had her other charges—so she was quite disappointed when no one challenged her when she came to the barricade. Her disappointment deepened when she found Rossthom's bloody remains sprawled next to the barricade. There were no marks on the muddy ground so she knew he'd died without a struggle. There were only his footprints and the depressions his body made as he flopped about while his attacker slit him from stem to stern.

Leiria dismounted and considered the situation. She thought it quite odd there was no sign of the enemy's approach. As carefully as she searched, there were no other marks on the ground. It was as if Rossthom had been attacked from above. She searched further and found the corpses of the other two sentries. Once again, there was no spoor left by the enemy.

She led her horse into a grove of trees overlooking Kyrania. In the light of the Demon Moon the fields and homes were quite clear. A few chimneys glowed, a few candles were guttering down in distant windows and far off she could hear a young rooster mistake the Demon Moon for dawn and crow an eerie welcome.

All in all, everything seemed quite peaceful. If it weren't for the dead sentries she might have thought her mad rush to Kyrania was not only a waste of time but a humiliating one at that.

Since she'd left Safar's side she had been making a decent if precarious living by selling her sword. Only a few weeks ago she'd been wriggling into the comfortable post as captain of a minor king's guard. The pay was good, the king's ambitions small and she had a comfortable room with a soft bed, easy access to the privy and a fireplace to warm her on a winter's night.

Then one night she'd had a dream. The dream had started well enough—she was in Safar's arms, snuggling up after making love and drifting off to sleep. This was a planned dreamed, a dream she'd conjured on many a night to carry her away from a difficult day.

On that particular night, however, the dream continued on. She found herself being pulled into another embrace. She went willingly, sleepily enjoying the caresses of her re-awakened companion. Then the arms holding her were suddenly somehow unfamiliar—but familiar—at the same time. It was not an embrace she welcomed. Leiria felt as if she had been drugged and had awakened in the arms of a monster.

In her dream, she opened her eyes and saw it was not Safar, but Iraj preparing to mount her. She shouted, catching him by surprise, then gripped his hair and flung him to the side. She came to her feet, grabbing a candleholder for a weapon. Iraj rolled away just in time as she hurled it at him and the heavy base thudded uselessly into the feather mattress.

Her sword was lying next to the bed where she always kept it and she snatched it up just as Iraj rose from the floor.

Except now it wasn't Iraj she was facing. Instead she was confronted by an enormous wolf! She slashed at it, but the bed between them was too wide and the wolf too agile.

Then it turned to her, red eyes boring in. The wolf opened its jaws to speak. She was too numb to be surprised when she heard Iraj's voice issuing from the wolf's mouth.

"Slut," it hissed. And, "Whore!" Then, "I gave you to Safar Timura. Now I want you back!"

Naked as she was, those words armored Leiria in the strongest mail. "I was given once," she said. "I won't be given again. Back, or otherwise."

And she hurled herself across the bed, slashing with all her might.

Then she was sitting up in bed, striking with her fists at nothing but innocent darkness.

Instead of confusion, however, Leiria had one thought fixed in her mind—Safar was in danger. She didn't question this thought, much less dwell on the nightmare. Her soldier's instinct said this was so and therefor she acted.

Two hours later she was riding for Kyrania. She didn't even bother to tell her employer, the king.

Now, looking down at the peaceful scene, she wondered for an instant if she'd gone mad. Love mad, that is. Had the dream been nothing but an excuse to be in Safar's presence once again? Admit it, Leiria, she said to herself, you still love him. But then she thought, No, I'm over that. If there's any love, it's because I love him as a sister loves a brother.

Then she had the skin-crawling awareness that there must be a spell on the trail to make her feel so confused about her mission. Behind her were dead sentries. Ahead of her was a seemingly peaceful village. Only a fool wouldn't realize that it didn't add up.

She moved closer to the hill's edge. Just below she could see Safar's home peeking out of the cherry grove that was Kyrania's unofficial boundary. There was a strange silvery glow streaming out of one of his windows. She frowned, remembering the layout. The light was coming from Palimak's room. At any other time she would have thought the child was up to some magical mischief.

But not this time. Not this night.

She loosened her weapons, took up her horse's reins and led it quietly down the trail.

Iraj turned back from his charges, sneering at Safar. "And what a friend you proved to be, Timura," he said. "To think I once swore a blood oath with you."

Then his eyes met Safar's and there was a long, frozen moment as the two enemies regarded each other from across the room. The only sound was the harsh breathing of the wolves and Gundara's frightened whimpers from his perch on Safar's shoulder.

Even through thick lenses of hatred, Safar could see that Iraj was as handsome as ever—muscular frame draped in black, white teeth glittering through his golden beard. A simple crown of black onyx encircled his flowing locks. But his eyes were fiery red—red as the Demon Moon. Red as the wine he'd shared with Safar when they'd pledged eternal friendship and brotherhood. Red as the blood that had stained Nerisa's snowy breast when Iraj slew her. And now Iraj had returned to threaten the life of the one he loved most. A sleeping child—half demon, half human—named Palimak.

Blood infused with shape-changer's hate, all senses heightened to the painful extreme—it was all Iraj could do to check his murderous rage. Safar's obvious good health and strength infuriated him. Safar should be diseased and mutilated, with barely strength to draw breath for what he'd done to Iraj. At the same time, Safar's strange blue eyes penetrated his heart and saw his shame and guilt, which made Iraj fear him—and hate him even more.

Safar exhaled and the moment came unstuck, slamming his emotional gate shut before those old wrongs could overwhelm him. Revenge was an unpredictable sword that cut in all directions. It was enough for Safar to recognize that Iraj was his enemy—an enemy so powerful he'd risen from the grave to confront him.

Quick—so quick Old Man Time Himself couldn't take its measure—Safar formed the killing spell and his little silver dagger rose to blast Iraj back into whatever hells he came from. The two wolves sensed the danger. As he formed the spell they growled and as the dagger rose they gathered to leap—long fangs dripping, claws anxious to rip out his heart.

They'd be fast, Safar thought, but not fast enough.

Iraj's mind, however, was racing ahead of the killing moment. He knew Safar, knew him well, and could see his enemy consider the murderous possibilities. Safar blinked, deciding, and Iraj immediately knew what he'd do next.

Iraj instantly visualized the action from Safar's point of view. Safar would attack Iraj first. Then the wolf on the right. Finally he'd whirl to confront the third creature. But it'd be too late and Safar would be ripped from throat to groin. However, in the killing the wolf would also die. Except Palimak would be safe and that's all that would matter to Safar.

Yes, Iraj thought. That's his greatest vulnerability. The child.

Safar had the spell set and had all but cast it when Iraj raised a cautioning hand.

"Beware, Safar!" he said.

Instantly, he turned on his companions, shouting, "Hold!"

And they held, snarling and gnashing their fangs. Eyes sparking in terrible frustration.

Safar stayed his hand as well. The dagger point dropped, but he only had to raise it less than an inch to hurl his spell.

"Consider before you act, Safar," Iraj said. He gestured at Palimak, who stirred in his spellbound sleep, moaning as if suffering a bad dream, saying, "Anything you do against me is certain to harm the boy."

Gundara stirred uneasily on Safar's shoulder. "He speaks the truth, master," he whispered. "One wrong move and Palimak is doomed."

As low as he'd spoken, Iraj's hearing was so acute he overheard. He smiled, saying, "If you won't heed me, heed your Favorite. And I promise you the child will not only die, but will suffer greatly in the dying."

Safar let the dagger point dip lower. It wasn't a surrender, but it was an admission of momentary defeat.

Small as the gesture was, Iraj was thrilled by it. His overcharged shaper-changer's emotions frothed over and he couldn't help the wild laugh that exploded from his throat.

Safar winced. "You look better than you sound, Iraj," he said. He was surprised when he realized he hadn't meant to be sarcastic, or wounding. It was simply a natural comment between old friends. Or old enemies, as the case seemed to be.

"Never mind what I sound like," Iraj snarled. He knew very well the laugh seemed like that of a jackal and felt humiliated by showing that weakness. It spoiled his momentary thrill of victory.

Grinding to gain the upper hand again, he said, "You should be worrying about what I want instead of thinking up empty insults."

"Very well, then," Safar said, evening the game by making his voice and manner mild, "What do you want with us?"

Another jackal bark. This time purposeful. "Why, I only want your misery, my friend," Iraj replied. "Whatever injures you is my pleasure." He nodded, indicating the wolves. "Or should I say, our pleasure! When you tried to destroy me, they were also injured most severely."

He gestured at the wolf on his left. "You remember King Luka, I presume?" Then to his right. "And Lord Fari?"

Safar remembered them very well. Luka had been the crown prince of Zanzair before he'd conspired with Iraj to overthrow his father, King Manacia. Fari had been Manacia's chief wizard and Grand Wazier. In their original forms both were not men, but demons.

"Where's Kalasariz?" Safar asked, dry. He was speaking of the old human spy master who had been his nemesis for many years. "It's my fondest hope he's absent from this impromptu party because I killed him."

Iraj let his eyes widen in mock surprise. "Of course you killed him, my friend," he said. He motioned, his gesture taking in himself and the others. "You killed us all! However, as you can see we've risen from the dead. Including Kalasariz. He's busy elsewhere and sends his regrets and apologies that he had to miss this reunion."

"Call him forth, then," Safar said. "I promise you this time there will be no messy resurrection."

As he spoke he let the dagger tip rise. He felt the weapon turn warm in his hand. He didn't have to look to know the point was white hot as if it had just been lifted from a forge.

Iraj saw what he was up to and laughed.

Leiria was rocked to the core when she peered through the window and saw Iraj.

Braced as she was by the dream that had driven her to Kyrania, she wasn't prepared to see her old lover in the flesh.

In the first shock wave of recognition her practical side was hurled into a gully of confusion. Battered logic rose to demand that her senses were badly mistaken. You're dreaming again, this practical side argued. In fact the whole thing is a dream. You never quit your post, much less rushed off on an insane journey to rescue Safar.

Nothing else made sense. Iraj was dead, wasn't he? Hadn't she seen his palace explode into flames with her own eyes? As well as the city surrounding it? Safar's spell was so powerful that nothing or no one could have escaped it.

She rubbed her eyes but the vision remained. Iraj was still hovering over little Palimak, two giant wolves standing on their hind legs on either side. Safar was still motionless in the doorway, Gundara chattering with fear on his shoulder. She saw the little magic dagger glowing in Safar's hand. She noted the ridge of concentration on his brow and knew he was gathering his strength to strike.

Mind racing with a thousand possibilities for action, all suicidal, she bent closer to listen.

"Let me tell you what I learned about dying," Iraj said to Safar, very calm as if the burning dagger presented no threat. "To begin with, it isn't necessarily fatal." He laughed again, bitterly. "Now isn't that a good jest?" he said. "One that few could make. Unfortunately for you, I am one of those few. And I owe it all to them."

Another gesture at the wolves. "Thanks to them we were already exploring . . . how shall I say it . . . new forms of life? Or afterlife, if you will. And when you struck we were able to escape into one of those forms—Shape-changers!"

Iraj was crackling with inner fire. As he spoke he seemed to grow larger, shoulders broadening, chest deepening, head rising almost to the ceiling. It wasn't posturing, but a spell he was making with the help of Fari and Luka. He was using that spell to strike fear into Safar's heart, attempting to hammer his enemy into submission.

He smiled, his long teeth making him look like a wolf. "We can move in and out of this flesh at will. It's a bit painful, but after time you learn that pain gives strength as well as pleasure. There's more hope in pain than you might guess, Safar. You can see things, horizons and possibilities you never dreamed of before. As a boy my greatest dream was to be King of Kings. Well, I achieved that dream. But great as it was, once won, it was nothing. I felt hollow, Safar. Empty of all achievement, even though I'd matched my boyhood hero, the Conqueror Alisarrian."

Protarus saw the dagger in Safar's hand waver. The spell was working! He pressed harder, pushing against Safar's defenses with all his might. The dagger point dropped lower still and it was all Iraj could do to keep from smacking his lips in anticipation.

Instead he gestured at the wolves who were Luka and Fari. "My friends saw this. They understood even more than I— even more than you—what I truly sought." He leaned closer, his breath hot on Safar's face. "Now, I can be King of Kings of both worlds—magical as well as mortal. I suppose I should thank you for opening the way for me. My ambitions, my dreams, have always been greater than the flesh that could hold them."

The spell was so strong that Safar—who was already stretched to the breaking by his twin effort to protect Palimak plus hold Iraj and the wolves at bay—was nearly overcome. Gundara sank sharp claws into his shoulder, hissing, "Master! Master!"

Safar rallied, beating back the spell. He said, "If you are so all powerful, Iraj, why don't you just do away with me now? Kill me. Kill the child. Blast Kyrania to dust with your most powerful spell. What's stopping you?"

Iraj forced laughter. He was shocked at Safar's swift recovery. This wasn't how it was supposed to work! On his right Fari growled, urging him to keep on.

"Think about it," Iraj said, swiftly trying to repair the spell. "The only thing that held me back from true greatness before was my lack of magical abilities. You were the one whose powers were so awesome even demons feared you."

"That's hardly my fault," Safar said, mentally brushing aside the spellweb. Looking for his chance. "I was born with those talents. And you weren't. What more can I say?"

"Still," Iraj said, "you could have given me those powers. They could have been a gift to your oath brother and king." He gestured at Luka and Fari, who growled at his motions. "They were certainly willing to give me such a gift. Why wouldn't you?"

"You won't believe this," Safar answered, "but even if I'd wanted to, I didn't know how. Not safely, anyway. With these two—plus Kalasariz—you formed the Spell of Four. Very powerful. But also a two-edged sword. It is dangerous not only to others, but to yourself. You don't realize it now—perhaps you never will—but the pact you made was your downfall. I did nothing to you. Not really. True, I made a spell of destruction. But it depended upon your own nature for it to work."

"You're right," Iraj said. "I don't believe it."

Safar shrugged. "I didn't think you would."

"As for destroying my kingdom," Iraj said, "it was only temporary. Even as we speak my armies are putting it back together again."

Safar ignored this. "You still didn't answer my first question," he insisted. "Why all this talk? It's really quite unlike you, Iraj. Why not just kill us now?"

"The answer is simple, Safar," Iraj said. "I'm here to collect your powers." He nodded at Palimak. "And the boy's."

Now, Safar thought. Now! And he let himself sag a little, as if in spell-induced shock.

Iraj's temples hammered with sudden elation. He gestured at the sleeping child, grinding in his perceived advantage.

"My friends and I are perfectly willing to drain those powers from your dying bodies. And put them to better use." He shrugged. "The result would be rather weak, but it'll do, it'll do. Alive would be better, of course. And with your full cooperation it'd be better still."

"You'd still kill us," Safar said. "Eventually."

Iraj barked humor. "Oh, I promise you that, old friend. As I said, I owe you much. But if you surrender now, I'll let the boy live."

"That's no bargain," Safar said, pretending unconcern. "I'd still be dead."

Iraj frowned, as if deeply concerned at an impasse that did not exist. "But I require the boy alive. He's the key ingredient to what I need to secure my new throne." As he spoke, he and his Brothers of the Spell poured all their powers into their assault on Safar's will.

"I know the child's just a foundling," Iraj continued. "So you probably don't have any deep feelings for him. You won't suffer greatly when I tell you we intend to make the boy's life as miserable as possible. And believe me, there's nothing about misery I don't know, Safar Timura."

Safar let a soft moan escape. Iraj grinned, excitement so great that he lost control of his human shape and a wolf snout suddenly erupted from his face.

"What luck!" he growled. "You do love the boy, you poor sad fool." He sniffed the air, licking his chops. "Marvelous," he growled. "I can already taste your pain."

Iraj sniffed again, liked what he found even more, and drew in a long breath, shuddering from the infusion of fear and servile misery Safar was pumping into the atmosphere.

I am small and weak, Safar thought, and you are large and strong. Mercy, Lord, mercy. If I must die make it swift. Mercy, Lord, mercy. And spare the child. I beg you, spare the child. Mercy, Lord, mercy.

Iraj gloried in the rich scent of Safar's humiliation. Grinned at the sour sweat running off of him in streams. It made a quite a heady concoction.

When he relaxed his guard Safar struck.

It wasn't his strongest spell. In fact, it was rather weak. But it was the best he could do without killing Palimak in the backblast.

A fiery arc leaped from his dagger point to Iraj's crown. There was a flash of light and a howl of pain as Iraj was hurled back by the force of Safar's attack, slamming against the far wall.

Hoping against all the odds Safar turned to his left, aiming a second blast at the demon wolf who was Lord Fari.

"To Palimak!" he shouted to Gundara.

The little Favorite leaped from his shoulder onto the bed.

Fari was almost on him when Safar let loose the next sorcerous blast. But it was weak, too weak and the demon wolf shrugged it off and kept coming. From the corner of his eye he could see Luka leaping for him. Just beyond Iraj was rising up, shaking off the affects of Safar's attack.

Then he felt a heatshudder as Gundara threw a protective shield over the spellbound Palimak.

He reached deep for his strongest spell but even as he formed it he knew he was too late.

All was lost but he kept going, praying his enemy would make the smallest mistake or misstep.

It was a foolish prayer because there were claws scything toward him and the euphoria of certain death leaked into his brain, numbing him for the shock.

Then there was a thunder of hooves bearing a chill war cry and the house shook as an enormous weight struck the wall.

Safar's three attackers stumbled about in surprise as the whole wall crashed inward—showering them with debris—and they hurled themselves to the side just as a mailed warrior on horseback smashed into the small room. And then everything was a confusion of flying hooves and slashing sword and shrill battle cries.

Iraj and his demon/wolves were flung apart. They roared in pain and fury as horse and rider whirled about, barreling into them.

Safar leaped back through the doorway as the horse swerved toward him. He glanced over at Palimak's bed and saw the boy was still asleep; Gundara crouched over him, his shielding spell keeping bed and boy miraculously untouched by the chaos.

Safar turned back to the melee. He had his killing spell ready but there was no clear target. A slight miss and his rescuer would die as well.

Then the equation became simpler as the two demon/wolves were driven through the shattered wall and horse and rider plunged after them. And then there was only Safar and Iraj, who was coming up from a pile of debris. As Iraj rose a powerful light radiated from his body. He began to transform into a giant wolf, black as a starless night with the fires of the hells in its eyes.

The wolf turned its huge head toward Safar, maw coming open. Their eyes met . . . and held for what seemed like an eternity. It was only a moment but it was time enough for an arc of recognition to leap between them. It was like two souls brushing together—souls from another place and another time when they were just boys, fast friends, with only clear horizons before them.

Then hate rushed back and Safar let loose his spell.

He meant to kill and held nothing back but when his sorcerous bolt struck there was a white hot flare, a loud crack of overheated air, and when his eyes cleared the demon wolf who was Iraj had vanished.

Cursing, Safar sagged back against the shattered door frame. Iraj had escaped unscathed. And he was certain to return—in one form or another—with even greater forces than before.

Safar looked over at Palimak and knew a small bit of joy when he saw the boy was still sleeping peacefully as if nothing had happened. There was debris all around the bed and spatters of blood on the lower frame.

Gundara stood over the boy, chest puffed up under his elegant little doublet, standing as tall as he could, a sharp-toothed grin gleaming in his little demon's face.

"Never fear, Master," he said, bold as can be. "Gundara is here."

Safar sighed and nodded his thanks.

He heard the clatter of hooves and the creak of harness and looked up to see the mounted warrior canter up to the gaping hole that had once been a little boy's bedroom wall.

The warrior reached up with a mailed glove and swept the helm away.

Safar was too numb for surprise and he barely reacted when he saw Leiria grinning down at him.

"Are they gone?" he croaked, exhaustion overcoming him.

"Vanished, is more like it," Leiria said, still burning with the odd joy battle fever can cause. "Good thing, too. They were coming at me from both sides and I thought I was in for a helluva fight. Then, poof! they disappeared."

At that moment Palimak sat bolt up in bed. He rubbed sleepy eyes and looked all around him, noting the destruction of his room.

He looked up at Safar, still a little dazed, a worried frown creasing his brow.

"I didn't do it, father," he said. "Honest, I didn't."

6
THE COUNCIL OF ELDERS

The funeral ceremony for Iraj's victims was depressingly easy to arrange. The village was still draped in black from mourning Tio. The wailing women's cheeks were well oiled for tears. This time, however, there were no swaggering louts shouting vows of revenge.

If Tio's death had shocked the villagers, the toll they now faced was beyond shrieks and tears and shouts. Besides the three murdered sentries Leiria had found, there were six others who had been surprised and killed by Iraj and his companions.

When the dawn came and the bodies were discovered there had

been so much blood they couldn't keep the children from seeing it. After Safar pronounced the funeral prayer and the boats were fired and launched, many of the young people became hysterical with grief. They clutched each other and wept, shouting the names of their dead friends. It was a scene that would haunt many a dream for years to come.

As soon as he could Safar retreated into the little temple. But there was no peace to be found in the dusty silence of his inner chambers. Solitude makes misery larger, not smaller, Safar thought. And when you are truly alone there's no one to curse but yourself. He was exhausted from his encounter with Iraj, so tired his limbs were ungainly weights and the air itself seemed formed of the thickest clay, resisting his every motion. It was as if he had been stripped of all spirit and will, leaving him so weak that if Iraj had suddenly appeared Safar would have surrendered gladly.

It made him ill prepared when his father entered the chamber, shamefaced and shuffling.

"You are my son," he said, avoiding Safar's eyes. "But it is my duty to speak to you not as a father, but as a member of the Council of Elders. Forgive me, Safar, for what I am about to say. It's their words, not mine, that I must speak. And you should know it is only out of courtesy that the Council is allowing me to carry them to you so the insult might be lessened."

Safar nodded. "That was good of them," he said. If there was sarcasm in his manner, it was unintended.

His father stiffened. "Safar Timura, son of Khadji and Myrna Timura, it is the wish of the Council of Elders that you report immediately to the Meeting Lodge. There you will wait while the Council considers the recent tragic events and the part you played in them. You have the right to address the Council before their final decision is made. However, you may not be present while that decision is being discussed. Do you understand?"

"I understand," Safar said.

Khadji's formal pose collapsed into that of a worried and awkward father.

"You know I'll speak up for you at the meeting, son," he said.

"Of course you will," Safar said, feeling like a child pretending to be an adult so he could reassure his parent.

Khadji added to the awkward moment by suddenly leaning forward as if to embrace him, then pulling back at the last instant, embarrassed.

"Your mother and sisters send their love," he said. Then, lower, "To which I add mine."

"Thank you father," Safar said, realizing the reply was weak, but under the circumstances it was the safest one he could manage.

He saved his father and himself further embarrassment by becoming occupied with a misplaced sash. While his eyes were lowered he heard his father let loose a long sigh of frustration.

It was a sigh best ignored, so Safar drew himself up, squaring his shoulders. "Tell the Council," he said, quite formal, "that I will be honored to attend them. And will abide by whatever wise action they deem necessary."

Khadji's eyes welled with tears. He stepped back, fighting for control. Unlike Safar, he was not a self-assessing man, so he didn't understand the difficulty he had with his son. A man of strong beliefs, rights and wrongs, blacks and whites, he assumed it was some glaring fault in the clay he was made of and berated himself for his failings. Safar had inherited many of his father's flaws. On sleepless nights, when good deeds are cracked in guilt's jaws to find the sinful center, he'd added greatly to that score. Still, he was a wizard with an instinct for striking for the truth and sometimes he was even lucky enough to find it. So where his father turned away, Safar looked deeper. Over time he'd come to understand that Khadji suffered from the ancient curse of all master potters. Under a potter's hands clay is a spirit demanding form and life. It also wants to be useful. It requires a purpose. What's more it insists that purpose and beauty be combined. To achieve this unity— which all potters desire above all else—perspective must be maintained at any cost. A potter loves the clay as deeply as any being can love. Yet he can never declare it. He must not let the barest hint of it come through. Above all things a master potter must keep his distance or he will lose his vision, hence control. Or else what he loves will become an ugly thing that bursts in the kiln at the first firing.

Unfortunately, Safar thought, understanding has less value

than a beggar's bowl when it stands alone, leaving him with nothing to offer when he looked across the chasm between himself and his father.

So he said, "How is little Palimak?"

His father laughed, more in relief than anything else.

"He thinks it was all a great adventure," he said. "He's even forgotten he was asleep the whole time." Khadji shook his head in grandfatherly amusement. "When I saw him last he was sitting in your mother's lap trying to make up a poem about the great boy hero, Palimak Timura, who drove away a hungry pack of wolves."

His father laughed again and Safar laughed with him. Then before the humor could lapse into an uncomfortable silence he used the skills he'd learned as a man of the royal court to send his father away feeling as comfortable as he could under the circumstances.

It didn't make Safar feel any better. However he looked at it, the Grand Wazier and Chief Wizard of all of Esmir had just dismissed—however politely—his own father from his presence.

Safar stood outside the meeting lodge while the Elders debated his fate. The village was silent, doors barred, windows shuttered. Even the dogs had been taken in and the only sound—other than the buzz of discussion going on inside the lodge—was the harsh sawpit song of a young cicada in lust.

At first he paced, then he realized the whole village watched through those closed shutters, and he stood as still as he could, trying his best to strike a noble pose. It made him feel clownish, like a young acolyte waiting to be punished for some bit of mischief. So he fussed with that pose, shifting from noble to manly unconcern and all the other contortions people go through when they know they're being watched but must pretend otherwise. In his days as a circus magician, Methydia, who had turned witchery into a crowd pleasing art, said the greatest trick when squaring off before an audience was to find something natural to do with your hands. It was a lesson he'd thought he'd learned, but as he waited for the elders' decision his schooling hid giggling in a corner while he shuffled his hands this way and that, feeling foolish, but not knowing what to do about it.

Leiria came hurrying down the lane, clutching a large jug in one arm. When she saw him she grinned and hoisted the jug onto her head. She walked toward him, exaggerating the swing of her hips so even in a soldier's costume of metal and leather she looked like a fetching village lass coming up from the well who'd rather tarry with the lads than go home to her mother. When she reached him she maintained the pose, swinging the jug down and coming up on her toes to offer it to him.

"I hope everybody is watching," she whispered.

"Wish granted, madam," Safar said. "No magic required."

He drank the cold well water as if it were the finest wine, surprised at how thirsty he was. When he lowered the jug Leiria stepped away, relaxing into her normal flat footed stance—right hand resting on the hilt of her sheathed sword.

"They could never figure out if I was a soldier or a slut," she said. "If anyone ever had the nerve to ask, I might have been more tempted to stay here."

"How would you have answered?"

"Simple. I'd have said, 'If truth be known, sir,' assuming it was a sir who asked, 'If truth be known, sir, I was once captain of the Imperial guard. But I was also once the king's whore. So I can claim both titles, sir. I stand before you, soldier and slut together. Lips and sword, sir. Lips and sword.'"

Safar laughed. "That speech sounds like it's had a bit of practice."

"I used it on my last master," Leiria said. "But I told him only one was for hire. I could tell he'd be trouble if I didn't put him straight at the beginning, so I made him guess which was which. Lips or sword? He could see right off the penalty'd be severe if he guessed wrong, so he took the safe road and hired my sword. And that was that!"

A loud voice from the meeting lodge interrupted them. They turned to listen in, but although they could tell it was Safar's father speaking, they couldn't make out the words. Then the voice stopped and the buzz continued.

Leiria was disgusted. "This is stupid."

"I'm not that sure it is," Safar replied. He was so tired almost anything seemed to make sense. "I told them exactly what'd happened. Iraj came here looking for me. And for Palimak. From their point of view the boy and I are responsible for the deaths of many fellow Kyranians."

"So what are they going to do about it?" Leiria asked. "Exile the two of you? Cast you out? As if that's going to solve anything."

"Maybe it will," Safar said wearily. "If we leave, maybe Iraj will let them be."

Leiria sneered. "That's ridiculous!" she said. "Iraj would never be satisfied so easily. He'd want to lay waste to the village as well." She snorted. "Typical leadership! Doesn't matter if you're talking about the leaders of the grandest city or smallest hamlet. They're all the same. I came to the conclusion long ago that to be a leader you must first drink the Wine of Stupidity. Followed by a hefty slug of the Brandy of Forgetfulness. And then a nice tot of Trivial Answers To Questions No One Asked for a nightcap."

She jabbed a finger at the lodge. "They know Iraj. He lived here when he was a boy. They sheltered him when he needed them most. It was Kyrania who brought Iraj here, not Safar Timura. You were only a boy, what did you have to say about it?" Another finger jab at the lodge. "I'd wager anything that your precious Council of Elders held a vote on whether Iraj was to be invited. Any trouble they have with him now comes from that decision.

"So who is to blame? The former members of the Council of Elders? Or Safar Timura, a young lad in a village so small you and Iraj were bound to meet?"

Safar made a wry grin. "You have a way of putting things in such simple terms," he said.

Leiria smacked her sword hilt. "Not so simple that they aren't true," she said. "Any ordinary person could see it. Those silly old men are in there trying to decide who to blame. Which will end up being you and Palimak. No doubt about that! Meanwhile, they're ignoring the real problem. Which is that Iraj will return—and in full force.

"Hells, the only reason they're meeting for so long is that they're faced with harming one of their own. Palimak will be easy for them. Half demon, half human. Bad luck all around and who else could be to blame? What they'll probably do is ignore you entirely and banish Palimak."

"But anyone who knows me would understand what that'd mean," Safar said, bewildered. "Which is that I'd have to leave as well. Adopted or not, half-breed or quarter breed, I'm responsible for the child."

Leiria rose up on her toes and gave him a quick kiss. "Of course you feel that way," she said. "That's why I fell in love with you. I didn't need the presence of Palimak to know that's how you would act if some sort of thing like that ever occurred. That's why I came back.

"Unless you missed it, Safar Timura, I have returned! Which in my mind—being the only mind I possess—is a damned remarkable thing and you are one hells of a lucky fellow!"

She raised her head and looked Safar straight in the eyes, catching them and holding them so there would be no misunderstanding. "But it's not for love," she said. "At least not that kind of love. I'm not only over that, but I've gone on."

Safar nodded. He had an odd feeling of sudden relief . . . and regret. "No need to be upset," he said, rather lamely. "I'm not expecting anything, or asking anything of you."

Leiria slapped her sword, angry. "Dammit, Safar Timura, that's not what I mean at all! I'm your friend. Ask me anything. That's what I want . . . maybe all that I ever really wanted. But ask me, dammit! Ask! Or go to the hells along with the whole damned world you're worried about!"

Safar didn't know what to say. He tried to make a weak joke out of the situation. "You never give me a chance to thank you," he said. "You keep saving my life before I can even shout for help."

Leiria nodded toward the lodge. The meeting had ended and his father was standing in the doorway beckoning him. "They're ready for you," she said. "The question is, are you ready for them?"

Safar's mind suddenly cleared. Resolve returned. Which had been Leiria's intent from the beginning.

"I'm ready," he said. "Now I know what to do."

Safar didn't wait for the Elders to settle into various poses of wisdom. He struck first. "I know you've already made your decision," he said, "but I also understand I have the right to speak before the ruling is announced."

A swift glance around the silent room showed him he was right. Except for his father, they all avoided his eyes. "All of us are not in agreement," his father said hotly, glaring at the other Elders. "So yes, son, a speech in your own defense would be most appreciated."

"But a vote has been taken, has it not?" Safar asked.

"Yes it has, Lord Timura," said Foron, the chief elder. The look on his face was that of someone who had tasted something unpleasant, but was required by circumstance to take another bite. "A vote has been taken. Your father was in the minority."

"Then I have absolutely no intention of defending myself," Safar said.

"Please, son," his father protested.

Safar raised a hand, begging his silence. "But I do insist on my right to speak."

"This is most unusual," Masura grumbled. "Not in the rules at all."

There were loud exclamations of agreement and disagreement. The Elders' debate still had them stirred up. Foron thumped the ceremonial pot in front of him. It made a booming sound like a large drum. Everyone obediently stopped. Safar noted with minor interest the speaker's pot had been made by a Timura long ago.

"Seems simple enough to me," Foron said. "In Kyrania all citizens can say what they want, when they want. Lord Timura is a citizen of Kyrania. Let him talk."

Masura tried to protest. "But this is a formal meeting of—"

"Oh, be silent!" Foron said. "We're not judges in some king's royal court. This is a village, not a city. Everyone knows Safar. Hells, most of us are even third and fourth cousins to him. Let him talk."

There was instant silence. Even those opposed to Safar were chastened. Masura opened his mouth to protest, caught the heavy scent of disapproval, and stopped.

Safar said, "No matter what your decision—be it in my favor, or not—I will leave Kyrania tomorrow!"

Khadji cursed and there were sounds of shock all around, even from the majority who had called for Safar's banishment. How could a Kyranian willingly leave his home? This was the blessed land. The Valley of the Clouds where Kyranians had lived for as many generations as there were stars in the sky. Where the Goddess Felakia reigned, rewarding them with her bounty because they were her chosen people. The people of the High Caravans.

Safar raised a hand for silence. "My decision," he said, "has nothing to do with these proceedings. Or any of the tragic events that have occurred. In fact, when we last met I was going to announce my departure. But it didn't seem the right time, what with all the panic over Tio. I was, however, going to ask permission to leave Palimak with you." He nodded at his father. "Under my parent's care, of course. The journey I have in mind is rather dangerous for a child."

The journey he was referring to was his half-formed, and therefore unspoken, plans to somehow make his way to Syrapis and investigate the vision in the demon wizard's tomb.

Masura snickered. "You must think we're fools," he said. "First, to believe that you'd already intended to leave us. Secondly, that we'd harbor that devil's—"

"Be careful, Masura!" the headmaster broke in, eyeing Khadji, who was about to come across the room after Masura to make him eat the insult. "This is no time for loose talk!" Foron turned to Safar. "Most of us like the lad, Lord Timura," he said. "At the time we would've granted your wishes." He shrugged, "But things have changed since then."

"What cowardly words!" Khadji broke in. "Say it plain, Foron. You voted with the majority—which consists of everyone but me!" He turned to Safar. "These cunning devils voted to exile Palimak," he said. "But not you. They figured if they banished him, you'd have no choice except to go with him."

Safar buried a smile. How right Leiria had been. Only now did he fully appreciated her subtle efforts to arm him against the elders, and to shoulder duty's burden and march on. A duty Safar was just beginning to make out. Dim as the outlines were, the undertaking would be enormous. If not impossible.

He had to go carefully, or he would stumbled at the first step. "Never mind them, father," he said. "It doesn't matter anymore. Because when I leave I'm taking Palimak with me."

There were murmurs of relief among the Elders. The issue was being settled for them. Possibly they could even forgo the announcement of the ban, which would be been controversial in the extreme. The Timura clan was as popular as it was influential.

It was the perfect time for Safar to play the next piece in a game whose rules he was making up as he went along. "I have only one request to make of the Council," he said.

Foron smiled broadly. With the pressure off he was eager to please. "Ask anything you like, Lord Timura," he said. "How can we help your journey? Is it supplies you need? Animals to carry them? Tell us exactly what you want from us and it will be provided."

"I want you to come with me," Safar answered, flat.

There was stunned amazement, which shattered as everyone shouted at once, some saying Safar must be insane, others that maybe he'd been misunderstood and should be given the chance to explain. Safar waited the small tempest out, noting the majority against him was hardly solid. Even though in effect they'd voted to banish him, Masura's trick of putting the vote against Palimak had only gone so far. Lord Timura had spoken. Mysterious as his intentions might be, they were used to listening to him with enormous respect.

At the proper moment Safar raised a hand and got silence. "Here's how I see it," he said. "I'm sure most of you think if Palimak and I leave, Iraj will ignore Kyrania and follow us."

Most of the men nodded agreement; that was the general feeling. "I mean no disrespect," Safar said, "but if you all think that, then you'd better spend a bit more time examining your logic. Because there is no way under the Demon Moon that haunts us all that Iraj will be satisfied with just my blood and Palimak's."

The Elders stirred as this truth sank in. "You all know as well as I," Safar continued, "that anyone who helped Iraj at any time will suffer for it. This is his nature. Kyrania once sheltered him from powerful enemies. Believe me, he'll destroy Kyrania for knowing he was once so weak that he needed our help."

"But he was just a boy," Foron wailed, the wail giving away the fact that Safar's logic had already smashed his own. "There's nothing for him to be ashamed of. We never harmed him."

"Neither did Tio," Khadji growled, "and look what happened to him!"

Cold dread filled the room and the men shivered at the memory of Tio's ravaged corpse.

Safar said, "There only one course. And that's to flee!"

"But where should we flee to, my son?" Safar's father asked, anguished.

Safar bowed his head. "There is a place I know," he said. "A place where we may all be safe. For awhile, at least."

Masura snorted again. "Bah! Why are we wasting our time with this? Read the child Palimak off the village rolls! Banish him! None of you but I had the nerve to make it Safar Timura we're tossing out. But we all agree it'll have the same purpose. Boot out the boy and Safar will follow. Then life can get back to being normal. No more damn demons stalking our hills, no more wolves killing our children, no more anything but sow our crops, tend our goats and face each season with as much cheer as the gods will allow. This is how we've always done things. I see no reason to change. And I sure as hells am not going to listen to foolish talk about leaving the place of my fathers."

A long silence followed this outburst. However, as embarrassed as everyone was by Masura's rude behavior, Safar could sense that most of the men agreed.

Before anyone could speak there came a familiar sound—caravan bells! Everyone stirred. Could this be? It had been ages since a caravan had visited Kyrania.

A boy burst through the door, shouting, "Caravan! Caravan!"

7

THE CARAVAN MASTER

The Elders rushed outside, Safar at their heels. Doors and shutters banged open as the excited villagers rushed from their homes, blinking at the wondrous animal train rattling into the main square.

It wasn't a large caravan—there were only a few camels and llamas and perhaps six ox-drawn wagons—but it was a magnificent thing to see on such a sorry day with all the banners flying, bells jangling and animals bawling. Everyone knew it would bring news from the outside world. People laughed and shouted, thinking the news must be good, else how had the caravan made it through?

Leading the cavalcade was a huge bearded horseman who rose up in his stirrups to bellow: "Greetings, O gentle people of Kyrania. It is I—Coralean of Caspan—who once again begs your hospitality!"

The Kyranians became even more excited, repeating the name to their neighbors as if they hadn't heard for themselves. An immense smile split Coralean's big face. He was an amazing sight; armored vest buckled about his rich merchant's robes, an immense sword dangling from his waist, his beard all bedecked with colorful ribbons.

"Coralean's heart is bursting with joy," he boomed, "that his old friends remember him with such kindness. He comes to you out of a wilderness of great trouble and sorrow. There was many a night when he didn't believe he'd live 'til dawn. And there was many a dawn when he doubted the blessed night would come again."

He thumped his mailed chest and it resounded like a ceremonial drum. "But here he is! Coralean, in the flesh! And damned be the eyes of all the devils who tried to strip it from me for their supper."

"What news?" someone shouted. Others took up the cry. "What news? What news?"

Coralean waved the questioners down. "Later, my dear people, I will tell the stirring tale of what has befallen this old dog since last we met." He shaded his eyes, searching the crowd. "But first Coralean must speak urgently with his old friend, Safar Timura. Will someone send for him, please?"

Safar stepped forward, the crowd parting to let him through. "Here I am, Lord Coralean," he said. "It's good to see you after so many years."

Safar was smiling, but he was not as overjoyed as the others. He liked Coralean, owed him much for past favors, but he knew the old merchant too well to trust him completely.

When Coralean spotted Safar he leaped off his horse and engulfed him in a mighty embrace, booming, "Safar, my old friend! How glad I am to see you!"

He pounded Safar's back, raising dust and a cough. Then he leaned forward and whispered, "You must call the Council of Elders together immediately!

"I bring word from Iraj Protarus!"

Once again the Elders gathered in the Meeting Lodge. This time it was to learn what the future had in store for them.

"Coralean would rather the gods had ripped his tongue from its roots," the caravan master said, "than be forced to speak the words I must say to such dear friends. I am here at the orders of King Protarus, who waits with an army not two days hence. The King sends his heartfelt greetings to all his dear friends in Kyrania and begs forgiveness for the misery caused by his struggles with the traitor, Safar Timura."

"Here now, I'll not have my son spoken of like that!" Khadji protested.

Safar patted his arm, silencing him. "Coralean means nothing by it, father," he said. "Those are Iraj's words, not his." He smiled at the old merchant. "Go on, my friend."

Coralean placed a meaty hand of sincerity across his chest. "I have sons and daughters of my own, so I understand full well that my words are wounding. As everyone knows, Coralean has the softest heart of any man in Esmir. Am I not easily moved to tears by a sad tale? Do I not shower charity on every beggar from Caspan to old Walaria? Why, the list of Coralean's generous deeds for the less fortunate could fill volumes, I tell you. Volumes!"

He looked fiercely about the room as if expecting argument. None came. "Nevertheless," he said. "I would be shunning my duty to you if I softened King Protarus' words, injurious though they may be to my old friend, Khadji Timura.

"The King commanded me to say he has no ill feelings toward the people of Kyrania. In truth, he says he has great love for them and fondly recalls the days when he was a lad and lived among you. He said he means no one here any harm. And he only asks that you lay down your arms and pledge your fealty to him. If you do this, he will reward you all greatly when he visits you with his army. And he will give much gold to the families of the young people who died in Kyrania's service to help compensate them for their great loss."

"What of Safar?" Khadji demanded. "And Palimak? I assume we're supposed to hand them over to Iraj as part of this . . . this . . . whole extortion!"

Coralean looked him full in eyes, then nodded. "As you say, my friend. As you say."

There was a touch of bitterness in Safar's laugh. "You've arrived with your message at exactly the right time," he said. "It seems that my fellow Kyranians have decided to exile me. And the boy, too."

Coralean stroked his beard, examining the faces of the other men. "That explains it," he finally said.

"Explains what?" Khadji asked.

"Why no one but yourself protested when I maligned your son," he replied.

Masura broke in. "Excuse me, Lord Coralean, but do you believe King Protarus speaks the truth? Will he spare Kyrania if we do as he demands?"

More beard stroking from Coralean. Then he nodded, "That's certainly what the King promises."

"But did he speak the truth?" Masura prodded again. "Come, my lord, you must have an opinion."

"Why, I have many opinions, my friend," the wily old caravan master said. "Sometimes my opinion is this. Sometimes it is that. All strongly held views, mind you. Coralean bows to no man when it comes to firm opinions."

Masura was exasperated. "And what is your opinion right now, please?"

Coralean grinned. "That you should seek an opinion other than mine, my good fellow. Better yet, form your own. This is the wisest advice I can give you."

He looked over at Safar. "I'm returning to Caspan when I leave here," he said. "You'll understand if I don't ask you to accompany me." He laid a hand on his breast. "Our King would not be amused."

"You're assuming that I intend to flee," Safar said, "rather than sacrifice myself to Protarus."

"Coralean admires bravery," the caravan master said. "He admires it above all things, save one," he tapped his head, "and that's a canny nature. It's a useful tool for cowards and heroes alike."

"What of Iraj?" Safar asked. "How did he seem to you?"

Coralean shrugged. "I can tell you very little," he said. "I'm not permitted to actually see him. They blindfold me and lead me into his chambers. There he addresses me. Asking for the news or commanding me to perform some errand. In return, I am given free passage through the lands he controls. What's left of his kingdom, after . . . uh . . ." he glanced at Safar, "you and he had your disagreement."

He shook his head. "If only someone had consulted Coralean. I could have negotiated a settlement that might have avoided this whole catastrophe."

"It wasn't a business dispute, my friend," Safar said.

"Nonsense," Coralean replied. "Everything is business. The world would be a much better place if only everyone realized it."

"He wanted too much," Safar said, surprised at the heat in his voice.

Coralean shrugged. "It was just a matter of price," he said. "And neither of you could see it because you had no one like Coralean to advise you." He sighed. "But what can be done about it now? We must all go on as best we can."

There was a time when Safar would have been angry at Coralean's remarks; reducing betrayal and murder to a simple business dispute and from there to crass price. He would have shouted, he would have railed. He would condemned Coralean as a hypocrite with a miser's cold lump of gold for a heart. But it was only a small moment, so small that it wasn't worth considering. He'd been a firebrand student of magic in Walaria—flirting with honey-candied idealisms like purity and truth. Then Asper had taught him there was a lie behind every truth and a truth behind every lie.

And so he said to Coralean, "You speak wisely, old friend. In the end good business is satisfaction for both sides, with the spice of promised profits on a greater scale in the future."

Coralean tapped his head. "It is a great thing to know," he said. "But unfortunately it is not always something that is acted upon." Another big grin split his face. "This is why Coralean, who is a poor man with many wives and children to feed, is not so poor as some of his competitors."

"I'm glad we understand one another," Safar said. He made a motion taking in the assembled Elders—his father included— their faces clouded with bewilderment. "All of us understand!" Which made the looks become even more bewildered.

"This is good," Coralean said. "Understanding is a virtue I praise above all others."

He plucked a long, fat leather-bound tube from his belt. It had hinged stoppers of brass on either side. He casually flipped it from end to end, then handed it to Safar.

"Here," he said, "a gift from Coralean to seal his side of the bargain."

Safar eyed him, but the old pirate's face was blank. He unsnapped one end of the tube, peered inside, then unscrewed a thick sheaf of parchment papers. He fanned them out, the other men bending close to look.

"Why they're maps," Foron said. "What do we need with maps?"

Coralean shrugged. "Worthless things," he said, "if you plan to stay in one place. But if you intend to travel, why I expect you might find them of some value."

"These are caravan maps," Safar said. "Worth a fortune to any trader."

"You will note," Coralean said, bending forward and poking at one of the maps, "the detail of these maps. They show all of Esmir, including the most secret trading routes favored by peace-loving merchantmen like myself. Why bother with bandits and greedy local overlords if you can skip them out by choosing another path? And if one were being followed by a fierce competitor, why you could quickly shake him off by using an unexpected route."

Safar quickly scanned the maps, which showed in detail the

whole northern region—from the Gods Divide to the port of Caspan where ships might be for hire to get him to Syrapis. He also marked the cities Asper had said he must visit on the way— Naadan and Caluz. It would be an extremely difficult undertaking, only made possible by the many hiding places along the route which were detailed on the maps.

He rolled the maps up and slipped them back into the tube. "What do you desire in return?" he asked.

Coralean slapped his knee and roared laughter. "Why isn't obvious, my good friend? I want your favor. If someday I stand before you a ruined man, I'll expect your help."

Safar made a thin smile. "In case things don't work out for Iraj, you mean?"

Coralean shrugged a mighty shrug. "Who can say what the morrow will bring, brother? At the moment, Iraj Protarus seems to have the upper hand. He's regained a good portion of his kingdom and nothing seems to stand in the way of his winning all of it back. Few kings dare defy him and those that do are guaranteed a horrid end.

"Also, his magic, I'm told, is most powerful. I've even heard rumors that he is a shape changer. Wolf and man in the same body. This could be true, it could be false. However you look at it, rumors are bad for business. And if he is a shape changer, why, how does an honest businessman know if he'll abide by his word? Did I make a contract with a man, or a wolf? Or something in between?"

Coralean sighed. "And so I come to my dearest friend, Safar Timura, for whom I have done many favors in the past. True, he is a wizard. But a most amiable one who has never meant old Coralean anything but the best. I'm sure a man as great as that will understand Coralean can do the bidding of Iraj Protarus and still look out for his good friend."

Now it was Safar's turn to slap his knee and roar laughter. "You win either way, right? No matter who loses, you win?"

Coralean made a long face. "I suppose you could look at it that way," he said. "But it would spoil the spirit of the bargain. I truly hope you win, Safar Timura. I doubt if you will, but there is a slight chance, considering that Iraj lost out to you once before. You will appreciate, I hope, the elegance of my bargain."

He gestured at the maps. "Coralean gives you freedom! In any direction you choose to take. I ask only your word in return. Your word that someday, if required, I may call on your favor."

"Consider it a bargain, my friend," Safar said. "And no hard feelings if it doesn't work out my way."

Coralean beamed. "I am most pleased!" he said. "I made a wise investment in you when you were young and I paid for your education in Walaria." He brushed his hands together and rose heavily to his feet.

"Please, gentlemen," he said to the Elders, "I hope you will forgive Kyrania's oldest and dearest friend, but I must be on my way. Please make my apologies to your people, but the caravan must not tarry. We're off to Caspan where Coralean's wives wait with much anxiety for his return. I'll leave some fine food and drink for you all, in hopes that you will toast Coralean's health. Bull that I am, I will need it desperately for my loving wives when they welcome me home."

Safar rose with him and Coralean grasped his hand, squeezing hard. "Before I depart, I will send a runner to Iraj's camp with my report. Unfortunately, the runner I have in mind—alas, the only man I can spare—is rather elderly and infirm, so it may take a little time for him to reach the king."

"What will the report say?" Safar asked.

"Coralean is not a man who lies," he said. "I will tell him that I delivered his proposal. And the Council of Elders is presently meeting to consider his magnificent offer."

"How much time do you think we have?" Safar asked.

Coralean shrugged his apologies. "Not much for you," he said. "But quite sufficient for me. I am a minor spot for Iraj to consider. His thoughts are full of you, so it isn't difficult for me to slip out the side door while he's thinking."

He made a face. "What can I say? I have a family to care for. Children enough to fill a villa with Coraleans and wives anxious to produce more." He sighed. "Few men appreciate the burdens I bear. The responsibilities are endless."

"Do you really believe," Safar asked, "that Iraj will wait two days or more for your messenger?"

Coralean lumbered to his feet. "That's another reason I must hurry on my way," he said. "Your former master has been known to apply a little pressure when he's negotiating. So if you will forgive me, my dear friends, I must say goodbye and make haste!"

The old caravan master stepped forward and embraced Safar in a great bear hug. "Good fortune, traveler," he said, in the age old blessing of the road. "Good fortune!"

Then he was gone.

Chaos followed as the Council of Elders turned into mere men—and frightened men at that! They all gathered around Safar, shouting questions and opinions and any nonsense that came into their heads. It was plain to them now that Iraj would attack no matter what they did.

Safar felt his energy creeping back, and with it, his confidence.

"Call all the people together," he said—no, he commanded, his old authority of office settling onto his shoulders like a royal robe.

"We must act now, or all is lost!"

8

BONES OF FORTUNE

They were the People of the Clouds; the men, women, lads and maids and wailing babes who made up Kyrania. When they gathered in the old stone fort there were just a little over a thousand of them. For many generations they had lived apart from the rest of the world. They lived up, up in that bowl of fruit and blossoms they called home where no evil could easily reach them.

But at long last darkness had descended and they were blind and stumbling, not knowing what to do.

Although he was one of them, Safar steeled himself against all empathy as they filed silently into the arena. There was no time for wasted emotion or leisurely debate by the tradition-bound Council of Elders.

If his people were to survive he must rally them to accomplish the impossible. First, they must defend themselves against Protarus. Second . . . Well, he'd get to what came next—the most daunting task of all—if they lasted the night.

He watched his people stream into the old fort and take their places on the big parade ground, pounded smooth by generations of young Kyranian boys who had trained here to defend their homeland. The fort had been built long ago, perhaps even before the time of Alisarrian, and only the battered walls and the remnants of ancient stone barracks were left.

Safar had dressed with care for the occasion. He was wearing his most glittering ceremonial robes. Never mind he no longer held the office, the robes were the ones he'd worn at King Protarus' most important court functions when Safar had been Lord Timura, the second most powerful man in all of Esmir. Upon his breast were all the medals and ribbons and awards Protarus had granted him for his many services.

He felt no sense of irony, much less guilt, as he raised his hands for attention, acting as much a king as Iraj. He'd forced himself to swallow a hefty draught of manipulative leadership. And now he had to act. The late afternoon sun made his robes glow, leaping off his medals and dazzling the crowd. Instead of friends and family, he made himself think of the gathering as an audience, with a group attention he could capture, then form to his will like good Timura clay into a good Timura pot. Adding to his regal display was Leiria, who stood next to him on the raised platform, the steel and leather of her harness and weapons burnished to a dazzling gloss. Between them was Palimak. He was dressed like a little soldier, complete with toy sword, breast plate and helmet.

As Safar gathered his mental forces, Palimak sensed the crowd's bewildered mood and whispered, "I like this father! I can make them do anything I want."

Thank the gods he said it a bare moment before Safar cast the amplifying pellet to the stone. Otherwise everyone would have heard. Instead, all they noticed was Leiria clapping her hand across Palimak's mouth, saying, "Sshhh!"

Just then the magical pellet burst and her admonishing "sshhh!" echoed loudly across the field. There was weak laughter from the crowd, who assumed Palimak had merely said something childishly clever.

Safar grabbed the moment and built on it.

"If Iraj Protarus heard that laughter," he proclaimed, voice resounding across the arena, "he'd be quaking in his boots. After all he's done, the people of Kyrania can still laugh at the antics of a little boy."

There were more chuckles, stronger than before.

Safar lifted his head as if to address the heavens. "Do you hear that, O Mighty King?" he roared. "Do you hear the spirit of the People of the Clouds? We are not afraid! We stand proud and defiant before you!"

Shouts of approval greeted this. Faces brightened, shoulders straightened and people lifted their children high so they could see better.

Safar smiled broadly at his audience, clapping his hands in congratulations. "That's the message we want to send to Iraj Protarus," he said. "He may do his worst, but our spirits will remain unbroken!"

This time nearly the entire crowd roared in agreement. Some even shook their fists at the skies as if Iraj were hiding in the clouds. Only some of his enemies on the Council of Elder appeared unmoved. They were knotted about Masura, whose face was swollen with fury because Safar had upstaged him and gone directly to the people. Safar was determined to change that look.

When the noise died down he said, "We're going to need that spirit in the days ahead, my friends. The future of all Kyranians depends on your strength.

"Nay, the world itself depends on it!"

There were murmurs and puzzled looks but Safar pushed on. His next words, he knew, would dash the little enthusiasm he'd won.

"Brave as you all are," he said, "you will need to be braver still. At this moment we are stalked by a great enemy. A royal enemy who has somehow escaped from the grave to become the king of the shape changers. He and his minions have killed innocent Kyranian children and young men."

Safar gestured at Masura and people turned to look at him. "I know you have all heard the controversy regarding those tragedies. It's said that the only reason Iraj Protarus brings such bloody actions to our peaceful valley is because he seeks revenge against me."

Masura jerked his head in dramatic agreement. Safar ignored him, signaling Leiria to lift Palimak high for all to see.

"You've also heard that Iraj demands we hand over this child," he said. "This is a child you all know. A child who is an orphan of the storms that ravage the outside world."

Not understanding the seriousness of the situation, Palimak kicked his heels in glee and shouted to the other children in the crowd—his playmates. "Look at me!" he laughed. "Look how big I am!"

Some people joined his laughter. But not enough, not nearly enough. Safar pressed on.

"It's true that Iraj demands my head," he said, "just as it's true that he requires you to hand over little Palimak. And if I thought for one minute that Protarus would spare you, pass the people of Kyrania by to savage other poor, helpless souls, I would march down the mountain to his camp and throw myself and Palimak on his mercy."

A few people, Safar's family among them, shouted, "No, no! We'll fight him. We'll never give you up!"

Safar smiled, pretending it was resounding chorus of majority approval. He took Palimak in his arms. "I'm overjoyed by your support, my friends," he said. "Palimak and I thank you for your loyalty and love."

Saying this made it so in many hearts and this time the cheers were louder as he passed the boy back to Leiria. When he turned back to speak the crowd grew quiet in anticipation.

"Unfortunately, the issues aren't so simple. The fact is, Iraj Protarus will not be satisfied until every Kyranian, from our oldest, most respected leaders down to our newborn babes are wiped from the face of Esmir. This is what we face, my friends. Not choices, but certain annihilation. This is how Iraj Protarus plans to repay you for your generosity to him when he was a boy."

Murmurs of fear ran thought the crowd. Even Masura looked grim-faced with sudden worry. Harsh reality was gradually boring through his vanity.

Meanwhile, Palimak was greatly moved by Safar's words. "Let's fight him, father," he cried. His shrill voice carried across the arena as if he were a giant's child. "To the death!" He raised his toy sword in defiance.

Fully half the crowd joined in the cheering that followed. Fired by a child's boldness, they roared for the chance to give battle and somehow bring Protarus down. Masura, however, seemed to have regained his composure and with it much of his former stupidity.

When the crowd sounds faded, Masura shouted, "You have no right to speak, Timura! You and the boy have been banished by order of the Council."

Since the vote hadn't been announced, some people were taken by surprise and started muttering among themselves. Masura and his supporters took advantage of the confusion, shouting, "Don't listen to him!" and "He's just trying to save his own skin."

Safar cracked another capsule of amplification, then spoke, voice so strong it drowned out his foes. "People of Kyrania!" he thundered, flinging his arms high. "Heed me!"

Everyone froze. Even Masura was cowed by the thunder of his voice. "Whether I leave or whether I stay, Iraj Protarus will come this night to slay you in your beds! Unless you act with me now, that is your fate. If you doubt me . . . then witness this!"

He snapped his fingers and there was a crack! like a glacier rock exploding in a campfire. At the same time his other hand shot out, snatching at the air. There were gasps of amazement as he drew first one long yellow bone, then another, from thin air.

Safar made a great show of it, displaying the casting bones for all to see. He fanned them out and a thousand pairs of eyes were compelled to count them, one, two, three, four, five!

Safar chanted, feeling his power growing over them with each word he spoke:

Has the day falsed us?
Promising nights
With strong shutting doors?
Did the light halt us?
From seeing skull eyes
Dark and void?

The bones made a ghastly rattle as Safar hurled them onto the platform. Two thousand eyes followed their progress, saw them bounce and scatter. The crowd was deathly silent as Safar peered long and hard at the ivory pattern.

"Will Iraj come?" Palimak asked, posing the question for all.

Safar raised his head. He looked first at the crowd, then Palimak, finally, straight at Masura. The man's eyes were bright with fearful suspense, his defiance smothered in Safar's hypnotic spell.

He stretched the moment to the fullest, then whipped out his silver dagger and jabbed its point at the jumble of bones. "Speak, O great spirits!" he commanded. "What is your answer?"

He waved the dagger and the bones floated off the platform. He motioned again and they reformed themselves, shifting from one pattern to the next, until finally they formed the skeletal head of a giant wolf.

"Speak!" Safar again commanded. "Speak!"

There were wild shrieks of alarm as fire burst from the wolf-head's empty sockets. The big jaws grated open, unleashing a blood-chilling howl! Suddenly, the head flew forward—straight at Masura! Howling and snapping its jaws.

Masura ran away, screaming, "Help me! Help me!" But everyone fled from his path, crying out in fear. At just the right moment Safar jabbed his dagger at the head and an explosion ripped the bones apart and they vanished into nothingness.

"There is your answer, my friends!" Safar shouted. "Iraj will come! The Fates have decreed it!"

Masura realized he was safe and fell to his knees, babbling, "Save us, Lord Timura! Save us!"

First Masura allies joined in, then the rest of the crowd, all shouting, "Save us, Lord Timura! Save us!"

Safar had won. The victory disgusted him.

Another sin to add to his ledger.

It was a warm night, a night that drew roiling mists off the lake. Under the Demon Moon the mists made ominous shadows, deep oranges and reds bleeding through fantastic black figures that spilled over hollow and hill and got caught up in the branches of trees where owls waited to hoot at darkening skies.

In the village all the homes were shuttered and dark. The chimneys were cold, the cobbled streets empty and the only sound was the belly rumble of a llama and the long soft tramp of its feet.

Renor was leading the llama, an old thing who had seen more of life than she liked but pressed on anyway from habit. She was carrying a heavy load of thorny brush that shifted painfully from side to side as she walked. The llama groaned and Renor dodged just in time as she tried her best to step on his foot.

"Don't bother complaining, Granny," Renor said. "I won't feel sorry for you no matter what you do." He shook his head at the swaying burden on her back. "I did my best to tie it down tight. But you blew yourself up like an old horse and now all the knots are loose. It's your fault, not mine."

The llama swung its head to the side, there was a rumble in its guts, and then it coughed up a good spit. Once again Renor dodged to the side and a stream of smelly stuff splattered against an alley wall.

"Threats won't do you any good either, Granny," Renor said, brushing away the few drops that had spattered onto his cloak. "You'll still have to carry this load all the way to the fort. And if there's time you'll have to go back and fetch another."

The llama grumbled in protest, but Renor was unmoved. "I don't know why Lord Timura wants all this wood," he said, "but if he says to fetch it, and the more the better, then we'd better fetch it!"

They rounded the corner and Renor saw the dark shape of the fort looming out of the gathering gloom. The llama stopped its complaining and quickened its pace.

"Ho! So you go quickly now, do you?" Renor said. "You think your day's work is over. Lazy old thing." He looked up at the Demon Moon, growing deeper red as night rushed in. "I sure hope you're right," he grudged. "I don't want to go back out into this again."

He thought of the huge mound of brush and timber already piled in the center of the fort. When he'd delivered his last load Captain Leiria had been directing people to spread the wood out into some kind of design. No one seemed to know its purpose. Only that Lord Timura had ordered it done and so they were doing it. Just like Renor and a score of other village lads were unquestioningly scouring the countryside for wood. Lord Timura had said it was to protect them from Protarus and after seeing the magical wolfhead chase after Masura, nobody was going to argue.

Personally, Renor hadn't needed any convincing. After what had happened to Tio and his adventure by Lord Timura's side in the meadow, he was burning for revenge. He imagined himself advancing on a cowering devil wolf, spear raised to strike.

Just then the llama bawled and Renor almost jumped out of his skin. The animal surged forward, breaking into a fast lope. Renor shouted at it and ran to grab the load, which was tilting dangerously to the side. As he reached for it he heard an ungodly howl.

The young man whirled and his breath froze in his chest when he saw the four huge gray shapes bounding toward him.

Renor turned and ran, scrabbling his sharp work knife from his belt. Behind him the four creatures shattered the night with their howls. He ran faster, catching up to the llama. Renor slashed at the ropes and the load fell away. The animal stumbled, bawling in terror, but he yanked on its halter, helping it keep to its feet.

"Run, Granny, run!" he shouted and the llama leaped away.

Heavy bodies, moving at a frightening speed, were closing on him.

Renor was only twenty feet from the fort entrance, but the beasts were coming on so fast it might as well have been a thousand.

Then he saw a figure leap from the ruined walls. It was Lord Timura! Safar landed in front of the entrance.

"Get down!" he shouted.

Renor dropped to the ground, bracing for the scything claws he was sure would follow.

Then there was a sound like the wind and a hot breath whooshed! over his body. Behind him the howls turned into yips of pain.

Renor looked up and saw Lord Timura beckoning him.

"Come on!" he shouted. "I can't hold them for long!"

Renor scrambled up and ran for it. He turned his head and saw a wall of hot light. Just beyond the four wolf shapes howled in pain and rage.

Then he was sprinting past Lord Timura into the safety of the fort.

People rushed to him, shouting what was wrong and was he all right and other such nonsense. Struggling for breath, Renor pushed them away and turned to see what was happening.

Just as he did he saw the wall of light—some sort of magical shield—vanish and the four wolf figures crashed through.

Lord Timura backed up quickly and at the same time Renor saw Captain Leiria and some men pushing a big cart of wood into the entrance.

"Now!" Lord Timura shouted and someone threw a burning torch onto the wood.

The wood caught and there was a great blast of white light, blinding Renor. Then his vision cleared and he saw the wagon was engulfed in eerie flames that sparked and shot off long tongues of fire.

Beyond the flames, which seemed to have sealed the entrance, Renor could no longer hear the howling.

A small hand tugged at his cloak and Renor looked down to see little Palimak standing beside him, his toy soldier armor glittering in the fire.

"We're safe now," he said. Still, he had a worried look on his face. "But I think they'll come back pretty quick."

It was like an omen, because as he spoke the howling resumed.

Safar crouched in the little tent, assembling his magical arsenal by candlelight. He was mixing herbs and votive powders in a strange little pot with a five-sided mouth, working quickly and expertly in the near dark. He was used to such difficulties. When he'd been a young acolyte in Walaria he'd often lacked the price of lamp oil and so he'd had to practice his spell making under similar conditions. Although it had been much more pleasant to hear the watchman call the hour, rather than listen to the incessant howling outside the fort.

Never mind he was fairly certain Iraj and his friends were merely waging a war of nerves while they gathered their strength for the next attack. If that were the intent, by the gods it was working. The awful sound of the howling had everyone's nerves stretched taut. Safar had the village busy with a myriad of tasks, trying to keep their minds off the four savage creatures bounding and baying about the walls. The Kyranians went about their duties silently, whispering prayers to the Lady Felakia.

When the attack came, Safar had no idea how much force Iraj could muster. The only thing he was sure of was that it would be entirely magical. Coralean had no reason to lie when he'd said that Iraj's army was two days distant. Safar guessed it was even farther away than that—the terrain they had to cover was all treacherous mountains. Also, if there'd been an army behind him, the massacre of Kyrania would already be over. No, tonight would be a night of horrors meant to intimidate the villagers. To soften them up for his army.

To help in his work Iraj had three of the most cunning creatures in the history of Esmir. Two had been demons in their previous forms and therefor magical by birth, although Prince Luka was nowhere near as powerful as Lord Fari, who had been chief wizard to several generations of demon kings. Iraj's other ally was the human spymaster Kalasariz, who had no natural magical powers but was so ruthless and clever he hadn't needed them. The three had preyed on Iraj's many weaknesses, promising him even greater powers then being the mere king of kings of all Esmir. The result was The Spell of Four—the shape changer's spell—that bound them together forever.

Safar poured a silvery liquid into the pot, whispered a chant until the mixture began to bubble, then set it aside for his next task. He slipped five heavy-headed war arrows from a bundle and dipped them into the liquid one by one.

The defensive spell he was concocting was much weaker than he'd like, but he had no choice. With over a thousand people to protect he was going to be spread very thin. A more powerful spell—a spell capable of doing any real harm to Iraj but still safeguarding the villagers—would be impossible to maintain.

His preparations done, Safar opened his wizard's pouch and lifted an amulet out by its leather thong. It was made of some rare black stone that had been carved into the shape of a wondrous horse. The amulet had once belonged to Iraj—a gift from Coralean for saving his life. Safar had received the silver witch's dagger at the same time and for the same reason.

He remembered the moment as if it were yesterday, instead of nearly twenty years before. Safar and Iraj had been mere lads then. Even so, they'd first warned and then rescued Coralean and his caravan from a marauding army of demon bandits who'd broken out of the Forbidden Desert.

The gifting had come at a meeting of the Council of Elders and both boys had been bursting with pride as Coralean praised them.

Safar slipped back in time, remembering . . .

"First, I must thank my friend Iraj," the caravan master said. He took out a black velvet pouch. Iraj's eyes sparkled as Coralean withdrew a small golden amulet. It was a horse—a wondrously formed steed dangling from a glittering chain. "Some day," Coralean said, "you will see the perfect horse. It will be a steed above all steeds. A true warrior's dream, worth more than a kingdom to men who appreciate such things. The beast will be faster and braver than any animal you could imagine. Never tiring. Always sweet-tempered and so loyal that if you fall it will charge back into battle so you might mount it again.

"But, alas, no one who owns such a creature would ever agree to part with it. Even if it is a colt its lines will be so pure, its spirit so fierce, that the man it belongs to would be blind not to see what a fine animal it will become." He handed the horse amulet to Iraj. "If you give this magical ornament to that man he will not be able to refuse you the trade. But do not fear that you will be cheating him. For he only has to find another dream horse and the man who owns it will be compelled to make the same bargain when he gives him the amulet."

Tears welled in Iraj's eyes and they spilled unashamedly down his face as he husked his thanks and embraced the caravan master. "When I find that horse," Iraj said, "I promise that I will ride without delay to your side so you can see for yourself what a grand gift you gave me."

A great chorus of howls, louder than before, broke through Safar's reverie and he jolted back to the present. He checked the arrow tips, but the potion smeared on them was still damp. A few more minutes and he'd be ready.

Safar glanced down at the amulet. Iraj had never found that horse. He remembered that Iraj had cursed Safar for that failing, as if he were to blame. Then he'd hurled it into Safar's face,

demanding that he take it in payment for Nerisa. At that moment
the war between them had begun.

"Ah, well," Safar said to himself, taking comfort from the
sound of his own sighing whisper. "Ah, well."

He tested the arrows again. They were ready.

Safar gathered them up, along with a sturdy bow, and slipped
from the tent to confront the night.

Leiria gritted her teeth as the next chorus of howling began. It was
a sound that first pierced the ears, then jabbed the brain with hot
spear points. All around her the villagers crouched down in
misery. Some wept and covered their heads to drown out the
sound, while others held their heads high in stoic defiance.

Palimak stirred beside her. She'd promised Safar that she'd
guard the child until the danger had passed.

"If I were bigger," he said, "I could magic their howls right out
of their throats." He lifted up both hands, cupping them into
paws like a cat's. Needle point claws emerged from his fingertips.
"I'd do like this . . ." and he slashed the air with his claws . . . "and
cut those howls right out!"

Not for the first time, Leiria felt a shiver when confronted with
the demon side of the child's nature. Claws and glowing eyes are
damned hard to get used to! She wondered, also not for the first
time, if she would've been able to adopt the child as her own as
Nerisa had done. The thought of Nerisa made her feel momentary
resentment. The woman had remained her rival even beyond the
grave. Then she remembered her resolve and smiled at the lapse.
She and Safar were friends, not lovers. So there was nothing to
resent.

Then the howling stopped. The silence came so abruptly it was
like falling off a cliff into nothingness. Leiria tensed for danger,
one arm going around Palimak.

"Look, Aunt Leiria," the child said, "there's my father!"

Her eyes swept left and she saw Safar walking from the small
shelter to the raised platform in the center of the field. People
called out to him as he passed and he had a quick smile and word
of reassurance for each of them, but he never paused, always
moving easily and quickly along towards his goal. Leiria remem-

bered when he'd done the same at Iraj's great court in Zanzair, giving cheer to his followers while hurrying to an appointment with the king. Except then he'd been moving through a dazzling royal chamber instead of a makeshift campground full of frightened peasants and their flocks.

Palimak struggled to get up. "I'd better go help him," he said.

Leiria gently pulled him back, saying, "Your father said you had to stay with me."

Palimak frowned. "Well, maybe he did," he admitted. "But I still think I ought to help. This is going to be a really, really hard spell. Maybe harder than he thought. I can feel it all the way over here."

His voice was mild, but Leiria could tell he was worried and a little angry with her for holding him back. His eyes were beginning to glow yellow and his little pointy claws were emerging unbidden.

"But if you disobey your father," Leiria said, "you might spoil his spell. I mean, what if he's so worried about you that he can't concentrate? Then what'll happen?"

Palimak sighed dramatically and slumped down. "I suppose you're right," he said. Then he brightened. "But we can be his . . . his . . . reserves, right?" he said. "Like they do in the army?"

Leiria chuckled. "That's exactly right," she said. She patted her sword. "We'll be his brave and loyal reserves. I'll provide the steel." She nodded at the stone turtle clutched in his hand. "And you can provide the magic."

Palimak chortled. He lifted up the little idol. "Did you hear that, Gundara? We get to be reserves. You too, Gundaree. Won't that be fun?"

There was no answer, at least any Leiria could make out. But Palimak seemed satisfied so the two little Favorites must have heard. She looked up and saw Safar mounting the platform, waving to the crowd, while at the same time directing some men who were quickly encircling the platform with a pile of wood. That circle was the center of a great four-pointed star also made of wood. Many barrels of oil, magically enhanced by Safar, had been poured on the wood, as well as on the mounds of additional wood scattered strategically about the field.

It would be a strange kind of fight, Leiria thought. Logs and bundles of brush instead of spears and swords. Like Palimak, she wished she could join Safar. Perhaps even more so. Finer feelings aside, Leiria had been Safar's personal bodyguard for many years. She'd turned away assassins' knives in the dark and had even charged into battle with him to protect his back.

Safar's orders, however, had been quite plain. If he failed—and all was lost—she and the two Favorites were to carry Palimak to safety. The child, he said, must survive at all costs. He'd entrusted her with one other thing, nearly as precious, he said.

Leiria patted her breast pocket. Inside was a small book, the Book of Asper. She was to keep that safe as well.

"Give it to the boy when he's old enough," Safar had said. "He'll know what to do once he's read it."

Just then, Safar made a gesture and green flame and smoke burst from the earth. The crowd went silent. Not a child cried, or a goat bawled. And when next Safar spoke his voice rang out like a great temple bell.

Leiria leaned forward, swept up like the rest.

"Gentle people," Safar said, "the moment is upon us, so listen to me closely. You will need courage and boldness this night, but you will also need your good common sense. No one here has had experience in magical battle, but I can assure you it isn't much different than the ordinary kind. There'll be lots of noise, smoke and confusion. The trick is to concentrate on your duties, whether it's to help me or assist a child or sick family member. Pay no attention to anything else and we'll be just fine when this is all over."

Safar saw all the wise nods his remarks drew, but he also saw the glazed, wide-eyed look in them that comes from facing a nightmare. He wondered if any of them really understood what he was saying. Hells, he wondered if they were even capable of hearing what he had to say.

As he struggled for words to break through their fear Iraj launched the first attack.

9

ESCAPE TO SYRAPIS

He was only a boy, too young to be alone in the mountains and he came out of the night crying, "Help me, Renor! Help me!"

The boy was a ghostly figure whose plaintive cry cut into every human heart gathered in the fort. His father collapsed, his mother shrieked and his brother shouted, "Tio! Tio!"

Kalasariz laughed as he manipulated little Tio's ghost. He put all the pain he could into its voice as it cried, "Help, me, please! Help me!"

He fed on the crowd's hysteria, straining to conjure up more ghosts. Kalasariz was new to shape-changer's magic and he found it difficult to concentrate.

Then Renor ran to the top of the fort's walls and clawed at the sky, weeping and flailing at nothingness in his effort to help his brother.

Kalasariz laughed again and made stronger magic.

Nine other ghosts faded into being.

They were the slain Kyranian sentries, with Rossthom at the their head, pleading with all their families and friends, "Help me, please help me!"

Now the crowd in the fort went from hysteria to blind madness. To Kalasariz' delight they rushed the walls wailing comforts to the dead.

The spy master's blood boiled with delight. As he liked to tell Luka and Fari—his demon rivals for influence over Protarus—native intelligence was more important than magical prowess. Even with his lesser magic, he could accomplish much by simply knowing his target's weaknesses.

He gloried at the agony he'd caused, drawing in more power from that pain and adding other little touches to his handiwork, like a bloody scar on Tio's face and a gory stump on Rossthom's right arm where a hand used to be.

Kalasariz struggled mightily and gave them all a voice, crying, "Help me! Help me!"

He basked in the misery, his black spirit wallowing in it—sinking and rising then sinking again in the heady musk.

And then he heard a voice shout, "Kalasariz!"

His spirit head jerked down, looking from sky to ground for the source of the shout—spectral eyes honing in like an eagle owl hunting a squeaking rodent. When he found the source of the squeak he would blast it from existence. But instead of a puny creature his eyes fell on a tall man with fiery blue eyes that cut across the great distance to sear his heart.

It was Safar, posing on a stone platform in the classic frieze of a bowman, heavy weapon bent tip to tip, string making a high-pitched whine as the flaming arrow leaped from the bow.

Kalasariz loosed his own killing bolt, but the fiery arrow speeding toward him made him jerk, spoiling his aim, and he desperately flung himself to the side.

In the fort Safar heard the boom! of his arrow exploding, heard Kalasariz wail, then swiveled, grabbing up another arrow as his eyes swept the skies for his next target.

Behind him, a huge gray wolf leaped onto the walls. The creature's claws gripped the rough stone and there was a flash as the wolf transmuted himself into demon form.

It was Prince Luka, eyes aglow, fangs bared, sword lifted high. Although people screamed warnings it was almost too late for Safar, who whirled, falling and firing at the same time. A tongue of flame arced from Luka's sword, but Safar's own arrow exploded simultaneously. He heard Luka shriek then felt pain sear his own back as the prince's bolt blasted close overhead.

He came to his feet with difficulty, stifling a groan as he picked up his third arrow and fixed it into his bowstring.

Lord Fari watched Safar shuffle in a clumsy circle, pain-dulled eyes searching for the next point of attack. But the canny old demon wasn't so foolish that he'd mistake his enemy's stumbling show for real weakness. Safar was hurt, yes, he could see that. But how badly? Long ago, when Safar was the prize jewel in Iraj Protarus' crown, Fari had noted Safar's talent at showmanship. It was a thing that Fari, who was a purist when it came to sorcery, particularly disliked in him. Still, he had grudging admiration for the way Safar used his magical theatrics to convince the entire royal court, demon and human alike, that he was a most powerful wizard truly deserving of the title Grand Wazier.

So Fari assumed that much of Safar's present difficulty was a sham to draw him out.

Instead of leaping onto the walls of the fort, Fari crept up on them. He put his spirit self into its demon presence and scrambled to the high point at the ruined gate. Then he made his spell, chuckling at his cleverness as he did so.

Even Leiria, who had seen all the terrible things a soldier could see, was shaken by what happened next. The stone walls of the fort came suddenly and horribly alive as the rubble was transformed into small mountains of gore that moved and squirmed and streamed torrents of blood. People screamed and fled this way and that, bouncing from one horror to the other. Then pustules of gore bloomed on the walls and each pustule became a face and each face was a Tio or a Rossthom or any of the other slain sentries.

But this time instead of begging for help, the ghosts snapped at their friends with long teeth and spewed obscenities.

Leiria gathered up a struggling Palimak and was preparing to flee when Safar fired his arrow.

Automatically her eyes followed its fiery flight and she saw it was hurtling toward the north corner of the wall. There were dozens of human faces there, shouting filth or begging for assistance.

Then she saw the target and the moment became quite still. Just below center, between two faces that were both Tio's, she saw Lord Fari. The demon was scowling with concentration, putting all his clever old ways into the apparition that was the wall of blood.

Safar's arrow flashed toward that face and Leiria had a jolt of pleasure when she saw Fari's yellow jaws widen with fear.

Then, crack! as the arrow struck. Flame running all around the walls. And then they were nothing but blank stone again. Leiria saw a spot of blood where Fari's face had been and prayed that Safar had done heavy damage.

On the platform Safar took his time as he fitted the fourth arrow into his bow. Iraj would be next, he thought. But from which direction would he strike . . . and in what manner?

The answer came in a great shout from above: "Safar!"

It was Iraj's voice and Safar's head shot up and he saw the face of the Demon Moon suddenly split down the middle and yawn open like a gigantic mouth. A ghostly cavalry charged out of that mouth, lead by a mighty warrior in golden armor.

It was Iraj.

And he shouted a challenge—"Safar!"

Iraj yanked back on his horse's reins and the huge ghost animal reared up, pawing the night, sparks shooting from its hooves.

Then horse and rider plunged down toward the fort, a horrid cavalry of demon riders sweeping after them.

Safar fired and the arrow arced toward Iraj. It exploded just in front of him and there was a blinding flash as magic collided with magic.

Iraj paused, but only for an instant. Then he and his demon riders continued their charge.

In the fort the crowd shrieked in terror. But Safar paid no attention to their panic. As calmly as he could he swept up his final bolt. As Iraj and his spectral army closed in he whispered the spell that brought the arrow into fiery life.

He drew back, aiming for Iraj, then at the last moment he swiveled and fired the bolt into the dry mass of wood encircling the platform.

The oil-soaked fuel ignited with an enormous blast that nearly hurled Safar off the platform into the roaring flames. He teetered on the edge, but recovered his balance just in time.

The soles of his feet prickled with the intense heat and his scalp hair bristled like so many hot needles. He smelled scorched cloth and knew it came from his own robes. They smoldered at the hems and sleeves and the smoke curled up to bite his eyes.

But now it was Safar's turn to laugh. He saw flame tongues leap across the arena, shooting along the paths of wood he'd laid out, leaping from place to place until the entire arena seemed to be engulfed—with Safar and the blazing platform at its center. The whole mass finally combusted into a blazing pentagram of magical flame that smashed upward like a massive shield.

It caught Iraj and his cavalry in midstride, lifting them up and up, hurling them back at the Demon Moon.

A clap of thunder, then the sky turned white. The white shattered and became snowflakes that drifted down and down until they struck the pentagram shield blazing over the arena and flashed out of existence.

The sky was empty and there was a momentary quiet as the crowd sagged in relief. Then the air was rent with cheers as the Kyranians congratulated themselves and Safar for turning back such a deadly force.

Safar shouted to them, his voice thundering across the arena. "It isn't over yet!" The cheers vanished, swallowed by this bad news. "Iraj will be back," Safar warned. "But we'll be ready for him, my friends! We'll be ready!"

Then he shouted orders and a select group, Renor among them, sprang into action. They ran to the spare piles of brush and fed them into the flames. The fiery pentagram took on new life, soaring brighter and higher, forming a sparkling shield above the fort . .

Iraj came again. As did Kalasariz and Luka and Fari. But each time the flaming pentagram hurled them back. Safar shouted orders until he was hoarse, urging his fellow villagers to feed the fires, whipping them past exhaustion while hour piled on hour and still the attacks were unrelenting.

Many horrors were lived that night. Many threats were posed, many ghosts were roused, but somehow Safar and the villagers managed to turn them back. They burned all the gathered wood, then broke up the carts and ripped off their clothes to feed them into the magical fires.

They were exhausted when dawn finally came and the attacks ended. The pentagram was nothing more than an ugly black smudge with foul smelling heaps smoking and sputtering in the morning's wet chill. People shuddered with relief and collapsed to the ground. There were no choruses of self-congratulation. The enemy had been defeated, yes. But all knew the defeat was temporary. Iraj would return, but now he'd be backed by a real army, not specters in the sky.

Safar slumped on the platform and looked around at all the spiritless people. It was as if they had been the losers, instead of Iraj. Even so, he had to rouse them, enthuse them, convince them that all was not lost. Then somehow he had to prepare them for a challenge far more daunting than Protarus and his army of demons and wizards and human savages. To do this he would have lie to them, manipulate them, then keep on lying and manipulating until either the goal was achieved or they were all dead.

Suddenly the whole thing seemed hopeless. His people's weary despair had infected Safar and now his plan seemed foolish, impossible in the extreme.

A voice cut through, "We haven't much time, Safar."

He looked up. Leiria was standing there, a sleeping Palimak in her arms. Her eyes were red from the smoke, her armor blackened. But her back was straight, shoulders square, and there was a gleam of determination in her tired eyes.

She nodded at the slumbering Kyranians. "We have to get them up and going," she said, gently lowering Palimak to the platform. There he curled up to sleep on, the stone turtle clutched between grimy paws.

"We have maybe two days at the most," she continued, "before Iraj shows up with his whole damned army."

"I know that," Safar said, a little sharp.

Leiria snorted. "Good for you," she said. "Now, would you mind enlightening me about what we're supposed to do next? All you've said is that somehow we're going to make an entire village of over a thousand people disappear." She chuckled. "I know you are a wizard above all wizards, Safar Timura, but that's magic I'm going to have to see to believe."

As she spoke, Leiria returned the Book of Asper. The sight of the book and the buzz of sorcery when he put it away firmed his resolve. A greater tonic, as always, was Leiria's presence. Her attitude had always been, show me the mountain and we'll both figure out how to climb it together.

Safar slipped Coralean's maps from his belt. "Actually, there's no magic to it," he said, unrolling the maps. "Well, not much, anyway. It's more of a trick, really. Sleight of hand, except with two thousand hands."

"That's still one hells of a trick," Leiria said.

"Not when you consider that Iraj will be dragging along of tens of thousands of soldiers," Safar said, "plus baggage trains that'll stretch from one horizon to the next."

He showed her one of the maps. "Look here," he said, tracing a finger north from the Gods' Divide to the Great Sea. "There are so many canyons and hills and secret roads and trails between Kyrania to the Port of Caspan we could hide a small city of people, much less a village."

Leiria studied the map, eyes narrowed. Then she nodded. "It could be done," she said. Leiria glanced over at all the people collapsed on the ground. "But I don't know if it can be done by them! They've lived in one place all their lives. They know nothing about life on the road, much less life on the road with the dogs of war on your heels."

"We can teach them," Safar said. "If you're still willing to help me, that is. A sensible person would laugh in my face and walk away with her skin still safe on her bones."

"I told you before, Safar," Leiria said. "That I'm with you. No matter what. So we've got two thousand miles or more between us and the sea. So there's who knows how many hundreds of sea miles more to go to reach Syrapis. And us not knowing if there'll even be ships to hire in Caspan to take us there."

She grinned. "If that's what his lordship wants, that's what he gets!"

They both laughed, although Safar's laughter was weak. Already his mind was running ahead.

Between skirmishes, Safar had managed to tell Leiria about his vision in Asper's tomb. Although he'd held some things back— like the mysterious side trips to Naadan and Caluz. He had two reasons for his silence. First, if it became too difficult he might skip them entirely and head straight for the sea. More important: whenever he'd been about to relate exactly what Asper's ghost had said magical alarms went off. All his sorcerous instincts warned him that by telling all he'd be putting Leiria in grave danger.

Safar was especially worried about mentioning Caluz. He knew something about the region from his days in Iraj's court. It was strange place where mysterious forces had been at work for eons.

"Come to me through Caluz," Asper had commanded. But Safar dreaded the moment of decision—if they lived to see it—when he finally reached the road that led to that dark region.

Lost in thought, he was surprised when he heard Leiria say, "There's only one thing that worries me, Safar."

"What's that?"

She indicated the villagers. "Maybe they can do it. Maybe they can't. The thing is . . . how are you going to convince them to try?"

"Magic," Safar said.

And he heaved himself to his feet and started getting ready.

An hour later, washed and refreshed, Safar once again stood before his people, Leiria and Palimak beside him.

Exhausted as the Kyranians were, they seemed to sense hope in the air and their faces were bright with expectation.

Safar cracked an amplifying pellet, then spoke: "You fought well and bravely, my friends. I'm sure that even now Iraj Protarus is cursing your courage and nursing a battle-sore behind!"

The laughter was weak. No one had to tell these people that Iraj wasn't done with them. Methydia used to say that the best way to get an audience in your palm was to make a dream for them . . . and keep them reaching for that dream. But first, she'd said, you have to scare them. Well, Iraj had done that unpleasant little job for Safar. Unfortunately, he needed to scare them in a whole different way.

"But I didn't rouse you from your well-earned rest to praise your courage, my good people," Safar said. "Besides, everyone knows that courage is something no Kyranian lacks."

Faces brightened, especially among the young bravos like Renor. He saw them flex their muscles and swagger from side to side.

"But it's another brand of courage I want from you today," Safar continued. "One that calls for even greater sacrifices than before."

The crowd stirred, a little fearful. What was he talking about? Wasn't dealing with Iraj Protarus enough?

"Not just your lives, but the lives of untold millions are at stake. In fact, the very world we stand upon depends on you, the Goddess Felakia's Chosen Ones, the People of the Clouds, the People of the High Caravans."

Safar definitely had their interest now.

"Behold!" he shouted, making a gesture and his magical dagger leaped out of nothingness into his hand.

Then, quieter, "Let me show you the world of the future, my friends. Even if by some miracle we could make Iraj Protarus and his forces vanish from Esmir, this is what the world would look like in not many years."

Safar made a circular motion with the knife, as if cutting a hole into the air itself. The crowd jumped as a fierce wind blew, shrieking through the hole he'd made.

Then a miniature tornado leapt off the dagger point. It swirled madly about the platform for a moment, then steadied, spinning in place like a top.

"Behold!" Safar shouted again and there was a loud pop! as the little tornado suddenly disappeared. The air where it had been shattered like glass, leaving a great dark hole gaping into nothingness.

There were gasps and fearful cries all around as everyone realized there was more than a blank void beyond the jagged edges of the hole.

"Look, my friends," Safar intoned. "Look hard and deep. See the world as it will be. With or without Iraj Protarus."

They looked and it was a terrible sight. A familiar range of mountains beckoned from the other side. It was the Bride and her Maids, but they had been shorn of all their glory and stood there black and wind-torn under a lunatic sky. There was not a patch of snow, tree, or blade of grass upon the range.

The scene shifted and there were fearful shouts as the crowd suddenly found itself looking down into the barren valley that had once been Kyrania. There were no fields or homes, or even the holy lake of Felakia.

Then the ground seemed to move and people shouted in horror

as they realized that millions upon millions of scaly insects made up the floor of their beloved valley. They swarmed over and under each other, feeding on rock and dust.

Just as everyone thought they could stand this nightmare no more Safar clapped and the scene vanished, the hole was healed and everything was the same as before.

"That is what we must prevent from happening," Safar said. "Only we can do it. Only the people of Kyrania have the will and the means. But to accomplish it, you must come away with me. You must come out of the clouds and walk the land and swim its rivers and climb its hills. We must walk until the land ends and there is only sea. And then we must find boats and cross that sea until we come to a new land, a place of safety and peace."

He jabbed at the air with his dagger point and again it shattered. But this time, instead of darkness, a warm yellow light poured out. Everyone looked and this time the gasps and shouts were of marvel, instead of fear.

A glorious island, looking like a wondrous emerald lizard, rose out of a shimmering blue sea. It had thick forests and high mountains on its back, with soft white clouds caught in the peaks. Silver streams coursed down the mountain slopes, leaping over cliffs and boulders and sending up fantastic rainbows from their spume.

"Friends and family," Safar said, "I give you Syrapis! The island of dreams!"

He clapped again and the vision dissolved. Safar turned back to the crowd. He took note of the faces. Some people's eyes were alight with the wonder they had beheld. These mostly belonged to the young. Others appeared withdrawn, suspicious. These mostly belonged to the old. Among the vast majority, however, was a mixture of the two, plus confusion.

Palimak piped up. "Was that our new home, father? Is that where we're going to live?"

Safar answered as if he and the child were alone, instead of surrounded by a thousand people. "If it pleases our friends to do so," he said.

"Is Syrapis very far?" the boy asked.

"Yes, son," he said, "it's very far. Farther than anyone has ever been before."

"If it's so far," he asked, "how will we ever find our way?"

Safar pulled the tube of maps from his belt. "Lord Coralean gave me these," he said. A quick side glance showed that Coralean's name was having a great affect on the Kyranians. All of it positive.

"These are secret maps that only caravan masters possess," Safar said. "They show every road and path in all of Esmir."

He raised his head slightly, making sure all heard. "You know how great a friend Lord Coralean is to all of us. He gave us these secret maps to save us from Iraj Protarus."

"Secrets!" the boy exclaimed, eyes glowing yellow in delight. "Does that mean if we go down those secret roads and paths no one will be able to find us? Even that . . . that . . ." Palimak automatically scanned the crowd for his grandmother's face. The words he had in mind would surely earn him a scolding. "That . . . wolf thing, or man thing, or whatever he is. He wouldn't be able to find us, would he?"

"It would be a pretty hard thing for him to do," Safar said. "And if he found us, we could always lose him again."

"Then what are we waiting for, father?" Palimak asked.

He turned to the crowd, putting his hands on his hips, looking like a circus midget in his little uniform.

"Who wants to go to Syrapis with us?" he shouted. "You get secret maps and a chance to save the world, and . . . and . . ." He spread his hands wide as if encompassing a huge world of wonders . . . "Everything!"

Everyone was laughing now, enjoying the show. In their laughter, Safar knew he'd found acceptance.

Palimak, however, wasn't satisfied. He stamped his little foot.

"You're not answering!" he shouted. "Who wants to go?

"Who wants to go to Syrapis?"

Part Two
Khysmet

10

THE COURT OF KING PROTARUS

The man's face was a bloody mask. "Please, master, please," he moaned, "we din't know no better, honest to th' gods we din't!"

Luka flicked a talon, making a greater mess of the man's face. "What a slimy little human you are," he said. "Everyone knows that Safar Timura is a desperate criminal, so why bother lying?" He flicked again and the man's shrieks echoed across the gloom that was the royal tent. "Even if I believed you, it wouldn't save your life. Your continued existence isn't at stake here, you filthy thing. Only how much pain you can bear before I send you on your miserable way."

Iraj shifted in his throne. Although Luka prided himself on his interrogation techniques, with lots of blood and moaning for entertainment, the king was clearly bored. As a shape changer some concentration was required to retain one form or another—whether human, or giant wolf. Iraj's concentration was visibly shattered by the proceedings; his body parts kept shifting back and forth from animal to human. Hand became claw, face grew a snarling muzzle, then crunched back again.

"Please, master!" the victim begged.

Iraj made a wolf snout. "Please, master, please!" he mocked, his voice a perfect imitation of the tortured villager's. His human face returned. "What a sniveling lot of fools I have for subjects. Always begging, never giving."

He turned to Fari, who sat to his left in a lower and smaller throne. "Tell my scribes," he said, "that in my next decree the phrase 'Merciful Master' is to be removed from my signature titles. King of Kings, Most Exalted Emperor of Esmir, Lion of the

Plains, etc., etc., and all the others should be quite sufficient."

"Noted, Your Highness," the old demon wizard said. "All will be done as you say. And in that spirit, I propose that we examine your other titles more closely as well. For phrases like 'Peaceful Protector,' and 'His Benevolence,' which would also be suspect."

Iraj agreed. "Peace, mercy, and benevolence are out," he said. "My subjects need to have a clear idea of who I am. That's the key to good leadership. And I blame you and Luka and Kalasariz for not reminding me of this."

Fari bowed, beating his breast to show his own quick acceptance of guilt. "It's as you say, Majesty," he said. "There's been too much talk of peace and mercy of late and we ought to end it."

Iraj was calmed and became fully human in appearance. "Exactly, Fari, exactly!" he said. "And by the gods it's undermining my kingdom and I won't put up with it any longer."

He gestured, his hand transforming into a claw to indicate the grisly scene before him. Besides the man Luka was tormenting, there were five others chained to stakes. All of the townspeople were horribly maimed, with only their soft moans and the quivering of their tortured flesh to show they were still alive.

"This a perfect illustration of my point," Iraj said. "They all begged for mercy, screaming and farting at every little poke Luka gave them . . . and what do we get for our pains?" Another wide gesture, paw becoming a hand again. "Nothing but a great deal of wasted time because we are unsure of their respect for me.

"I tell you, Fari, we're losing far too many taxpayers to get at the truth! If I learned anything from Safar, it was that! I mean, genocide is all very well for an ordinary king recapturing an ordinary kingdom. But if you want to be truly great, you must pay a mind to the royal treasury."

Fari bobbed his big scaly head with the ease of one who had tended to the moods of many kings. "I agree entirely, Majesty," he said. "All your wishes will be put into force immediately."

"That's good, Fari," Iraj said. "We don't want to give out too much hope, you know. Another thing I learned from Safar is that hope is a coin more precious than any metal, including gold. So let's give out hope sparingly, if you please. Let's make it count."

Across the tented room, Luka did something to the prisoner

again and the sound of his pain rasped against the scab of Iraj's boredom.

"Enough!" he shouted. "Enough! This exercise is making no progress whatsoever . . . No matter what we do, the fellow's only going to repeat what the others said."

"As always, your Majesty," Lord Fari replied, "your instincts are on target. This is the township's mayor, after all. And I don't know why Prince Luka left him for last. In my experience the post requires a good deal of moral cowardice, so the truth and pulled fingernails will out, as they say."

He made a lazy wave at the mayor, who was gibbering protests and squirming against his restraints as Luka delicately cut his flesh away. "In the end he'll confess to the same thing as the others. He'll claim that Lord Timura and his ragtag army of villagers arrived one day and forced the town to sell him food and supplies. He'll say they had no choice but to comply. And that he is as surprised as we are that Lord Timura insisted on payment."

Fari hefted a small sack of gold in his talons. "Our friend paid quite handsomely too."

"So what's the point in listening to this fellow's whining, then?" Iraj demanded. He raised his voice so Luka could hear. "Kill him and be done with it!"

The prince shrugged, cut the mayor's throat, then ambled back to his seat on Iraj's right, wiping his talons on a rag as he went and dropping it to the ground. Luka had no doubt that his work had been discussed by the king and his old rival, Fari. So he automatically protested.

"I understand your impatience, Majesty," he said, "but we should have probed deeper. After all, we still don't know where Lord Timura went when he left this township. We don't even know which direction he took."

He rattled his talons on the arm of his chair. "One thousand people, gone, vanished. Or at least that's what these fools told us." He indicated the chained forms. "Someone had to have seen what happened," he said. "A thousand people just don't disappear. There's no wizard in the world who could do such a thing."

"Whatever the explanation, my prince," Fari said, "this is hardly the first time Lord Timura has accomplished the trick. When we showed up in Kyrania with the army, all we found was a smoking ruin. The homes and fields were burned, so there was nothing for our soldiers to scavenge. And all the people had vanished."

Iraj glowered at the memory, wolf jaws grinding in frustration. "Where could they have gone?" he growled. "They were there two days before."

Fari shrugged. "That remains a mystery—as Your Majesty is well aware. Our trackers found the northern trail they took through the mountains from Kyrania. But once into the desert they lost it in a warren of rifts and barren canyons so complicated only a devil god could have been the creator."

He indicated the map board posted near their thrones. All the major cities, Naadan and Caspan included, were clearly marked. As were all the known roads and byways. However, unlike the special maps Safar had received from Coralean, none of the secret caravan tracks were shown. From the point of view of Iraj and cohorts, there was nothing but an impassable wilderness in those areas.

"Not only our trackers, but all my wizards have been confounded ever since," Fari continued. "We've been hunting Lord Timura for months without success. Sometimes he reappears at a town or city with a band of raiders to resupply his people. But when our troops reach there, he's vanished again without a trace. The next time we hear of him weeks have passed and somehow he's several hundred miles away."

To Luka's immense displeasure, Iraj smiled at Lord Fari. The demon wizard's calmly put litany of what was already known soothed the king somewhat and his face was back to normal.

"You have summed up our difficulties most succinctly, my lord," Iraj said. Then he immediately grew angry again, glaring at Luka. "At least Fari's using his gods given mind," he said. "Unlike some fiends I know."

Fari openly gloated at the demon prince. And Luka thought, you'll never change, you old fraud. First my father, now Protarus. Always posing as the all wise one, trying to appear superior at my expense.

But what he said, was, "Lord Timura will make a mistake by and by, Highness. They always do. It's the nature of such things."

Fari shifted tactics and nodded in wise agreement, "Quite true, my prince," he said to Luka. "Quite true."

But he was thinking, you're just like your father, you young fool. Nothing but cold porridge for brains.

Iraj's dark mood returned and he glowered at them both. Such useless creatures, he thought. Always quarreling and backstabbing. Telling lies to win his favor. If it weren't for the unbreakable Spell of Four that chained them all together, he'd have them taken out by his soldiers and beheaded. That would shut them up once and for all!

"Enough excuses!" Iraj rumbled. "The point is we've failed. Despite the fact that I've had an entire army pursuing these peasants. Why, I'll soon be the laughing stock of all Esmir."

You already are, Luka thought, wishing not for the first time that it was he who wore the crown.

But all he said was, "I'll fetch some more prisoners, Majesty. Perhaps we'll have better luck with the next batch!"

Iraj slammed his fist on his throne arm! "Nonsense!" he roared. "All of it, nonsense! You've turned my tent into a charnel house for nothing!"

He leaned forward in his throne. "Let me make myself completely clear, brothers mine," he said. "We must have this man, Safar Timura, and his ridiculous child. And we must have them immediately. I will brook no more excuses, do you hear me?"

"We hear, Majesty," both demons muttered, bowing their heads and hating him and each other.

Just then there was the sound of bootsteps, sentries snapped to attention and Kalasariz was ushered into the big tent that was Iraj's traveling palace. The spy master was leading an old woman by a long chain that was locked about her waist.

"I've brought you a little present, Majesty," Kalasariz said, yanking the chain hard so the old woman stumbled. "For your afternoon pleasure, if you will."

Iraj was so surprised that his lower face erupted into a wolf's snout. "What kind of present is this?" he growled. "A skinny old woman with bones so brittle I'd choke on them."

"I'm not for eatin'!" the old woman exclaimed. "And if yer thinks yer gonner get any fun from tormentin' a poor old soul like me, yer gots 'nother think comin', Majesty! I'm so frail that if yer touched a hair on my head I'd up and die on yers."

"How amazing," Luka murmured. "The gift talks. Not very well, but it's amazing just the same."

"And now that's she's seen us," Fari said, "we'll have to kill her. How tiresome. Like she said, she's so elderly she'll be no sport at all."

Kalasariz ignored his enemies, addressing his rebuttal directly to Protarus. "She isn't for sport, Majesty," he said, "but for gain. And as for seeing us, it surprises me that ones so perceptive as Prince Luka and so intuitive as Lord Fari haven't noted the woman is blind. Ergo, she isn't here for killing, but for your Majesty's possible edification."

Kalasariz shot quick gloats of victory at Luka and Fari, thinking, There you go, you sons of pig lizards. Root around in that trash and see if I've left anything tasty behind!

Iraj peered at the woman, noting for the first time her disfigured eyes, which were entirely white as if they had been permanently rolled up into her head. The king's wolfish features dissolved into something quite human, featuring the same bright and handsome smile that had once won him so many ardent friends and supporters.

"She really is blind," he said, smile growing broader. "I like this. Now the question is entirely open on whether we kill her or not. It's been a long time since precedent was challenged."

Iraj leaned an arm on his throne, cupping his chin in his palm. He studied the old woman for a moment, noting that although her dress was stained with dirt, the material was quite expensive. "Tell me, Granny," he said, "What do you have to say about all this?"

"Same as I said 'afore, Majesty," she replied. "Old Sheesan ain't for killin'. And never mind I'm blind. Don't take eyes to know yers're shape changers. Old Sheesan can smell the wolf in yer!"

"Let me kill the old bitch, then," Prince Luka said. "Since there's no longer a question of her lack of sight saving her."

The old woman snorted and turned her blind face toward Luka. "Beggin' yer pardon, Lord," she said, "but that'd be about the stupidest thing yers could do. Yer should count yer blessin's that I'm even here 'afore yers."

Kalasariz laughed. "It's true," he said. "We didn't capture her, you know. She turned herself in and demanded to see someone in charge." He tapped his breast. "Which is when I stepped in."

He turned to Iraj. "In case you haven't noticed, Majesty," he said, "the woman is a witch. She claims she can use her witchery to help us track down Safar Timura."

Luka and Fari made derisive noises, displaying rare agreement. Iraj made no comment, but he stared at the old woman in disbelief.

Finally, he said, "Are you saying that this hag can do what all of us combined haven't been able to accomplish?"

Kalasariz started to speak but the old woman beat him to it with a prolonged bout of cackling and coughing.

"Hag, you say?" she chortled. "Just an old bag of bones with a hank of hair on top. That's what'cher thinks of me, does yer?"

Then she composed herself, crossing her arms over wizened breasts. "All's it'll cost yers is a purse of gold, Majesty," she said. "A nice fat one, if yer please. And I'll deliver Safar Timura to yers soon enough."

"I can't believe I'm listening to this," Luka said. "An old woman dares to ask a price for what she should give us freely. What is Esmir coming to? Is there no dignity left in this court?"

"If it's dignity yer wantin', Me Lord," the old woman said, "it'll cost yers two purses, not one. Dignity spells don't come cheap, 'specially when I gots some fiend like yerself fer a client. No insult intended, I'm sure. I'm only speakin' the facts, here." She sniffed at the air and wrinkled her nose. "Shape changers make such a stink," she went on. "Can't do nothin' 'bout that. Even if yer was to give me three purses of gold."

While Luka was choking on this insult—to the vast enjoyment of the others—the witch turned her blind face to Iraj.

"Purse a gold's me price, Majesty," she said. "But most of it won't be fer the likes of me, if it gives yer comfort. Be lucky if I can keep a coin fer meself, as matter of fact. The rest'll go to me dear sisters of the crucible."

Iraj gawked at her, then he looked at Kalasariz. "What in the blazes is she talking about?" he asked. "Purses of gold and sisters of cups, or whatever. Is this a jest, my lord? If it is, it's in damned poor taste."

The old woman started to speak again, but Kalasariz yanked viciously on the chain, silencing her.

"It's quite simple, Majesty," the spy master said. "This remarkable woman is not a thing of beauty, I admit; or at least not in any conventional sense. She's beautiful enough, however, when judged by her position and talents.

"It seems that this . . . this . . . creature . . . is quite an influential person in her own sphere. It so happens that Old Sheesan is an elder in the Witches' Guild, which has members in every city and hamlet in Esmir.

"What she proposes to do is to contact every member of her Guild, promising fat rewards for any and all sightings of Safar Timura. The earlier we get notice, the richer the reward. Finally, if a witch should trap Lord Timura, or one of his key people, there will be a special bounty above and beyond all other rewards."

Old Sheesan raised a finger. "And I'll be wantin' commissions on all's a them," she said. "Includin' the bounty."

"What a greedy thing she is," Lord Fari said admiringly. "But she makes such good sense I'm inclined to recommend it." He bowed to Kalasariz. "A remarkable find, my good fellow. My congratulations."

"Well, I don't like it at all," Luka grumbled.

The old woman sniffed. "What's not to like? A bit a gold gets the whole sisterhood in yer camp. Witches all over Esmir'll be on the lookout for this Safar Timura feller. And they'll be at it day and night, I tells yer. Day and night. Sniffin' ever stranger comes to their village, tossin' bones or lookin' into their crystals for some sign of him.

"Time's are hard for witches just now. What with droughts and plagues makin' money so scarce. Use to get a bit of silver for yer spell makin'. Curin' boils, or castin' the evil eye and such. Now, yer lucky if yer can get a skinny chicken for yer pot. Which is why yer gettin' us so cheap, Me Lords. A whole army of witches for a single purse of gold."

At first Iraj had been merely amused by Old Sheesan, but the more she talked the more amusement dissolved into intense interest. As he stared at her, Iraj suddenly caught a flash of someone quite different than the toothless hag standing before him. It was as if curtains were momentarily parted to reveal a shimmering creature of incredible beauty. Then the curtains closed and the image was gone.

The old woman cackled knowingly—as if she had just shared a great secret with the king.

Iraj gripped the throne arms, so overcome by emotion that his wolf snout erupted through his face.

"Woman," he said, "if you bring me Safar Timura's head I will make you richer than any queen."

The old woman giggled, sounding remarkably girlish. "Imagine that," she said, primping her greasy hair. "Old Sheesan a queen!"

And Iraj thought, yes, yes I can imagine.

11

MISSION TO NAADAN

The demon glared down at Safar, fangs bared, yellow eyes narrow with suspicion. "State your business, human!"

Safar staved off nausea as the soldier's foul breath washed over him and forced his most jovial smile. "Profit and entertainment, sergeant," Safar said. "If not the first, why we'll settle for the second. Especially if it comes with ale."

Beside him, Leiria smacked her lips. "I hear Nadaan makes the best ale in all Esmir," she said.

The demon soldier peered at her, noting her dirty mail and even dirtier sword. His eyes swept on, taking in the ox-drawn wagon and the three heavily-laden camels. Besides Safar and Leiria, who were both leading horses, there were four other humans—a driver for the wagon and three men to tend the camels. There was something decidedly shabby about the group. Their clothes were unkempt, the animals' fur was clotted—even the canvas covering of the wagon was filthy.

The demon snorted in disgust. "You call this a caravan?"

Safar sighed, leaning against the portable barricade blocking the road. Five soldiers—three of them human and all wearing the uniforms of Protarus' troops—guarded the barricade. About a mile beyond were the Naadan city walls.

"It's a long story sergeant," he said. "And not a very pleasant one, either. A year ago I was sitting pretty. A dozen wagons, a score of camels plus horses and men and . . ." he glanced at Leiria, lowering his voice, " . . . And I had a proper guard, if you know what I mean. Six outriders and a retired captain of the king's own to lead them."

He let his voice rise again. "But you don't want to hear my tale of woe, sergeant. Times being what they are, there's hundreds of poor merchants just like me all over Esmir. So broke we clatter like a glazier's cart on a badly cobbled street. All we ask is a chance to get back on top again. Hell's, I'd settle for just staying even!"

The demon shrugged, massive shoulders rising like mailed mountains. "What do I care, human? You and your entire shabby lot can turn into dust and blow across the desert, for all it means to me."

He jabbed a taloned-thumb at the gates of Nadaan. From beyond came the caterwaul of bad music and the babble of a great crowd. "Besides, rules'r rules. If you wanna to sell your trash at the Naadan Fair you gotta have a permit. No riffraff allowed. And that's my job—to keep out the riffraff."

Once again his eyes swept Safar's ragged outfit, but this time his look was more meaningful. "Smells like riffraff to me," he said.

Safar slipped a fat purse from his sleeve. He gave it a good shake so the silver rattled.

The demon's long, scaly ears perked up at the sound.

"Are you sure we can't come to some sort of arrangement, sergeant?" he asked. "Hmm?"

As they came to the city gates Leiria cantered closer to Safar. "You're getting to be such a good liar," she teased. "Aren't you ashamed of yourself?"

Actually, he was. As far as Leiria and the others knew they were in Naadan on a routine raiding mission. Which was far from the truth.

"I'm not ashamed one bit," Safar laughed. "But I am damned thirsty. In fact, before we get down to the business of robbery why don't we try some of that famous Naadan ale?"

Leiria wrinkled her hose. "I was just looking for something nice to say," she laughed. "Actually, I hear their ale tastes like mare's piss," she said. "But he looked like the sort of creature who liked mare's piss, if you know what I mean."

She made a rueful face. "Guess I'm getting pretty good at lying myself."

Safar flinched and looked away so she didn't see the guilt in his eyes.

Inside the gates all was madness. It was the last day of the fair and the streets were packed with revelers. Traffic was a great drunken weave with no apparent purpose or goal. There were tribes and villagers from all over the vast high desert region. There were painted faces, scarred faces, veiled faces, faces with filed teeth, faces pierced with jewelry, and, yes, even a few faces that would have been ordinary except they stood out among so many exotics.

Until recent years the Naadan Harvest Festival—which the fair celebrated—had been a minor event that drew only nearby farmers and herdsmen. It certainly hadn't been large enough to entice Methydia to stop with her circus when she and Safar had passed this way. The circus had instead gone to Silver Rivers, a much larger and richer town and many miles distant. But a series of disasters had reduced Silver Rivers to a ghost city, where the only inhabitants were bandits. Silver Rivers' misfortune, however, had been Naadan's good luck. Five years of rich harvests—so rare in recent times that it seemed a miracle—had turned the city into a thriving center of life and commerce.

The once sleepy water hole in the middle of the Northern Plains now enticed people from hundreds of miles around—including Safar Timura and his band, who quickly unburdened themselves of their paltry caravan by simply walking away from it. Sharp-eyed thieves led the wagon and animals off before Safar and the others had melted into the crowd. Just as the shrewd demon sergeant had noted the caravan was worthless. The goods were trash. The animals spavined. They were all surplus booty from an encounter that had gone badly for a group of seedy bandits.

"So much for my debut as a merchant prince," Safar joked, after they'd all found a grog shop and had ordered up mugs of cold wine. "Shed my whole caravan and didn't earn a clipped copper for my troubles."

Renor, who had been driving the wagon, snorted. "Oh, I don't know about that, sir. We couldn't throw the stuff away or bury it because it'd give us away. And the animals were not only useless, but eating us out of hearth and home. Hells, we made a profit just by getting rid of them."

He took a long happy drink from his mug. "Least, that's how I see it, Lord Tim—" and one of his companions elbowed him before he could get the whole name out.

Realizing he was in the middle of a packed bar, and someone might overhear him, Renor blushed and ducked his head. "Sorry," he said. "I'm not used to so many people about."

A man staggered into their table, sloshing his drink all over them. "That's what I tole him," the man roared into Safar's face. "An' if he dares say the same thin' to me again, while I'll spit in his face! The dirty son of a . . ." and then the man realized Safar was a stranger and his voice trailed off. He burped and pulled back. "You're not my friend," he said, surprised. Then he shrugged. "Just don't tell nobody, right?"

"Right!" Safar said and the man staggered away. He turned back to Renor. "No need for sorries," he said. "In this place we're as safe as in the middle of a forest."

Unnoticed by them, across the room the drunk suddenly straightened. He looked back at Safar's table, measuring with sober eyes. Then he smiled and exited the tavern whistling a merry tune.

Back at the table, Safar refilled everyone's mugs, saying, "You're in charge of this little expedition, Leiria. Why don't you give us our orders now so we can drink up and be on our way?"

Leiria nodded. "This should be fairly simple," she said. "Easier than most, as a matter of fact, because we have a good map of Naadan, thanks to that little trove of maps we got from Coralean.

"You've all got your copies, right?" The men all nodded, but just the same they patted their pockets to make sure. "And you all know which area you're to do your snooping in, right?" More nods.

"Fine. Now, here's what to look for. If you have barracks in your sector, check to see how many beds they have. That'll tell us the exact number of soldiers on hand during normal times. My guess is that most of the soldiers we're seeing are here temporarily for fair duty and will be gone within a day or two.

"Also, if there are any storehouses in your area of search, see what kinds of grains, food, clothing, etcetera are inside. The more portable the better. Pay close attention to this, because we want to have a good shopping list drawn up when we show up here with our army to talk things over with the king. Quintal, I think his name is.

"We also need first hand knowledge of all the ways in and out of the city. Maps are good, but they aren't always up to date, or even accurate when they are. We don't want to have to beat a hasty retreat, then find that the gate we're heading for—a gate clearly indicated on our map—has long since been covered up. Or was just a royal architect's dream that never got funding."

She looked at each man. "Is that all clear? You understand what you're supposed to do and how to do it? I know we've gone over it all before, but I want to make sure. We can't afford any mistakes. Protarus' soldiers are none too bright, but they can be as error-prone as they like. For us one mistake might be a death sentence."

Everyone said they understood. Then, to avoid suspicion by getting up and leaving en-masse, they drifted away one-by-one, until only Leiria remained. She stared at him, eyes narrowed with sudden suspicion.

"What's going on, Safar?" she asked

"Going on?" Safar said, all innocence. "Why, what ever do you mean?"

She kept staring, eyes ferreting for some sign beneath Safar's bland features. Finally she sighed. "Never mind," she said. "I'm sorry I asked."

And then she was gone. Safar caught a serving wench by the elbow and ordered up another jug of wine.

His assignment was to investigate the city's central arena where the sporting matches were going on—and to get a close look at the Naadanian king. At least that's what Leiria thought. Actually, Safar's mission was much more difficult.

Asper had bade him to go to Naadan. For what purpose, he

hadn't said. Safar grimaced, wishing the master wizard had given him the smallest hint of what he was supposed to accomplish in Naadan. All Safar could think to do was go about his thieving business and pray for a sign.

Then the wench came with the jug and he set about the impromptu task of restoring his confidence. He settled back in his chair and let the warm sounds of the tavern flow over him. It had been a long time since he'd been in such easy company. When he was a student in Walaria his happiest hours had been spent at the Foolsmire, a tavern catering to the student trade that was known for its cheap wine and even cheaper books.

Safar took a big gulp of wine, enjoying the feel and taste of it going down. Strange thing—he remembered liking wine in those days, sometimes in excess if truth be known. But he didn't remember needing it. This wine he definitely needed.

And with good reason, he thought. At one time, the odds against him ever reaching Naadan had seemed insurmountable.

He drank his wine, remembering . . .

It was an epic flight, an odyssey of terror. Panic lurking like cliff edges on every side as Safar used all his tricks, plus inventing scores more, to keep himself and his charges alive and out of Iraj's clutches.

The first days were so desperate that Safar didn't have much memory of them. Everything was a blur of hysterical people and animals and badly packed baggage trains careening from one mountain pass to another. Safar had a vague route in mind to confuse their pursuers, but it was all Leiria and her scouts could do to keep the Kyranians on the right track.

The journey might have been made easier if Safar could have commanded the leading party—his presence alone tended to calm people. But out of necessity he had taken up position well in the rear with Renor and his friend, Sinch, to assist him. He peppered the trail with magical spells and traps to confound the enemy. He also triggered a whole series of avalanches, blocking not only the passes they'd pushed through, but all others as well so Iraj's scouts couldn't tell which way they'd taken.

Luck was also with them. As they were coming out of the

mountains into the northern wastelands an unseasonable storm roared in from the Great Sea, hammering the ranges with icy blizzards and bringing all of Iraj's forces to a miserable halt. Meanwhile, the Kyranians were safely in the rocky foothills and Safar and Leiria only needed to keep the villagers moving through the heavy rainstorm.

When the rains stopped they found themselves in a bleak landscape of blasted stone. Oddly formed peaks burst out of blackened ground that was cut by hundreds of ravines and gullies, many so deep and broad and filled with storm-swollen creeks and rivers it took days to negotiate them.

It was in these badlands that Safar performed the greatest nonmagical tricks of his life. Food was scarce and water came only in amounts that were treacherous—swift moving streams that could sweep away a wagon and its contents, or tracks that remained waterless for day after throat-parching day. To shake off Iraj he relied on Coralean's maps of all the secret caravan routes that crept through the north country from the Gods Divide all the way to Caspan and the Great Sea. All the main trade centers were also well-documented, including routes meant to avoid the clusters of bandits that prowled the outskirts of civilization.

The sheer number of Kyranians, plus their lack of experience on the road, nearly defeated Safar at the start. Fortunately they had reached the relative safety of the badlands, with all its switchbacks and secret trails, before Safar was overwhelmed by the sheer logistics of the expedition.

When they'd abandoned and burned their village, the Kyranians had fled with little thought of what they ought to carry away with them. Some households tried to transport all their worldly goods—from kitchen stoves to festival dinner service. Others only snatched icons off the wall, cats from the hearth seat and lucky cicada cages made of dried reeds that buzzed like supportive orchestras when the insects sang their songs of romantic longing. The Kyranians pressed everything into service that could carry weight for their flight—from lumbering ox-powered freight wagons down to sledges drawn by goats. They also tried to take all their animals—goats by the hundreds, oxen by the score and llamas and camels by the dozens. Even favorite horses long retired from toil were brought along. The consequence of this chaos was an enormous unwieldy mass of people and animals spread all over the landscape. Heavily-ladened wagons broke down, animals scattered and were lost, one pregnant woman and a several elders died of exhaustion.

But when all seemed lost, Safar dug keeper into his sack of leadership secrets to rally his people and put steel back into their spines. The villagers stripped themselves down to the barest necessities, burying tons of abandoned goods and household items in places where Iraj's scouts couldn't find them. When they set out again they were a disciplined force that got better with each passing day. Thanks to Leiria and Sergeant Dario, most of the young men were being turned into a skilled fighting unit, so they had little to fear from bandits and rogue soldiers.

When supplies ran low Safar used Coralean's maps to find secret routes to the richest towns and cities and after he'd raided them the Kyranians were able to vanish with ease into hidden passes and deep ravines.

To keep his people going, Safar dangled the vision of Syrapis before them—a paradise to replace the one they'd lost. Meanwhile, he kept edging them toward Naadan. The city was to the north, as was the Great Sea, so no one guessed his intentions.

It didn't hurt that Safar wasn't that sure of them himself. However, after worrying on that bone until it was splinters, he gave up. Frustrating as it was, he had to let the winds of fate carry him where they would—as long as they headed north. To keep his will focused he reduced everything to a simple mantra: Naadan, Caluz, Syrapis. Naadan, Caluz, Syrapis. Naadan, Caluz . . .

. . . Syrapis!

He wondered what waited for him there. Prayed that whatever it was, it would at long last answer the two questions that had haunted and driven him his entire adult life:

What was killing the world?

And how could he stop it?

Safar downed his wine and poured another. At the rate he'd been traveling, he thought, he'd die of old age before he reached that fabled isle.

What was Asper's line? Oh, yes, " . . . All who dwell 'neath Heaven's vaults . . . live in dread . . . of that monster, Time . . ."

Monster, indeed.

He got up to leave, nearly stumbling over a skinny little crone who had been leaning, unnoticed, against his table.

"Pardon, Granny," he said politely. But as he spoke he felt a sudden prickle of magic sniffing along his skin.

The crone grinned a toothless grin, saying, "Alms, master. Alms for a poor old woman."

Safar kept his features mild, showing no reaction to her witch's magic. He cast a spell to ward off her snooping, fishing in his purse for a few coppers to cover his actions.

"Here you go, Granny," he said, plopping the coins into her outstretched claw. "Make your prayers sweet for me tonight."

He moved on, pushing through the crowd until he reached the door. As he went out he turned sideways to peek at the witch's face. She looked most disappointed. Just beyond her he saw a familiar figure. It was the drunk who had bumped into his table not long before.

You don't need a Master's License from Walaria University to figure that one out, he thought as he walked down the street. Obviously, the witch was looking for him and that fake drunk was in her employ. Iraj had offered a fortune for Safar's head and this wasn't the first time he'd encountered reward seekers. They were easily spotted and avoided, so normally he didn't trouble himself. However, he'd never encountered a bounty-hunting witch before and it made him wonder if some new element had been added to the game.

By the time he reached the arena he'd decided it was only a coincidence that this particular reward seeker was a witch. He bought a ticket at the gate and went inside, putting the crone from his mind. He did go more cautiously, however, his magical senses wary for more signs of danger.

The highlight of the Naadan Fair was the wrestling tournament, an ancient sport taken to a high art in this region. Hundreds competed in the opening matches but their numbers were whittled down as the festival progressed until the final day when the last two men competed for the championship.

Safar bought a bowl of hot peppered noodles from a vendor and joined the spectators in the stands. Some were cheering the action on the big grassy field, but others paid no attention at all—gossiping or eating or scolding unruly children, while on the field several pairs of beefy champions grappled with one another, heaving and hauling as they attempted to hurl their opponents to the ground. In Naadan wrestling matches often went on for hours before a winner was decided, so the spectators behaved accordingly, becoming only fully absorbed at key moments in the matches.

While Safar ate his noodles he casually searched the stands until he found the wide stone box with its gaily colored awning shading King Quintal and his family. The royal box was just across from him, so he could see the king quite clearly. He was a big man, a once muscular man who had gone to fat. His face was puffed and red in the places his gray-streaked beard didn't cover. While around him his children and wives cheered the match, the king watched sullenly, drinking deeply and frequently from his cup.

"Looks like the king's drunk again," said the man sitting next Safar. He turned and saw a pleasant little fellow with a pudgy face and a wine-stained robe. "Seems like Quintal's always drunk these days."

Pudge Face lifted up a leather bag and shot a stream of wine down his throat. He wiped his mouth, cleaned his hands on his robes, which were of a rich material, then said, "Bad example for our children, if you ask me."

He offered Safar the wine bag. After he drank, Safar passed it back, saying, "Glad I'm not king. Can't think of a more boring life. Being a good example, I mean."

Pudge Face chuckled. "No chance of that for me," he said. "But I never wanted to be champion, much less king. Got a nice little shop, a good wife and five hard-working daughters to keep it running while I do what I like." He slapped the wine bag. "And what I like is this."

Safar glanced around at the crowd, many of whom were as red-faced with drink as Quintal. "I'll wager Naadan is as silent as a temple vestry when this festival is over," he said.

Pudge Face laughed. "Whole city will be passed out for at least a week," he said. "Nothing, but nothing gets done after a harvest festival. Nobody on the streets, that's for sure, unless they're on their way to a healer to get something for their sick heads and bellies. Hells, even the taverns are closed because the innkeepers are as bad off as the rest of us."

Safar was delighted with this intelligence. The festival was officially over tonight. That would give him a day or two, if needed, to track down the answer to Asper's mysterious command. It'd also make the supply raid much easier. They could ride right up to the king's palace and face him unopposed. The escape ought to be just as easy. Few would see them go and those who did would be in no shape to follow.

The crowd burst into cheers and Safar looked up to see the reason for the sudden mass interest. Out on the field there were only two wrestlers left. Their victims were being helped away by officials in flowing red robes with yellow sashes and high-topped boots.

The victors were huge men, wearing only short leather breeches with wide belts. Their bodies were streaked with so much blood that it was hard to tell the difference between them and the losers who had already been carried off the field. They stumbled as officials led them into the center of the field for the final match. The crowd shouted its appreciation and everyone seemed to be scrambling to get a bet down.

"What's going on?" Safar asked his new friend.

"This is what we've been waiting for!" Pudge Face said excitedly. "Finally, we're going for the championship! Won't be long and we'll see who's the new Titan."

He pointed at the wrestlers. One was entirely bald, the other shaggy as a bear. "The hairy one's Butar," he said. "The other's called Ulan. He's the most popular wrestler in Naadan. And favored in this match. Hells, Ulan could be king himself one day. Which would be a big improvement over Quintal, that's for certain."

"What's the prize?" Safar asked, wisely skirting the political issue of who'd make the better king.

"Whoever wins today," Pudge Face said, "gets to put Brave Titan in front of his name. He'll also be rich for life. Plus, this year, there's a special prize. To thank the gods for it being such a good harvest year."

At that moment Safar felt a tingling sensation against his chest and his hand came up unconsciously to touch the horse amulet dangling beneath his shirt. To his surprise it was quite warm and was growing warmer by the minute. He clutched it, wondering what was happening.

Just then six riders dressed in flowing, calf-length robes, rode onto the field. They appeared to be some sort of honor guard and they pranced about showing off to the crowd. What they were presenting soon became apparent as two men trotted out, leading a magnificent horse onto the field.

Safar felt a shock jump from the amulet to his skin and he nearly cried out—not from pain, because the shock was more surprising than hurtful. His entire attention was suddenly fixed on that horse.

It was the most remarkable animal he had ever seen. Safar was a man of the mountains and no great horse lover. Plainsmen like Iraj, who spent their lives on horseback, practically worshipped the animals. To Safar they were merely useful creatures under certain circumstances—circumstances rarely met in the snowy passes of the mountains. He liked them well enough and had even encountered a few with interesting personalities. On the whole, however, he thought a good goat or llama was far more valuable to a Kyranian.

But this creature seemed to exist on an entirely different plane than all other animals of its kind. He was almost godlike in beauty, so handsomely muscled he seemed like a great work of art from a master sculptor. He was tall, taller than any horse Safar had ever seen. He was the color of fresh cream, a deep and glossy off-white so full of depths he seemed to glow. His feet were black, as if he wore short boots on his hooves and he had a lighting bolt of black on his handsome forehead.

He ignored the crowd as he came out, giving off an aura of royal aloofness. When he came to the center he tossed his head high and pawed the ground as if he were anxious to be off on more important business than mere adulation.

Then Safar had a second shock as the horse turned his sculpted head and looked in Safar's direction. The look flew across the distance and found him and he had a sudden feeling of warm and glad recognition. It was as if two souls had met and in the meeting an instant bond had been formed.

Safar whispered, "Hello, old friend!" And the horse rose up on its hind legs, pawing the air and shrilling a glad greeting.

And he thought, this is it! This is what Asper wanted me to find.

Then all was confusion as the horse was led to the side and trumpets announced the final match. The last note had barely faded away when Ulan The Bald rushed his opponent. It was as if the sight of the horse had given him new life and he grasped Butar by the belt and hoisted him off the ground. The crowd screamed in ecstasy as all the days of suspense ended in a quick, breath-bursting second as Ulan slammed his opponent onto the ground. Trumpets blared, drums rolled and big kites of every color were launched into the sky, carrying exploding fireworks in their tails.

Safar didn't see any of it. He was concentrating solely on the horse, who stood patiently in solitary splendor at the far side of the field.

"Now we'll see if there's going to be a challenge," Pudge Face said.

Safar, half in a daze, turned to him. "What do you mean?"

"Anyone can challenge the champion," he said. "At least that's the fiction. In a minute the king's gonna ask the crowd in if there is anyone among us who can best Ulan." Pudge Face took a drink, laughing at the same time and making a bigger mess of his robe. "As if any of us could outwrestle a Brave Titan!"

"What happens if someone does?"

Pudge Face laughed again. "Don't be ridiculous," he said. "These men are not only giants, but they train all their lives. They know all the tricks."

"Still," Safar said, "what if such a thing occurred?"

"Then they'd win the title, plus the riches, plus the horse. But if you're considering some sort of wager, keep your money in your purse, my friend. No challenger has ever defeated a champion in the history of the games."

Pudge Face looked over at the horse. "More's the pity," he said. "A stranger could keep the horse for his own."

"What do you mean?" Safar asked.

"Well, this particular horse is meant for sacrifice. That's Ulan's gift to the gods."

Safar jumped at this, as if stung. But the little man didn't notice. He'd just tried to take a drink but found his wine sack was empty. He sighed, regretting his generosity. But that couldn't be taken back, so he looked across the field at the horse and gave still another sigh, but deeper. Sometimes life seemed so terribly unfair.

"Ah, look at that!" he said. "I'm as religious as the next person. Praise the gods once a week and try to do right in between. But the sight of that beautiful creature prancing about so proud . . . and knowing the poor thing's fate . . . is enough to make you wonder if the gods are right in their heads.

"Does our heavenly family really want to see this handsome creature handed over to thin-lipped priests with sharp little knives?" He shuddered. "Holy purpose or not, what a horrid fate for something so magnificent."

He turned to Safar. "With a little drink in you it makes you wonder if the gods even—"

Pudge Face stopped in mid-flow. The seat beside him was empty!

As Safar raced down the stairs he didn't notice the old crone reach through the crowd to snatch at his tunic with her long nails. He only felt resistance and he tugged hard. The fabric ripped and the witch snatched back a claw full of shredded cloth. He ran on, while behind him the witch chortled in glee.

"It's him!" she cackled. "I jus' know it is!"

Out on the field, Safar trotted toward Ulan. The officials stood back, incredulous. Who was this lowly creature who dared challenge a Brave Titan? Safar stripped off his shirt and as he ran the amulet bounced on his chest. Each time it struck he felt a warm glow. It was such a strong feeling that any misgivings dissolved before they were fully formed.

As he approached Ulan he heard the stallion whinny and he saw the two minders grappling with the animal, who was struggling mightily against the ropes.

Then he was standing before Ulan, who grinned at him through bloody gums and shattered teeth. Ulan stared down from a great height. Safar was tall for a Kyranian, but Ulan took him by at least a foot. Safar was slender, but broad of chest and shoulder. Against Ulan he seemed puny, a weakling with wrists that could be snapped easily and a slim bow of a backbone that could be crushed under Ulan's mighty feet.

The wrestler's bloody grin grew wider. He rose up, blowing his body out to intimidate his opponent. His brow beetled, making his eyes as small as spear points. He clapped his horny hands together, making a sound like thunder.

"Who are you, little man," he intoned, "to challenge the great Ulan?"

"All I want is the horse," Safar said, trying to throw his enemy off the mark. "You can keep everything else after I defeat you."

Ulan's big head split in two and he guffawed a great guffaw. "You can wish in one hand and defecate in the other and you'll soon see what comes out in the balance," Ulan said.

An official locked a wide belt around Safar's waist. "You know the rules," he said.

Safar shook head. "Actually," he said, "I've never done this before."

Both the official and Ulan were incredulous. "What a fool you are, little man," the wrestler said.

The official shrugged. "It's your life," he said to Safar. "You can do what you want with it." Then: "The rules are simple. Kicking, punching, gouging, neck breaking, whatever, are permitted. The fight ends when one man lifts another off his feet by the belt, then throws him to the ground. Getting knocked to the ground or slipping and falling doesn't count for anything. Got it?"

Safar gulped. "I think so," he said.

The trumpet blared and Ulan advanced on Safar, enormous arms outstretched to catch him whichever way he dodged.

Safar cast a spell of confusion and leaped to the left. Ulan lofted a clumsy swing, missing with a blow so strong that Safar heard the punch explode the air as it sailed past his head.

Ulan made a lumbering recovery and Safar grabbed him by the big leather belt and heaved.

Ulan looked down on him, amused. He spread his feet and became a weight that could not be moved. "Heave away, little man," he mocked.

Safar gasped, but it was like trying to pick up a mountain.

Then a blow like an unleashed siege machine sent him flying. As he sailed through the air he heard the stallion nicker in alarm. It gave him strength and as Safar hit the ground he tuck-rolled to his feet.

The Brave Titan of Naadan bellowed and swept down on him like an avalanche.

12

SAFAR IN CHAINS

"Uh, oh!" Palimak said. "Looks like my father's in trouble."

"Let me see! Let me see!" Gundara demanded, pushing forward.

"Will you please!" Gundaree complained. "You are such a rude Favorite! Mother would be so displeased!"

"Just shut up about Mother!" Gundara shouted. "You hear me? Shut up!"

Palimak, who was crouched on the tent floor peering into a wide, silvery bowl, looked up at them with an expression of utter disgust on his elfin face. The two Favorites could only appear together in his presence. But they squabbled so much sometimes he wondered if it was worth the extra strength he got from them.

"Stop your arguing this instant," he said, copying the scolding tones adults used when chastising him.

Gundara pointed at his twin, tiny demon's face all screwed up in outraged innocence. "He wouldn't let me see," he whined.

Gundaree sneered, his little human face a portrait of lordly condescension. "I only asked him kindly not to shove," he replied.

Palimak sighed. "Why do you two always make everything so hard?" he said. "Now, look. There's plenty of room for everybody." He pointed to one end of the bowl. "You stand here," he said to

Gundara, making his high child's voice as commanding as possible. "And you can stand over there," he told Gundaree, indicating the opposite side. "And hurry up, please. I told you my father is in trouble. Big trouble!"

Chastened, the Favorites obeyed. When they were set Palimak waved his hand over the bowl and a cloud of blue steam hissed up.

Gundaree sneezed. "What an awful odor," he said in cultured tones.

"Just shut up and look," Palimak said.

"Don't say shut up," Gundara admonished. "You're not supposed to say shut up."

Palimak snorted, but didn't reply. Instead he peered into the bowl. The smoke vanished and the whole inside of the bowl became a miniature of the Naadan Stadium. The audience cheered from the stands, which ran all along the side of the bowl. At the bottom was the grassy wrestling field where his father grappled with Ulan.

"I wonder why he's fighting?" Palimak mused.

"Who knows why the Master does anything?" Gundaree said. "Except, show him an impossibility and he'll attempt it."

Gundara winced as Ulan struck again and Safar was knocked backwards. "Ouch!" he said. "I'll bet that hurt!"

"We have to help him," Palimak said.

"That's all very well and good," Gundaree said. "But the question, Little Master, is how?"

Safar scrambled to his feet, dodging just as Ulan reached for him. He came around, joining his fists together into a club. He swung, connected with Ulan's kidney and heard a satisfying grunt of pain.

But the giant wrestler was used to much worse punishment and just as Safar was forming another spell of confusion a huge hand snatched out and caught Safar by the belt.

The crowd roared. The final moment had come. Now that Ulan had a grip on Safar's belt all he had to do was lift him off the ground then slam him into the earth. That would certainly be easy enough— compared to the massive Ulan, Safar was less than a feather.

Safar heard the horse shrill as Ulan hoisted him on high.

Without warning a great wind swept into the arena and

bowled them both off their feet. Safar landed on top and he heard the breath whoosh out of Ulan. Some kind of miracle had just occurred, but Safar wasn't thinking about miracles just then. Instead he was backing up as fast as he could because Ulan was already bounding to his feet.

Another blast of wind struck, this one bearing rain. It hit them like a tropical torrent and in moments the whole field was turned into a slippery river of mud.

Ulan kept coming, looking like a sea god as he burst through all that rain. He didn't look so godlike when he reached for Safar, skittered in the mud and fell backward, sending up a dirty spray that struck Safar full in the face.

Safar sputtered, rocked back and then his feet abandoned him and it was his turn to go arse over hearth kettle.

He tried to rise but it was like walking on a boatload of fish and he was flailing wildly, arms and legs going every way except the intended direction. Safar finally rested on his back. Through the heavy rain all he could see was the hazy outline of the cheering crowd.

Safar sensed Ulan moving toward him and he flopped over, pushing himself to his hands and knees. He found himself looking straight into the wrestler's giant face. The Titan of Naadan was also on his hands and knees—nearly incapacitated from laughter.

"What a match, little man!" Ulan roared. "A match that will never be repeated in a thousand years. Nay, ten thousand, if the world should live that long." He reared back, muddy hands gripping Safar by the belt. "Unfortunately, it's time for this match to end, my small friend," he said.

And he lifted Safar over his head, then gently dropped him to the ground.

Safar had lost.

Ulan was helping him to his feet when the rain stopped as suddenly as it began.

The crowd cheered and the wrestler pounded his back, knocking the wind from him. "What a brave little man you are," he said. "But let me give you some advice. If you should visit us next year, don't try it again."

"Believe me, I won't," Safar promised. "I feel as if I've been run over by a freight wagon."

He smiled at the big man, but his thoughts were on the cause of his sudden madness. Safar glanced over at the horse who was looking straight at him, head jerking up and down. The animal's hide was shining from the rain, sun dancing on the high gloss. Safar sent a silent promise that he'd be back no matter what and the horse seemed to understand for it reared back and pawed the air, whinnying loudly.

"Here, what's this?" Ulan shouted.

Safar turned to see a group of guards descending on him. Rough hands grabbed his arms and twisted them back behind him.

"This is no way to treat a challenger!" Ulan roared. He stepped forward, threatening.

"Don't do anything you'll be sorry for, Ulan," said one of the men—an officer from his rank tabs. "We have reason to believe this man is a great criminal. Wanted by Iraj Protarus, himself."

Ulan stopped. He looked at Safar with sad eyes. "Is this true, little man?" he asked. "Are you indeed a criminal? If you're not, speak up! You have won the respect of Ulan, the Titan." He gestured at the guards, all strong, tough men. "And I will break their heads for insulting you."

Safar sighed. "Don't get yourself in trouble over me, friend," he said. "I'll be fine after all this is straightened out."

As they dragged him away a familiar old woman came scampering up. "Yer've just made this old granny a rich woman, Safar Timura," she cackled. "Thankee very much fer that!"

"Oops!" Gundara said.

Gundaree grimaced. "What a terrible development," he said.

Palimak groaned. "What'll we do?"

Gundara shrugged. "Not much we can do," he said. "Oh, well. He was a good Master, as masters go." He saw Palimak's sad face and try to cheer him up. "But we still have you, Little Master."

"Now, there's a silver lining if I ever saw one," Gundaree said in his mocking voice. "I'm sure Palimak is just so pleased to hear the news that he's about to inherit."

"Oh, shut up, you!" Gundara grumbled. "I was only trying to be thoughtful."

"What if we made it rain again?" Palimak said. "Except this

time, we don't let it stop." He stretched out his hands. "For a long, long time."

"What good will that do?" Gundara asked.

Palimak frowned, thinking. "Well, if it keeps raining . . . they can't do anything to him, right? And they can't send anybody to tell that damned old Iraj, either. I mean, if we make it rain hard enough the roads will be too muddy. Then Aunt Leiria will have time to rescue my father."

"I don't know if I'm up to it," Gundaree said. "I'm faint from exhaustion as it is. Rain isn't easy. Especially a prolonged rain."

"What a puny," Gundara scorned. "Tired out from a little cloud squeezing."

Gundaree slapped his forehead in exasperation. "Why must you always contradict me?"

"I don't," Gundara said.

"Yes you do."

"No I don't."

"You're contradicting me now."

"That's because you're stupid, stupid!"

"What about this?" Palimak broke in. "If I get some bread and cheese for you, Gundaree. And some honeyed figs for you, Gundara. And you ate them all up. Why, you probably wouldn't be tired anymore, right? And we could keep on making it rain."

Both Favorites were delighted at this solution.

"I must say, Little Master," Gundaree commented, "you do have the makings of a most remarkable diplomat."

Palimak frowned. "What's a diplomat?"

"I'm not sure," Gundara said. "But I think it has something to do with always having lots of nice treats for your Favorites."

Palimak snorted. "That's ridiculous. Who'd make up a word to mean something like that?"

"Some very wise men, Little Master," Gundaree said. Then, to Gundara, "Amazing how sensible you can be sometimes, brother dear."

"Oh, shut up!"

The guard aimed his crossbow straight into Safar's face. He fingered the trigger that would send the bolt crashing forward. "Don't try anythin' funny," he said, "or I'll put this right between your eyes!"

Safar rattled his chains and laughed. "What am I supposed to try?" he said. "You've got me shackled, manacled and chained to my bench." He indicated the others in the cell. "Plus, I'm surrounded by six crossbowmen who have been commanded never to leave my side."

The guard beetled his forehead, looked at Safar who was weighed down with twenty pounds of chain, then at his companions who were all relaxing on barrels that had been dragged into the cell for makeshift seats. They were grinning at him, amused.

"Jus' remember what I said," he growled. But he lowered the bow.

"Yer better watch out, Tarz," one of the men teased. "He might bust outta all them chains and kiss yer!"

"Aw, stuff a dirty loincloth in it," Tarz shot back. "He's a wizard, ain't he? Wizards can . . . well, you know, do stuff." He thought. Then, "Real bad stuff, too." He nodded, firm.

"If I really were a wizard," Safar said, "why would I be here in chains? Why would I allow myself to be captured?"

Tarz shrugged. "How the hells do I know?" he said. "Maybe yers messed up. Made a mistake, like. Makes no never mind to th' likes of me."

Safar had no answer for this. The man, dumb oxen that he was, had hit the nail squarely. Safar had "messed up" as the man said. And at the present time there was nothing he could do about his dilemma.

Outside thunder crashed and rain drummed against the steel roof of the cell compound. Thank the gods for the rain, Safar thought. Or else he'd already be on the road to wherever Iraj was camped. Then he smiled to himself. Thank the gods, indeed! And here he was a man who firmly believed the gods were all asleep and paying no attention to human affairs. It was enough shake a man's faith in his disbelief.

He glanced at Tarz and the other men who perched on their barrels quietly talking among themselves. Very well, he thought, however he'd come by whatever time the storm provided, he'd best start putting it to some good use.

Safar examined his surroundings. His cell was one of twenty contained in a single story stone building with a steel roof and heavy bars on all the windows and doors. The whole building had been emptied of prisoners, mostly rowdies arrested during the festival. The six guards normally assigned to oversee the compound were now gathered in Safar's cell to provide air-tight security.

He shifted, sneaking looks at the heavy padlocks on his chains. Those he could open. As for the rest, they probably wouldn't be that difficult once he was free of the chains. If he started gesturing and muttering spells he'd have six crossbow bolts in him at the blink of an eye.

Then he felt the amulet grow warm on his chest and he thought of the fantastic stallion who was destined to be sacrificed when the rain stopped. He had absolutely no doubt now that the horse was the reason Asper had sent him to Naadan. He had to act quickly, or all would be lost. All I need, he thought, is some small advantage. A means to divert their attention so I can cast a spell. It wouldn't take much for one man. But six!

He felt a tickle on the back of his hand and he looked down to see a mosquito getting ready to drill. Safar was about to brush it away, then realized the sudden clatter of chains might accidentally get him drilled by something much worse than a mosquito's beak.

Then necessity wed inspiration and he quickly made a fist, trapping the mosquito in the tightened skin. He closed his eyes, pretending to sleep, but instead he was focusing inward, making his mind slender and sharp like the mosquito's beak. He pierced an artery and went snaking along through his own blood stream suddenly filled with the knowledge of all the loops and turns so he was ready when he shot into the heart, felt the immense pressure of contraction, then was released and hurled onward. He raced to the place where the mosquito's beak came through and then he released his fist and let the insect draw his spirit self up along with the blood.

His world became a place of powerful odors and strange lights and images, but somehow it all made sense when he realized he'd become the mosquito. And he wasn't a he, but a She! And this she was ravenous. She could smell the hot blood all around and it was driving her mad with hunger. Safar tightened control and gave her a mission first. A mission that had to be accomplished before she could feed.

The mosquito buzzed through the cell bars, vertical massifs from her point of view, gleaming with oily moisture. She called to her sisters, a high pitched whine of a song. A song of a place of plenty, where the prey was huge and slow and clumsy. And full of hot blood, rivers of it, torrents of it, floods of the stuff of life.

They came to her, lifting up from stagnant pools in the nooks and crannies of the cell house. First by the scores, then by the hundreds. Her song grew louder, clearer, and the little mosquito larvae in those pools burst wings and legs through skin and became full grown adults who joined their sisters by the thousands. She led them all to the cell, a swarm so thick with flying insect life that it looked like a black wall moving along the corridor. They were all singing together now, singing the blood song and the sound of them all was a shrill skin-crawling wail.

At that moment Safar snatched his spirit self back and he became fully aware, eyes opening just as the guards were turning to see what was happening. He made a quick warding spell as the hungry black cloud swarmed into the room and attacked. The men slapped at themselves, cursing. Then the slaps became frantic and the curses wild. More mosquitoes poured in, all ignoring Safar and going for the guards. They were rolling on the floor in agony now, or curling up into balls of pain.

Safar came to his feet, chains rattling in odd counterpoint to the mosquitoes' song. He made a simple spell, then clapped his hands together, shouting, "Sleep!"

The guards all sagged, unconscious. The black cloud of insects settled onto them, covering them like a blanket. But this blanket was alive and ravenous, draining them of their blood.

Safar took pity on them. He quickly whispered an unlocking spell and the chains fell away and the cell door clacked open. Then he snatched a torch from its bracket, whirled it around his head until it was sparking and shouted, "Begone!"

He hurled the torch to the floor, white smoke exploded upward and outward, filling the cell with a harsh, oily odor. Then the smoke cleared away and all the insects had vanished. The guards were sprawled out on the floor in whatever position the sleep spell had caught them.

Safar smiled at them. "Pleasant dreams," he said and slipped out into the corridor.

He went to the main door, barred inside and out for extra security, and peered through the peephole. It was night and the rain was so heavy he couldn't make out the guard post at the main gate.

When he'd entered the compound he'd seen a dozen soldiers led by
a lieutenant. He'd assumed they were to secure the outside of the
small prison in case someone tried to rescue him. At the moment,
Safar guessed, those soldiers would be huddling in the guard shack
sipping tea and trying to keep dry and warm. He'd counted on that
when he'd worked the mosquito spell, figuring they wouldn't hear
the cries of their victims. So far it looked as if he'd guessed right.

He motioned and both locks, inside and out, fell away. He
cracked the door a few inches, saw no one about, and went out,
shutting and locking the door behind him. With luck his escape
wouldn't be noticed for a few hours until the sleep spell faded and
the guards woke up and found him gone.

The rain was falling so hard he was soaked through within seconds. He made his way gingerly across the muddy ground, trying
to work out a plan of action for when he reached the guard shack.
He still needed another bit of luck to complete his escape.
Actually, he needed more than a bit. He strongly suspected that to
overcome twelve soldiers a mosquito just wouldn't do.

When he got close he heard a thump and a groan, then the sound
of a heavy weight splashing onto the muddy ground. Safar had
frozen at the first sound, pulling back into a dark recess. He heard
bootsteps going into the yard and tried to make himself smaller.

Then he saw a familiar form leading four men toward the cell
building.

He sagged in relief.

It was Leiria!

13

THE BLOOD PRICE

The priest chanted a prayer, swinging his censer by the chain, lid
clack-clacking, incense smoke billowing through the altar room.

King Quintal gagged on the smoke, making the painful throb

in his temples drum harder and he cursed the very gods the priest was invoking. Quintal was sick—sick with fear, sick from too much drink and trebly sick from enforced sobriety on this most horrible of mornings.

Two other priests joined the others in sing-song prayer, adding their censer smoke to the too-sweet perfume that already infused the air.

Quintal shouted, "Get on with it you pack of shrieking eunuchs!"

The head priest protested. "But Your Majesty, this is a solemn occasion. Everything must be properly purified."

"Well, I'm purified up to my behind," Quintal roared. "My bowels are bursting with your damned purity. If you want to keep your head you'll get that horse out here right now. Let's kill it, and be done with it!"

The frightened priest issued orders and a moment later the stallion was brought out by sweet-faced boys dressed in white robes. The executioner followed, a broad ax resting on his shoulders.

Sick as he was, Quintal couldn't help but admire the animal. Besides its classic form, the stallion seemed quite calm. Not placid—his head was up and his eyes were alert. Confidence, that's what it was. Despite circumstances that would panic most animals, this one acted as if it were in complete control of the situation.

To Quintal's right a bulk as large as his own stirred uncomfortably. It was Ulan, sitting in the traditional place of honor. He was also the sole public witness to the event. Other than the principals, the sacrificial chamber was empty. The room was large enough to hold several hundred and normally it would be packed with dignitaries and honored guests. The priests began to pray over the horse and Ulan shifted again, the ornate seat groaning under his weight.

"I don't like this, Majesty," he grumbled. "Don't seem right to kill a great horse like that. And in such a hurry, too. With nobody around, so it's like we've got no respect for him."

Quintal flushed, angry, but he bit off a royal curse. Ulan was the most popular man in Naadan. Not only was he a Brave Titan, fresh from victory, but he was well-known for his many kindnesses to the poor, his temperate lifestyle, and for speaking up when ordinary people were wronged. In short, he was Quintal's rival for the throne. And if the king wasn't careful he find himself deposed.

Quintal pretended sympathy. "I know, I know," he said. "I've been in your place—declared Brave Titan of Naadan with all the honors and glories. And you want your friends to see. And your family, too. They'll all be proud and damned disappointed as well they can't be here."

"I don't care about that!" Ulan said. "Killin' the horse is what bothers me. I already offered to put up a sacrifice double his value. That should satisfy the gods. I won him fair. And I oughta be able to do what I like!"

It was all Quintal could do to keep from calling the guard to punish Ulan for his impertinence. But he needed the wrestler's support. Especially now.

"I can't take a chance on pissing off the gods," the king said. "Especially right now!"

Ulan was not mollified. "So why're we doin' it this way, Majesty?" he asked. "In secret and all. Like we're ashamed of something. I don't like the smell of this!"

Quintal looked about to see if anyone could overhear him. Then, desperate to win Ulan's backing, he leaned closer to say, "I'll tell you what's happening. But I've got to swear you to secrecy."

"Done," Ulan said. "You've got my word as a citizen, brother wrestler and fellow Brave Titan."

Quintal hesitated, then said, "A terrible thing has happened. Safar Timura has escaped."

Ulan gaped. "How?"

Quintal sighed. "It doesn't matter how. He just did. I haven't told anyone other than my closest advisers, otherwise the whole city'd be in a panic."

Ulan grimaced in painful understanding. "When King Protarus hears about it they'll be the hells to pay."

"Exactly. I haven't sent runners out to tell him yet. I'm trying to decide what to do and how to portray it. But I can't delay much longer because Protarus will think I've conspired with Lord Timura."

He pointed at the horse. "That's why I'm doing this so quickly and so quietly. My priests tell me the faster we make the sacrifice, the faster we get the gods' blessings. Which we'll need when Iraj

Protarus hears what's happened. But my generals said if any kind of crowd was gathered together—especially a crowd of such important Naadanians—word was sure to get out. Then we'd have public hysteria on our hands at the same time Protarus showed up."

Ulan frowned. Like most Naadanians of late, he thought Quintal a drunken fool. Now, it seemed he'd become dangerous as well. If Iraj Protarus was about to pay a visit with blood in his eye, they ought to be doing more to get ready than killing a poor horse in some stupid secret ceremony. Ulan was never one to keep his deep-felt beliefs silent.

The big wrestler was weighing a reply, when a voice broke through: "Perhaps I can solve your problem, gentlesirs!"

The men jolted around and saw Safar standing there, hands on hips, wizard's cloak thrown back to show a gleaming breast plate, steel blue eyes boring out from a face darkened by the desert sun.

Then a second jolt as they saw the tall warrior woman standing by his side, crossbow cocked and ready. Behind her were at least ten other bowmen, all poised to strike.

Quintal jumped as the executioner saw the group, let out a berserker's roar and charged, swinging his ax over his head.

Leiria fired and the bolt dropped him in midstride and he crashed to the floor, dead.

Ulan was coming to his feet, but Safar stopped him with a shouted, "Hold, friend! I mean you no harm!" The giant wrestler sagged back.

Safar turned to Quintal, saying, "I'm sorry for that man. He was only trying to protect you. Now, let's make certain no one else makes such a tragic error. Tell your people to keep quite still and when our business here is done we'll be on our peaceful way."

Quintal gave the orders, although he saw it wasn't really necessary. The priests and boys were frozen with fear. Then the horse nickered, pulled free and trotted over to Safar. To the king's amazement the two seemed to know one another. They acted like old friends, too long apart. Safar touched the horse, hesitant at first, then it snorted with joy and nuzzled him. Safar patted and stroked and whispered into the horse's ear.

Then he looked up, blue eyes moist. "Does he have a name?" His voice was husky.

"Khysmet," Quintal said. "He's called Khysmet."

Safar's eyes widened. The vision in Asper's burial vault leaped up and he once again heard Asper's ghost whisper, "Khysmet!" He blinked in sudden realization.

He smiled, patting the big stallion, "Khysmet. Khysmet. Yes, now I understand!"

Then, to Quintal, "This is why I'm here. For Khysmet."

Dazed, Quintal waved a hand. "Then take him!"

"We're not thieves," Safar said. "I don't intend to steal him." He turned to Ulan. "Besides, he belongs to you."

"I'm with his Majesty," Ulan said. "If that's what it takes to get you out of here, he's yours. We've got troubles enough on account of you. Call him a gift, call him anything you want. Just take him and go!"

"Actually," Safar said, "I had a trade in mind." He lifted the horse amulet from his neck. He came forward, Khysmet trailing him like a big dog.

Safar handed the amulet to a puzzled Ulan. Then puzzlement turned to surprise. "It's warm," he said. "Like it's been toastin' next to the heart."

"It's an old witch's charm," Safar said. "The story is that whoever owns it will someday find a great horse, a magical horse." He nodded at Khysmet. "Like him." The horse rubbed its head against him like a cat. "As you can see, that part is true. So the next part must also be true." He indicated the amulet. "Someday you'll find such a horse and the owner will have no choice but to trade it for the amulet. And so on and so on."

"Who cares?" Ulan snapped. "Don't matter one way or the other if it's magic or not! Iraj Protarus is maybe gonna come down on Naadan like a hammer 'cause of you! Thousands of innocent people could die for somethin' that wasn't their fault!"

Quintal groaned and Ulan turned to him. "Isn't that right, Majesty?" he said. "Naadan's in big trouble all because of——" The rest was cut off when he saw Quintal slumped over in his throne.

"Ah, hells!" Ulan said. Ignoring Leiria and her warriors, he stalked over to the throne and bent to listen to Quintal's chest. After a moment his head came up and he announced grimly, "He's dead! Guess this was too much for him." He straightened, shaking his head. "Can't say as anybody'll be sorry. Even his kids didn't like him much."

Before Safar could speak, the high priest wailed, "But who will speak for us now, Ulan? Who will plead for us to King Protarus?"

Ulan thought a minute, then thumped his chest. "I will!" he said. "I'll tell Iraj Protarus what happened here! And if wants a head for revenge, he can take mine. And godsdamn his eyes!"

"I can help you with Iraj," Safar said.

Ulan peered at him. "Oh, yeah? How?"

Safar pointed at the amulet around Ulan's neck. "That used to belong to him," he said.

Ulan jumped, snatching at the amulet. Safar laughed. "Don't worry, I came by it honestly. Though not the way the charm is normally supposed to work."

"So what about the amulet?" Ulan growled impatiently. "How will that help?"

"Give it to Iraj as a gift," Safar said, "and all will be forgiven. I guarantee it."

Ulan stared at him, hard. Then: "You've got no reason to lie about that. So I'll take your word for it. But don't expect any thanks."

"I don't," Safar said, taking Khysmet's reins and preparing to lead him away.

"One other thing," Ulan said.

"What's that?"

"If you're ever in this region again . . ."

"I'll give Naadan a pass," Safar finished for him.

"Yeah," Ulan said. "Like that!"

The escape from Naadan was slow going. Supplies were low in the main Kyranian encampment and Safar had tarried long enough to force Ulan to sell him all the goods they could haul away. Now there were so many wagon and camel loads of food and other badly needed things that they had a fairly large train. Plus there was a herd of goats and fresh horses to tend, so they barely made it into the hills by nightfall. Safar didn't know how much time they had. He assumed the worst. Ulan was clearly no fool and Safar suspected the new king would send runners to Iraj the moment they cleared the gates.

Once in the hills, Safar and his companions only rested a few hours. They set out again before dawn, using the stars to guide them and the Demon Moon to light the way. Their goal was the main camp, where all the villagers were well hidden in a woody ravine.

When first light came Safar dropped back to the rear of the column, where Leiria and her best men were positioned.

Leiria waved at the rumbling wagons and slow-moving camels. "We'll be a week at this pace," she said. "We never counted on the expedition taking that long."

"We'll be fine," Safar assured her.

"Are you soothsaying, or just trying to make me feel better?" she said, but she said it with a smile.

"Neither one," Safar said. "I was merely expressing my faith in you, Leiria."

"Then we're lost for certain," Leiria laughed.

"I'm supposed to be the wizard in this group," Safar said, "but you're the one who's had all the magic." He nodded at Renor and the other men, weapons at the ready, alert for any danger. "They were all just farm lads and goat herders not many month ago," he said. "But you've turned them into a real force to be reckoned with. As professional a group as I've ever seen, even when Iraj was at his peak."

"It wasn't that difficult," Leiria said, with not a trace of false modesty. "In a way they're better than professionals. They have a greater reason to fight than money or ambition." Once again she indicated the caravan. "They're fighting for their own. You can't ask for a better goad than that."

Safar agreed and was about to praise her more, when she said, "All right, Safar, you've got your horse . . . Khysmet . . . and you've rather belatedly told me that he was the reason we were in Naadan. That it wasn't just a routine raid. Fine. Wonderful. Asper speaks and we obey, whether we know we're obeying or not! Now, what else are you holding back?"

"I can't say," Safar replied. "I've already told you why."

Leiria groaned. "I know! Wizard business!"

"It's not that simple," Safar said. But before he could go on Renor whistled a warning.

They turned to see an ominous cloud of dust puffing up on the horizon.

Leiria examined it with expert eyes. "Not that big a force," she said after a moment. "But it's coming up fast."

Safar frowned, concentrating until he caught a whiff of purpose in the oncoming cloud. "I think it's a scouting party," he said. "Iraj's men, that's for certain."

"Doesn't look like there's enough to mount any kind of serious threat," Leiria said. "I'll get some men together and ride out and meet them. Make them sorry for being so stupid."

Safar started to agree, then hesitated. "That's not necessarily a good idea," he said. "You'd have to catch or kill them all. If you failed, Iraj would be able to pinpoint us exactly for the first time since we left Kyrania."

Leiria was irritated. "What are we supposed to do," she said, "let them follow us all the way back to camp?"

"What are your chances of getting them all?" Safar asked.

Now it was Leiria's turn to hesitate. After a bit, she sighed and shook her head. "Not very good," she admitted. "They're most likely Iraj's best scouts. They'll be smart. They'll be fast. And they'll never forget that mission takes precedence over all else."

Safar nodded, then said, "Give me your water."

Leiria was startled. "Water? What are you talking about."

"I have an idea," he said. "Their prime mission is to capture me, right?"

"Rii-ght." Leiria wasn't sure where this was going.

"Fine, then I'll ride out to meet them," Safar said, "wag my tail and get them to chase me. I'll lead them off in some other direction, lose them, then meet you either on the trail or if it takes longer, at the encampment."

Leiria gave him the hells for even thinking of the idea. But Safar persisted and in the end she saw he was determined.

Safar patted the stallion. "Besides," he said, "I've been wanting to give Khysmet his head and see what happens. Both of us have been going crazy with this slow pace."

"One fall," Leiria warned, "and you're done for."

"We won't fall, will we Khysmet?" Safar said to the horse. The stallion whinnied and pawed the ground. "I don't think it's possible for him to stumble," Safar said to Leiria. "I can't explain how I know this. I just do."

"Great," Leiria said, "You get to play and I get to trod along the common path."

Her voice was heavy with sarcasm but Safar could see it was to cover real worry. "What a lucky man I am," he murmured, "to find a friend like you."

"Just you remember that, Safar Timura," Leiria scolded as she handed over her water bags. "If you let something happen to you I'll track down your ghost and kick its behind from here to Hadin."

Then Safar was riding away, looking like a warrior prince on his great horse.

A large piece of Leiria's heart went with him.

14
HORSE MAGIC

Iraj dreamed of horses—a great wild herd flying across the plains. He sailed with them, moving at breathtaking speed, the air full of fresh spring currents, the horizon a joyous thing of blue skies meeting lush green earth. He felt like a boy again, a fully human boy with innocent dreams and youthful yearnings.

He was skimming just above the herd, which moved in graceful unison like a flock of birds flying to some glorious home that was free of all earthly cares.

Iraj quickened his pace, moving along the herd until he came to the leaders. There were two of them, the first creamy white, the other hearthstone black, and both were so magnificent he loved them at first sight. The black was a fiery mare, the white a tall, noble stallion.

He chose the stallion and settled down, down, and just as he touched the world spun and he suddenly found himself crouched in a canyon, the stallion standing next to him. Now the horse was saddled and harnessed and he was holding the reins loosely in one hand.

Iraj heard the sound of fast-moving riders and he knew his enemies were hunting him just over the ridge. He didn't know or care who that enemy was, but he thrilled at the prospect of an encounter. The horse nickered, sharing his excitement. Laughing, Iraj came to his feet and vaulted into the saddle.

Astride the horse he felt strong and swift, a man who feared nothing. The horse was magic under his hands, moving with easy fluidity. It was as if he were part of the animal and it was part of him.

Blood sang in his ears and he shouted in glee as he and the horse surged forward. They practically flew up the steep sides of the canyon, dust and rocks boiling behind them as they plunged up and up and then they were over the rim charging across a hilly plain.

When he spotted the scouting party he brought the horse to a skittering halt. Iraj was startled at the animal's quick obedience. He'd barely touched the leather straps and the horse had stopped on a skinned copper. It was as if the action had been communicated by thought alone. Now the stallion stood trembling under him, ready to charge into the fight, or turn and run like the winds.

Iraj waited, keeping a rein on his own high-pitched emotions. He felt wonderful. Full of life and spirit and clean purpose. Gone were the ravenous urges of a shape changer. He had no overpowering lust for blood and misery. No fiery dreams of grand thrones and bowing subjects. He didn't even hate his enemies who were thundering toward him. He only wanted to bedazzle them, confound them. That would be enough to make a joyous victory.

He patted the horse, soothing it as the scouting party came closer. There were twenty: six main scouts astride fast horses in the lead, and eighteen demons, bristling with arms and riding the huge, cat-like beasts that could take a charge and turn it back with their ferocity.

When the scouts were near enough to see him, Iraj raised his fist high in challenge. He stood his ground until he heard excited shouts of recognition: "It's him! Don't let him get away!"

At the last moment Iraj wheeled the stallion and raced away across the plain, the soldiers in thundering pursuit.

It was a ride like no other and Iraj whooped in joy as they sped over rocky ground as if it were meadow grass, leaping wide ravines as if they were merely narrow clefts. Sometimes he got too far ahead of the soldiers and he had to turn back to swoop just outside of their range, then wheel and charge away again.

He led them far from the main track, through rough hills, barren valleys and dusty canyons full of tricky switchbacks and false trails. He never stopped, riding on through the night, the horse never tiring under him. The scouts grew weary, their animals ready to drop. Laughing at their plight, Iraj gave them no mercy, prodding and teasing whenever they tried to rest.

He rode that way for many a day, until he finally abandoned the soldiers, exhausted and lost in the middle of a desert.

A few hours later he came to a small wooded area with a creek running through. A tall willow shaded a pool where the creek widened. He dismounted and led the horse to the pool for a cool drink and shady rest. The two of them drank long and deep, a warm feeling of comfort and satisfaction shared between them.

Iraj splashed water on his face, breaking the mirrored surface with his cupped hands as he sluiced dust and grime from smooth cheeks.

Strange, he thought, I remember a beard.

Curious, he peered into the water and saw a wavery reflection floating up at him. He couldn't make it out at first, but then the surface calmed and the image resolved itself.

With a shock he realized he was looking at the face of Safar Timura!

Safar jolted back, nearly losing his balance and falling into the water. Khysmet nuzzled him, wondering what was the matter.

"It's nothing," Safar said, stroking the soft nostrils. "I'm just tired, I guess."

Even so it was with some trepidation that he leaned forward again to peer into the water. Floating there was the reflection of his own smooth features.

A moment before he would have sworn an oath that he'd seen

the face of Iraj Protarus staring back at him. The illusion, surely caused by exhaustion, had been so strong he'd even felt a beard under his fingertips when he washed.

Ridiculous as the notion was, Safar was vastly relieved. To calm himself he washed and groomed Khysmet, then gathered some sweet grasses for a treat. He also found berries all fat and full of juice and he fed them in alternating handfuls to Khysmet and himself. Then he slept. It was a sound and dreamless sleep and when morning came he felt refreshed and full of energy. Khysmet evidently felt the same, for he pranced about and kicked up his heels like a colt. Safar was eager to get into the saddle and be on his way. He had many miles to cover before he reached home. Although it was nothing more than a tented encampment soon to be on the move again, home was how he thought of it and so home it was.

As they cantered out of the woods, Safar thought of his wild ride—the ride that seemed as if it would never end. Khysmet snorted, tossing his head, as if sharing the memory and enjoying it equally. Then Safar thought of the soldiers he'd left in the desert. They were so exhausted and so lost he doubted they'd survive. To his surprise he felt not one pinch of pity for them. They'd chosen the wrong side and too bad for that.

It was a cold, just so, feeling and it was discomforting how easily it sat upon his soul.

And he had a flash of awareness of what it was like to be Iraj.

In Iraj's most private quarters the king paced the room, fighting to control his emotions and retain his human form. He kicked at the pillows and snarled at a terrified serving wench to fetch him some wine and make it quick or he'd tear her heart out.

The dream was gnawing at him. Although to call it a dream would be an exaggeration, because Iraj never slept. That was one of the things he missed most about his previous life. Sleep, blessed sleep. As a shape changer he only dozed, or, as Fari explained it, he entered a neutral state where he was vaguely aware of his surroundings but was resting.

Iraj knew all this, but he still thought of the experience as a dream. And it had left him with a feeling of great loss. Normally, if normal it could be called, Iraj's neutral state was full of quick, bloody images mixed with snatches of voices; some screaming, some wailing, some babbling, some shouting in fury. When he came "awake" he was angry, always angry and the only relief was causing pain. The greater the pain the closer he came to a state of—joy? All that had somehow been welded to his overweening ambition and combined into a ferocious desire to always be on the move—doing something, crushing something, killing something.

It was like a furnace, Iraj thought, an immense furnace straight out of the hells that could never be satisfied.

But the dream, ah the dream, if only he could capture it and make it into a potion then drink it down and quench that angry fire.

Wine was thrust into his hand and he drank and paced and drank some more, letting the dream spill out. The horse! That magnificent creature, a plainsman's treasure unmatched by any Iraj had ever seen. And the ride! By the gods that was a chase to end all chases! Iraj chuckled, remembering how he and the horse had fooled the soldiers. Most of all he remembered the feeling of being whole and human again—the sense of freedom so strong it was like being lifted up to the skies.

Then he came to the uncomfortable part, the part that had smashed him out of his dream into dismal reality.

He thought of the moment when he'd stared into the pool and seen Safar's reflection instead of his own. Everyone knew dreams sometimes had deep meaning, but what was that all about? The strangest thing was although seeing Safar had been a shock there had been no feeling of hatred for him. And for certain Iraj hated Safar with passions only a shape-changer could know. Iraj hated him now as he paced and thought and wondered, thinking, if he had Safar in his grasp at this moment he'd rip off his limbs and devour them before his still living eyes.

However, for a brief span, just as Iraj was recovering from his surprise at seeing Safar, there was no hate. In fact, the first thought he had was being glad that he'd met an old friend in his dream.

He was still worrying that bone an hour later when Kalasariz begged an audience. The spy master entered, cool and smooth as ever, with only a few spots of wolfishness to show his inner excitement.

"I bear good tidings, Majesty," he said. "Our witches' net has proved itself already. There's still some rough spots, such as communications, to burnish, but I do believe we are on the right path with this."

"A sighting of Lord Timura?" Iraj asked, nerve endings burning with interest and he remembered his bargain with the strange witch known as Old Sheesan.

"Better than that, Majesty," Kalasariz said. "A witch over in Naadan not only sniffed out Lord Timura in a festival crowd of thousands, but she was able to alert the authorities in time so he could be captured."

Caught by surprise, Iraj's wolf snout erupted from his face. "You mean, we have him?" he snarled.

Kalasariz sighed. "Unfortunately, he was able to escape, Majesty," he said. "His magic was too strong and his kinsmen were too clever for the local king. Disappointing perhaps, but only when looked at from a certain angle."

"And how should we look at it?" the king growled. "How can Lord Timura's escape be viewed as anything other than abject failure?"

Kalasariz had been ready for this. "Why, Majesty, Old Sheesan only just set up the witch network. And already we have proof that no city in your kingdom is safe for Lord Timura." He shrugged. "Nest time we'll get him! We only have to improve the response of the local authorities. They have no experience in dealing with wizards."

"You'll see to that?" Iraj demanded.

Kalasariz smiled. "Gladly, Majesty," he said, "except I fear I'd be treading on Prince Luka's territory. He's in charge of dealing with local authorities, if you recall."

Iraj looked at him coldly. "You've certainly managed to wriggle off that hook," he said.

Kalasariz acted hurt. "Why, Majesty," he said, "you've misconstrued my intent. I was merely reporting what I thought was the best news since this whole exercise began."

Iraj decided to ignore this large chunk of dissembling, saying,

"Tell me the details. Exactly what happened in Naadan?"

Kalasariz reported as fully as he could, from the tavern encounter to Safar's strange challenge of the wrestler, Ulan, to his capture and eventual escape.

"Now, here's where it really gets interesting, Majesty," he said. "We nearly had him twice. The Naadanian messenger was on the road to this camp and luckily encountered one of your scouting parties a few miles from Naadan. They went in pursuit."

"Yes?" Iraj said.

Kalasariz took a long breath. This was another dangerous area to be bridged. Then, "Well, I can't say what happened exactly after that. The soldiers never returned. I suspect they were ambushed by Lord Timura's forces."

Iraj was rocked by the news, his features becoming more wolflike. Not at the defeat. He was thinking of the dream, the mad chase into the desert. The soldiers—his soldiers!—in pursuit. Could this be true? Had it been a vision, not a dream?

"There's another way Prince Luka can aid our cause," the spy master went on. "We should post similar scouting units in each city, backed by sufficient troops to prevent another ambush. Then we don't have to leave things to chance."

Iraj was drifting now, not really paying attention. He was thinking of the dream in a completely different light, which had an odd calming effect on him.

It was a human hand that he waved at Kalasariz, saying, "Yes, yes, tell Luka to do all that."

"And the witch, Majesty?" the spy master asked. "Old Sheesan? Shall we increase the reward? I'm a great believer in financial incentive."

"Fine," Iraj said absently. "Double it if you like." He paused. "And send for the witch. I want to speak with her."

"Yes, Majesty, it will be done, Majesty, just as you say." Kalasariz hesitated. He'd won every point thus far and was willing to try his luck once more. "One other thing, Majesty."

"Say it."

"Prince Luka informs me he plans to punish Naadan for allowing Lord Timura to escape."

"Whatever he decides," Iraj said.

"Yes, Majesty," Kalasariz said, "except Naadan is such a rich area—one of the few bright spots in your kingdom that can pay real taxes, instead of chickens and scrawny goats. And the king who was responsible for letting Lord Timura get away—King Quintal—suddenly died. He was probably scared to death. Ulan the wrestler is king now."

Iraj shrugged. "Luka knows my views on that issue. I assume he took them into account when he made his decision."

"Yes, I'm sure he did, Majesty," Kalasariz said, "and I meant no criticism."

He slipped an object out of his sleeve and held it up for Iraj to see. "However, I don't think he took this into account, Majesty," he said.

Iraj goggled at the object. It was the horse amulet he'd given to Safar long ago! Hurled it at him, actually, in his anger at Safar's defiance over the woman, Nerisa.

"King Ulan sent this to you as a gift, Majesty," Kalasariz said, "and he begs you to spare his people."

Iraj took the amulet with trembling hands. He had no doubt the spy master knew the tale behind the amulet. But Kalasariz could have no idea that it now had even deeper meaning.

"It's true," Iraj murmured. "The horse really exists."

"Pardon, Majesty?" Kalasariz asked.

Iraj shook his head. "Leave me."

"But what about Naadan, Majesty?" the spy master asked. "Shall we spare them?"

Iraj snarled, "Yes, dammit! Now get out of my sight!"

Kalasariz left, vastly pleased with himself. He cared nothing about Naadan's fate. However, he'd just won a major victory over Luka by having his orders reversed.

When he was gone, Iraj hung the amulet about his neck. He felt the warm glow of its magic against his chest. Once again he was astride the great horse running free with the winds. The reverie ended with a crash and he shouted for his officers.

They came running and he issued orders to break camp immediately. He would march within the hour, never mind there wasn't time to rouse the whole army. "They can catch up to us later," he said, dismissing the men.

The furnace in his belly was burning full force. He knew exactly where to go to pick up Safar's trail. Somewhere outside Naadan there was a canyon where Safar had lain in wait for his soldiers.

Iraj had no doubt he'd recognize the spot the moment he saw it.

Palimak felt like he was swimming in camel curds, which he hated more than anything, especially if the milk camel had grazed in an onion field and then it was really awful because all the onion juice seemed to concentrate in the curds. Grandmother Timura said it was good for him and made him eat it anyway, but why was she making him swim in the stuff? It was thick and slimy and hard to swim in and he kept on bumping into big pieces of curd and then he'd sink down and down and get it in his nose and mouth.

Then he thought he heard voices. He wasn't sure whose voices they were but he heard his name so he turned over on his back and floated on the curds to listen.

"Palimak's been sick since the storm," he heard his grandmother say. He knew she wasn't really his grandmother, although she acted like one and talked like one and cuddled like one, and scolded like one, so that's what he called her.

The same with Grandfather Timura and that's who he heard talking now. He heard him say, "We've been scared to death. First it was a fever, which seemed to hit when the rain stopped."

"I got the fever down just fine," his grandmother said. Her voice quavered. "Then he went to sleep and we haven't been able to wake him up." She sniffled, trying to hold back tears. "It's been more than a week, now."

Someone answered but Palimak couldn't tell who because he sank under those stupid curds again and he was swimming and swimming and then he was whirling around and around in all that onion tasting stuff and then . . . Nothing. A long, long time of nothing. Then he smelled incense, except not just one kind because there were so many layers of scent—rose and sage and lemon and cinnamon—that it was like he was smelling a rainbow . . . if only you could break off a rainbow hunk and put it in an incense burner. Then he sensed light and he heard someone chanting, but they were whispering so he couldn't make out what the chant was all about.

He thought, talk louder, please! and just like that someone said, "Wake up, Palimak!"

The boy opened his eyes to find his father bending over him. His threw his arms around his Safar's neck, crying, "Oh, father, I'm so glad to see you!"

Safar hugged him back and told him what a good boy he was, and brave too, and other things like that until the world was whole again.

Then Palimak remembered and became alarmed. "What about Gundara and Gun- daree?" he asked, fumbling around his bed-clothes for the turtle idol. "They've been sick too!"

"Don't worry," his father said, slipping the turtle from his sleeve. "I had to take care of you first." He laid it on Palimak's chest. "Just leave it there for awhile," he said. "Before you know it they'll be out here driving us crazy again."

Palimak giggled. "They will, won't they," he said. "Saying 'shut up, shut up' all the time." Then he remembered something else and the giggle turned into a full-bodied laugh. "You sure looked funny in all that mud, father," he chortled. "Falling down, splat! And that big wrestler, boom, splat!"

"So you were the one who made it rain," his father said, laughing with him.

"Sure," Palimak said. "Well, not just me alone. Gundara and Gundaree helped too. It was pretty hard to do. You have to sort of catch clouds and keep squeezing them to get all the water out." He made wringing motions with his hands. "And then you have to blow real hard to make a wind." He puckered his lips to demonstrate. "At first it was fun. Then we had to keep going and going until you got out of that dungeon and it wasn't fun any-more."

He shrugged. "I guess that's why we got so sick," he said. "But it was worth it. You escaped, right?" More giggling. "All those mosquitoes!" he said. "That was really, really disgusting, father. Would you show me how to do it someday?"

"Soon as we can find some mosquitoes," his father promised. Then, "When you're well again," he said, "perhaps we'd better talk about doing great big spells, like making it rain. You can see for yourself that it can be very dangerous."

"It was the only way I could help," Palimak said.

"I know, son, and I thank you for it. You were very brave and very smart and you might even have saved my life."

Palimak squirmed with pleasure. "Did I really save your life, father?"

"Absolutely," Safar said. "And I wasn't criticizing you for doing it. I was only saying that you have to learn how to be careful about that sort of magic. We have to go slowly, son. Sometimes you'll even have to help me keep up with you. Even though you're still a boy, there's things you can do that I can't." He smiled. "Like making such a big rainstorm!"

"Oh, sure you could, father," Palimak said, feeling quite manly in his reply. "You're much stronger than me!"

"Only because I'm older, son," his father said. "And I've studied very hard all my life. You'll catch up to me one of these days. Plus more. Much more."

"That's because I'm half demon," Palimak said with much satisfaction. "It's better than just being one or the other, right?"

"That's right, son," his father said.

Palimak had a sudden thought. "What about the horse?" he asked, worried. "Khysmet, right?"

His father looked surprised. "Yes, that's his name."

"Is he here? Did you bring him back?"

"He's outside the tent eating a big basket of corn and rye."

"That's good," Palimak said, quite solemn. "He deserves it after riding around all over the place."

His father frowned, then, "Did you see that too, son? Me on Khysmet and the soldiers chasing us?"

Palimak hesitated, then, "I guess I did, but not the same way I saw you in Naadan. It was after I got sick and I had these strange dreams. One of them was you and Khysmet."

"That was a vision, son," his father said. "Not a dream. I was wondering when you'd start having them."

Palimak wasn't listening. He was thinking of something else. "The really, real strange thing was that you weren't always on Khysmet," he said. "Sometimes somebody else was riding him."

His father's blue eyes narrowed. "Who, son? Who else did you see?"

Palimak remembered and his heart gave a bump. "It was Iraj Protarus, father!"

"I'm no wizard," Leiria said, "but that sounds worrisome to me."

Safar nodded. "Exactly why I wanted to talk to you before the meeting," he said. "There's no sense getting everyone alarmed when I don't know what it means myself. I'm sure Palimak had a vision. And in that vision he definitely saw me playing my little game with Iraj's scouts. But I don't know what to make of him seeing Iraj as well. Hells, that might not even have been part of the vision. Perhaps it was a dream attached to the vision. It happens sometimes. It's the magical equivalent of the tail on a kite."

"We'd be safer assuming the worst," Leiria said. "Although only you know what that could be."

Safar thought a moment, jumping from worst case logic point to the next and so on, face growing grimmer with each leap. The moment he'd proposed that Ulan give the amulet to Iraj, he'd known that he was making Iraj's task easier. Still, with so many lives at stake he had no other choice. He considered the gloating witch in the arena who had torn off a piece of his cloak. That, too, might help Iraj. On the other hand, the magic of human witches was weak. It would take an extraordinary sorceress to make any use of it. And those were very rare, indeed. Still . . . still . . .

"The safest thing," he said finally, "would be to run as far and as fast as we can."

"You think he'll track us here?"

"Taking the bleakest view, yes."

"Then that's what we should do," Leiria said. "Run." She sighed. "At least we're ready for it," she said. "We're supposed to move out at first light."

"True," Safar said, "but we just might want to change which way we go and how." He unsnapped the map case from his belt. "We'd better get the route plotted before the meeting. Otherwise our beloved Elders will want to debate the issue for a week."

"Honestly, Safar," Leiria said, "I don't know why you put up with them. I know the Council of Elders is a proud Kyranian tradition and all that. But they aren't organized for this kind of life. They've rarely had to decide on anything more important than when to let out the pigs and geese to keep the streets clean.

"This is war and they're just not suited for it. You need to organize some kind of military leadership. People who can think quickly, argue when its time to argue, and no matter what they think to shut up and fall in to march with the rest of us when the final decision is made."

"You don't understand, Leiria," Safar said, unrolling the maps and picking through them. "This is the system we've always had. I'm loathe to interfere with it, much less change it. We're nomads now. But I hope that doesn't last much longer than a couple of years. In Syrapis, with luck, we can start a new life. A new Kyrania. If we set up some sort of military command it might be hard to change things back to the way they were."

He grimaced. "From what I've seen of most places, with all the kings and generals, it's nearly impossible to get rid of them once they're installed."

Leiria pointed at the maps. "Even so, the Elders don't get to choose now, do they?" she said. "I mean, we're going to work the whole thing out in advance, right? Then you'll convince them they thought of it themselves. Why, you're already leading them by the nose. So what's the difference?"

"Simple," Safar said, "I don't like doing it."

Leiria thought a minute, then smiled. "To split a hair like that, Safar Timura," she said, "your conscience must own a damned sharp sword."

In the tent with the Elders, Safar spread out the map and placed a stone on each corner. He moved casually, although inside his anxiety was mounting. After studying the maps he knew exactly where they had to go next. He didn't like it, but it was the only thing to do. The moment he'd been dreading for months had arrived.

"It seems to me," Safar said to the Elders, "that Naadan was very lucky for us. For the first time since we left Kyrania we have enough supplies to last us for several months."

"Only if we live off the land," the always argumentative Masura replied.

Khadji growled. "I suspect that's what Safar meant and you know it, Masura," he said. "The supplies we have on hand, plus living off the land. That's how we've been doing things for close on to a year!"

Masura grumbled. "I just want to make sure things are clear to everyone," he said.

"Actually," Safar said smoothly, "I did mean that, my friend. And I'm glad you brought it up. We don't want to miss anything and the supply situation is just the sort of crucial mistake we want to avoid."

Satisfied, Masura gave Safar's father a dirty look as if to say, see, I was right to ask. Your own son says so.

The headman, Foron, peered at the map. He put one finger on the ink blot that marked their current position and another on Kyrania. There wasn't much distance between them.

"I don't like that," he said.

Then he measured the distance to Syrapis. He grunted with effort as he made the stretch. It was two thousand miles away. "I like that even less," he said.

Foron scratched his head. "What if we took advantage of our luck to really cover some ground?" he said. "Instead of dodging and ducking and hiding out all the time, we could make one long dash for it."

Masura coughed. "We'd never make it all the way to Syrapis," he said.

Safar gave his father a signal and Khadji groaned. "For the gods sake, Masura," he said. "Foron wasn't saying anything of the kind. He meant we should try to get as far as the supplies will take us."

Khadji moved to the map, just as he and Safar had planned, and studied it. He pretended to search for a moment then put his finger on the prearranged spot.

"My guess is we wouldn't need new supplies until we reached here."

Everyone craned to see, including Safar who acted as curious as the rest.

"It's the Kingdom of Caluz," said the headman. Then, to Safar, "Have you heard of that place, Lord Timura?"

"Only that they have a famous temple there," he lied. "I once approved funds for a temple restoration project in Caluz. For the life of me I don't remember anything more about it. However, it must have been a rich area to possess such a temple."

Safar thought, if they only knew! He hadn't even told his father why Caluz had to be the choice. After finding Khysmet in Naadan, Safar had greater reason than before to heed the words of Lord Asper's ghost: "Come to me through Caluz!"

"If Caluz is that rich," he heard his father say, "then we can get new supplies without much trouble."

Everyone murmured agreement and the decision was made. There would no ducking and dodging and hiding in the months ahead. Instead they would strike straight for Caluz and resupply there.

"Actually," Safar observed, "Caluz might be the last place we have to raid." He indicated the map. "A short run from Caluz should put us at the Port of Caspan. On the shores of the Great Sea."

The headman smacked fist into hand. "Then it's on to Syrapis!" he exclaimed.

"Well, there's a sea to cross first," grumbled Masura. "Don't forget that!"

The men roared laughter and teased Masura—which had been Safar's intent all along.

Then wine was passed around and everyone drank to the journey ahead.

Two weeks later Iraj's army entered the wooded ravine where the Kyranians had camped. It was night and the sky was alight with the thousands of torches they carried to show the way.

The Kyranians had gone to great pains to wipe out all signs of their presence, but an advance party of Iraj's scouts had found an iron horseshoe nail, which led to the uncovering of the thrown shoe itself. From there it was only a matter of more detailed searching and enough other small signs were discovered to give the Kyranians away.

Now the army was coming, led by Prince Luka and his demon cavalry of mailed warriors astride the great cat-like horrors they used for mounts. Behind them was a huge armored elephant bearing King Protarus' royal howdah, all gold and bejeweled and with blood red curtains drawn tight so the king could not be seen. The king's army sprawled back from there, starting with his royal guard of crack troops, both human and demon. There were archers and slingmen, demons who fought with giant battle axes and short spears, fierce human tribesmen who fought on horseback with crossbows they could fire at the gallop, and long curving blades so sharp they'd slice through chain mail as if it were paper.

The army stretched for miles, torches and lanterns all gleaming in the night, back to the farthest reaches where the big supply wagons groaned like captive giants put to the rack.

In the howdah Iraj sniffed the air with excitement, wolf's snout bristling. Old Sheesan cackled in the corner, waving a scrap of cloth about like a tattered flag. "I paid her handsomely fer this," she said. "But it's right off Lord Timura's cloak, so it's worth ev'r bit a gold I could scrape together."

Iraj licked his chops and tossed her a purse of gold. "I'll give you another," he said, "if you can sniff out his spoor."

If the old witch only knew, he thought, she could get a cartload of gold from him as a reward. In all these months this was the closest he'd ever come to finding Safar. First he'd retraced the route he'd taken in the vision, finally coming to the desert spring where he'd seen Safar's reflection. His plan had been to have his scouts follow Safar's trail to the main Kyranian encampment. But his old nemesis had been too canny, using both physical and magical tricks to obscure his passage. Several times his hopes were raised when he'd caught the scent of the great dream horse he'd ridden in the vision. It was the amulet that made this possible, heightening his powers to pick up the stallion's musk. Then some spell of Safar's would interfere and the scent would be gone, his hopes dashed.

It was then that Kalasariz had showed up with Old Sheesan in tow and the witch had presented him with the scrap of cloth she said would put him on the trail again. Iraj had his doubts—the dirty old hag was hardly a figure to inspire confidence—but he'd given her the chance and now he was vastly pleased with himself for doing so. Using the cloth and her witchy powers—which even Fari had grudgingly admitted were "most remarkable . . . for a human!"—she'd picked up Safar's trail and carried it many miles forward until Safar confounded them again with another trick.

The trick, however, proved to be flawed. Iraj had merely scoured the area in a twenty mile radius and this time luck was with him, not Safar, and his scouts had stumbled on the ravine.

Yes, Old Sheesan had proved her value. In his wolfen state it was difficult for Iraj to think deeply. Even so, he felt an sense of affection for her and even . . . trust? That was strange! Iraj had only trusted one man in his life—Safar. And look what that had gotten him! Still, every once in awhile, when the witch was in repose, he caught a glimpse of that remarkable creature he'd seen for an instant when they'd first met. Who was this woman who called herself Old Sheesan? Was she a beautiful woman hiding behind an ugly facade? Or a filthy old hag through and through . . . and the glimpsed visions of beauty a product of his imagination?

Just then he heard a voice whisper in his ear, low, and musical and full of seductive promise: "Together . . . together . . . we can achieve all . . . together . . ."

He jolted around, but only saw the witch sniffing at the scrap from Safar's tunic, beaked nose twitching.

She lifted her head, cackling triumphantly. "This is his place, yes it be, Majesty," she chortled in voice totally unlike the whisper he'd heard. "Lord Timura slept here, ate here and he left it not long ago. The scent's that strong, it is. Not more'n two weeks gone, is Old Sheesan's guess, Majesty."

Iraj concentrated, transforming fully into his wolfen state. He strained to catch Safar's spoor, but he didn't have the witch's powerful magic nose, with a long lifetime of experience to separate and interpret what she sniffed.

Suddenly the amulet glowed, so hot it nearly scorched his chest and he growled with delight at the pain, pressing it tighter against his wolfish hide to feel all the more.

Then Iraj caught the spoor of the great dream horse and he lifted his head and howled with delight.

15

THE SPIRIT RIDER

Once out of the wilderness the Kyranians dared the main caravan tracks for the first time since they'd fled the Valley of the Clouds. They were amazed at the pace they could maintain, averaging nearly thirty miles each day—a distance a trained army would covet. What's more, they were able to command the entire length of that thirty miles. With scouts ranging far ahead and behind their control was extended even farther—a hundred miles or more.

It was Safar's practice to alternate between both scouting parties when they were on the road, seeing little of Palimak and the rest of his family during that time. Sometimes he found himself too far away from the caravan to rejoin it at night and would miss seeing them altogether for days at a time.

He regretted this, particularly when it came to Palimak whose boyish experiments with magic could be worrisome. He'd learned, however, that even a wizard couldn't be all places at all times so he locked the feeling away with all the other regrets that make up a life.

Thanks to Khysmet, he was at least enjoying these lonely but necessary missions more than in the past. It was not only a joy—and sometimes a breath-taking thrill—to ride him, but the stallion was remarkable company as well. Like an old friend, Khysmet knew all his moods and how to deal with them. When Safar became absorbed in thought, usually about what might await him in Caluz, the horse took control of the journey. Uncannily guessing the route Safar intended and becoming extra wary, sensing that Safar's mind was far away from present dangers.

Once when Safar was digging into Asper's book for a spell he could use in a swamp he became so absorbed in the demon wizard's theories he forgot where he was. When he became aware again he was startled to find himself on the other side of the swamp. Somehow Khysmet had found the way even though it was riddled with pits of quicksand deep enough to swallow a team of oxen, wagon and all.

Khysmet also proved to be a bit of a practical joker and Safar had to be wary when he squatted by a stream to drink, lest Khysmet butt him into the creek. When Safar came up out of the water sputtering and swearing Khysmet would rear back, snorting and pawing the air in delight.

There was also a strange kind of magic emanating from Khysmet. Oh, he couldn't suddenly sprout wings and fly, or scratch out a spell with his hooves like a witch's goatish Favorite. But on a long run, just when Safar felt he could no longer go on, he'd feel a sudden surge of energy and purpose radiating from Khysmet and then he could continue on for as long as it took to achieve his goal. As for the stallion, Safar had yet to see his limits.

There was the smell of the earth in Khysmet's magic: tall plains grasses golden in the sun; swarms of bees and locusts swooping this way and that, all of a single mind though there were thousands of them; small birds darting through the insect clouds to feed; and sharp-eyed hawks and eagles floating above it all, watching for their chance.

Safar strayed so far away from the others that Leiria admonished him, saying it was his duty as their leader to keep himself safe. Safar knew she was right, but despite several promises to stay close he kept forgetting and giving Khysmet his head and then there was no telling how many miles he might travel before he remembered his last promise.

One day she swore she'd stay with him herself and she brought along a spare horse so she could switch back and forth to keep them both fresh. By nightfall she'd worn out both animals and herself and it was all she could do to prop herself up to eat when dinner was ready.

Safar had gone to some trouble for her, catching a brace of pheasants and roasting them over the fire with wild herbs to sweeten the flesh.

She sighed, saying, "This is when I miss palace life. All those servants to tend your every need. If we were in Zanzair right now, I'd snap my fingers and order up strong wine and a good massage and then I'd have them carry my poor boneless body to the bed, where'd they'd tuck me in for the night."

"I can help you with the wine," Safar said, popping the stopper off a flask and pouring her a cup. He handed it to her, grinning. "I'd best not offer my services as a masseur. Not if we want to remain just friends, that is."

Leiria laughed. "A lot of good it would do you," she said. "I'm so tired you'd be sleeping with a corpse."

"There's nights when that wouldn't stop me," Safar joked, "and let's just say this is one of those nights."

Leiria gave him a look. "You don't want to start something you can't finish, Safar Timura," she said. "So don't tease a woman who still has delicate feelings for you."

"I know that, my dear, dear Leiria," Safar replied. "It's only how I'm feeling tonight, which I can't help."

Leiria yawned, sleep suddenly very hard to resist. "We need to find you a woman, Safar," she said. "We need to . . ." and she fell asleep in midsentence.

Safar watched her for awhile, admiring her clear strong features and inviting figure. He thought of the days—and nights—when they were lovers, then the memories became too disturbing and he rolled up in his blanket and tried to follow her into sleep. He drifted for a time, thinking of nothing, then he heard Khysmet nicker, soft, not in alarm, but calling, calling . . .

. . .And Safar was astride Khysmet, riding through a soft wood full of trailing ferns and sweet mosses. The air was misty, almost raining. They came upon a small glen filled with wildflowers and nourished by a musical brook.

Khysmet whinnied and Safar saw something moving through the mist and then it swirled away and the most marvelous woman he'd ever seen floated into view. The mist parted more, like a veil being drawn back, and with a shock he saw she was riding the remarkable black mare he'd seen in the vision.

Then his eyes were drawn back to the woman. She was achingly, exotically beautiful. She had long limbs and ebony skin with long waves of hair tumbling to her waist. She was nearly naked, wearing only a loin cloth and a light chain vest that swung open as she rode, showing her long torso and small, shapely breasts. She had a bow over her shoulder, along with a quiver of heavy arrows. Strapped to her waist was a short, broad-bladed sword.

Khysmet snorted, shifting back and forth as his blood warmed at the sight and scent of the mare. Then the rider and her steed sensed their presence and froze. Both turned to peer through the mist.

Safar felt a thrilling jolt as his eyes met the woman's. They were large and dark and full of wary interest as she examined him in turn. Her face was long, with high cheekbones, brows like black swallow wings, a slender nose slightly hooked over a sensuous mouth.

He saw that mouth twitch with humor and then the woman raised her hand to him as if in greeting.

Safar waved back and started forward, Khysmet quivering under him, filled with burning thoughts of getting closer to that mare.

The woman laughed—it was a rich husky laugh, a laugh out of the deep places in the forest, full of mystery and delight and no little danger. She wheeled the mare about and plunged back toward the wood and the mist swallowed her up. Safar heard the laughter trailing behind her and he urged Khysmet forward.

The stallion didn't need the urging and he exploded after the mare, crossing the meadow in a single jump and plunging into the mist.

It was a delicious chase, a chase full of thrills and near encounters that only added to the fire burning in both man and horse. The mare was Khysmet's equal and the woman was more than Safar's match when it came to pure riding. She led him on a merry hunt through the forest. Sometimes she'd let him draw near then dash away under branches so low Safar was nearly swept off, while she ducked down and easily evaded them. Or she'd disappear for so long he'd be hurled into depression thinking he'd lost her, then she'd burst out of a grove, hold the mare just long enough for Safar to get near, then wheel and dash away again.

Finally they came to the forest's edge and the mysterious horsewoman cantered out. There was a long patch of narrow ground bordered by a steep cliff. Safar's heart tripped when he saw she could go no further.

Then she turned her mare to face him, dropping the reins as if to show the chase was over. The mare nickered for the stallion and Khysmet trotted forward, eager to join her.

The closer Safar came, the more beauteous and exotic the dark stranger seemed. Her long arms and legs were remarkably graceful. Her ebony skin gleamed as if it were burnished and her smile was a bright welcoming light. But it was her eyes which captivated him most, so wide and dark and full of humor.

When he came within twenty feet or so, she raised her hand again. "Please stop," she said, in a voice that was low and full of warmth.

Safar did as she asked but his heart was with Khysmet, who grunted in protest when he reined him in. He obeyed but with great reluctance and once again Safar was struck by the horse's strength of purpose. Any other stallion would have thrown Safar off and hurled himself upon the dancing mare.

"So you're the famous Safar Timura," the woman said. She looked him up and down and seemed to like what she saw. "I must say, I'm certainly not disappointed."

"Who are you, my lady?" Safar asked. "Please grant me the boon of your name."

She laughed and shook her head. "Why, I can't tell you that," she said teasingly, "for if you knew it I could deny you nothing."

Safar's mouth became dry, his throat parched as a desert thicket.

The woman tossed her head, tresses floating in the wind. "Oh, but I probably shouldn't worry about that," she said. "If I were pleasing to look upon, perhaps I'd have reason to worry. But as it is . . ." a graceful hand swept down and up, indicating her lovely form . . . "I fear I'm too plain for one such as you."

"Who said you were plain?" Safar said. "Tell me and I swear that great liar will soon lack a tongue for so offending you."

Another musical laugh. "Only my sisters, Safar Timura, and it would be a vast relief if I had sisters without tongues. They're such dull-witted chatterboxes. But I think my mother would object, so, alas, I must refuse your kind offer to rid them of the means to torment me."

"I am the one in torment, my lady," Safar said. "To be kept in ignorance of one such as you is the deepest of miseries. If you can't find it in your heart to say your name, at least tell me your reason for being here. Are you lost? Is there some way I can assist you?"

Her ripe lips twisted in amusement. "Lost? I think not. A Spirit Rider is never lost!" A small laugh. "Although one of my sisters was confused for a month or two. But that's because she dallied with a handsome lad and forgot her duty. My father punished her—much too mildly in my opinion."

Safar goggled. Spirit Rider? He'd never heard of such a thing.

"As for assisting me," she continued, "it's my duty to assist you, Safar. My father sent me to warn you of grave danger."

Now it was Safar's turn for amusement. "Danger? How unusual." he said dryly. "What, pray tell, could be a greater danger than Iraj Protarus?"

The woman frowned, "Protarus? I don't know this name." Then her face cleared. "Ah," she said, "you mean the strange one who pursues you."

"The very one," Safar said.

"I can't say if you will survive this Protarus fellow," she said. "He's a shape changer in league with other shape changers so it's impossible to predict the outcome."

"Then I repeat the question, my lady," he said. "What could be worse than Iraj Protarus?"

"You will meet it in Caluz," she said. "There you will face a challenge as great as the shape changer and all his armies."

Safar's heart raced. "But I must go there!" he said harshly. "Lord Asper commanded it!" Intuitively he knew she understood who Asper was.

"Of course, you must!" the woman exclaimed. "Otherwise you'll never reach Syrapis."

"Then what's the sense of the warning?" Safar asked. "I already know Caluz is dangerous."

"It's much worse than you think, Safar Timura," she said. "Whatever preparations you have in mind—double them!"

"I will," Safar said.

"One other thing," the woman said. "My father bade me to say that what you seek to defeat your enemy—this Iraj Protarus, I presume—can be found at the temple in Caluz."

"You mean the oracle?" Safar asked. "The Oracle of Hadin? I know something about—"

She stopped him with a raised hand. "I can say no more. Go to Caluz just as you planned," she said. "Accomplish what you intend to accomplish. But remember, Safar Timura, in Caluz all is not as it seems. Seek the truth beyond the veil of lies."

Suddenly the woman and the mare began to fade. "I have to go," she said.

"Wait!" Safar shouted.

She shook her head, becoming fainter and fainter until she was like a ghost. She waved to him.

"Farewell, Safar Timura," she cried, then turned the mare and plunged toward the cliff.

The woman and her steed were translucent, now. At the cliff's edge the mare leaped high.

The woman shouted, "Until we meet again!"

"Where shall we meet?" Safar cried after her. "Where?"

She vanished, but her answer was left floating in the air:

"Syrapis!"

Safar came awake with a start. Across from him, Leiria was still sleeping peacefully. He glanced at the campfire and was surprised to see it exactly the same as when he'd fallen asleep. The vision had seemed so long, yet only a few seconds had passed.

He rose quietly and went out to where Khysmet was tethered. The stallion perked up his ears as he approached, but he stood quietly, as if his thoughts were elsewhere.

Safar laid his head against the horse, stroking the sensitive nose. "Were you there?" Safar whispered. "Did you see?"

Khysmet huffed and stamped his feet, switching his tail back and forth.

Leiria called out. "Is something wrong, Safar?"

"No, Leiria," Safar answered. "Nothing's wrong. Go back to sleep."

He stroked Khysmet. "Syrapis," he whispered. "Syrapis."

Palimak was bored. Day after day he rode with the small group of wagons making up the Timura family caravan with little to do but get into mischief. The roadside scene passed so slowly and with so

little change that the smallest thing became major entertainment.
A rodent dashing across the track, an ox lifting its tail to defecate
and birds taking a dust bath were among the more stirring sights
he'd seen that day.

It wasn't so bad for the older children, he thought. They got to
run around the wagons, or dash off into the fields to explore and
play games. Sometimes they'd disappear all day and wouldn't
catch up to the main caravan until nightfall. Oh, how he wished
he could go with them. Why one of his cousins had seen a bear and
her cubs just the other day. Now, wouldn't that've been something
to see? Maybe he could've made a pet of one of the cubs, or at least
played with it a little, What really offended him was that his
cousin was a girl. This made life seem even more unfair.

There was little privacy when on the road, so he couldn't play
with Gundara and Gundaree as much as he'd like. The Favorites
hated it when so many people were around and tended to be
grumpy when he summoned them. Always complaining that
people could peek into the covered wagon anytime they wanted.

To Palimak it seemed as if he was always getting into trouble,
especially when he played with his magic. Although he never
meant any harm, sometimes things just didn't go as planned and
he was always being scolded as if he'd done it on purpose.

He was still sulking over an incident earlier in the day. After
his grandmother had put out the wagon fire he'd explained quite
plainly that he'd only been trying to help. But she didn't listen—
they never listened!—and he'd gotten the scolding of his life and
was banished to the smelly old supply wagon.

"Now, let's see what mischief you can get up to in there,
Palimak Timura," his grandmother had said in her most scornful
tones. "I'm sorry there's nothing but moldy flour and wormy corn
to occupy your Lordship. Now maybe you'll have time now to
think about all the heartache and worry you're causing me."

"I'm sorry, Grandmother," he'd said in his most contrite
manner. Unfortunately, she wasn't so easily soothed.

"I'm sorry, I'm sorry," she mocked. "When I'm in my grave
from the worry you've caused me you'll know what sorry really is!"

Palimak poked a finger at a damp floursack. He didn't know
what she was so upset about. It hadn't been that big of a fire, after

all. And he could easily have put it out himself. If he could've remembered the fire putter outter spell, that is.

He still didn't know what had gone wrong with his experiment. The whole idea had originated with his grandmother's and aunts' complaints about how dark it was in the wagons. There was always a lot of mending to be done and they said they were going blind from sewing in such dimness. Because of the danger of fire and the roughness of the road no one was permitted to burn an oil lamp while the wagons were moving.

Bored as he was, Palimak became intensely interested in their difficulties. Interest turned to a child's concern for his loved ones. What would his grandmother do if she were blind? And his aunts, what if they couldn't even see their children to kiss them? So he'd turned his agile little mind full force on the problem.

Instinctively, he went at it backwards. What was the result he wanted? That was easy, he wanted light without having to burn anything. There were two ways to go at that, he'd decided. The first would be to take the light out of the fire and throw the fire away. You could then pour the light into bowls, or something, or even glass jars with stoppers on them so the light couldn't escape if it were so inclined. Probably the jars would be best, he thought. For reasons he couldn't explain he imagined light might be pretty rebellious and would always be trying to run away.

The second method would be to somehow trap the light. You could catch it in some kind of net, or whatever, as it ran away from its source—the sun or a campfire—then you could store it in great big casks with spigots like wine barrels. Then whenever you needed some light all you had to do was turn the spigot and fill up a jar.

He could envision his grandmother and aunts with jars of lights all around them, sewing away with no trouble at all and praising him for being such a smart and thoughtful little boy. The image pleased him immensely and he worked even harder.

He'd quickly dismissed the idea of trapping light and storing it. The trouble with light was that it was even runnier than water and much thinner so you'd have to have really big, big barrels, maybe even bigger than a house—which was the largest object he could imagine—to hold just a little bit. Which wouldn't last very

long either, so that was really stupid. Fine, then. He'd try to separate the light from fire and see what happened.

This feat proved to be surprisingly easy. Oh sure, Gundara and
Gundaree helped, but it was his idea and he'd done most of the
real work. One night after everyone had gone to sleep he'd filled a
bowl with oil, lit it with a candle, then summoned his Favorites.
After a few false starts due to the usual quarrels between the two,
he'd cast the spell.

"Come out, little light," he crooned. "Come and play with
Palimak. We'll have lots of fun and good things to eat and you
won't have to smell that stinky oil all the time. Come out, little
light. Come out and play with Palimak."

He scooped his hands forward, skimming across the wavery fire
and to his amazement he suddenly had a double palmful of light
spilling onto the tent floor. It made little glowing puddles with
scattered drops all around. Then the light began to fade—running
away, as Palimak thought of it—and he quickly turned a jar upside
down over the largest puddle. Inside the jar the light was only a soft
glow at first, then it suddenly became much brighter.

Palimak clapped his hands with glee. He'd done it! He looked
over at the bowl of oil. There was no light coming from it now.
But he could smell the burning oil and when he put his hand close
he could still feel the heat of the fire.

That night Palimak slept the peaceful sleep of a smart little
boy, a kind little boy, a boy who'd just saved his grandmother and
aunts from blindness. He'd smiled to himself as he slept, the jar of
light clutched in his arms, dreaming of all the hugs he'd get and
all the nice things they'd say about him.

When he awoke the light was gone. Palimak was in a panic
trying to figure out what had happened. The stopper was on tight.
The spell he'd used to enforce the jar's light-holding properties
was still strong. Then he'd looked at the bowl of oil and saw that it
was empty and the invisible fire was no longer burning.

Palimak frowned. It seemed obvious that although he'd sepa-
rated the light from the fire, some connection had remained.
When the fire had burned up its fuel the light in the jar had gone
out. Well, that was no good. You still had the same problem as
before, which was that you can't have a fire in a moving wagon.

But, wait! Nobody said anything about outside the wagon.

Palimak had labored until late that night working on the solution. The next morning—this very morning, in fact, this most boring of all days with its almost squashed rodent, stupid oxen and dusty birds—he'd put his plan to its first, and final, test. A brass burner was suspended beneath a rarely used wagon. A fire was lit, a small one so no one would notice. Light went into a jar. And the jar was hidden under Palimak's coat until the caravan set off and he was alone in the wagon. Then out it came, glowing very nicely, although maybe only enough for one person to sew by. So what? That was no problem! He could make a jar for each of them, being sure to hang the same number of burners under the wagon. Then when the light got dim all somebody had to do was jump off the wagon, toss more fuel into the burners and the light would be strong again. Palimak figured he'd volunteer to do the jumping off to start with. Later on someone else could do it, like that cousin of his who thought she was so smart because she'd seen a bear with its cubs. As if anybody couldn't do that!

It would have worked just fine too, Palimak thought, if the driver hadn't gone over that bump. And the bottom of the wagon had caught fire. Real fire you could see and smell and which could burn everything up! Palimak was trying to think of a spell to put it out when his grandmother came running from her wagon and beat it to death with a wet broom. Scolding and punishment followed swiftly.

Deep in the gloom of his supply wagon exile, Palimak gave a long, heartfelt sigh. It was so unfair. The more he thought about it, the sadder he became. So sad he thought he might even let himself cry, although he was probably too old for that and if somebody saw him he'd never get to run in the fields and play just like everybody else.

A tear was leaking down his cheek, with more due to follow, when his grandfather opened the back flap and jumped into the wagon.

"If you're not busy, son," his grandfather said, "I could use a little help."

Palimak hastily wiped the tear away and composed himself. "I'm not busy," he said. "What do you want me to do, grandfather?"

"I'm taking over the lead wagon," Khadji said. "We just added a new ox to the team and she's so green she's going to need some watching. I can't mind the road and her at the same time. Not very well, anyway. And I thought I could use a real good pair of eyes to help me."

"I've got real good eyes, grandfather," Palimak said, spreading the lids wide and looking this way and that. "See?"

"You're just the man for the job," his grandfather said and in a few minutes Palimak was ensconced on the seat of the lead wagon, glaring for all he was worth at the worrisome ox.

"Now, I feel much better," his grandfather said, cracking his whip to get the team moving. "No telling what a green animal will get into its head."

"But she's white, grandfather," Palimak said, pointing at the young ox. "Why do you keep saying she's green?"

Khadji buried a smile and pretended to examine the ox, which, as Palimak had said, was white as snow. "Hmm," he said. "Now that you mention it, she is white. I must have been looking at her in the wrong light. Thanks for pointing that out to me, son. I might have missed it."

Palimak was disappointed. "Then you don't need me to help you watch her anymore?" he said. "Since she's white, I mean. And it's the green ones that give you all the trouble."

"Oh, white's worse," Khadji said. "Much worse than green. Give me a green ox any day, but spare me the white." He gave Palimak a nudge. "You just watch her extra hard," he said. "Now that we know she's white."

Palimak glared at the ox even harder, so hard his eyes started to burn. "Why don't you take a little rest for a minute, son," Khadji said when he noticed the boy blinking fiercely. "I think she'll be all right for a mile or two now that she knows you're along."

The boy relaxed, easing closer to his grandfather and enjoying his company. A long silence followed. It was comfortable at first, but then it extended and expanded, making room for alarming thoughts, like the unfortunate matter of the wagon he'd set on fire. His grandfather stirred and Palimak had the horrible thought that Khadji was about to bring up the subject. Which was just awful. Everything was so peaceful and nice but it was going to be spoiled by another scolding. And maybe other punishment, as well. You could never tell with adults. They were like, like . . . the white ox, which his grandfather said was worse than even the green ones and you never knew what they'd do next.

By way of preamble his grandfather hawked, then turned and spat into the dust and Palimak knew he was in for it.

"I don't know about you," his grandfather said, "but ever since we took the main track I've been going crazy with boredom."

Palimak gaped in surprise. "Me too!" he said.

"I don't want to dare the gods for more trouble than we already have," his grandfather continued, "but when we were running and hiding all the time at least things were interesting. Sure, we might have been caught by Iraj, but that just made it more exciting. Our minds were always busy thinking up new things, or tricks, or guessing what Iraj might be up to." He glanced at Palimak, smiling. "Right?"

"Right!" Palimak nodded hard for emphasis.

"So here we are on the main track," his grandfather went on, "and they tell us we're making excellent time. Thirty miles a day!" He snorted. "Feels more like a thousand before the day is done."

He shook his head. "Nothing to do and all day to do it in," he said. "It's hard to bear sometimes, I tell you. Very hard to bear."

Another sigh, this one longer. "In fact," he said, "I'm feeling like that right now. Like I can't stand it anymore."

He paused, as if thinking, then, "Here," he said, "take over for a moment, will you?" And he handed Palimak the reins.

The boy was stunned at this display of trust. He straightened up and tried to snap the reins. It came out as a disappointingly slow wave that died before it reached the first oxen, but his grandfather nodded in approval.

"That's the way to do it," he said. "Nice and gentle. A wise driver is careful not to frighten his animals."

Heartened by the praise, Palimak sat taller still. Khadji fumbled in his pocket and took out a small lump of moist clay wrapped in oil cloth.

"Here's what I like to do to keep from getting bored to death," his grandfather said, working the clay between his hands.

Palimak gaped as his grandfather squeezed and pinched, turning out one little figure after the other—a goat, a bear, an ox and even a camel with such a long neck and silly expression on its face that the boy burst out laughing.

"May I try?" he asked.

He'd seen Khadji and sometimes even his father make pots and jars and dishes. All useful things, but dull as mud as far as Palimak was concerned. It'd never occurred to him you could create such interesting figures.

"Why not?" Khadji said. He fished another oil cloth packet from his pocket. "I've been saving this for something special," he said. "So far I haven't thought of anything, but maybe you can."

He traded the reins for the packet and watched from the corner of his eye as Palimak opened it. The boy's face brightened when he saw the unusual color of the clay. Instead of a dull gray it was a lustrous green, so deep that it was almost black when looked at from certain angles.

"It's beautiful!" the boy breathed. He looked up at Khadji. "Can I make anything I want?" he asked. "Anything at all."

"Of course you can," his grandfather said. "It's yours, now."

Palimak stared at the clay long and hard. Then his face cleared. "I know!" he said. And he started squeezing and molding in the clay.

"What're you thinking of making?" Khadji asked.

"I can't tell you," Palimak said with a sly grin. "But I'll give you a hint. It's a surprise for somebody.

"A really big surprise!"

16

PALIMAK'S REVENGE

Kalasariz moved cautiously through the night forest, keeping a discreet distance between himself and his quarry. His shape changer senses were tuned to their highest pitch and he could smell the sulfurous odor of the witch clinging to the brush lining the narrow trail. It was so powerful it nearly obscured the king's spoor, that mixture of fresh blood and old graves that marked all shape changers.

Behind him, sprawled on a great field, the army slept. Except for a few key sentries—all in the pay of Kalasariz—no one knew the king was out this night.

The spymaster seethed as he followed the king and Old Sheesan through the forest. Unless they were of his own making, Kalasariz detested all mysteries. And this midnight journey certainly fit that definition.

He wasn't as worried about what they were up to as he was at being left out. From the outset he'd given Old Sheesan explicit orders she was report every word and movement the king made when in her presence. This was the main reason he'd introduced the witch to Protarus. He was much more interested in knowing his king's most secret thoughts than he was in finding Safar Timura.

The witch, however, had proven to be cannier than he'd thought and now he was losing control. Old Sheesan's reports had become perfunctory, vague and of little value. She hadn't started outright lying to him yet—other than lies of omission—but he suspected she'd begin soon enough. And then he'd have to go to a great deal of bother and no little danger in getting rid of her.

The forest's edge reared up with no warning and Kalasariz nearly gave himself away as he stepped out onto open ground into the light of the Demon Moon. Hastily, he pulled back and found cover. He stayed quite still for a moment until he was sure no one had noticed him. Then he gently parted some branches and peered out.

Old Sheesan and the king were walking along a narrow strip of barren ground that seemed to be edged by a cliff. The forest was silent so the spymaster could hear the swishing of the witch's robes as she moved and the creak of Protarus' battle harness. They paused at the edge of the cliff. The witch gestured at a point on the ground.

"More magic there," Kalasariz heard her say. "A woman, methinks."

"A witch?" Protarus asked.

"No, she weren't no witch. Somethin' else, for certain. I can't quite put me finger on it."

She turned and pointed back at the forest where Kalasariz was hiding. He was so alarmed he nearly fled. But then she said, "Both of 'em come through there. Lord Timura was on that horse that's been givin' yer Majesty fits of envy. The woman was on a mare— and that was somethin' special too. Animal magic all over the place."

"Yes, yes," Protarus said, sniffing eagerly at the air. "I can smell it myself!"

The witch chortled. "Soon yer won't need the likes of Old Sheesan to ferret out mischief," she said. "And then where will this poor old granny be?"

"She won't be poor at any rate," Protarus said. "Not after all the gold I've been dumping in her lap."

"Gold's not ever'thin', Majesty," the witch said. "Least that's what they say. Although they leave out the part about exactly what's missin' that gold won't cure."

Kalasariz made a mental note to find out where the witch had hidden all this gold she was talking about. If he removed her little treasure cache she'd be more dependent on him.

"Anyways," the witch went on, "they came out there and rode up to the cliff where they stopped to palaver awhile. Then Lord Timura went off that way." The witch pointed to the most distant edge of the forest.

"What about the woman?" Protarus asked.

"I don't know," the witch said. "There's no sign of her after that. It's like she rode her mare off the cliff, or somethin'. Whatever she did, she didn't go with Lord Timura."

"Is that all?" Protarus asked, impatient. "When you urged me to go with you tonight you said you'd made a great discovery. Where is it? I see Safar's trail, which we've been following all along, so that's certainly no 'great discovery.' He met a woman! So what? A romantic interlude, I suspect. He's probably tired of Leiria by now and wanted something different. Again, so what? As for the woman's disappearance, if I don't care about the woman, then what do I care what happened to her?"

"Yer got it exactly, Majesty," the witch replied. "A romantic inter-lude! Yes, indeed, that's what Lord Timura was up to." She gave a nasty giggle. "In more ways th'n one, yer old granny suspects."

She gestured wide. "There's lust in the air, that's for certain," she said. "A prancin' stallion and a willin' mare. A lusty young man and a hot-blooded maid. What could be more natural, like? Then add magic: the man's a wizard, the maid's maybe a witch. Stir the pot well, mixin' in the horse and the mare, both magic too, and we gets us a delicious broth, yer Majesty.

"We're gettin' close to Lord Timura, Majesty. Catch up to him within a week, is Old Sheesan's guess. And yer needs to be prepared when that time comes, if yer don't mind me sayin'."

"What's to prepare for?" Protarus asked, curt. "I have an army. He only has a few hundred peasants."

"But he's slipped yer grasp afore, Majesty," the witch said. "So he might do it again. More important—how's he gonner fight back? Ferget his soldiers, good or bad. Don't matter. Neither does yer army. We're talkin' about a wizard, here. Most powerful wizard in all Esmir, some say, demons included.

"Why, it's said it was Timura The Wizard that brought down Zanzair, Majesty. And yer had a bigger, meaner army then. And yer weren't a shape-changer, neither, was yer, Majesty? That's how bad he hurt yer, ain't it? Hurt yer real bad he did, this Timura the Wizard and if yer ain't careful, he'll get yer again!"

"And you have a solution, I take it." Protarus said.

"Indeed I do, yer Majesty," she said, lifting up her blind face to him. "I can give yer power over him when yer meets. We can make a spell here and now that'll do it."

"Then cast the spell, woman," Protarus demanded. "Get on with it!"

"That's all I needed to hear, Majesty," the witch cackled. "Yer had to order it, first!"

With that she raised her hands and began to twirl. Around and around, like a slow moving top. In his hiding place, Kalasariz snorted in disgust when he saw her raggedy robes rise up and show her bony knees. Then she went faster, turning still faster, and both Kalasariz and Protarus gaped as she became a blur. The blur began to glow, radiant sparks flying off into the night. Then the witch slowed and the blur took form.

Kalasariz gasped. For instead of an ugly witch there was a wondrous woman standing before Protarus. She was pleasing of form and face, with long golden hair and a gossamer gown of black that displayed all of her beauty.

The spymaster heard a growl of lust, thought it was his own being voiced, then realized it was Protarus.

The witch laughed, but instead of a harsh cackle it sounded like tinkling bells. "Come to me my sweet," she said, voice silky and smooth. "And we shall make such a spell!"

She opened her arms and Protarus gave a great howl and bounded forward to take her.

Kalasariz crept away. Before he'd been angry and worried. Now he was merely frightened. He had to come up with something quickly, before the witch had complete control over the king. What really frightened him was that it might already be too late.

If the spymaster had tarried he would have seen greater reason to fear the witch.

After she had drained Iraj of all his strength, she made herself more beautiful still, curling up to him, whispering poisoned words into his ear.

"You are a mystery to me," she said. "You are so strong, so wise, and yet you allow yourself to be guided by fools."

Iraj stirred. "If you mean my spell brothers," he said, "I don't have any choice."

The witch cuddled closer, pressing her luscious form against Iraj. "Is that what they told you?" she asked. "That once the Spell of Four was cast, you were locked to them forever?"

Iraj sighed. "Yes," he said. "Forever."

"I can show you how to be free of them," she said. "I can teach you how to break the chains."

Even in lust, Iraj's suspicions were aroused. "Why would you do this?" he asked. "What is it that you expect in return?"

"Only to be your queen, Iraj Protarus," the witch answered. "I have waited a lifetime for one such as you. I have powers—more power than any witch in all of Esmir. But I want more. You understand what I mean by that, don't you? To want more?"

"Yes," Iraj whispered. "Yes!"

"Together," she said, "we can have it all! Together we will at last be satisfied. But first . . . we must set you free from the Spell of Four."

Iraj turned to her, eyes bright with hope. "How?" he asked. "Show me!"

"First we have to catch Safar Timura," the witch said. "It would help to have the child, but it isn't absolutely necessary."

"Teach me now!" Iraj demanded. "I don't want to wait!"

The witch giggled. "So impatient!" she said. "Just like that stallion after the mare!"

He tried to take her again, but she avoided his embrace, saying, "First swear to me that you'll make me your queen."

"I swear it," Iraj said huskily. As he spoke he felt a strange sensation burn through his body and knew a magical pact had just been made. This was one promise he'd have to keep.

Sheesan smiled, eyes aglow with victory. "When the time comes to confront Lord Timura," she said, "you must make certain that your Spell Brothers are close by. The casting will not only free you, but kill them, as well as Timura. Do you understand?"

Thrilled at the prospect of all his enemies being destroyed at one blow, Iraj nodded eagerly that he did.

"Go on," he urged. "What's next?"

Laughing, the witch drew Iraj into her arms again and they made even wilder love than before. When they were done she bathed him with cool water from a forest stream. And when Iraj was entirely human—too spent from lovemaking to be overcome by his shape-changer's side—she taught him the spell.

He was amazed at how simple it was.

Leiria watched the horizontal smear of light inch toward her. The smear broadened and deepened as it came, like a slow moving storm creeping along the earth.

"No doubt about it," she said to Safar. "It's Iraj. The way he's going he'll be on to us within a week."

The two were crouched on a hill overlooking a swift moving river crossed by a sturdy bridge wide enough for two large freight wagons to pass with room to spare.

"He's moving more quickly than I expected," Safar said. "With an army that size I thought the most he could do was keep pace with us."

"It's because he's marching all night," Leiria said. "I was on a campaign with him once when he used that trick. We'd set out at dusk and march until late morning. Then hole up in the afternoon to rest. Surprised the hells out of the enemy when we showed up at his door two weeks before we were expected."

"Why didn't you tell me about that trick before?" Safar asked, a bit exasperated.

"You had enough worry on your mind," Leiria said. "Besides, there's nothing we could've done about it. We're going as fast as we can. Scary stories wouldn't make us move any faster."

Safar sighed. "I suppose you're right." He studied the horizon a little longer. Then, "How long can he keep that kind of thing up before he exhausts his army?"

Leiria shrugged, then gestured at the approaching light. It was bright enough now to obscure the lower heavens. "In this case," she said dryly, "he's in little danger of that."

"Let's do our best to give him a nice long rest," Safar said. He pointed at the bridge. "Remove it and his engineers will need at least a week to bridge the river. From the map of this area, there's no other place to cross for miles."

"And I suppose O Great Wizard," Leiria teased, "that you have some amazing magical spell that will do the job."

Safar laughed. "Absolutely," he said. "I call it fire. Perhaps you've heard of it? It's especially effective on wooden bridges."

"My, haven't we been jolly lately," Leiria said. "If I didn't know better I'd say there was a woman involved."

When he didn't answer Leiria looked up sharply and caught him blushing. He muttered something unintelligible, mounted Khysmet and cantered down the hill to the bridge.

Leiria puzzled over this as she hurried to catch up to him. Had she somehow stumbled on a little secret? But that didn't make sense. Where would he meet a woman way out here?

Gundara and Gundaree were perched on a keg of honey, sucking on their fingers while they watched Palimak fuss over his master-piece.

"Looks like a dog," Gundara said. "If you put some ears on it, that is."

"It's not a dog," Palimak scorned, "and it doesn't have any ears because I haven't made them yet."

Nevertheless, the next thing he did was form small pointy things on the odd-shaped lump of clay.

"Oh, now I understand," Gundaree said. "You're making some sort of an animal. Yes, now that I look at it that way I can see four legs, a tail, a neck, and I suppose that's some sort of head, right?"

"With ears," Palimak said, showing him.

"The ears were my idea," Gundara sniffed. "Pretty stupid dog, if it didn't have ears."

"I detest dogs," Gundaree said. "Filthy creatures. Always sniffing around our little home."

"Remember the one that made water on us?" Gundara said.

Gundaree shuddered. "Like it was yesterday, instead of six hundred years ago."

"It was seven," Gundara corrected.

"Six," insisted Gundaree. "I remember because our master was—"

"I told you," Palimak broke in, "that it's not a dog!"

He held up the object. "It's a horse! See?"

Both of the Favorites studied the object, scratching their heads.

Finally, Gundaree said, "I can see why you asked for our help. I hate to say this, Little Master, but your skills as a sculptor need a bit of honing."

"I still say it's a dog," Gundara said. "A big black dog."

"Maybe a little more green than black," Gundaree said.

"All right, it's a greenish blackish dog," Gundara said. "But it's a dog just the same."

"I don't care what you say it is," Palimak scolded. "I thought horse when I made it, so it's a horse. I even put a horse hair in it from Khysmet's tail."

He picked up a sharp twig and poked holes in the clay for eyes. He examined his work and nodded in satisfaction. "All I have to do is write my name on its stomach," he said, flipping the clay over and sketching the letters with the stick.

Palimak plumped the "horse" down on the wagon bed. "Now, we can make it pretty," he said. "Make it so he can't help himself when he sees it and he'll just have to pick it up! Then he'll flip it over . . ." Palimak demonstrated, turning the clay so the belly and writing was exposed. " . . . And when he spots my name he'll read it aloud."

"And that's when the surprise comes in?" Gundara asked.

"You guessed it!" Palimak said. "That's when the surprise comes in!"

Kalasariz watched the engineers hoist the last timber in place and start to nail it down. In an hour or so the bridge would be complete and the army could march again. As he considered the rough but sturdy structure that spanned the raging river, he couldn't help but feel grudging admiration for the king.

Not long ago, when the scouts had returned with the news that the bridge had been destroyed, Kalasariz thought the task was hopeless and the canny Safar had foiled them once again. To his amazement, Iraj had been vastly amused.

"It's good see you in such humor, Majesty," the spy master had said. "Enlighten me, please, as to its source so I can join in your laughter."

"Safar just made a mistake," came the reply. "He's playing to my strength."

"To your strength, Majesty?"

"Yes, to my abilities as a general. And there's no man or demon who can match those."

Then without further explanation he'd shouted to an aide, "Call the chief of engineers! Tell him his life depends on how quickly he obeys my summons!"

A few moments later a badly frightened old demon had stumbled into the tent to get his orders.

That had been four days ago. Now Kalasariz watched that very same demon crouch with the work crew, closely overseeing the finishing touches. What Iraj had done was order the bridge built while they marched. Freight wagons were cleared out for the carpenters to work and the bridge was built in parts and by torchlight as the army moved on through the night. By the time they'd reached the river it was nearly done and only a little more time was needed to erect it over the stumps of the old stanchions the previous bridge had stood upon.

Kalasariz heard horses approaching from the other side of the bridge and looked up to see a group of weary scouts coming in to report to their officers. It was ironic, Kalasariz thought, that the first group to cross the new bridge was coming from the opposite direction.

But the spymaster wasn't here for humor and certainly not to admire Iraj's brilliance. He smiled to himself as one of the scouts saw him and made a signal unnoticed by the others. Very good, Kalasariz thought, nodding to acknowledge his spy. Then he signaled back. They'd meet in an hour at the usual place.

One and a half turns of the glass later he was back in his tent examining an object under his brightest lamp. Gleaming up at him was the small figurine of a black horse, so beautifully wrought that it could only have been produced by a master potter. He turned it over and made out the name sketched in the hard-fired clay.

"Palimak," he read. The spymaster's eyes glittered. It was from the boy—the half-breed Iraj was hunting along with Safar.

The figurine was not only beautifully fashioned and fired, but it buzzed with gentle sorcery, as if it were meant to be a magical pet. The child was obviously some sort of prodigy. Not only in magic, but in the arts as well.

What great luck, Kalasariz thought. Somehow the boy had lost a prized, personal treasure. One he'd made himself, so it would be of incredible value to Fari and his wizards. It was a direct magical link to Palimak—and where the boy was, Safar would be nearby.

I'll present it to the king myself, Kalasariz thought. I'll wait a day or two and pretend I found it abandoned on the road. Which is where the scout said he'd found it. He said it was lying next to a broken keg of honey and the whole ground was so swarming with ants he'd almost missed it. Kalasariz would tell the same tale, but with himself as the hero. It wouldn't solve his problems with Old Sheesan, but it would put him in such favor with Protarus that her advantage would be slightly lessened.

In Kalasariz' world slight was a great victory. Slight could be made into a gap and the gap could be widened into a ravine. Slight had won many battles for him in the past and in crucial moments when his life had been at stake, slight advantages had saved his neck.

He was about to send a messenger to the king to beg an audience when a second thought crept in. Kalasariz always heeded such things, placing second thoughts above even slight advantages as plums to his trade. Second thoughts kept you wary, second thoughts gave you special insights, second thoughts kept you alive when all else failed.

What if there were some trick to this? What if Safar Timura's mind was behind the crafting of this magnificent creation? That made more sense. Lord Timura was a master potter as well as a wizard, after all. The more he thought about it, the more this scenario seemed likely. Even a child was unlikely to lose such a beautiful magical toy. He'd keep it close to him always, checking for it when he went to sleep, looking for it first thing when he awoke and patting his pockets wherever he went to make certain it was still there.

If this were a trick he could be ruined. However, if it wasn't and he didn't present it to the king opportunity might be lost. Never mind that if the king found out he'd withheld any kind of a clue, ruin would be the most pleasant thing that would happen to Kalasariz. Yes, he'd bless the possibility of mere ruin from his chains and beg to be lifted to such a high plane as the king's torturers worked on him.

They wouldn't kill him. He was bonded to Protarus by the Spell of Four so they couldn't make away with him or the king would suffer as well. As would Fari and Luka. But they could keep him barely alive. Keep him imprisoned in perpetual pain with one of Fari's spells.

Then the solution came. Old Sheesan! Ever since the night he'd seen her reveal her true self to Protarus, he'd pondered how to regain the upper hand. After the initial shock, his old confidence had returned.

A wily master of setting plots within plots, Kalasariz had never met his match in sheer cunning. Well, Safar Timura, possibly. But he didn't like to dwell on that. But this woman—this witch—was not Safar Timura. He didn't care how much magic she possessed. Kalasariz had something better—a mind full of so many tricks and turns that he could confound mere magic and run her as easily as he ran all his spies.

He sent a messenger to the witch, politely begging her attendance.

A few minutes later she joined him in his quarters to examine the figurine. She turned it about in her hands, feeling every inch of it, blind face furrowing in concentration.

Finally her brow cleared. "It's jus' as yer guessed, me lord. Made by the boy, Palimak, himself." She rubbed scratched letters on the belly. "Don't need to see the name to know it's his work." She tapped her nose. "I can smell him, I can."

"And it's of some use to you, I hope?" Kalasariz asked.

She cackled. "Sure it is," she said. "All kinds of spells to get at a body if yer gots somethin' real personal of his. Shrivel his head or his parts, assumin' he's old enough to have parts, that is."

"Excellent, excellent," Kalasariz said.

He took the figurine from her, pulling slightly to make the greedy old thing give it up. Blank as she kept her face, the spymaster had long experience in reading hidden things so he could tell she was seething with jealousy.

Good. Now for the next part.

Kalasariz wrapped the clay figurine in a piece of silk, then, to the witch's immense amazement, he put it back into her hands.

"Perhaps you wouldn't mind delivering it to the king," he said. "I'd consider it a personal favor if you would."

Old Sheesan was instantly suspicious, just as he knew she'd be. "Why the likes of me?" she asked. "Why not take it to him yerself. Yer deserves the credit fer findin' it."

"Actually," Kalasariz said, "much as I'd like to be involved I can't. I came by it by means I wouldn't want to get around."

"'Specially the king, right?" the witch said, knowing he was talking about revealing the extent of his network of spies.

Kalasariz laughed, wagging a finger at the witch. "It's not nice to pry in other people's business," he said. "But you did get the general idea of my problem."

Her suspicions satisfied, the witch made the figurine vanish into her raggedy cloak.

"I'll see he gets it, I will," the witch said. "And thanks fer thinkin' of Old Sheesan, me lord. Yer've made a better friend than yer know."

"That was uppermost in my mind, Madam," the spymaster replied. "Uppermost."

Old Sheesan made a remarkable transformation when she entered Iraj's tent an hour later. Instead of a cackling hag, she was once again the beautiful, sensuous woman Kalasariz had seen in the forest. And just as before her blindness was miraculously "cured."

She curled up against the king, purring like a sleek cat. When he fumbled for her she laughed a musical laugh and drew away.

"Wait," she said in a most melodic voice. "I have a surprise for you."

"A surprise?" Iraj asked, vastly pleased. Kings and queens are like children when it comes to gifts. "What is it?"

She handed him the cloth package containing the horse figurine. "Oh, just a little thing I found on the road," she said lightly. But her eyes, which were a deep shade of violet, danced with excitement.

Iraj unwrapped the package. He reacted strongly when the fantastic miniature of the black horse was revealed.

"What's this?" he said, trembling with excitement. "Is it from the boy?"

"Turn it over and see for yourself," the beautiful witch said.

Iraj flipped the horse upside down. He immediately saw the clumsily scratched letters.

He spelled them out. "P-A-L-I-M-A-K." Iraj grinned, wolfish teeth gleaming.

"Palimak!" he said aloud.

Safar and Leiria were once again hidden on the hill overlooking the bridge. They'd been bitterly disappointed Iraj had foiled their plan so easily and now they were frantically wracking their brains for some other means to stop him.

"This is the only place for miles where we can do any good," Leiria said, not bothering to whisper.

Although Iraj's army was at rest, there was so much activity going on no one could hear them. Off in the night they could hear armorers hammering, animals bawling and supply sergeants barking at their lazy charges.

Safar peered at the big tent set up in the middle of the camp. Iraj's flag flew overhead, fluttering in the light of the Demon Moon.

He shook his head, grim. "There's nothing that can be done," he said, getting to his feet. "Come on. We'd better catch up to the others and warn them."

At that moment a large explosion rent the air. The two turned to see a fiery shower bursting into the night sky.

Iraj's tent was in flames and frantic men and demons were rushing from all over to put it out

Leiria could barely keep from doing a dance. "What incredible luck!" she hooted.

Safar was thoughtful, examining the dancing flames. "It wasn't luck," he said at last. Then he smiled. "Someone's been up to some mischief again," he said.

"Palimak?" Leiria asked, incredulous.

"Who else?"

Palimak and his Favorites were peering at the small lump of clay he'd pinched off the original before he'd made the horse.

Suddenly it flared and Palimak yelped with glee. "We got him! We got him!" he shouted. He smacked his knee with a small fist. "That'll teach that mean old Iraj Protarus!"

Then the bit of clay shattered into dust. Palimak's joy turned to dismay.

"Do you think he's still alive?" he asked.

Gundaree stroked his handsome chin, examining the patterns of clay dust on the floor. "I fear so, Little Master," he finally said.

Gundara was looking over his shoulder. "But we killed somebody," he said, trying to sooth Palimak's feelings. "At least we did that."

"So what?" Palimak said, still gloomy. "It was probably just some stupid soldier."

"It wasn't an entirely cheerless event, Little Master," Gundaree said. "We did manage to hurt the king. Enough to keep him out of action for awhile."

Palimak brightened. "That's all right, then," he said. "Maybe we didn't kill him, but at least we slowed him down."

Kalasariz watched with much satisfaction as the burial party carried the still-smoking remains of Old Sheesan to the river and dumped them in without ceremony.

In the medical tent he could hear Protarus howl in pain as Lord Fari treated his burn wounds with magical ointments and spells.

"I want that child found and killed!" the king shrieked. Another how of pain, then, "No, don't kill him! I'll skin the man or demon alive who harms a hair on his head!

"I want him for myself, do you hear? I want him for myself!"

Once again the spymaster whispered thanks to the dark god who'd overseen his birth. Without the native caution of second thought, it might have been Kalasariz' body that was being so roughly treated.

Oh, sure, the spymaster was sorry the hunt for Safar would be delayed while the king healed. But in his opinion—the only one that ever really counted to Kalasariz—that was a small price to pay for survival.

There was also a bright side—possibly even outweighing the near disaster. At least I rid myself of that witch, he thought.

He looked down at the roiling river and saw a blackened lump of flesh snagged on the shore. A freshwater crab scuttled out from a hole in the bank, snatched the flesh up in its claws and dashed out of sight.

Good riddance, you old bitch, Kalasariz thought. Then he strolled into the night, humming to himself while his agile mind searched for new plots to hatch.

Part Three
Covenant of Death

17

INTO THE BLACK LANDS

Three weeks out of Caluz Safar led his people into a region so desolate, so barren that even vultures shunned the ashen skies. Black peaks vomited sparks and sulfurous smoke over a dark, cratered plain littered with gigantic heaps of rock. Here the Demon Moon shone strong and bright, casting strange shadows that seemed like pools of old blood.

Tornadoes rose up like disturbed nests of dragons, roaring from one end of the plain to the other, destroying everything in their path. The craters proved to be entrances to deep caverns and at night millions of bats swarmed out. They hovered in dense black clouds, then flew away to some distant promised land where plump insects abounded. The bats returned each dawn, descending into the craters in great swirling columns as if they were being sucked into the Hells.

Everyone became fearful, starting at the slightest sound, continually casting nervous glances over their shoulders, trembling hands never far from a weapon. Although surrounded by hundreds of fellow villagers, each person felt oddly alone and vulnerable to the vagaries of evil chance.

Then they began to run low on supplies, especially feed for the animals. In the long, sustained dash to Caluz there had been little chance for the animals to forage. Now the stores of fodder were dangerously scarce and there was no place to stop and let the beasts fill up on the bounty of the fields. Nothing grew in that bleak land where even a thorn could not take root.

The alarmists on the Council of Elders wanted to abandon

some of the wagons, killing and butchering the oxen, then drying the meat so they'd be certain to have enough food to reach Caluz. Their reasoning was that the wagons and animals could be replaced when they reached their goal.

Safar successfully argued that it was too great a risk. "What if something happens in Caluz that prevents us from buying more?" he'd said. "Then we'd be caught in a trap of our own making."

Actually, he was fairly certain there'd be no chance at all of replacing the wagons and animals. But if he told them what he really knew about Caluz he'd be hard pressed to keep them from running like the Hells in the other direction.

If truth be known, it wouldn't have taken much for Safar to join them in mad flight. From the moment he stepped foot into the Black Lands his wizardly senses had been assaulted by sudden magical disturbances—a rippling of the surface of the other-worlds, that made him feel unsteady, sick to his stomach. On a few occasions he was hit by a feeling of the deepest foreboding that something quite terrible was going to happen if he continued and it was all he could do not to order an immediate retreat.

If it weren't for the memory of the mysterious and beautiful Spirit Rider who'd come to warn him in the vision, he might have succumbed. True, she'd said he faced grave danger in Caluz. However, she'd also confirmed the necessity of the visit. The two things combined to give form to the dangers they faced. Thus strengthened, he was able to cast shields to protect the other Kyranians from the worst of the rogue spells that made all seem so hopeless.

Palimak didn't seem to be as affected. The boy's growing powers seemed to shield him from the worst. Since they'd entered the black lands Palimak's eyes were a constant glowing yellow and Safar could feel currents of power flowing from him.

Most surprising of all, the boy had a fairly good idea about what was happening.

One night Safar rode in from a scouting mission and found Palimak lying awake waiting for him. When he entered the tent the boy held up a finger urging silence.

He pointed at the stone turtle, whispering, "I just got them to sleep." He put a pillow over the idol, made a magical gesture to soften sound, then said in a normal voice, "There. That ought to do it."

"What's wrong?" Safar asked.

Palimak shrugged. "Gundaree and Gundara don't like it here," he said. "I don't either, but what can you do? Like grandfather says, 'this is the way the road goes so you just have to put up with it.'"

Safar nearly pinched himself. The boy frequently sounded like a miniature adult, but this was beyond the wisdom of a good many of the full grown adults in the caravan.

"You seem to be learning a lot from your grandfather," he said.

"Oh, sure," Palimak replied. "I was surprised myself. I didn't know he knew so much, being kind of old and everything." He frowned. "I don't mean old is dumb, but sometimes it is pretty cranky. And cranky people don't seem to think very well. They just get mad for no reason and say 'get out of here,' instead of trying to find out what's happening."

Safar smiled. The child was plainly speaking of his grandmother, who tended to have less patience with the boy. How ironic. When Safar was a child it was his mother who was full of understanding and his father who, in Palimak's words, was "pretty cranky."

He held out his arms and Palimak scrambled into his lap and snuggled against him. He stayed there for a time, breathing deeply and Safar remembered the comfort he'd felt in his own father's arms many years ago.

Then the boy rose up, saying, "Is it a machine that's doing it father?" he asked. "Making everything feel so bad, I mean?"

Safar was mildly surprised. "How did you guess?"

"Oh, it wasn't so hard," Palimak said. "I was just thinking about what could be causing all that bad magic and I couldn't see a person doing it. You know, like a wizard or a witch. Even a whole lot of them together couldn't keep on making so much magic all the time. So then I thought, maybe a machine could do it. A great big machine."

He shook his head. "The only thing is, why's it doing it? It's just sort of shooting off lots and lots of power and a whole lot of spells that don't seem to do anything for any special reason.

Except make people feel really bad. Why would a machine want to do that, father?'"

Safar hesitated, then said, "I suppose I'd better tell you, so you know what's ahead. But first you have to promise to keep it a secret."

Palimak was excited. "I'm good at secrets," he said. "Ask anybody. Ask Grandfather, even. He'll say I never, ever tell." Then he frowned. "Except I guess you can't ask him or anybody else," he said. "'Cause they'd know there was a secret, which would spoil the whole thing."

"Don't worry," Safar said, smiling. "I'll take your word for it."

"Does Leiria know?" Palimak asked.

"Some of it. But she's the only one. I didn't want to frighten people."

"Is Caluz a bad place, father?" the boy asked.

"I'm afraid so, son," he said. "You've seen how everything looks around here. I honestly didn't know it would be like this. So I have to think that Caluz might be worse."

"Is that where the machine is?"

"Yes."

"And that's what's causing all this?"

"There's other things involved, but yes, it's mainly the machine."

"But if Caluz so is so awful, why are we going there?"

"There's an oracle we need to visit," he said. "For reasons so important that I think it's worth the risk we're taking."

"Will it help us with Iraj?"

"I'm not sure. Possibly. But that's not my sole purpose."

He saw the boy's puzzled look. Safar knew he was wondering what could be more important than escaping Iraj Protarus.

"I'll tell you the story," Safar said, "and then maybe you'll understand."

He settled back, remembering when he'd first heard of Caluz and its oracle. "It started long before you and your mother came to Zanzair looking for me," he said. "I had just been appointed Iraj's Grand Wazier . . ."

. . . Day was fading to night and from his hilltop home Safar could see the oil lamps blooming all over the ancient city of Zanzair. The dying rays of the sun danced on the gold demon-head towers of the Grand Palace, where Iraj had been recently crowned king of all Esmir. He had made his main court in the old demon seat of power to symbolize that he was king of demons and humans alike. Even so, with an influx of humans seeking opportunity in the capital of the young and progressive king, Zanzair remained stubbornly demon. It was a place of mystery and secrets that were already swirling about the throne just as they had in the days of the demon kings. Safar had learned quickly to trust no one and always to mind his back. So when one of his gate guards became ill and was replaced by a stranger from the royal barracks, Safar decided to keep an eye on him to see if there was some hidden purpose behind the illness and the replacement.

He noticed right away the fellow was erratic about who he would admit to see Safar and who he wouldn't. Safar's duties were wide and in this climate of constant double dealing he need to keep his door open to anyone with legitimate business. He'd admonished the man the night before, so he was particularly watchful that day, peering out his study window whenever he heard someone approach.

At first everyone seemed to be properly handled, then Safar saw a man approach riding a little donkey. He was a tall man, with an unkempt beard and dusty, much-patched robes. He made a comical figure as he approached, sitting crossways on the donkey's back, sandals dragging across the cobbles. The guard barred his way and although the man argued strongly, Safar could see his employee's mind had been made up and nothing the visitor could say would sway him.

An argument ensued. Safar couldn't hear the details at first, but then the visitor lost his temper, shouting, "How dare you treat me in this manner! I am a priest, I tell you! Here to see Lord Timura on important business!"

The guard responded by shoving the man toward his donkey and ordering him to leave. At that moment Safar decided if the guard were a spy, he was not only an incompetent one but rude to boot, so he sent his majordomo to intervene. A few minutes later the guard was summarily dismissed and the visitor was brought to Safar's chambers.

"Please accept my apologies, kind sir," Safar said, "as well as the hospitality of my house. Anything you desire is yours. Food. Drink. A bath and a place to sleep. Whatever you require."

"I require nothing, My Lord," the man said, "other than to beg your attention on a matter of utmost importance."

Nevertheless, Safar sent for refreshments and a servant with hot towels and perfumed water and waited until the trail grime had been wiped away and the man was sitting in a comfortable chair with a glass of brandy in his hand.

"Now, speak to me," Safar said after the man had taken his first drink and he'd seen color flood his cheeks. "Tell me of this urgent business."

"I am called Talane, my lord. A priest in the temple of Caluz. The High Priest has sent me all this way to tell you of the calamity that has befallen us and to plead for your assistance."

He gestured at his raggedy robes, which when examined closer still retained the faint symbols of a priest's robes. "You would never know to look at me, lord, but I started out for Zanzair over a year ago with an entourage of scholars and soldiers and wagons loaded with rich gifts to place at your feet. Alas, after many misadventures on those bandit-infested roads I now possess only these robes. The wagons are gone, the soldiers dead or vanished like the cowards many of them were. As for the rest of my priestly colleagues, only I survived to complete the journey."

Immensely interested, Safar urged him to continue. Not long before he'd encountered a reference to Caluz in Asper's book. The demon wizard had speculated that the area was a source of much natural magical activity. Word had come from the human lands that a fabulous temple had been erected at a place in the Black Lands where two rivers joined. It was said to be near a small village named Caluz. The temple, Asper said, was shaped like an immense turtle and it rose out of the place where the two rivers became one. Water rushed through the center of the turtle, he said, rotating a huge wheel which in turn operated magical machinery inside the temple, sending out a constant stream of spells that nourished the spirit as well as the land.

There was one other thing Asper had said about the temple.

"Forgive my ignorance, holy one," Safar said, "but wasn't Caluz once known for its famous oracle?"

Talane nodded. "It still is, my lord," he said. "It's called The Oracle of Hadin."

Safar felt something move in his pocket, then a little voice whispered, "Ask him about the turtle." It was Gundara, stirred from his home by the mention of Hadin.

"What did you say, my lord?" Talane asked. "Something about a turtle?" He sighed and took a sip of his brandy. "I fear my ordeal has affected my hearing. All of a sudden your voice became quite faint."

Safar pretended to cough. "My fault," he said. "A chill coming on, I think. But, yes, I did use the word turtle. I was referring to your temple, where the Oracle keeps her home. Isn't it in the shape of a turtle."

"Yes, my lord. It's in honor of the turtle god who carries Hadin on its back. That's on the other side of the world, you know."

"That's my information as well," Safar said dryly.

"Sorry. Of course you would know that. I'm told you are a great scholar. A learned man as well as a master wizard."

Gundara snorted. "If he only knew!" the little Favorite whispered.

Talane gave Safar a look of sympathy. "The chill again, my lord?"

Another cough. "Yes. Forgive me." Safar gave his pocket a warning tap. Once more and Gundara was in for it.

"I'm sure you also know of the old tale that there is a holy force—you would probably call it magical—that runs between Hadin and Caluz. Like a river running straight through the world."

"I've heard that tale before," Safar said. "Although never in detail." Actually he had only just guessed it. The priest's comments, plus Safar's years of studying Asper had led him to the conclusion. Talane told him about the temple and the great wheel inside that had churned out magical spells for many centuries.

"Our land was once a poor place," he said, "a bleak place of wild storms and mountains that spat fire. But then a holy man, whose name is lost to us, found the magical springs running under the place where the rivers join. No one knows what he did there, but somehow word got out and other holy men came. The first man vanished, the others stayed and built the first temple—the one standing now is much larger and more powerful. They cast spells to bless the land and when the wheel began to turn a miracle resulted. The land became rich, the weather tame, the mountains silent."

"And the oracle?" Safar asked.

"Yes, the Oracle of Hadin came into being during that time. People came from all over Esmir to consult it. Even Alisarrian made a pilgrimage on his way to conquer all of Esmir."

"She gave him a glowing forecast I take it?" Safar asked with a touch of sarcasm. Methydia had taught him that there were notorious frauds in the oracle profession.

"Actually, my lord," Talane said, "it is written that the Oracle warned Alisarrian he would someday be betrayed by those closest to him."

Which is exactly what had happened to Alisarrian—betrayal, death and the eventual destruction of his kingdom. At that moment Safar began to take the Oracle seriously.

"What do you require of me?" he asked. "As the Grand Wazier I can authorize many things to assist our priests. Construction funds, increased temple subsidies, scholastic endowments. That sort of thing."

Talane lowered his head as if in shame. "What we need, my lord," he said, "is a means to make the wheel stop!"

Safar was surprised. "But why would you want to stop something so wondrous?" he asked. "The very source of all your happiness and wealth."

"It is now the source of the greatest misery, lord," Talane said bitterly. "Something terrible has happened. Only bad spells, malicious spells, are being churned up now. Our fields are barren, our newborn deformed and one of the mountains has even begun to spit fire."

"I'm desolate to hear of your people's misfortune, holy one," Safar said, "but what's the difficulty? Why can't you stop the wheel on your own?"

"Perhaps we could have done it once," Talane said. "But now

anyone who approaches with such an intent is killed the moment he touches the wheel."

"What does your oracle say?" Safar asked.

Talane sighed. "Only that she warned us this would happen and we didn't listen."

"Perhaps you'd better tell me exactly what happened," Safar said.

The tale was a simple one of human greed's many victories over common sense. It happened some years back—about the time, Safar guessed, he'd had his youthful epiphany in the mountains above Kyrania. Talane said one day the Oracle summoned all the priests. When she appeared she was weeping, which frightened everyone. She said a great disaster had occurred in Hadin. And that tragedy would have so great an affect on the world that she couldn't see the future after a point not many decades hence. What she did foresee was that Caluz would be among the first to suffer. Their only hope, she said, was to prepare for the worst. Store food and drink and carefully husband all their resources in hopes they could weather the bad times to come. But most of all, she urged them to stop the wheel. Her final warning came as a great shock to everyone. Oh, they'd been frightened by her dire predictions and mysterious remarks about the disaster in Hadin. But in reality those things seemed so distant, so surreal, they couldn't imagine them.

The wheel was a different matter. All they could see was that the moment it was halted all the good things that made Caluz so rich would stop as well. Fortunes were at stake and important men were not pleased when the priests brought them the news. A great argument ensued, settled when the king ordered a royal commission to meet and study the Oracle's remarks closely. Perhaps the priests had misinterpreted her. Maybe she meant some other wheel. All kinds of alternatives were suggested, each one more foolish than the others. Years passed, the commission continued to meet, but nothing was ever done. Early on a young priest was so scandalized by the blasphemy against the Oracle that he attacked the wheel with an ax. He'd chipped a large hunk of one blade off before they stopped him and carried him away to the dungeons.

"That's how we know it was once possible to destroy the machine," Talane said. "But when a team of engineers tried the same thing two years ago, every man was blasted on the spot by some mysterious force. All seven were killed, may their ghosts be at rest."

Safar thought a moment, then said, "I can't see how I can help you find a solution from such a distance, holy one. I'd need to visit Caluz and consult with your High Priest and best scholars. I'm not opposed to making such a journey, mind you. Even if I were so unfeeling that I didn't sympathize with your plight, I have personal reasons to come. Unfortunately, it will be several months before I can take leave from my king."

Talane became agitated. But not over the delay. "Oh, but you must not come, lord!" he said. "The Oracle warned us you would want to, but she said you must stay away at all costs."

Safar's eyebrows shot up. "Why is that?"

The priest made a weary shrug. "She didn't say. Oracles aren't always that forthcoming, you know. But she was most insistent. She said you shouldn't come until the machine is stopped."

Safar was mightily confused. "I don't understand," he said. "You want my help, yet at the same time you say I'm barred from giving it. What other way can we halt that wheel?"

Talane took a deep breath, then, "By changing the course of the rivers that drive it."

The rescue project Caluz proposed was not only costly, but an enormous engineering feat. Two rivers had to be forced to leave their natural beds and find a new course to the sea. Safar spent many hours with the priest, who came armed with facts and figures and memorized plans that he sketched on scraps of paper as he talked. In the end Safar was convinced it could be done.

Several weeks later Talane departed for Caluz with royal promissory notes and decrees calling on neighboring cities to provide all necessary assistance. Safar and the priest said their final farewells at the main gate. Outside the walls they could hear the caravan master cry his last warning that he was ready to depart.

"There's one other thing I should tell you, my lord," Talane said. "Forgive me for withholding it, but I wasn't clear on the Oracle's meaning. I was already ladened with so many confusing things to relate to you that I feared it would only make explanations more difficult."

"Tell me now then, holy one," Safar said.

"The Oracle said to tell you this: 'He who seeks the way to Hadin must first travel through Caluz.'"

Talane scratched his head. "It still doesn't make any sense to me, lord," he said. "Do you know what she means?"

Safar shook his head. "No. But I hope to find out one day."

Palimak stirred in his lap and Safar looked down to see if the boy had wearied of his story. Instead, Palimak's eyes were huge and glowing with interest.

"Imagine that!" he said. "Making two whole rivers change which way they go." Outside a volcano rumbled with pent up gases and his elfin face turned serious. "I guess it didn't work," he said. "The machine's still going."

"Actually, it did work," Safar said. "They labored for several years building dams and digging an alternate bed for both rivers to flow into. The wheel stopped and the bad magic with it. The people of Caluz sent me many proclamations of thanks and praise. I even had a note from Talane saying the city was going to honor me by naming a day after me. I don't know if they did, because not much later I was fleeing Zanzair with you and Leiria. And I haven't heard anything since."

"Something must have happened, father," Palimak said, "because the machine's going again."

"Apparently," Safar said, "all that work turned out to be just a temporary fix. We'll find out what happened when we get to Caluz."

Palimak was alarmed. "But what about the Oracle's warning?" he asked. "If the wheel's going, you might get hurt. Or even . . . you know . . . killed or something!"

Ever since Asper's ghost had bade him to travel to Caluz Safar had considered that point himself. But he smiled at the boy, saying, "Don't worry. I know a lot more about such things then I did in Zanzair. A wizard gets stronger as he ages. Why, think about how much more powerful you are now then when we left Kyrania. You've made storms from small clouds, saving my life, I might add.

"And that trick you played on Iraj was masterful. It gave us valuable time to get away."

Palimak frowned. "That's what everybody says. And I guess maybe I'm a hero, like I wanted to be. They're all saying, 'Oh, Palimak, you're such a brave boy! And 'How can we ever thank you enough.' Things like that. But, I don't know. I don't feel very good about it."

He gave Safar a look of great frustration. "I was trying to kill him, father!" he said. "That's how it was supposed to work. But it didn't. It was sort of like the rivers. A temporary fix."

Safar ruffled his hair. "That's all we needed," he said. "So it doesn't matter."

Actually it did matter to Safar, but not the way Palimak might have thought. He was secretly glad the boy had failed. Evil as Iraj might be, Safar thought his murder would be too much for a child's soul to bear. There would be plenty of opportunity in the years ahead for such scars to accumulate.

"Will you let me help you in Caluz, father?" Palimak asked. "I'm really strong, just like you said. See?"

He flexed one of his little arms by way of demonstration. Safar smiled and felt the small lump of muscle. To his surprise it was hard and sinewy and quite unchildlike.

"You certainly are," Safar said. "I was nowhere near as strong when I was your age."

Palimak shrugged as if indifferent but he was secretly pleased. "I think it's because I'm part demon," he said matter of factly. "They get stronger faster, right?"

"Right," Safar answered.

"Stronger in magic, too, right?"

"Right."

Palimak's face turned sly. "Then you'll let me help you, right?"

"Right again," Safar said.

The boy looked startled. Had his trick worked? Then he became concerned.

"Do you really mean that, father?" he asked. "Or are you just saying it and then you'll make up a reason later why I can't?"

"Yes, I really do meant it, son," Safar said. "To tell the truth, I was sort of counting on it. That's why I told you the story, so you'd be ready when we got there."

Palimak's face lit up with supreme pleasure. "Will it be dangerous?" he asked.

Safar turned serious. "Very dangerous, son. So you have to pay close attention to everything I say. No more little tricks and experiments on your own, right?"

"Right!" Palimak said. "Right, right, right. And three times right makes it so!"

Sergeant Dario eyed the road ahead. The old Kyranian fighting master was not pleased with what he saw, or actually, what he couldn't see. They'd been traveling for weeks on the barren plains of the Black Lands, but as forbidding as they were, he thought, at least a man had an uninterrupted view of any danger he might face.

Here, however, the great caravan road narrowed to accommodate a passage hewn straight through a mountain. Dario figured it had once been a natural ravine which was widened by gangs of slaves working for some greedy king determined to bring the caravans to his realm.

Whatever the origins, Dario definitely didn't like the way the road snaked into the dim passage, then vanished entirely beyond the first bend.

"If I was thinkin' of settin' up an ambush," he said to Leiria, "I'd pick somewhere's in there. You could trap the whole damn caravan."

"I was thinking the same thing," she replied. She looked up at the towering, blank-faced mountain. "I wish there were a route around it, or over it," she said.

Dario leaned away from his saddle and spit, which Leiria had learned over many miles was a signal that he was thinking. His leathery old face, which drooped like a jowly dog's, was a permanent, emotionless mask he kept for the world. But Leiria could see a glint of worry in his eyes as they darted this way and that, probing the depths of the passage.

Finally he settled back in his saddle. "Had a cap'n once't," he said, "who knew all there was to know 'bout ambushes, 'cept for one thing. And that killed him so I never did find out what he was missin'. Make a long story short, he taught me what he know'd afore he ate that arrow, so I'm a pretty fair hand at ambushes."

Leiria laughed. "Except for the kind that got the captain," she said.

Dario grimaced, which was his way of smiling. "Hells," he said, "there's always one more for a soldier. One more hill to climb. One more meal you ain't gonna eat. One more sword lookin' for your guts. Same with ambushes. There's always one more waitin' somewhere's that's gonna get you."

Leiria laughed. "Isn't that the truth! What's the old barracks' saying? No matter how bad the shit gets, it's only the second worst thing that's going to happen to you."

Dario grunted his enjoyment. Then he gestured at the pass, saying, "Why'nt I slip on in there, Cap'n, and see what's what? Maybe you could sorta linger a bit behind me to guard my back."

Leiria nodded agreement. "Wait up a minute," she said, "until I talk to the boys."

She trotted back to where the other scouts, including Renor and his friend, Seth, waited. She told them the plan and then said, "In all likelihood we're worrying about nothing. But if we should trigger an ambush the last thing I want is for any of you to come running to our rescue. Leave one man here to watch and the rest of you ride to the main column for help. Renor, you're in charge, so you choose who's going to stay and who's going to ride. Got it?"

"Yes, Captain," Renor said, squaring his shoulders as if suddenly feeling the weight of command settle on to them. "But, how about if I send somebody back now, so Lord Timura and the others will know what's going on up here?"

"Good idea," Leiria said, feeling a flash of pride at how far Renor had come since Kyrania. He was going to make one fine soldier someday—assuming he lived long enough. "In fact, instead of waiting to see if we need help, ask Lord Timura to send up a platoon now just in case."

She rode back to the pass where Dario was stripping himself and his horse of all unnecessary weight. She did the same, then they helped each other tie rags around their horse's hooves to muffle the sound. When they were ready she nodded at Dario to proceed.

The sergeant grimaced a smile. "If somethin' happens," he said, "tell my old woman to put a jug out for my ghost tonight. Way I hear it, dyin's damned thirsty work."

And then he rode into the pass.

She waited until he reached the first bend. At his signal she moved slowly forward. Dario took up temporary position at the bend, keeping watch in both directions until she reached him. While she stood guard he moved to the next point, scanning the high walls of the canyon for any movement.

They leapfrogged like that, going deeper and deeper until the light became so dim that all was in shadow and they relied on hearing and instinct more than sight. The high canyon walls were old and rotting, showing dark wounds where they had given away to tumble down onto the road.

There was no wind and the air was hot and stale. Sound was intensified, almost unnatural; the horse's muffled hooves seemed like distant drums, their breathing harsh and gasping like a dying beast's, and once in awhile some far off landslide would break, sounding like slow rolling thunder.

Sweat trickled down Leiria's back, increasing the prickling sensation she'd experienced after passing the first bend. She felt as if she were being watched, a sensation she'd normally heed. But the atmosphere was so bleak she thought it might be her imagination. Adding to her wariness was the fact that there was simply nowhere for anyone to hide—no perches on the faces of the cliffs, no rubble so dense or high enough to provide cover. Each section of road they cleared should remain cleared. It was only common sense.

Then she saw Dario signal frantically. She halted the horse and swiftly fit an arrow into her bow.

Dario held his hand, keeping her in position. She saw him lean forward, as if listening.

Then she heard it—the heavy, measured tread of many boots. Dario reined his horse back, quickly slipping an ax from his belt. He came slowly, eyes forward, listening to the tromp, tromp, tromp of the approaching boots.

Suddenly, from behind her she heard the same measured tread. Leiria came about, heart hammering at this impossibility. She lifted her bow, staring at the bend, waiting for the first face to show.

The boots came closer, moving in from both sides as if closing some gigantic pincer with Dario and Leiria in between.

She sensed Dario at her side and they moved together, the noses of their horses pointing in opposite directions.

The sound of marching boots grew louder and louder until they were like kettle drums. Then a great horn blew, the boots went stamp . . . stamp . . . stamp . . . three times, hard on the last, and stopped.

Silence.

Then the air shimmered and out of all that nothingness appeared a long column of huge, mailed warriors. Their skin was white as death, lips blood red, and their eyes were great empty sockets as black and deep as caves.

Leiria took a chance and glanced behind her. And her eyes confirmed what mind and heart knew.

The pincers had closed.

They were surrounded.

18

THE ROAD TO CALUZ

Lord Fari watched with mild amusement as the soldiers tormented the two prisoners. A man and a woman, both stripped naked, were staggering between two ranks of cheering warriors. One side was human, the other demon, and they were hurling rocks and sticks at the couple, trying to drive them toward one group of soldiers or the other.

The game would go on like this, with some interesting variations, until the prisoners had been ripped to pieces. Then those pieces would be used in stirring games of fiendish polo, pitting mounted demon and human teams against one another as they whacked gory parts about the field with clubs made of bone.

It was all great innocent fun, Fari thought, and he was pleased to see the young soldiers engaged in such vigorous, morale-building activity.

The woman fell a few feet from the demon side and long talons reached for her. She screamed, dragging herself away, long trails of blood raking along one thigh where they'd caught her. The soldiers roared laughter, giving the woman time to stagger to the middle of the wide gap between the ranks of tormentors. They howled louder still when she fell next to the man and he embraced her with bleedings arms trying to comfort her.

"Oh, good show! Good show!" Fari cried, rapping his skull-topped cane against the ground. Beneath him, a husky demon slave shifted patiently under Fari's bulk, alert to his lord and master's every movement.

There was a lull in the game as wineskins were passed about to slake all that happy thirst and Fari sent a runner with a bag of gold to add to the stakes and the excitement.

The rough playing field was set up on the edge of the Black Lands where Iraj had camped his army while he considered his next move. Fari frowned, absently reaching out a taloned hand—instantly filled with a cup of wine by a demon maid who was as comely as she was attentive.

Actually, time for consideration had little to do with the king's planning. Protarus was in one of his moods again, so black no one dared come near him except his slaves and they had no choice in the matter. He'd already killed more than a dozen for infractions so small even Fari was startled. Lord Fari was known to have hard views about spoiling slaves. He even approved of the occasional act of casual violence to keep them anxious to please. Besides, a slave on a gibbet in front of your house was a good thing for an enemy to see when he came to visit.

There was no similar artifice in Iraj Protarus' actions, however. He didn't even kill them out of anger, Fari noticed. It was more like a fly had been buzzing about, interrupting his melancholia. It was a melancholy so deep and so dark the king seemed to find a strange comfort and escape in it, as if sorrow were a thick, warm coverlet he drew over him to blot out the world. Then came the buzz of the fly—a smile when he didn't want to see a smile, a solemn face when he wanted a smile—and he would flick it away. Claws erupting from his hands, snatching out a throat, then becoming hands again as the king returned to his thinking, eyes only blinking when the body struck the floor.

Protarus had been like that since the attempt on his life by the boy, Palimak. Fari scratched his horn with a long, contemplative talon. It had been a very good spell, he thought. One that even he, a master wizard, could admire. The only error the child had committed when he'd composed the spell was to leave a link between the giver of the amulet and the taker. So when the king spoke the word "Palimak" aloud, triggering the spell, it was the witch who took most of the killing force, not the king.

The king had suffered enough physical harm to delay the march for several weeks while his wounds healed. He'd been left with only one scar no magical treatment could erase, even when applied to the self-healing body of a shape changer. It was a small scar that lifted one corner of his lip into a permanent smile. It wasn't a sneer or a grin, but a sly tilt that made you wonder if he knew some secret that did not bode well for you.

As time went by it soon became apparent the king had suffered a deeper wound. Without warning, he'd suddenly fall into a black mood and call the army to a halt, only to retire the into the depths of his harem. When the mood ended he'd suddenly rise up and order the march to resume, cursing at the delay as if it were the fault of others.

The consequence was that they were far behind Safar Timura and his refugee caravan. So far the magical trail they were following was very weak and would soon fade out entirely. And Lord Timura would have eluded them once again—possibly for all time. The forced hunt could only go on for so long. Eventually, either all the supplies would be exhausted or the kingdom would become so neglected Protarus would have to pause to put things in order.

For the first time since the hunt began, Lord Fari didn't care. It didn't matter to him if they won or lost the race. He had different goals now. Goals which only coincidentally involved Safar Timura. In short, Lord Fari had a new view on things, a new way of thinking. Shorter still, he was thinking only of himself.

The game resumed with a blood-curdling scream as a rock struck the male captive. Fari glanced up, red demon's tongue flicking out at the prospect of renewed amusement. This time, however, he found himself bored. The man and the woman were barely conscious, so there was little sport. Fari snorted. The youth of today, he thought, have even less patience than they have imagination. Some other torments should have been used well before now. The trick was to keep the game alive and interested as long as you could.

Fari hoisted himself up on his cane. It was something he no longer needed—the transformation to shape-changer had rid him of all the ailments old demons suffer. But he used the cane anyway, out of habit, and as a badge of authority. He strode away, his slaves scrambling to keep up. The one who served as his stool ran the hardest. When Lord Fari decided to sit, he would sit. The slave's most constant nightmare was that he wouldn't be there, hunched on all fours and steady as a rock, when Lord Fari took it into his mind to rest.

Fari climbed a short hill, stopping at the crest and leaning on his cane to take in the view. His slaves scrabbled around him, the stool ready to leap into any position, the shade unfurling the wide umbrella over Fari's horned head, the fan swishing the air with her feathery plumes, the maid at the ready with cup and jug. Spread out behind him were guards and runners and bearers carrying small comforts he might desire while taking the air.

Fari glanced back, taking rare notice of his entourage. The king had more, he thought, much more. So many to tend his whims it beggared the imagination. Fari shrugged. What did it matter? It was better to be Grand Wazier than king. He gazed out at the Black Lands, where tornadoes rutted a ghastly terrain and volcanoes spat their fire, poisoning the air with their stench. To Fari it was a place of beauty and promise that soothed his old demon's soul.

When Lord Fari first saw the Black Lands he felt as if a veil had been lifted from his eyes. For too long he had been held in the grip of the wild emotions and sensations of a shape changer. It was difficult to think clearly, to plan beyond the immediate goals and challenges. A demon of more two hundred feastings, he had seen many kings come and go. He'd survived them all by always being attentive to their moods, guessing which way they would leap next and racing ahead to that point so he could be there when they lighted. Not unlike the living stool Fari now sat upon. Court intrigue was second nature to the old demon. Many a knife had been aimed at his back by his rivals. Many a deadly plot hatched with Fari's removal at their core.

He was not a fiend normally driven by emotions of any kind—other than fear, that is. Fear alone was to be trusted. Fear kept a fiend wary. Fear could see into shadows. Fear could creep around corners unnoticed. Fear could read the lips of whispering conspirators. Fear could divine the deepest thoughts of a king. Fear had been with him as long as he could remember. It was his father, his mother, his brother and sister and most loyal friend. Fear was his lover whom he ardently embraced every hour of every day.

When he looked out over the Black Lands and felt the constant pounding of magic gone wild, Fari realized he had been without fear for much too long. He'd allowed himself to be overcome by his shape changer's heart where only bloodmust raged. Fari felt a little ashamed of himself when he realized that. The old Fari, the Fari who had kept his head while thousands of others were losing theirs, would have made better use of the new powers he'd gained when he became a shape changer.

It was Fari who was the architect of the Spell of Four, after all. It was Fari who'd drawn Prince Luka and Kalasariz into the conspiracy to seduce the king into the shape changer's bond that had saved them all from Safar Timura's great spell of revenge, which had turned Zanzair into a molten ruin, killing all but the new brotherhood Fari had formed. The trouble was, he had forgotten his original intent. At the time it had seemed as if he were losing control. Safar Timura was the Grand Wazier, not Lord Fari. What's worse, Timura was such a powerful wizard Fari had no hope of competing against him. It was no secret. Everyone knew it. And in the game of Grand Waziers, second best is a shadow away from an assassin's blade.

The old demon sighed and lumbered about, his entourage shifting with him, those who might impede his view falling to the ground to let him see what he wanted to see. The king's banner—silver comet collapsing onto the red demon moon—hung limp over the huge pavilion that housed his court and quarters. From the hilltop Fari could see the three smaller pavilions that made a half moon frame for the king's traveling palace. One was his. The others belonged to Prince Luka and Lord Kalasariz.

Each had his own fear, his own driving ambition. Each sought not just to find favor with the king, but to control him. To master him. To Lord Fari it only seemed right and just that it should be him. But how to go about it? How to slip past the canny Kalasariz? And Luka. What about him? His hate for Fari was long and deep. His ambition also burned brighter, because Prince Luka wanted nothing less than to be king himself. Something Fari could never allow him to achieve. It suddenly occurred to the old demon that Luka and Kalasariz might naturally seek an alliance. He wondered if they'd realized it yet. He wondered if their minds had become clear before his own.

He snorted. Not likely. He was not only wiser and cannier, but he possessed more magic than any of them. But then he thought, Just in case, my dear Fari, just in case . . . you'd better plan for the worst.

Then he straightened as he thought of a course of action. He'd begin with the king. All else should follow after that. First he had to shake the king from his melancholy. He needed to put the hunger back into Iraj Protarus. To rouse the hunter from his sleep.

A final, piercing shriek caught his attention and Fari looked over at the field, a smile curling up from his fangs. The soldiers had finished off the victims and were gleefully ripping them to pieces so the next game could begin. Actually, he thought, they'd done quite well. Considering their two captives were so young—barely in their teens—it was really quite a feat to keep them alive so long.

Then he saw a tall demon holding up the heads, the greatest prize of all. Many cheers greeted this gory sight.

Lord Fari grinned as the idea dawned. He rapped his cane for one his aides.

He tossed him a purse of gold, saying, "Buy me those heads."

Renor and Sinch sat easily in their saddles, nibbling on dried fruit while keeping a casual watch on the entrance to the pass. They'd neither heard nor seen anything amiss since Leiria and Dario had set out to investigate the Caluzian Pass.

Renor chuckled. "Old Dario had me about ready to wet my breeches with all that ambush talk," he said. "But I guess that's all it was—talk." He stretched, yawning. "At least he's not wastin' our time for a change. We get to rest up while he and Cap'n Leiria scout the trail for us."

"I don't know if it was such a big waste of time," Sinch said. He waved at the dark entrance of the pass. "Sure looks like ambush pie to me. And the only way to find out is to dig into it." Despite his comments, Sinch felt a sense of great ease and cheer.

"The sergeant's a good sort, don't get me wrong," Renor replied. "He just goes on and on, is all. You've got to listen to the whole history of the Tarnasian Wars, or some such, before you come to his point."

Again he stretched and yawned, really enjoying it. For the first time since they'd entered the Black Lands Renor felt safe and quite comfortable sitting here talking his friend about nothing in particular.

"Oh, I don't know," Sinch laughed. Actually, it was more like a giggle. "Depends on what sort of story he's telling. Like the kind you wouldn't want your little sister to overhear. The other night he told me one about an old lamplighter in Walaria. Did you hear it?"

Renor laughed in anticipation. "No, I haven't," he said. He nodded at the pass. "Nothing happening there. So go ahead."

Sinch chortled, remembering the jest. "Anyway," he said, "there was this old lamplighter in Walaria named Zenzi. And old Zenzi had been lighting lamps faithfully in one neighborhood for nearly thirty years. And now it was time for him to retire and collect his pension from the king.

"Comes his last night and when he gets to the first house the family comes out with food and drink and a few silvers to thank him for all his years of service. Same thing at the next house and the next. Everybody liked Zenzi, so they were piling on the gifts and making his last night something really special.

"Then he comes to the last house on the street and a slave comes to fetch him, saying her mistress wanted to speak to him. The slave takes Zenzi by the hand and leads him into the house and up the stairs, where he is pushed into a bedroom, the door closing behind him.

"You can imagine his surprise when he sees there's a beautiful woman waiting for him—dressed in nothing but a filmy gown and a big smile. 'My husband is away for the night,' she says, real sultry, then she takes him to bed and they make mad passionate love. The greatest love poor old Zenzi had ever experienced. Then the woman claps her hands and the slave brings in a wonderful dinner of the best kabobs and sherbet and all the other delicacies the rich get, but Zenzi had never tasted before. When he is done the woman pours him some fragrant tea.

"Zenzi starts to reach for the cup, then notices a copper coin sitting beside it."

"'Pardon, my dear lady,' Zenzi says, 'but everything has been so wonderful. The hours of love. The food. The drink. Everything. But what's this copper coin for?'"

"The woman smiled and said, 'Well, yesterday I told my husband this was your last night after thirty years of service. And I asked what we should give you. And my husband answered, 'Screw Zenzi. Give him a copper!' The woman shrugs. 'The dinner,' she says, 'was my idea!'"

Renor roared laughter, slapping his thigh and looking quite unsoldierlike when Lord Timura came riding up on his great stallion, accompanied by thirty men.

"I thought there was an emergency here," he said, blue eyes fierce under his dark brows. "Instead I find my best men lolling about like tavern sops. Laughing and making merry."

Renor shook his head, amused. "This is a pretty funny situation if you think about it, my lord," he said, chuckling. "Here we are telling jokes—dirty ones, at that. And then you ride up and—"

"Where's Captain Leiria?" Safar barked, breaking into Renor's babble. He glanced around. "And Dario! Where's Sergeant Dario?"

Renor grinned and motioned toward the entrance. "Checking out the pass, Lord Timura," he said, choking back laughter. "To see if there's . . . ha ha ha . . . an ambush! Ha ha ha."

Sinch snorted laughter. "Did you hear the one about the guys who ate the frogs?" he asked.

Safar slipped his silver dagger out. He mumbled a spell.

Renor shook his head, laughing so hard there were tears in his eyes. "No," he said.

"Well there was this plague of frogs, see . . . And—"

Safar sliced the air, casting his spell, and the two young men were suddenly left gasping and flailing the air as if they'd been drenched with icy water.

Renor was the first to recover. His eyes were wide with shame and fear. "I'm sorry, Lord Timura," he said, voice trembling. "I don't know—"

"Never mind, lad," Safar said gently. "It wasn't your fault. Now, join the others. You too, Sinch."

The young men did as he said. At Safar's signal everyone formed up and checked their weapons and gear.

He turned back to the entrance of the Caluzian Pass, probing with his magical senses. Khysmet chuffed and shifted under him, as if he too were investigating. Safar pushed harder. It was difficult to "see" in the constant hail of wild magic that pelted the Black Lands, but whoever had cast the spell of amusement on Renor and Sinch had left a faint trail. In Safar's magical vision it looked like a silvery path left by a snail. But it faded away just before it reached the first bend in the road.

To Safar it seemed obvious that whoever, or whatever, had tricked the young scouts was trying to keep their attention away from what was happening down that dark avenue through the mountain. Not for the first time he wished he had Gundara with him. The little Favorite was an expert at snooping out such things.

He gritted his teeth, forcing his mind away from what might be happening to Leiria. And Dario, oh yes, mustn't forget Dario.

But it's Leiria, dammit, Leiria! She has no stake in this whole thing . . . except for me. Then Khysmet pawed the ground and Safar jerked back. He knew immediately he was being seduced by another sort of spell and he shook it off like clinging moss. Quickly, he raised a magical shield over himself and his men so there could be no other such surprises.

Safar leaned forward, patting Khysmet and whispering, "Who needs a Favorite?" The horse jerked its head up and down as if agreeing.

Then, without a thought passing between them Khysmet moved toward the pass and Safar signaled for his men to follow.

They made their way much as Leiria and Dario had done—leapfrogging from one cleared section of road to the next. Although the passage was narrow, it was still wide enough to carry caravan wagons and so Safar had little concern he might encounter an overwhelming force. There was plenty of room for him to deploy his men in strength, and either fight their way through or retreat to safety, dealing out much death and injury to whoever opposed them.

Khysmet moved easily over the rubble-strewn ground, finding firm footing in places where the other animals stumbled. Safar was left free to concentrate solely on the task at hand. His eyes pierced every shadow, his hearing was acute and his magical senses kept up a slow sweep for any sign of danger.

It came without warning—the heavy tread of many boots marching toward them. Khysmet whinnied alarm and Safar heard his men shout. With a start he realized the sound of marching came from both before and behind him!

As the air shimmered he scrabbled for a blocking spell, mind yammering that there had been no sign of a magical attack, but it was coming just the same.

Then he saw what Leiria had seen: long columns of huge mailed warriors marching toward him, closing the jaws of the trap.

He reared back to blast them, praying he had the right spell. But just before he struck he heard a shout:

"Safar!"

Safar blinked. It was Leiria's voice.

She called again. "Over here, Safar!"

He looked in the direction of her voice, then realized he could see through the warriors as if they were ghosts.

And there, just beyond, he saw a small golden pavilion. And in that pavilion, sitting at their ease before a table filled with food and drink, were Leiria and Dario.

Leiria waved to him. "Just push on through, Safar," she said. "They're harmless. Come and meet our hostess."

Lord Fari fussed with the heads, pushing a stray curl away from the woman's dead eyes, wiping a spot of blood from the man's pale lips.

"Perfect, your Majesty," he said. "Just perfect. We couldn't have asked for better heads."

Protarus gloomed at him from his throne, eyes hollow, features slowly changing from man to wolf to man again. Scarred lip twitching in all forms.

"What's so special about these heads?" he asked in a deadly voice.

"Exactly what I was wondering, Majesty," Prince Luka said.

He glared at the old wizard, who stood between the two posts that held the heads. "The king is ill," he said to Fari. "Why are you disturbing him with such nonsense?" And he thought, what an old fool you are. I've been waiting for you to slip. Now I'll boot your arse the rest of the way down the stairs.

Fari sneered at Luka. "His Majesty will soon be able to judge for himself whether this is nonsense or not," he said. And he was thinking, You haven't a brain in your noggin, my prince. You were bred to fight, not to think. Your father was right not to trust you.

Kalasariz shifted his glance from one demon to the other, highly amused at the barely disguised hate between them. He kept silent—ready to jump to whichever side most benefited him.

Protarus motioned. "Get on with it," he said. His voice, however, was less threatening than before. The game between Fari and Luka had sparked his interest more than Fari's urgent call for a meeting.

"My mission tonight is most vital, Your Majesty," Fari said. "If

I am successful in my experiment we will know the whereabouts of Lord Timura within the hour."

Iraj shifted in his throne, black mood momentarily abated by this news. His features becoming wholly human.

Luka sneered, exposing many rows of gleaming fangs. "I suppose the heads are going to tell us," he said. "We've tried that sort of thing before. But Timura's shields are too strong to get past."

"That's true, Lord Fari," Protarus said, mildly amused. He was thinking of various torments he could apply to the old demon after he failed. "It's never worked before. Why now?"

Fari raised a talon, looking a bit like an old demon school master. "In a moment, Majesty," he said, "all will be clear."

He busied himself with the heads, taking jars of magical oils and powders from the stand beside him and sprinkling the heads.

"For most of this hunt, Majesty," he said, "Lord Timura has been dashing all over the landscape. Going in first one direction, then another, then back again. It made it more difficult to find him, because we couldn't determine his eventual goal."

"He had no goal," Luka snorted. "Except to live another day. He's running, that's all."

"Do you think that's true, Majesty?" Fari asked, daubing a bit of ointment on the woman's head. "Does this sound like Lord Timura? You know him best."

Protarus frowned. "Not one damn bit," he said, surprising himself a little by his answer. "Safar always has a goal. A direction."

Luka was alarmed. "Well, of course he has some eventual goal, Your Majesty. But that's only to find some place of permanent safety for his people."

Kalasariz thought it time to insert a neutral comment. "He has been moving generally toward the northwest," he said. "Taking in all miles traveled, that is."

"That's most likely accidental," Luka protested. "We're the ones doing the driving. He's fleeing in the only direction left open to him. Which just so happens to be northwest."

But to the Prince's dismay, Protarus had already gone past that point. "I wonder what he's looking for?" he mused. "What's in that region?"

Fari pretended to be busy, hiding a smile as he poured golden oil over each head.

Kalasariz thought it was safe for another neutral answer. "Eventually, Majesty," he said, "there is only the Port of Caspan. And then the Great Sea."

Luka took heart, smacking one taloned fist into the other. "Exactly!" he said. "In the end, there's nothing but the sea. And if we keep going like we are we'll have him pinned against it. With nowhere to go."

Protarus shook his head, his scarred smile making Luka's heart jump. "Not likely," he said.

"There's one thing we've all overlooked, Majesty," Fari said. "I blame myself for not seeing it before."

"What's that?" the king prodded.

"Until a few months ago everything Prince Luka just said appeared true. Lord Timura was behaving exactly as described. Dashing this way and that with no other apparent purpose than to escape us.

"Then everything changed. Just before the, uh . . . " he gave Protarus a sympathetic look, " . . . the uh . . . most unfortunate attack on Your Majesty . . . he leaped onto one road. And then stayed on that road, never varying his direction or using his usual tricks."

Kalasariz cleared his throat. "Actually," he said, "it happened after Naadan. We tracked him to the ravine. He tried to escape, but we had the, uh . . . the uh . . . " he glanced at Protarus "the, uh . . . Lady Sheesan to help us. Then he got on this road and went like the hells."

"He must have made some kind of decision in Naadan," Protarus said. Then he grimaced, remembering the magical stallion. "Or maybe even before. Perhaps he meant to go to Naadan all along. And then . . . and then . . . " He shrugged. "My logic takes me no further. So he travels through the Black Lands. What does that tell us? Nothing."

He sighed, adding, "Except that Safar is as brave as ever. We have two hundred wizards with us. He has only himself. And yet he dashes across the Black Lands while we stand here afraid to set our toes in it."

"It's the machine, Majesty," Luka pointed out. "We know that somewhere out there a great magical machine has gone wild. We have to be sure we have the right spells before we proceed. It's the prudent thing to do, isn't that right, Lord Fari?"

The old demon brushed away Luka's desperate clutch to rejoin him on the side of safety. "I don't think our esteemed Majesty wants to hear about prudence right now, My Lord," he said.

Kalasariz, the most cautious of men, agreed. "Bold action is the only course," he said, aligning himself with Fari. Thinking, *you cunning old foul-breathed devil. I just know you have something up your sleeve. Now, let's see it.*

He was startled when the king, as if reading his thoughts, said, "Let's see it, Fari! What are you leading up to?"

"Why, the heads, Your Majesty," Fari said, "The heads." He gestured at the completed pair. "Beautiful, aren't they?" He said this as if they were the greatest works of art, instead of two ghastly things with dead eyes and slack mouths.

Luka found reason to murmur appreciatively, as did Kalasariz. The king only frowned, impatient.

"It's like this, Your Majesty," Fari said. "The Black Lands have confounded us for a few days, no doubt about it. But they also give us an opportunity. With all the magical insanity raging out there, it's highly unlikely that Lord Timura could maintain his usual shields. Why, all my wizards together couldn't do it and as great as Lord Timura's reputation might be, I suspect he's met his match with that machine.

"So he'll be going naked, as it were. Using all his powers just to throw up a small ring of protection around his people. There's nearly a thousand of them, if you recall, Majesty. That is an enormous amount of people for one wizard to shield, especially in the Black Lands."

He gestured at the heads. "These people were captives from a nearby village. They were born and raised next to this region, continually bathed in all the sorcery leaking out. They had no magic of their own, of course, but when I saw our soldiers making sport with them, it came to me that they would be very sensitive to it." He shrugged, "That was my guess, at any rate. Subsequent experiments proved my theory."

"Now I understand," Kalasariz said, smiling, feeling pleased he'd jumped in the right direction. To seal his position he hastened to explain, whether anyone needed the explanation or not.

"Lord Timura is not only vulnerable to a casting," he said, "but those are the ideal devices for the casting spell."

"As always, My Lord," Fari said, "you are most astute even in matters that aren't your expertise."

"You are too kind, My Lord," Kalasariz murmured.

Luka said nothing.

"Enough!" Protarus barked. "You're mooning over each other like a pair of harem girls. Do the casting, dammit! Let's see what Safar's up to!"

Safar goggled at the scene, not sure which was real and which the apparition. The threatening horde of warriors, or Leiria and Dario laughing and waving in greeting.

Then he had even more reason to goggle as a large figure rose from the table, saying, "Welcome to Caluz, Safar Timura. We have been waiting many a year for your visit."

The speaker was female—a demon female. And as she spoke she made a motion and the ghostly soldiers vanished.

She was a spectacular sight. Even taller than a large male demon, she was dressed entirely in red—a red gown of the finest Sampitay silk; red shoes beneath that gown with the sheen of a rare jewel. Her talons were painted red, as were her lips curling up in a red painted demon smile above fangs like spears. A ruby crown was set upon her jutting forehead—just above her ivory white demon horn, which was decorated with red magical symbols.

Big as she was, demon as she was, none of these things were the true reasons for Safar's amazement. What had his complete attention was her gown, which was embroidered with a startlingly familiar decoration. The winged, two-headed snake that was the sign of Asper.

She came toward him and Safar whispered assurances to Khysmet, who was still uneasy, then swung off the saddle to greet her.

Safar had never been aboard a ship, but in his imagination the demon queen—for her bearing left no doubt she was a queen—looked like a ship as she came to him, red gown billowing like great sails. Despite her size she was incredibly graceful, moving with smooth and sweet femininity. An odd side of him, a primitive side most men would rather not discuss, took note of her remarkable figure. She was large, yes. A demon, yes. But her shape was the perfect hourglass that dumbfounds all human and demon males.

When they came together, pausing for the formal greeting, Safar felt shamefaced, like a boy.

She held out her claw, dainty as a maid, saying, "I am Hantilia. Queen of Caluz. And chief priestess to the Oracle of Hadin."

In Protarus' court Lord Fari was making his final preparations.

"I'll need your help, Majesty," he said. He motioned to the others, Prince Luka and Lord Kalasariz. "All of you must help. To ferret out Safar Timura we need the full powers of the Spell of the Four."

Everyone leaned forward, concentrating, as Lord Fari made magical motions over the heads, chanting:

Speak, my Brother.
Speak, my Sister.
Speak, O creatures of the Shades!
What road does Timura take?
What goal does he seek?
And what is his heart's desire?

Soul numbing shrieks shattered the air as both heads came alive. Their eyes burned with pain and they screamed to the heavens as they relived their final moments on the sporting field. Their anguish was so deep that it pierced Iraj's shape changer's heart and struck at the core that was still human.

Their wails echoed throughout the royal chamber, hammering at his ears and rattling the small, scarred thing he called a soul. He wanted to shout at Fari to end their agony and his misery, but he clipped it off, gagging on guilt. To do otherwise would show a dangerous weakness.

Then, thankfully, Fari waved a claw and the wailing stopped.

Two pairs of haunted eyes turned to regard the demon wizard.

"Speak, my sister," Fari chanted. "Speak, my brother. Grant us this boon and we shall release you from all your cares."

The woman spoke first, voice quaking with pain. "He is near!" she said. "He is very, very near!"

Then the man, in equal agony—"Yes, he is near! Run my friend, run from these devils!"

The woman shouted—"No, don't run! Please don't run! Save us, Safar Timura! Save us!"

Fari chortled. "What willful heads," he said to Iraj and the others. "No matter. They're very young and so it's to be expected."

Then, to his victims—"Lord Timura can't hear you. And even if he could, there'd be no help. You are in our care, my lovelies. Only I can help you. Now speak. What road does Timura take?"

And the woman said, "The king's road."

"What king?" Fari pressed. "Tell us his name."

"Protarus," the man croaked.

"Timura and the king," the woman said, "travel the same road."

Fari was clearly puzzled. Luka, seeing slender hope, said, "I knew this was nonsense from the start."

But Protarus shouted, "Silence, you fool!"

The outburst surprised Iraj as much as the demon prince. Mysterious as the answers were, they made ghostly, skin-prickling sense.

Emboldened, Fari continued. "What goal does he seek?"

"Hadin," the woman said. "The Land of Fires."

And the man said, "Two were together. But now there is one."

Iraj shuddered as the words unleashed memory's flood. Suddenly he was a boy. And Safar was with him, casting the demon bones to see what the future held.

He remembered the red smoke hissing up, rising like a snake. Then out of the smoke a mouth formed, curving into a woman's seductive smile. Then she spoke, and he could hear the words clear echoing down the long corridor of years:

"Two will take the road that two traveled before. Brothers of the spirit, but not the womb. Separate in body and mind, but twins in destiny. But beware what you seek, O brothers. Beware the path you choose. For this tale cannot end until you reach the Land of Fires."

Then he was jolted back to the present as Fari asked the final question:

"What is his heart's desire?"

And the woman said, "Love."

And the man said, "Hate."

And Fari shouted, "Answer clearly, or I'll blast your souls to the Hells!"

But once again Iraj could glimpse cloudy meaning and the two words, "love" and "hate" churned about in his guts.

Kalasariz spoke up. "Some of my spies are like that. Ask the time and they count the grains of sand in the glass. Perhaps our questions are too general."

Fari took heart and tried again. "Tell me brother, tell me sister, where is Lord Timura now?"

"Caluz," the man answered.

Fari was pleased. "Who does he seek there?"

"The Oracle of Hadin."

"Now it makes sense!" Kalasariz said. He turned to Iraj. "There is a famous oracle at Caluz. Called the Oracle of Hadin, I believe."

Fari could see his victims were tiring. He wracked his brains for a last question.

Then, "Tell me brother, tell me sister, what is Lord Timura's purpose in Caluz?"

The answer came in a ghastly chorus: "To kill the king."

Then their eyes went lifeless, their lips slack, and blood gushed to the floor.

Fari turned to address the king, rattling his talons in glee. But when he saw the state Protarus was in, he kept his silence. He noticed Kalasariz and Luka were also staring in wordless fascination. The king was flickering from one shape to the other at a blinding rate, claw and maw and handsome human profile winking in and out of existence.

Iraj knew his emotions were an unchecked torrent, but he couldn't help himself. The announcement that Safar sought his death had unaccountably ripped him from his moorings. He suddenly felt as if he were the hunted, instead of the hunter. He knew this made no sense. Safar was the deer, Iraj the bowman. Still, he'd felt a chill run down his spine when the words were spoken: "To kill the king."

Then fear turned to mad outrage. This was betrayal! Safar was his friend! How could he possibly plot to assassinate a friend? Never mind that Iraj tried to kill Safar long ago and had sought his death since. Never mind that Safar had struck back furiously, nearly killing Iraj and destroying his kingdom. Deadly blows had been exchanged many times over the years. Safar Timura was clearly his enemy. But why did Iraj still feel he was also a friend? A friend bent on betrayal and murder?

All these thoughts and emotions stormed about his heart and brain, then anger took root and bloomed into a mighty tree, spreading strong branches of rage all through his body from toe to nape.

With anger came cold reason and purpose and fully human now, he rose to his feet. Golden beard and head and crown glowing in the torch light. He was Iraj Protarus, by the gods! The King of Kings. Lord of the Shape Changers. Greater even then the Conqueror Alisarrian, who was a mere mortal, wizard though he had been.

"We all owe you a great debt, my lord," he said to Fari, who visibly preened, not caring if Luka or Kalasariz noticed. "Now we know not only exactly where Safar Timura is hiding, but we know that Caluz has been his goal all along.

"Timura is not a man to just run and hide. He was mountain born and people who live so high above us all have courage and will bred into them. They breathe air so thin it would make you faint. I lived among them once, so I know. I was weak and light-headed for days before I found my footing. In fact, I think that's the reason for it. The reason Safar and his Kyranians have managed to defy us for so long.

"It's the air, dammit! And I curse myself for missing it all this time. I'm a man of the plains. The air is thick and healthy on the plains. Now water, that's scarce and all our wars rise from that. But water is nothing compared to air. Can you imagine living in a place where you had to fight for the very air to sustain you?"

No one answered. The king's anger made speech unwise.

"They can also see! Oh, by the gods can they see! Up in that eagle's nest they called Kyrania, they could see the most amazing horizons. Horizons so distant they confounded me. Me, a simple man of the plains where all is flat and you drown in the air and you can't imagine what it really is to see. All the way around you—all the time. That's what separates Kyranians from ordinary mortals. The power to see.

"That's another thing we must remember. Safar is the greatest Kyranian of them all, for he can see the future. And sometimes I think he can imagine more. If there is a place that lies beyond the future, Safar can see it.

"But he has to kill me first." The king slammed his throne over, shattering the wood against ground.

He turned to Fari, who was frightened, no longer so desirous of the king's attention.

"Tell me, Lord Fari," he said, his tone fearfully close to the one the demon had used addressing the heads, "And tell me true. Does Safar have to kill me to get to Hadin? Isn't that what your heads were telling us?"

Fari called on all his skills to slip to a middle course. He shrugged.

"Who can say, Your Majesty?" he said in his most oily voice. "Our casting was not plain on that point."

The king merely nodded, so Fari braved thinner ice. "We should be practical about this, Your Majesty," he said. "Hadin is so far away it was known as World's End by the ancients. Surely, this place is out of anyone's reach.

"Far-seeing though he may be, I think it would be wiser to surmise that Lord Timura's goal is more reasonable. Forget about World's End. Think of Esmir, only. It would be far seeing enough of Lord Timura to conclude that his answer was in Caluz. In the center of the Black Lands where a magical machine has gone wild.

"He must overcome the devil machine, the desolate land, the low spirits of his people—everything—to consult with the Oracle of Hadin. And there he must pray that he can find a means to kill the most powerful king in history."

He snorted. "Come, now, Your Majesty! That is seeing very far, beyond not only the future, but hope itself. And as for the business with the air, Highness, I think he's breathing something very thin indeed to conjure up such an impossible task."

"Here, here," Luka said, making the king smile and gaining back a bit of grace.

"Lord Fari speaks wisely, Majesty," Kalasariz said, tipping a wink at the old demon that meant, 'We must talk.'

Although no plan had been set, the unholy three, as Iraj had come to think of his brothers, acted as if victory had already been won. They called for food and drink and music and dancers to celebrate. Iraj tilted his scarred lip, making them believe he was fooled by their actions.

Oh, but he was cold, so cold. Damnation he could see it clear. Like Safar could see distant horizons.

Iraj was no fool—even though he was a king, and kings, it is said, make the grandest fools of all. He knew what was going on. His brothers of the spell conspired against one another and they all conspired, separately and together in various alliances, against him. Sheesan had warned him about that.

He felt a pang, thinking of that strange, beauteous witch. How could she have borne appearing like such a crone, when she had been a woman of such beauty and wonder. She had her own designs, of course—some of which she'd even admitted. But that hadn't bothered him. Iraj had learned early that no one addresses royalty without base motives. Even Safar, pure, humble, "I'm only a potter's son," Safar, had something he wanted when he joined Iraj in his mission. He wanted Iraj's power. Safar was jealous because Iraj Protarus was favored by the gods! Destined at birth to be king of kings.

But what was it Safar claimed he wanted? Oh, yes—to save the world. What a lie that was!

Iraj scraped at his chair with a heavy ring, smiling at his false brothers as they drank and made merry jests about the human and demon maids who danced for their pleasure. They pretended to chatter happily about their king, their wise, strong king, and how they would stretch every tendon in his effort. Talking about this plan of attack and that.

Fari was saying something about gathering all his wizards to cast a spell to protect them all from the wild magic of the Black Lands. Luka was laying plans to create the greatest mounted shock force in history. As if the Kyranians were the half million demons Iraj once defeated to gain his crown, instead of a handful of hastily trained peasants. And Kalasariz— Damnation! Safar warned me about him, I'd better be careful—Kalasariz was slipping up to Fari, saying this and that and glancing in Luka's direction. What Iraj would have to watch for was when Kalasariz looked in his direction.

In some ways Luka and Fari were easier to understand, he thought. They were demons. Conspiracy came easily to demons. But Kalasariz—oh, be careful of Kalasariz—was of a different cut. The least of which was that he was human. And humans, Iraj thought, were superior to demons in hatching a conspiracy.

I should know, he thought. I am the result of conspiracy— from whom my father would bed on a royal night, to my mother's scheming against his harem. His mother had been a gentle sort, loathe to use poison. But when it came to her son and dreams of being mother of a clan leader, her hand was steady when she poured.

Iraj's mother had taught him about secrets. Keep your own counsel, she'd said, no matter who tells you what is closest to their heart. They are lying. Know this, son, and build greater lies and you will be safe.

Iraj had such a secret. He'd guarded that secret more closely than even his love for his mother. If she were here he'd lie to her face and know she'd be proud of him.

His secret was that thanks to the witch who desired to be his queen, he had the means to break free of the loathsome bond he'd made with these fiends. He ached for the moment when he could cast the spell she'd taught him and destroy them.

But first he'd have to catch Safar. Oh, yes, I must not forget— and his scarred lip twitched—the child, Palimak. Before she died the witch said the child wasn't really necessary. Although the spell would be more powerful if Iraj had them both—like the heads on Fari's stake.

Then I can be free, Iraj thought. Free!

A winsome demon maid pranced in front of him. She was half

again his size and of a form he'd only killed before, not caressed. But he suddenly found himself desirous of her and so he motioned and she came to him, pressing strange but somehow familiar parts against him.

He plunged into her embrace, thinking, I wonder what Safar is doing now?

I wonder how he finds Caluz?

19

THE VEIL OF LIES

Leiria and Dario waved their wine cups and chorused—"Long live Queen Hantilia!"

Then Leiria whacked Safar on the shoulder, saying, "What do you think of Queenie, here?" She made curving motions with her hands, then winked. "Nice package, don't you think?"

Dario whacked his other shoulder, then leaned in, sloshing wine into his boots. "She likes you, me lord," he stage whispered. He hiccuped, covered his mouth, then said. "Couldn't help but—hiccup!—notice."

Safar smiled, then turned to Queen Hantilia. "Are they drunk or in your spell?" he asked.

"A little of both," the queen answered. She flicked up two talons—rather daintily, Safar thought, considering each was a curved ruby dagger six inches long. "First, you'll have to admit that the wine is rather good."

She toasted Safar and drank. He eyed his own glass, cast a spell to search for ill intent, found none, and so he shrugged and drained his glass. It was delicious, as if all the fruits of the Valley of the Clouds had been turned into the rarest of wines.

"Ambrosia!" he sighed. He hooked the jug onto the table, asking, "Shall we have a little more?" She nodded, and Safar refilled their cups.

Leiria and Dario started sniggering and whispering to one another like excited children.

"Now that we have the drunk issue settled," Safar said, "tell me about the spell."

The demon queen shrugged, well rounded bosom lifting her gown most delightfully. "It's completely harmless," she said. "I just didn't want them to have to worry until I talked to you."

She gestured, saying, "The same with them." His men, hardened scouts all, were sprawled next to their horses, laughing and drinking wine served by giggling maids, many of whom were demons. They wore red robes like Hantilia's, although not as fine, also bearing the twin-headed snake symbol of Asper.

"Trust me, it's a harmless spell," she said. "Their troubles and worries have been momentarily interrupted. That's enough to make anyone drunk—no wine required, my dear Safar. And I promise you there will be no ill effects when they awaken."

Safar glanced around and saw that other than the maids, the queen had no guards, no royal entourage. "I could lift the spell myself, your highness," he said, half-teasing, "and cast a few of my own. Then the tables would be turned. And it would be you and your servants who would be in my thrall." He smiled. "I'd make it as pleasant as possible, of course."

Hantilia lifted a claw to her mouth, covering pealing laughter. It was quite musical, Safar thought. Strange that a demon should sound so melodious.

"But you are already in my thrall, my dear, dear Safar," she said, chuckling. "Haven't you noticed?"

Safar drank a little more wine, measuring his faculties as he did so. The queen spoke the truth, he thought. He sensed danger, but he felt cheerful about it. He found her company most . . . stimulating? And he was anxious to learn more.

"You're right," he said. "The wine is good. The spell is good. No harm intended."

Hantilia smiled. "And the company?" she asked archly. "Do you find that pleasant as well?"

Safar grinned, raising his cup. "It was boorish of me not to praise my hostess," he said. "Yes, I find the company most charming. Mysterious though she may be."

Hantilia held out a claw. "Come with me, Safar Timura, and all will be revealed." She gently took his hand and led him toward a shale outcropping bulging from the cliff face. "We'll start with Caluz."

Safar glanced down the caravan road. "I thought it was in that direction," he said, pointing. "Through the Caluzian Pass."

Hantilia shook her head. "That way was barred by the Guardians long ago," she said.

Safar puzzled. "The Guardians?"

"Those ghostly warriors who greeted you," the queen answered. She pointed at the many cave mouths that pocked the walls of the passage. "For generations the people of Caluz buried their mightiest heroes in those walls. They are called the Guardians because their ghosts protect the city from any who might come against her."

Safar made a face. "So they aren't harmless," he said.

"Not at all," Hantilia replied. "As you would soon have learned if your intent was other than peaceful."

Then without further ado she waved at the outcropping and Safar felt a jolt of magic. "Open," she commanded—and the rock face dissolved into a misty curtain.

"This is the new road to Caluz," she said. "In fact it's the only one. Even with the Guardians assisting us, we've had to close off the other pathways to defend ourselves from the nasty business going on these days."

For some reason this comment had a false note to it. But before he could consider further, she let go his hand and stepped through the mist, vanishing. Safar hesitated, glancing back at Leiria and Dario, who were still happily under the spell. He followed.

Safar felt a slight chill, then a tingling sensation and suddenly he was shielding his eyes from a bright sun. There was a warm breeze carrying the scent of flowers and ripening fruit. His wizard senses were also pleasantly entertained with fragrant spells carried on gentle magical breezes.

"Once again, Lord Timura," Hantilia said, "welcome to Caluz!"

His vision cleared to be treated to a marvelous sight. They were standing at the crest of a road that curved down to meet a small, graceful valley. There were farms and fields and wooded hills nourished by two rivers that ribboned down from high blue mountains. On a bluff near where the rivers joined there was a beautiful city, all silver with a grand palace towering over the walls.

Below the castle was the Temple of Hadin—a huge stone turtle crouched at the end of a peninsula where the rivers met to form a single stream. The turtle was identical to the miniature idol that was home to Gundara and Gundaree down to the red painting on its back of a volcanic isle topped by a fire breathing demon. Blissful magic streamed from the temple, churning out spells of health, happiness and prosperity.

All in all Caluz seemed a wondrous place where birds always sang, butterflies sweetened the air and its inhabitants happily tilled the fields, tended the markets, or fished the rivers.

As he looked, the warning from the Spirit Rider rose up and he heard her whisper, "In Caluz, all is not as it seems. Look for the truth beyond the veil of lies."

"How perfect this world is," Safar said. And then he couldn't resist adding sarcasm: "The only thing missing is a fat pink cloud hanging over the rivers."

Hantilia grimaced. "I told them you'd ferret it out soon enough."

"I suppose the real Caluz is down that road you told me was barred," Safar said.

Hantilia frowned. "Yes, it is. I'm sorry I lied to you." She shrugged. "My priestesses and advisors were afraid you would turn back if you knew the truth. Immediately, that is. I assure you I had no intention of keeping it from you for more than a few days."

"You mean, until I had brought all my people here," Safar said. "All one thousand of them."

Hantilia sighed again. "Am I so transparent?" she asked.

"No," Safar said, "it's only that I've had much experience with royalty. Even when they have the best of intentions, kings and queens have a certain way of thinking. I merely followed that route."

He laughed. "Also, wouldn't I be fairly dim-witted if I didn't notice such things as the absence of certain large celestial bodies."

He pointed to the bright blue sky. "Such as the Demon Moon." Hantilia said nothing. She only looked more embarrassed. "Finally," Safar said, "there's the machine itself." He pointed at the great turtle idol. "That is certainly not what's causing all the misery in the Black Lands."

"Actually, it is," Hantilia said. "Except what you are looking at is a manifestation of the real machine. A mirror image, so to speak. It's the result of a spell the Oracle cast just as Caluz was being destroyed." She waved at the city and the pleasant valley. "As is all this."

"What of the original inhabitants?" Safar asked. "Such as the priests who asked my assistance long ago."

"They're all dead, it grieves me to say," Hantilia replied. "But you'll be pleased to hear a few of the former inhabitants escaped here. Into this false Caluz."

Safar perched on a rock, then took off his cloak and placed it on a flat spot next to him. He motioned to Hantilia. "Why don't you make yourself comfortable," he said, "and tell me the tale? From the beginning, if you please."

Once she was settled she said, "Just as I told you, I am Queen Hantilia and I really do rule here. I'm also chief priestess of the Oracle. But it wasn't always so. I am a pilgrim like you, Safar Timura. My kingdom was in a distant land, a realm so small and so peaceful that when Manacia was king of the demons he barely knew we existed.

"There, I was also the high priestess of the Cult of Asper."

"Pardon," Safar said. "I've never heard of such a thing."

"There are few of us," Hantilia replied, "but our origins go back very far." She nodded at the temple. "For instance," she said, "one of our myths is that Lord Asper discovered the magical properties of this place and set the forces in motion that led to the creation of the temple and the machine.

"But back to my tale. Scarce as we were, when the barrier fell between demon and human lands the way was opened for our religion to spread. Soon there were small groups like us all over Esmir. We mingled together, humans and demons, all in the spirit of Asper's teachings."

Hantilia blushed—her skin turning a deeper shade of emerald.

"Some even became lovers. A few married. Fewer still managed to bring forth a child."

Safar's heart bumped. Hantilia saw his reaction and said, "You have one such child with you, I understand. The Oracle spoke of him."

"Yes," Safar said. "His name is Palimak."

Hantilia frowned. Then her brow cleared. "Ah, now I understand. It is in the Walarian tongue. Palimak means promise, does it not?"

Safar nodded. "Yes."

"A lovely name," she said. Then—"It is quite likely the child comes from just such a union as those I described. In fact it is impossible for it to be otherwise. And I'll tell you why.

"When the Demon Moon rose and ill befell the land many of us were forced to flee our homes because of sickness and starvation and evil things crawling out of the earth. My kingdom was one of the early victims and my people and I became refugees, wandering Esmir, finding our living where we could. The others of our cult did the same. Many did not survive. I suspect Palimak was the child of such a couple—demon and human—who met with misfortune during that time and he eventually came into your care. Someday you must tell me that tale."

Safar bit into the bitter memory of Nerisa and grimaced. "Someday," was all he said.

The queen saw his discomfort and steered her remarks past that desolate trail. "The day arrived when things were at their worst," she said. "I didn't know how I would find food and shelter for my people. Then the Oracle appeared to me."

"The Oracle of Hadin?" Safar asked.

"The very one. You'll meet her soon enough. At least I pray you will agree to such a meeting. But to go on. The Oracle appeared and commanded me to make my way to Caluz. She said the fate of the world depended on it. I learned later she made many such appearances to members of our cult throughout Esmir.

"Soon all of us were streaming toward Caluz. Our strength grew as we came together and the journey was made easier because we no longer had to fear bandits. We arrived in Caluz just before it collapsed. The city was in a panic because the Oracle was issuing dire warnings. But the Caluzians only became more hysterical with each passing day. And so all the things she urged them to do were left until it was too late."

Safar frowned, remembering the old Caluzian priest who'd told him his people were of that temperament. "The last I heard," he said, "the city leaders were going to divert the rivers, which would effectively shut off the machine. It seemed like a good plan to me. What went wrong?"

"The Demon Moon," Hantilia said. "No one took its tides into account. At the time the plan did seem like an artful solution. After the dams were built and the new channels dug the machine fell silent for a long time. Then the influence of the Demon Moon became more powerful.

"The river tides began to rise, overflowing their banks. This went on day after day, the floods reaching higher each time. The people filled bags with sand and stacked them along the riverbanks trying to halt the flow. Finally the currents jumped back into their original courses and the machine returned to life. This time worse than before."

"I saw the Black Lands," Safar said. "I saw what the machine has done."

"As I said," the Queen continued, "the Oracle warned of the disaster all along. She'd urged a course of action, but only the priests listened. This is when I arrived in Caluz with my followers. And at the pleadings of the priests—and the Oracle's command—we did all we could to help construct her spell."

Hantilia paused, lines of sadness creasing her face. She wiped an eye with her claw, then said. "I have seen many things in my life. Horrible things. But the day we cast the spell overshadowed all the horrors I'd seen before. It is too painful a memory for me to recount.

"Suffice it to say, Caluz was destroyed and the priests all died nobly, staying until the end so the rest of us could escape."

She gestured at the lovely scene that was the false Caluz. "And we've been here ever since. Waiting for you."

Safar sighed. "What do you want of me?" he asked.

The Queen's eyes glittered. "Only to save our lives, Safar Timura," she said. "For without your help all of us will be dead within the month."

* * *

Leiria was mortified. Although her memory was hazy from the moment she met Queen Hantilia until the spell was lifted many hours later, she had flashes of seeing herself and Sergeant Dario behaving like two tavern sots.

"I don't like this," she said to Safar, who was riding beside her on Khysmet. "We're trusting everything to a complete stranger."

Safar chuckled. "You're only embarrassed," he said. "Don't be angry with Hantilia."

"I'm not angry!" Leiria snapped. "I just don't know the bi— uh, know anything about her. Oh, I understand the spells were the gentlest way she could handle us. And that certain things were done because the Oracle of Stupid Hadin wanted it that way. So I have nothing to hold against her. In fact, I quite like Hantilia. For someone I only met, that is."

She suddenly grinned at Safar, a devil's glint in her eye. "Although a certain friend of mine—who shall remain nameless, but whose seal bears the letters S.T.—seems to have gotten a great deal more out of that first meeting than I did."

"Ouch!" Safar laughed. "Come on. You're just jabbing at me to relieve your own frustration. Go back to being embarrassed. See if I care. You're right. You were a total fool and should be ashamed of yourself. There. Chew on that, my sweet Leiria."

"You can't get off that easily," Leiria parried. "Admit it. You're attracted to her."

Safar blushed. "A little," he said.

"Even though she's a demon, right?"

Safar's reply was a muttered, "Right."

Leiria snickered. "Now you know how Palimak was made," she said. "First hand, or claw, or whatever."

Another mutter—"Whatever." Then, firm—"Do you feel better now, my dear Leiria? After putting me in my place?"

"Sure I do," Leiria said, eyes dancing with fun. "But what about you? And Hantilia? What do you intend to do about it?"

Safar squared his shoulders. "Nothing," he said. "Except note it as a curiosity of nature."

"Don't make me laugh," Leiria chortled.

"You are laughing."

"Well, who wouldn't?"

"All right! All right!" Safar snapped, switching moods with Leiria. "Let's talk about something else. Something depressing and morbid like your premonitions of doom and betrayal."

"I didn't say that," Leiria retorted. "I only said we were trusting an awful lot to someone we don't know. We're fetching the entire caravan to Caluz. Or whatever that place is. You say there's two of them, I'll take your word for it. Anyway, we're throwing ourselves on the mercy of these people." She shuddered, remembering. "And those . . . Guardians! I'll never forget how helpless I felt when I realized they were all ghosts. And they could hurt me, but I could do nothing to them!"

"Don't worry about the Guardians," Safar said, matter of factly. "I can take care of them."

"Sure you can, or at least I believe you when you tell me something like that. You're a mighty wizard, and all. But we'll still be outnumbered. They can overwhelm us at will."

"That's true," Safar said, "but you're forgetting something. They need me to stop the machine."

Leiria became angry. "I just don't want you to get killed, Safar!" she said. "That's all. What's down in that damned temple? Who is the Oracle? She could be the great devil queen of all devil queens, as far as we know. What if it's a trap?"

Safar started to laugh. "Thanks," he said. "I feel much better now."

"What are you talking about?"

"You just reminded me of the worst thing that could happen."

"You're damn right. Death is what could happen."

"No, the worst thing that could happen is that we'd be killed by Iraj."

Another laugh. "And can you imagine how angry he'd be if we died in Caluz before he could catch us? If I could see his face just as I died, I'd go to my grave a happy man."

"I never thought about it like that," Leiria said, smiling. "You're right. It does make you feel better."

They came to the top of a rise and reined in to let the others catch up. Some miles away they could see the caravan crawling across a barren plain to meet them. It was late afternoon—the worst time of day in the Black Lands—and the heat was intense, the air thick with sulfurous fumes from the distant volcanoes.

"At least the air is sweeter in Caluz," Leiria said. "They'll be glad of that."

Safar didn't answer and she turned to see him drawn up stiff, peering hard at the caravan.

"What's wrong?" she asked.

"I'm not sure," Safar said. He pointed. "But look at that crater. Just to the left of the wagons."

Leiria found the crater. Although large, it was only one of hundreds scattered across the plains. The road skirted them all, so after a time she'd grown used to their presence.

"I don't see anyth—" Something swirled in the entrance and she broke off.

Then the swirl became an immense cloud of bats flying out of the crater—rising in a thick column.

Leiria relaxed. "It's just the bats," she said. "They fly out every night about this time."

"It's . . . not . . . just . . . the . . . bats!" Safar gritted. Then he shouted, "Come on!"

As he charged down the long hill he had a flicker of memory of another such time. Iraj had been with him then.

Racing down the snowy pass to save the caravan.

Palimak was dreaming of the machine. He was asleep, almost in a stupor from the heat, and in his dream he saw the machine as a huge turtle, a gigantic clockwork toy with immense snapping jaws and it lumbered toward him on mechanical feet.

He jumped into a lake and made himself a fish and swam away. But the turtle came after him and its legs became like revolving oars and it churned through the water at an amazing speed. He swam faster, fast as he could, but the turtle got closer, closer, jaws snap snap snapping, snap—

"Wake up, Little Master!" came a voice. "Wake up!"

Palimak's eyes blinked open and he saw two small frightened faces hovering over his chest—Gundara and Gundaree.

"What's wrong?" he mumbled, rubbing his eyes.

"Can't you feel it?" Gundara said. "Something's watching!"

"And it isn't a very pleasant something, either," Gundaree added. He shuddered. "Kind of oily."

And that was it! Palimak could feel it, feel something watching, something big, something mean and something . . . oily! But thick. Real thick. And hot! How could it live and watch and be so hot?

"Let's go!" he said, jumping up.

The two little Favorites fled back into the stone idol. He pocketed it and leaped out the back of the slow moving wagon.

The Timura wagons were about half way down the long line, herd animals straggling behind the last wagons with boys driving them along. Beyond them was the rear guard. Perhaps twenty armed men. Up front—past the lead wagons—was another force of fifty. In between and along the both sides of the road, people and children walked, talking listlessly in the heat, burping babies, or flicking sticks at goats and llamas to keep them together.

Palimak stood in the road, letting them pass by. He turned, searching for the source of his discomfort. Then he caught it. On the other side of the road!

He ducked under a camel, swatting its jaws as it tried to snap at him like that damned turtle. Oops! Shouldn't say damned. It made Grandmother mad.

Then he saw the bats streaming out of the crater. He looked up at the huge black cloud swirling above the caravan. Normally the bats flew away. But this time they were staying in the same place! Millions of them!

"Is it the bats?" he asked.

Gundara's voice came from his pocket. "It's not the bats!"

"Definitely, not the bats!" Gundaree added.

"Quit repeating everything I say!" snapped Gundara.

"I wasn't repeating. I was emphasizing."

"Oh, shut up!"

"Don't tell me to shut—"

Palimak slapped his pocket. "If I get killed or something," he said, "you'd better learn to like oily stuff. Because that's what your new master's going to be. Big and oily!"

"And hot," Gundaree said. "Don't forget hot!"

Palimak sighed, "Okay, he's hot! But where is he?"

Then he caught it. A filthy presence at the crater's edge. About fifty feet away. And he could feel it oozing out.

"There he is!" Gundara said. "We'd better get you out of here!"

"Lord Timura will kill us if we let something happen to you!" Gundaree added.

"What spell should we use?" Gundara asked his twin.

"I'd suggest running," Gundaree said. "We can think of one while we're running!"

"Good idea. Do you hear that, Little Master? Run! Run like the Hells!"

But Palimak was already running as fast as his little legs could go. But he wasn't running away. He was racing toward his Grandfather, who was driving the lead Timura wagon.

"Grandfather!" he shouted. "We have to get out of here!"

Khadji heard the boy and turned to see Palimak running toward him. "What's wrong?" he shouted.

Palimak twisted his arm to point, still running. "Back there! It's coming!"

Khadji jumped off and swept the child up. He was startled to see his eyes glowing fiercely yellow and he could feel the boy's sharp little claws biting into his arm.

"What's coming?"

Palimak calmed himself down, eyes flickering back to normal. "It's a great big magic thing, Grandfather," he said, spreading his arms wide as he could. "And it's going to get us all if we don't run."

He squirmed to be freed and Khadji let him go. He landed lightly on his feet, like a cat.

"Quick, Grandfather!" he shouted. "Sound the alarm!"

"Calm down, son," Khadji said. "Let's see what it is that's bothering you."

He looked around, saw the bats, smiled and looked down at the boy. "It's just the bats," he said. "They won't hurt us."

Palimak stamped his foot. "It's not the bats!" he snapped. He pointed at the crater. "It's in there. And it's coming out and you'd better blow the stupid horn!"

He saw his grandfather flush with anger and realized he wasn't getting through. To Khadji he was just a little boy who'd suddenly become very rude.

But there wasn't time to fool with that adult stuff. He didn't have time to argue or explain. He knew what he could do, suddenly felt the knowledge and power to go with it. Still he held back, reluctant to take action. This was his Grandfather, after all!

"Please, Grandfather," he said, "Please, please, please. Blow the horn!"

"I'm losing my patience with you, young man!" Khadji said in the tones adults used when they'd had enough.

"I'm sorry, Grandfather," Palimak said.

And then he cast the spell, right hand shooting out, claws uncurling from his finger tips, eyes glaring yellow.

Khadji twitched as the spell hit him, stiffening to his full height. He looked down on his grandson with fond eyes. Such a wise little boy.

"Please blow the horn, Grandfather," Palimak said as nicely as he could.

"Sure, son," Khadji said, a broad smile on his face. "Right away!"

Khadji jumped up on the wagon and grabbed the long warning horn that every family leader kept nearby at all times. He blew three blasts—the signal for everyone to go like the blazes and ask questions later. Palimak knew this wasn't the best plan of escape, but it was all he could think of. Other horns picked up the warning and joined in the cry. People shouted, whips cracked, animals bawled, and the caravan surged forward at a much greater speed.

Khadji smiled and waved happily at Palimak as he drove the wagon away. The boy waved back, feeling very bad about what he'd done.

"All right, Little Master," came Gundara's voice, "so you don't like running. I hope you can think of something pretty quick."

"Frankly," Gundaree added, "we're out of suggestions."

20

BEAST OF THE BLACK LANDS

Palimak walked slowly back to the crater. Wagons and animals streamed past, people running beside them, horns blowing, camels bawling, geese shrieking, children wailing, parents shouting, a whole cacophony of panicked flight.

As fast as they were moving, he could tell it wasn't fast enough.

It was getting darker and oil lamps and torches flared into life, so the caravan became like a stream of stars flying low across the land. A passing wagon hit a rut and a lamp came flying off, shattering against the ground to leave a small pool of flaming oil.

"This thing is hot," Gundara said, "but he doesn't like fire."

"Fire is absolutely not one of his favorite things," Gundaree added. "Apparently he's rather vain about his appearance."

And then a great voice shouted: "Hate!"

It echoed across the bleak plain, striking lightning on the highest rocks. Overhead, the immense swarm of bats shrieked and Palimak's heart jumped so high he thought it was going to fly out of his throat.

Again came the shout: "Hate!"

And then Palimak was trying his best to catch and swallow his heart as the crater began to bubble and froth, foul steam rising to meet those shrilling bats.

A scum formed, cracked and then a mighty head emerged, all tarry and stuck this way and that with the white bones of angry things that had died long ago. Skulls made its eyes. Ribbed spines its nose. And its mouth was a graveyard clutter, opening wide, bone dust expelled in a cloud as it shouted:

"Hate!"

It rose out of the crater, shoulders following head, then arms and trunk and limbs, climbing higher and higher. A massive black tarry beast, all pitted and scarred with oil bursting from those scars and bleeding down the sides.

The creature's head moved slowly, looking for the cause of its terrible wrath.

Then its eyes, all aboil with grinning skulls, fixed on Palimak.

Safar rode full out, urging every ounce of speed he could from Khysmet. Even so, when he saw the beast rise from the crater to confront Palimak he feared he'd be too late.

Far below he could see the crush of fleeing people and wagons and animals race up the hill toward him, flooding the road from bank to bank like a solid wall of onrushing water. He'd never break through to get to Palimak.

He saw a narrow trail to the side that looked like it might lead in the right direction. He shouted for Leiria to meet the panicked horde and guide them, then turned down the trail, praying he'd made the correct decision.

Palimak was frozen with fear. His whole being fixed on those ghastly eyes and bony mouth splitting open into a horrible smile. In the background he could hear sounds of panic as the caravan fled the horrible presence.

Then Gundara said, "You should have run, Little Master."

And Gundaree said, "It isn't nice to say, 'I told you so.'"

"Shut up!" Palimak shouted to them both, breaking from his trance.

He ran to the pool of flaming oil. He made a scoop of his hands and skimmed through the heart of the fire. The light came off, spilling out in beads, but Palimak quickly make a glowing ball of them, holding the ball firmly between his hands.

And the beast shouted—"YOU I HATE YOU!"

Palimak jumped, burning himself on the invisible flame, but he kept his concentration. Pulling up the spell, putting together all the parts of it—light and fire, it was hard, a lot of pieces don't fit. Hurry! Hurry! Don't pay attention when he shouts. So what if he's close—oh, boy is he close!

"Listen to me," he said to the Favorites. "Remember the spell we practiced? Fire follow light?"

"That's a good spell," Gundara said.

"I don't know if I feel like it," Gundaree grumbled. "He said 'shut up' to us. Which was a very rude thing to say."

An immense shadow fell over them. Palimak hunched his shoulders, holding the ball of light close to his stomach.

"I apologize, all right?" he said. "Sorry and double sorry. Now, do it!"

He turned—looking up and up, head craning back, feeling like such a small boy. Standing beneath a living mountain of tar and bone. So close that when the pustules of oil broke they ran down the smoking skin to pool at his feet.

The creature's breath was a hot, foul wind of gritty magic blasting away at his senses. But he closed his eyes and stuck out his chin taking the wind full on his face.

And he chanted:

"Palimak, Palimak,
Here I come!
Demon boy,
Or people boy—
Guess which one!"

He threw the ball of light as high he could, casting the spell, feeling Gundara and Gundaree push in behind it. Blowing it bigger and bigger until it looked like a watery sun when it crashed into the beast's face.

Dazzling light splashed into the creature's eyes and he reeled, screaming as if the light had been acid.

And Palimak shouted, "Fire follow light!"

The Favorites fed him their powers and Palimak's right hand speared out, pointing finger becoming a long, sharp talon. There was a searing from within as the fire leaped from the oil pool to his body, then shot out of his talon, racing to join the light.

A huge blast followed as the two forces were rejoined and the beast roared in pain, stumbling back, head bursting into flame. It beat at its skull trying to put the fire out, but then its hands caught and it was shouting and wailing in agony. Flailing and screaming helplessly.

"Got you!" Palimak shouted.

"I wouldn't be too sure about that, Little Master," Gundara cautioned. "You might have just made him madder."

"Maybe you'd better consider running again," Gundaree added.

To his horror, Palimak saw the beast had managed to put out most of the flames and was recovering.

What would he do now? The spell had left him drained and he was frightened that even if he could think of another spell he'd be too exhausted to cast it.

"Wait!" Gundara said with sudden excitement. "Here comes help!"

He no sooner spoke than a score of mounted warriors rushed onto the field to do battle. Shouting Kyranian battle cries they charged the beast, firing arrows and waving swords and battle axes.

"Let's think about that running option again," Gundaree said. "There's just enough time."

Still, Palimak didn't budge. Frightened as he was, he'd determined to make a stand.

"Such a stubborn child," Gundara said.

"I'm definitely going to tell his father," Gundaree said.

For a moment it looked as if the mounted charge was having some affect. Pierced by arrows and spears and slashing blades, the beast shrilled pain, bleeding oil from many wounds.

"Hate!" It shouted. "Hate!"

Then it suddenly drew itself up, towering three times the height of the warriors. The beast's mouth yawned open, a great black hole ringed by white skeleton lips.

First smoke belched out, thick, evil-smelling clouds that burned the eyes and seared the lungs.

Then it vomited boiling oil. A great steaming river of it, splashing over the attacking men.

Their cries were terrible, but only a few caught the full blast. They were left groaning on the ground, while the others wheeled about and fled.

* * *

High above, Leiria had commanded a position at a bend in the road, shouting into dazed faces, smacking panicked men with the flat of her sword.

"Get them in order! Get them in order!" she shouted, hauling the calmer ones out of the crowd and pointing at the hysterical mass.

Gradually, some order took form as her deputies waded in to straighten out the confusion. Then a camel reared up, frightened and bawling and lashing out with its front feet. It came down, nearly smashing over a wagon, but people caught the rim and tilted it back up. As it crashed to the ground the camel panicked even more, roaring in fear and trying to bite anything in sight.

Leiria leaped over two men who were scrambling to get away from those flat, deadly teeth.

The camel's head snaked toward her, eyes wide and glazed, bloody gums and teeth exposed in a panicked snarl.

Leiria ducked, letting the head sweep past her, then jumped for the rear.

She caught the animal as it came about, jabbing the camel in the hind quarters with her sword. It bawled and galloped up the hill, caroming off of several wagons, bowling over a few people, then disappearing from sight.

Leiria turned, shuddering relief. Then she saw the beast and the fleeing men. Saw the wounded flailing on the ground.

And Palimak, very small, very alone, looking up at the beast.

They was no way she could reach him. Groaning, she looked this way and that, wondering:

Where is Safar?

The beast looked down at the injured men and horses. He held up a tarry hand, belching wreaths of smoke.

"Kill later you!" he thundered. "First kill hate!"

He stepped over them, coming toward the road, eyes sweeping the ground for his small enemy.

Then once again the beast settled its awful eyes on Palimak. Bone cracked as its mouth opened into a ghastly grin.

"I'm going to miss you, Little Master," Gundara sniffed.

"It'll be a thousand years before we find somebody as nice as you," Gundaree added.

And the beast shouted—"Hate! You I hate!"

It stomped forward, ground rumbling under its weight and Palimak conjured up all the power he could find. The Favorites rushed to help him, squeezing out every drop of sorcerous energy, but it was only a slim trickle and Palimak felt as if he was lifting an infant's fist against a giant.

He heard someone shout his name and he turned to see a glorious sight charging toward him. It was his father and Khysmet flying across the plain, the red Demon Moon grinning behind them.

"Pa-li-mak!" his father shouted, voice stretching across the distance between them, long and slow and sweet like grandmother's taffy. "Pa-li-mak!"

And the beast said, "Hate! Kill you hate!"

An immense hand swept toward him, tarry fingers the size of ancient swamp stumps, opening wide to grasp.

Palimak closed his eyes.

Then there was a rush of sound and sensation and a hand grabbed him by the collar.

He was lifted up, but so slowly, hells it was slow! Like he was coming up from the same dreamlike depths where the giant turtle had pursued him. Someone—someone he loved, someone who loved him possibly even more—was heaving, kicking, fighting the heavy drowning weight, turtle jaws going snap, snap, snap, kicking hard for the surface.

The dream shattered and everything sped up. Real sensation returned, but in quick jerks—A rush in his ears. Snatched from the ground. Beast spitting Hate! Blistering splatter across his legs as he was snatched to safety. Then all was normal—but upside down normal—as he opened his eyes and saw the ground racing past beneath him.

It nearly made him sick.

He tried to rise, but his father pushed him down with one hand as Khysmet plunged away—contorting his body as he dodged from side to side. Palimak felt like a huge ungainly weight that shifted wildly as Khysmet avoided attack. He saw torrents of smoking oil shoot past, curl into them, then be hurled away as Khysmet changed course, bending as if he were double-jointed.

Then his father reined Khysmet in and the halt was so sudden Palimak's stomach hit an unforgiving wall. Acid contents splashing about, then racing for his throat.

His father dropped him to the ground and he fell on his knees, spewing.

Palimak wiped his mouth and looked up. His father's eyes were bluer and deeper than he'd ever seen them. Wells of blue, dark seas of blue, so sad and all-seeing in the moment passing between them that Palimak nearly wept.

His father spoke. "Stay there, son. I'll be back as soon as I can."

He held the reins tight as spoke, steadying Khysmet who was pawing the earth, anxious to get on with it. Then he whistled to the stallion and they whirled in their tracks and charged back to face the beast.

"Get ready," Gundara said.

Palimak fell from safety to fear so fast he thought he was going to throw up again.

"Ready for what?"

"As I see it—tell me I'm wrong if you think differently . . ." Gundaree said, so slow in his reply that Palimak thought he'd go mad, watching his father and Khysmet plummet toward the hideous creature. " . . . but in my view we have two choices."

"Run," Gundara broke in.

"Yes, we could run," Gundaree said, impatient with the interruption, but keeping his temper so he could make his point. "Running is still a very good idea," he said. "A course we've urged all along."

"I hope you tell your father that," Gundara said, "because he's going to be really mad when this is all over. And it wasn't our fault."

"Never mind fault," Gundaree said, such an uncharacteristic statement from him that Palimak's attention was riveted. "The point is, we're looking at life and death, and who our new master is going to be if something isn't done right away. The beast is stupid. I don't mind that. We've had stupid before. But he's also really, really dirty. An affront to all civilized beings. I definitely do not want that . . . that . . . thing, for a master!"

Palimak saw his father closing on the beast, the huge, hideous figure turning to fix on them.

"Soooo, if we're not going to run—" Gundara began . . .

" . . . Which we still advise—" Gundaree poked in . . .

" . . . We might consider helping the Master," Gundara completed.

And the beast shouted, "Hate!"

Palimak saw Khysmet rearing up, hooves slashing the air, bolts of lightning cracking out. He saw his father reach behind him, scrabbling at the saddle, then plucking a javelin from its sheath beneath the cantle lip.

As his father reared back to throw, he saw the javelin tip flare. The flare leaped to join the crackling fire from Khysmet's hooves, shooting up toward the beast.

Palimak dug down, clawing past layers he never knew existed, finding untapped reservoirs of magical power. The effort took everything the boy had and he fell to his knees.

"Now!" the Favorites shouted in chorus.

The beast was reaching for his father when Palimak cast the joining spell.

He was so empty he had no mind, no soul of his own. Everything was focused on the spell. He leaped onto the spell's back, clutching as tightly as he could, magical winds buffeting his face. Palimak collided with his father's spell, burst through the walls, then was swept onward and upward at a heart-stopping speed.

Then he entered a never-never state where he was floating like a high meadow moth on a spring wind. He could see all the parts of his father's spell, a wondrous flock of soaring birds with more colors, it seemed, than there were rainbows in the world to make them.

Palimak turned, relaxed and lazy, still speeding along, but feeling easy about it. Time to think. Time to consider. Time to marvel at the complex beauty of the spell, but marveling more at the elegant simplicity of its core.

His father's spell made him feel as if he'd just lost his childhood. Everything before this moment had been a game. A silly little boy amusing himself.

Now he could see what real magic was. See it and admire it through the eyes of an adult. He was confounded and excited at the same time. Tone deaf at one moment, acute musical hearing the next, with all those magical notes spurting out like a harp played by a madman. But then it all made sense. He could see it, hear it, feel his bones throb with it.

Magic as it should be.

And he thought: So that's what it's like to be a wizard!

His father shouted a warning and Palimak kicked away just in time, spirit self plunging back into his mortal form. Then he was a small boy again, watching the white hot spear sink into the beast's face.

It thundered agony, grasping the magical spear between both mighty hands. The beast heaved, screaming louder still, then there was a great blast of light and the beast exploded into flames. The force was so great it hurled Palimak away and for a moment he thought he was his spirit self again, flying with the sorcerous winds. Then he struck, landing heavily on his back, the air knocked out of him.

He fought for breath, desperate to get up, to get moving before the beast struck back.

Then he found his father standing over him and relief rushed in along with returned breath and he shuddered in all the air he could hold. Safar knelt beside him, trying to smile to cover worry and feeling his limbs for signs of injury.

When Palimak could speak again, he asked, "Did we get him?"

Safar glanced over his shoulder at the scattered pieces of the beast. Hot tarry lumps, big and small, with white bits of shattered bone showing through.

He turned back. "We sure did, son," Safar said, scooping him up. "As good as any pair of wizards could."

Palimak grinned weakly, proud to be included. A moment later he was aboard Khysmet, nestled against his father and they were riding slowly after the caravan—back in order now and climbing the hill.

He was tired but his mind was abuzz with all kinds of thoughts and possibilities roused by his experience.

"I want to learn to be a real wizard, father," he said. "Like you."

"I've already been teaching you, son," Safar said.

Palimak frowned. "Maybe so," he said. "But I don't think I've been listening real well." He sighed. "There's so much to know," he said, thinking of the elegance of his father's spell. "So I'd better hurry and learn before I get too old."

Safar chuckled but didn't answer. Then a sudden thought struck Palimak and his eagerness turned to dismay.

"I think I'm going to be in big trouble," he said.

"I kind of doubt that," his father said. "You're the hero of the hour, son. You saved the caravan."

Palimak shook his head. "But I had to do something really bad," he said. "I was mean to my grandfather."

"He'll forgive you," Safar said. "Whatever it was."

"He wouldn't listen to me," Palimak went on. "So I put a spell on him and made him do what I said."

Safar looked down at him, his eyes unfathomable. Palimak thought he even looked a little sad. Then he saw a glitter in the depths.

"When I was going to wizard's school," Safar said, "they had a special class for first year acolytes called 'The Ethics of Magic.' Naturally, it only lasted a week, and no one ever attended." He snorted humor. "In fact, it was the only class at the Grand Temple of Walaria where students were expected to cheat. You could buy the tests from the teacher for six coppers. Four if you were on scholarship."

"Did you cheat, Father?" Palimak asked. "Did you buy the test?"

"I confess I did, son," Safar said. "I didn't have any choice. The master of the course didn't attend either and the only way you could take the test was to buy it with a set of answers. But I did feel guilty about it. And I suppose that's the best you can do. Keep a good, healthy sense of guilt at hand."

"And then still do what you think have to do?" Palimak asked, troubled at this new and very difficult world being revealed to him.

Safar squeezed his arm. "That's the closest to the truth that I can get," he said.

"But what about the gods?" Palimak protested, thinking of the lessons he learned at the Temple in Kyrania. "Don't they tell you that one thing is right, and another thing wrong?"

"I've never had one tell me," Safar said. "Only their priests. And priests are no more honest than the rest of us. Maybe even less, since there's so much temptation about when you make your living from sin."

Palimak was amazed. Each level of this larger world obviously became more complicated and confusing the higher you climbed. Or maybe he was going down. Maybe to know wasn't up, but down, down, and then down some more. All the way down a long flight of dark stairs that descended forever.

He looked up at the boiling skies of the Black Lands and the grinning Demon Moon.

"What's wrong with the gods, anyway?" he said, a little angry and self righteous. "Can't they see? Can't they warn you? Are they asleep or something?"

Palimak felt his father suddenly tense up. What had he said wrong? Then Safar relaxed.

"I'll tell you a riddle," he said. "When you figure it out, you'll know as much as anyone in the world about what the gods are up to."

"I'm good at riddles," Palimak said. Then he frowned in exaggerated demonstration. "Go ahead," he said. "My riddle machine is all the way on."

And so Safar recited the Riddle of Asper:

"Two kings reign in Hadin Land,
One's becursed, the other damned.
One sees whatever eyes can see,
The other dreams of what might be.
One is blind. One's benighted.
And who can say which is sighted?
Know that Asper knocked at the Castle Keep,
But the gates were barred, the Gods Asleep."

Palimak listened closely, setting his sharp little mind to work on the pieces. But no matter how hard he tried, the puzzle refused to make itself clear. Finally, he gave up.

"I suppose you have to think about it a real long time," he said.

"I suppose so," Safar answered, dry.

"Do you know the answer, Father?" he asked.

Safar shook his head. "No I don't son," he said. "No I don't."

Then from overhead came the cry of many bats and Safar looked up to see that the black swirling cloud was still there. Except now the bats seemed more excited than before, shrieking and flapping excitedly as if suddenly disturbed.

"What's wrong with the bats?" Safar asked.

Palimak yawned, exhaustion suddenly overcoming him. "Nothing, Father," he said. "It was never the bats!"

He fell asleep, but Safar kept his eye on the bats as he rode along, wondering at their odd behavior.

Far away at the edge of the Black Lands, four giant wolves prowled a hilltop. A great spellfire swirled in the center of the hill, shooting off sparks and spears of flame. The wolves paced about the fire, sometimes on all fours, sometimes on hind feet, growling and grinding their teeth.

Their huge glowing eyes were fixed on the heart of the spellfire, where an image of the Black Lands wheeled about. They were looking down from a great height, gaping crater to one side, a wide track running along it. They could see the blasted remains of the beast. And far up ahead the lights of a caravan were winking on, curving up a long hill.

But immediately beneath them, trotting along the track after the wagons, was the sight that had them growling with delight, shape-changer's hunger stoked into hot-bellied pain.

It was Safar Timura, riding a magnificent horse, carrying a sleeping Palimak in his arms.

Then Timura looked up—staring right at them. It was so sudden they were startled and drew back, growling warnings as if Safar's image were about to attack.

The image became clouded and confused as their spell concentration weakened.

"Kill him!" they snarled. "Kill his brat! Kill his bitch woman!"

The creature who was Iraj Protarus recovered first, roaring at the image, "Enough! I've seen enough!"

And the image shattered.

Safar's hackles prickled as the huge black swarm of bats suddenly broke apart. Their cries were wild, hysterical, as if they had been asleep and now danger had suddenly awakened them.

Then, just as quickly as it began, the hysteria ended and they formed up again and flew off in an orderly fashion. A great long, blunt-tipped arrow aimed out of the Black Lands.

Safar shivered and at the same time Khysmet quickened his pace.

The hunters were out and it was time to get off the road.

Iraj paced the edge of the hill, staring out into the Black Lands, scarred snout moving this way and that as he searched the barren plains.

In the background he could hear his spell brothers howling orders and his great army muscling into life. Demon steeds shrieked and clawed at one another as their masters booted them into formation. Humans threw their shields over their shoulders and settled their battle harness and weapons for the march. Cooks and supply men were scattering the campfires and loading the wagons. Demon and human whores fought each other for space aboard those wagons, slapping or comforting frightened children and kits, depending on their temperaments.

Iraj ignored all this, searching the glowing skies beneath the Demon Moon. The wait seemed interminable. His anger and blood lust grew by the minute.

Then he saw it—the huge cloud of shrieking bats, streaming out of the Black Lands.

His senses exploded into exquisite life and he howled in joy at the sight. Then the bats were overhead, wheeling about the sky, once, twice, three times. Then they flew off again, heading back the way they had come.

Like an unleashed bolt Iraj charged forward, bounding down the hill after them, howling for his prey. His spell brothers charged after him, fanning out to sweep up anything and everything in their great snapping jaws and deadly talons.

Behind them came Protarus' army. The first elements had already topped the hill and were pouring down the other side. They were led by five hundred mounted demons, their spears making a deadly forest, their battle cries ululating across the lightning blasted terrain.

Within moments the whole plain was swarming with men and demons—led by the four immense wolves who were their masters.

It was a juggernaut aimed straight at Caluz.

21

DARK PARADISE

After a year of desperate flight and miserable camps, the Kyranians fell into the embrace of Caluz as if it were the softest and deepest of pillows. They were warmly welcomed, with hundreds of people and demons streaming out to greet them with gifts of choice food and delicious drink and all manner of clothes and goods to replace their trail-worn things.

Queen Hantilia provided them with a large, lightly wooded field to make their temporary home and supplied them with every luxury imaginable, until soon the field seemed more like a pleasure camp for royalty enjoying a few weeks in the bracing outdoors. They settled into colorful pavilions filled with thick carpets and pillows. Cheery cooking fires were scattered among the pavilions, each with tables and benches so the Kyranians could imagine they were at home, gossiping and sharing leisurely meals.

Portable bath houses were set up along the river and the Kyranians reveled in an orgy of hot soapy baths, soaking away months of grime in steaming kettles big enough to hold a family. Then they all donned their new clothes and strolled through the trees, or along the nearby river bank, feeling clean and without care.

Special attention was paid to the soldiers and horses hurt in the encounter with the beast. The Queen sent her best healers to treat them with magical herbs and ointments and soon they were up and about, injuries fading, enjoying their new home as much as the rest.

Every day was a glorious day in Caluz. The sun always mild, the nights pleasantly cool and the remarkable absence of the Demon Moon made everyone feel as if a large weight had been lifted. Children played, lovers swooned, mothers and fathers enjoyed many stolen moments alone, as did the grandparents. At night those who could make music made it and everyone danced and sang away their troubles.

It was a grand holiday for one and all—except Safar, who disappeared for several days of intense conferences with the Queen and the top Caluzian priests and scholars. His absence only made everyone's mood lighter. For a short time they could forget about Iraj Protarus, prophecies of a doomed world and their desperate journey to far off Syrapis. Safar was dealing with such things. And when he decided what they should do next he'd come and tell them. Who could say when that would be? So let's enjoy life, grab what we can from it for the dark days will return soon enough.

Yet there was a ragged edge to their joy. Snatched as they were from a place where fear had become ordinary, the Kyranians went about their pleasures at a frantic pace. Leaping from one activity to another. Always glancing over their shoulders, waiting for the predestined shadow to fall.

Only Palimak and Leiria were unaffected. Only they saw the mirror cracks in the perfection that was Caluz. Leiria because she was a soldier and had a soldier's healthy suspicion of all things. Palimak because he was a newly serious boy, a self-appointed wizard's apprentice to his father, whom he was worried would leave him out of the main action. Whatever that was going to be.

One evening while they were walking together along the river looking for a likely fishing spot they came upon a small park with a dozen or more Caluzians—both human and demon. Some were taking the air alone, some in company, and there were several family groups with children or kits.

As soon as they saw the two Kyranians they all rushed over to bow and smile and murmur greetings. Saying, "How is the Lady Leiria this evening?" Or, "Does the Young Lord Timura find himself well, we pray?" And "May the blessings of Lady Felakia be with you!"

As they spoke they spontaneously handed the two little gifts, a bracelet or necklace for Leiria hastily stripped off by the owner, a small top or a ball for Palimak, willingly given by smiling children. Leiria and Palimak made polite replies and tried to fend off the gifts but it was no use, so they stuffed them in their pockets, thanking everyone and grinning until their jaws ached.

A moment later the Caluzians all chorused farewells and trooped off, pleasant laughter trailing in their wake.

Leiria looked about the empty park. "They certainly left in a hurry," she said. "I feel like we brought something odorous to a party."

Palimak snorted. "They're just so nice they make me sick!" he said. "But they never really want to talk to you. Or play with you. They just say, 'How are you, Young Lord Timura?' And 'May the gods be kind to you!' Things like that, but soon as you try to say something back they pretend they're busy, or going someplace in a hurry, and run away."

"I thought I was the only one to notice that," Leiria said. "I went into the city the other day and you should have seen the fuss everyone made over me. Then they suddenly melted away and all of sudden the street was empty and people were closing their doors and shutters.

"The same thing happened when I went into a tavern to get a drink and some company. At first they were all my friends, buying me drinks and welcoming me to Caluz. Next thing I knew the tavern was empty and the innkeeper was making excuses about having to close up early."

"What's wrong with them, Aunt Leiria?" Palimak asked.

"I don't know, my dear," she answered. Then, thinking she might be neglecting her auntly duties, she tried to sound more kindly. "Maybe they're all just very frightened and trying to put a brave face on things. The gods know they have a right to their fears. From what your father said they're under some curse and don't have much longer to live, unless he helps them."

"Maybe . . ." Palimak said doubtfully. He thought a minute then said, "What if they have to be really nice and happy all the time because that's the way the machine wants it? What if they don't have any choice?"

He waved at the idyllic scene around them, taking in twittering birds and flitting butterflies. "Look at it, Aunt Leiria!" he said. "Everything's too nice! It's not natural. It has to be the machine!"

Reflexively, Leiria turned to look upstream at the great stone turtle squatting over the place where the rivers joined. Water poured out its mouth, thundering into the wide basin below, sending up a mist laced with many rainbows.

For a moment she thought she saw something. A flicker of another scene laid on top of this idyllic vision, but black like a shadow cast. In this, the turtle god was the size of a mountain with lighting crackling on its back. And instead of water pouring from its mouth, there was a river of fire. Then the vision vanished and all was the same again.

At first she thought she was imagining things, but then Palimak said, "Did you see it, Aunt Leiria?" His voice was excited with just a touch of fear. "Did you see it?"

"Yes," she said, almost in a whisper. "I saw!"

High above in Queen Hantilia's silver palace Safar was having his own problems.

He paced the lush waiting area outside the Queen's courtroom, a little red-robed serving maid trotting behind him with a silver decanter of wine to fill the glass he clutched in his hand. Behind the closed doors he could hear the low murmur of the Queen's aides, discussing his request. A request he had made three days before and still had no answer.

His mind was buzzing with all manner of questions and half-formed conclusions. Many of them quite similar to Leiria's and Palimak's.

Yes, the Queen and her subjects were strange, yes, the wonderland spells emanating from the Temple of Hadin were too good to be trusted, and, yes, the citizens of Caluz faced eventual doom from the machine and had every reason to be frightened in the extreme, but somehow they spent their days with pleasant smiles pasted on their faces as if life could be no sweeter.

Safar paused at the window, which looked out over the Temple of Hadin. If he could have seen far enough he might have spotted Palimak and Leiria strolling along the path by the river. He sipped his wine, thinking, piling still more questions on his plate.

For instance, there was the matter of the twin Caluzes—one good, one evil—which made things complicated to the extreme. When he'd queried the Queen's wizards and scholars about the phenomenon, they became blank-faced, uncomprehending. Their own situation was too complex to fathom, much less factor in such minor things as the cause of it all. Their main worry was that Safar would refuse, or be unable to help them. So they coated every difficulty with such a sweet layer of honey Safar came to doubt most of what they said.

In the courtroom there was a hush as the Queen spoke and Safar turned his head to listen. But her voice was so low it was swallowed by the thick silver doors that closed off the chamber.

Safar let the serving maid refill his cup, giving her an absent smile by way of thanks.

Hantilia was as serene as her subjects, he thought, but seemed more willing to speak her mind. Her magical resources were great, so she wasn't quite as affected as the others by the dream-spinning machine. Possibly it was because she was spinning so many of her own—and all were aimed directly at Safar. It was an innocent thing, an unconscious thing, or so he supposed. Although she was a demon and he was human, she found him attractive and was sending out many signals and spells that made her alluring. How he should or would react remained to be seen.

He pushed all this aside for another time—if there ever was to be such a time. There was urgent business to attend to before he began to plumb this and the other mysteries of the odd mirror worlds that made Caluz.

Safar resumed his pacing. He'd rarely been so frustrated. He'd expected to be rushed off to the temple immediately where he would consult with the Oracle he'd come so far to see. The queen said the Oracle of Hadin and all her people had been waiting for his arrival, so one would think they'd be just as anxious for the foretold visit to begin. Except there was apparently more to consulting the Oracle than just marching into the temple and announcing his presence. He was told there were elaborate purification ceremonies that had to be performed first. Ceremonies and spell castings that would take a week or more. So he was bathed and oiled and suffered so many hours in incense filled rooms that he felt like smoked meat.

Meanwhile, he fretted and gnawed at his growing worry that all would be for naught.

Uppermost in his mind was what to do about Iraj. The question wasn't if his enemy would show up, but when. The flash of awareness Safar had caught of Iraj's presence had been very strong—as if Protarus had been newly energized, stronger in purpose and determination than ever.

Safar would just as soon not be here when Iraj and his spell brothers showed up with their vast army.

The only reason he had tarried in this cursed place was because Asper's ghost had said the way to Syrapis was through Caluz. How this could be, he didn't know. But he had to take the chance. Safar was more convinced then ever that only in Syrapis would he find the key to the disaster that was overtaking the world.

The disaster blowing on poisoned winds in far Hadinland.

The serving maid offered more wine. Safar hesitated, then shook his head, no, and returned his now empty cup.

He smiled, thinking, many things besides Iraj Protarus could stop him from reaching Syrapis. Life being what it is he might even choke on a wine cork and that would be the rather foolish end to the saga of Safar Timura, son of a potter who rose to become the king's chief wazier, only to die trying to get at his drink.

Just then, while he was grinning at his own imagined clownish demise, the doors boomed open and a troop of robed priestesses with serene eyes and pleasant smiles came to escort him into the Queen's presence.

He tried to read Hantilia's expression as he approached the gilded throne, but all she presented was a sweet smile on her oddly—to him—beautiful demon's face. He also couldn't tell from the atmosphere of the courtroom if a decision had been reached. The Caluzians only watched his progress down the main aisle, murmuring little pleasantries as he passed.

"My dear, Lord Timura," the Queen said after he'd reached her and bowed his respects. "Please know that we've given your proposal our full attention. We've discussed it for many hours. But, frankly we find ourselves in a great quandary."

"What could be so difficult, Majesty?" Safar asked, keeping his tone as formal and distantly polite as hers. They'd met many times since his arrival, but always in more intimate surroundings. "I only want to make a casting—under the close guidance and full assistance of your best mages—to determine when we can expect Iraj Protarus.

"I've not only promised, but shown magical proof that he will be unaware of this casting. It will in no way draw his attention, or the attention of his wizards."

Safar raised his hands, turning them palm up. "What could be simpler than that?" he asked. "Or more vital? After all, you must be as concerned as I am that an army will soon show up to knock on your doors."

"I don't agree," the Queen said. "We are well hidden. How will this Protarus find us through the secret gate? You saw for yourself how well hidden it is. Only the cleverest wizard would ever find it, much less unravel the spell locks."

"Don't make that mistake!" Safar said, emphatic. "Believe me when I say that Iraj will find the way. It may take him awhile, but he has more than enough magical resources at his command."

"You forget the Guardians," the Queen said. "They will protect us now, as they always have. Nothing has ever managed to get past them! Only those we favor are permitted through, such as pilgrims and innocent wayfarers escaping the Black Lands."

"And I'm telling you that you don't know what you're facing," Safar said, deliberately letting some of his anger show. "Iraj Protarus is an enemy who once conquered all of Esmir. And he's quickly bringing it back under his command. He will hammer your Guardians into ghostly dust and crack your gates open and spill you out like an egg.

"Finally, Your Highness, this something I simply must insist on. If no one here will take the threat seriously, I'll have to gather my people and leave before Protarus arrives. And there will be no meeting of Safar Timura and your blessed Oracle of Hadin, a meeting that I am now beginning to think was a big mistake on my part for ever even thinking about."

Safar's bluff got the result he intended. There were gasps in the courtroom. The Queen gave him a look of great concern, clutching her robe at the breast. "But you don't understand, my dear Lord Timura," she said. "We aren't refusing you out of some mean-spirited motivation. Our survival is at stake as much as yours, after all. The real fear is that the casting will ruin everything we've done. You're almost ready for your meeting with the Oracle. What if your spell conflicts with the magical preparations we've already made?"

"Why didn't someone say that was the worry, Your Highness?" Safar asked, bewildered. "Why all this unnecessary secrecy? Let me meet now with your best scholars and we'll have the answer within the hour."

The Queen shook her head, no. "I'm sorry," she said. "That isn't possible. You would have to delve into things that are forbidden for you know in advance."

"I've never seen a situation in which ignorance is good for anyone, Majesty," Safar said sharply. "And if this decision is final, I really must take my leave. My people and I will be on the march again by tomorrow at dawn."

"But where will you march to, my dear?" the Queen said, finally calling his bluff. "There is only one way out of Caluz. And that's the way you came. Back through the Black Lands to face an oncoming army. As I said before, the road ahead is blocked. What I kept from you then was that we sealed it because it leads right into the heart of the real Caluz, the mad Caluz, the Caluz where no mortal could possibly exist for more than a few moments."

He caught an odd note in her tone as she spoke the last, but when he tried to catch her eyes she averted them.

"So you see, Lord Timura," she said, "there is no escape for your people. They are trapped here, it grieves me deeply to say, along with my own subjects. And what happens to us will happen to them."

At that moment Safar fully understood the nature of the trap he'd been drawn into. And if he failed in his mission here, there was no getting out.

"I'm sorry, Safar, my dear," Hantilia said, low. "But you see how it is?"

Safar saw. Just as he saw there was no malice intended by Hantilia or anyone here. It was just so.

"All of us came here at great cost," she went on. "It was and still is a holy mission. We must trust and we must believe, or everything is lost. Not just for us, but for the world itself. Perhaps it's made us a bit mad. I'm sure you think that when you see us smile when there is only reason to weep."

Safar thought they probably all were mad, including Hantilia. Then it came to him there was more to it than that.

"When we cast the spell that made this place," Hantilia said, "the Oracle warned us we would not be the same as before. She said we would leave part of ourselves in the real Caluz, the city we fled."

Somewhere in the courtroom someone giggled. There was an hysterical edge to it. Hantilia nodded toward the sound. "It's easier to bear than weeping," she said, "so I suppose we can't complain."

Safar knew he was defeated. He had no choice but to go on. "When will I see the Oracle?" he asked.

"In three more days," the Queen answered. "After I have undergone my own purification. I won't be able to see you until then."

"What about the boy?" Safar asked. "I'll need Palimak, you know."

"When I send for you," she answered, "bring him along. He'll only need a few hours of preparation."

Safar stared at her, realizing there was still a great deal more he didn't know.

He made one more attempt. "There is one other thing I'd like to ask," he said. "Something that has mystified me more than anything else."

"And what is that, my lord?" the Queen asked.

"You are all adherents of Asper," Safar said. "You wear robes with his symbol—the two-headed snake. You speak his name with zealous reverence. You even describe yourselves as members of the Cult of Asper. True?"

"Quite true," Hantilia said. "But what is the question?"

"Why is it none of your are curious about what I know of Asper?" he asked, noting the sharp reactions all about. "I have studied him most of my adult life. I doubt there is a mage in all Esmir who knows as much about his teachings as I do. I've even shown some of you his book, which I have in my possession."

He slipped the little book of Asper from his sleeve and held it up. "This is quite rare, you know," Safar said. "I got it at great personal cost. And yet none of you have asked to see it. I would have thought you'd have a team of scholars and clerks awaiting my arrival so you could copy down his words."

Hantilia sighed wearily, then said, "We are forbidden to speak of it to you. I can say no more."

"Yes, but do you have anything like it?" Safar pressed, waving the book. "If not, do you possess any artifacts from Asper at all?"

Another long silence, another shake of the Queen's head. "Again," she said, "I am forbidden to answer."

"Yes, yes, I know," Safar said, not hiding his disgust. "Have patience and all will be revealed."

Hantilia sighed, then leaned forward from her throne. Safar felt her cast the gentle spell that made her perfume headier, her presence soothing with just a hint of sensuality. But he pushed it away. She drew back and for a moment he thought she was offended. Good, he thought. That's how I meant it.

Then she sighed again. "It's the best I can do, Safar," she whispered. "Please trust me."

Safar was in a dark mood when he entered the Kyranian encampment. It was made fouler by the holiday spirit in the air, music and dance and hilarious chatter in the face of what he knew to be a most questionable future. Khysmet caught his bad temper, laid his ears back and nipped at the barking dogs.

They made a gloomy pair riding through the camp and when

people saw them they stopped what they were doing—music and laughter cutting off in mid-peal—and stared as they passed, faces turning dark with worry. His kinsmen's plummeting emotions startled Safar from his mood and he felt guilty for being the cause of it.

He could see the dread in their eyes that maybe he'd returned to announce their brief stay in paradise was ended and they must once again resume their fearful journey.

Safar hastily pulled on his old entertainer's personality, waving and laughing and shouting jokes and words of cheer. Khysmet did the high step as if born to the circus march and soon everyone's joyous mood returned. He pushed on, smiling until his lips ached, until he came to the place where his family had set up camp.

All his sisters and their husbands were gathered about a big, rough plank table, eating and making merry while the children played games under the trees. In a little potter's shelter his mother and father were making small clay necklaces as gifts for the young ones—painted jesters, with skinny limbs and peaked hats riding jauntily over long beaked noses. Toys in the shape of the Jester God, Harle, were an ancient favorite of Kyranian children.

His mother, who was running leather thongs through holes bored into the caps, was chatting gaily with his father when Safar rode up and dismounted.

When she saw him her face lit up she dropped what she was doing. "It's Safar, Khadji!" she cried. "Come home just in time!"

She ran over and embraced him while his father looked fondly on. "We're having a celebration, dear," she said. "And I was so hoping you'd come."

Myrna pulled back, eyes shining. "Thanks to you," she said, "we're safe at last. And in such a beautiful place! Why, it's almost as beautiful as home!"

Safar didn't know what to say, so he embraced her and murmured the usual loving evasions sons and daughters use when they believe one of their parents has lost all touch with reality. Such as, "I'm happy that you're happy, mother, dear." Or "Yes, I've missed you too."

And so on until his mother rushed off to fetch him a plate of the tastiest morsels from the feast. When she was gone, he eyed his father, who was painting smiling faces on the toy jesters.

"You've made your mother very happy coming home today, son," he said. "She and your sisters worked hard on this feast."

"What is she celebrating, father?" he asked, still smiling, still trying to hide his concern.

"Why, our deliverance, son," his father said brightly. "Didn't you hear what she said?"

Safar was finally tested too far and his smile dissolved. "Of course I did," he said. "But that's ridiculous."

To his surprise his father's eyes seemed to glaze over and like a child shutting out harsh words it didn't want to hear he started humming a bright little tune.

Safar kept going, trying to break through. "For the gods sake, father!" he said. "No one's been delivered. No one's safe. You know that as well as I do. Why are you letting mother think differently?"

But the whole time he spoke his father kept up the humming. When Safar finally realized he wasn't getting through and gave up, Khadji broke off and resumed his side of the conversation.

"It's such a relief to all of us that you found this place, son," Khadji said. "To think we no longer have to go all the way to Syrapis to find our new home. The people here are so wonderful and generous. Why, I heard only yesterday that the Queen was selling you a good bit of land so that we can rebuild Kyrania right here."

He blinked back tears of joy. "You can't imagine how proud you've made your mother and me," he said.

Safar gave up. It was clear his family and friends had been afflicted with the same insane but merry spell as the Caluzians. He would have to do something about that soon, but just now he didn't have the heart. So he hugged his father and kissed him. Then his attention was drawn to the pile of completed jester necklaces. He picked one up to examine it and felt a faint buzz of mild magic.

"Where did you get the clay for these, father?" he asked. "They're quite . . . uh . . . unusual."

Khadji pointed up the river. "There's a nice bed of it around the next bend," he said.

He grabbed some up from a pail, skilled fingers forming another jester. "Palimak discovered it," he said. "And I must say I've never seen clay as perfect as this. A nice neutral gray color, not too sticky, not too spongy, and it fires in no time at all. And not one shattering out of the scores I've already made."

Khadji scratched his head, thinking. Then he smiled. "In fact," he said, "it was Palimak's idea to make these jesters for the children." He chuckled, "Such a thoughtful boy."

Safar narrowed his eyes when he heard that. He looked down at the large pile of completed jesters. There were also several trays of others ready to go into the oven. Plus, Khadji was painting several dozen more.

"There's a lot more here," he pointed out to his father, "than there are Timura children."

More chuckling from Khadji. "Well, after we talked about it for awhile, it seemed like such a good idea that we decided to make enough for everybody."

Safar goggled. "Everybody?"

Khadji nodded, firm. "Before we're done every Kyranian, down to the newest infant, will have one. The best of luck from Harle, the king of luck, hanging about our necks.

"Now isn't that a grand gift for everyone?" his father asked.

Safar nodded absently, puzzling over all this. What was Palimak up to? "Sure, father, sure," he said.

"Well, it's nice talking to you son," his father said. "But I'd best get back to it. I've got more than a thousand of these to make."

He started getting busy, pinching out more jesters and laying them on a firing tray. Becoming so absorbed in his work he seemed to forget his son's presence. Safar gently took his arm, stopping him. His father blinked at him, awareness coming back.

"Where is Palimak, father?" Safar asked.

Khadji again pointed up the river. "At the claybed," he said. "He's with Leiria, so you don't have to worry. They're fetching more material for the jesters."

Safar just smiled, gave his father another hug, and swung up on Khysmet. "Tell mother," he said, "that I'm off to see Palimak. And to save us some of that delicious food."

His father didn't hear him. He was humming merrily again, totally absorbed in his work. Safar shrugged and headed up the river.

He eventually found them standing on a hill, supervising a half dozen willing lads who were digging up buckets of clay from the river.

"Be sure and clean it real well," Palimak admonished two young men who were washing the debris from the clay.

"You there," Leiria called to another group. She pointed to several pails of finished clay. "Grab a couple of those buckets and trot them down to Khadji. He should be getting pretty low by now."

The lads took all this with such good nature that Safar was immediately suspicious.

When Palimak and Leiria spotted Safar they both jumped in startled guilt. Palimak ducked behind Leiria.

"I take full responsibility," Leiria said. She said it boldly, but he detected a quivering note of embarrassment.

Safar sighed and pointed at the working youths. "Let them go," he said wearily.

"Yes, father," Palimak squeaked. Then, his voice a little firmer, "But you have to let me do it my way. If they wake up too quickly they're going to feel pretty bad."

"Go ahead," Safar said.

Palimak ventured out from behind Leiria enough to wave a hand at the boys. "You're suddenly all feeling very tired," he said, trying to sound commanding. The boys all stretched and yawned. "That's good," Palimak praised. "Really, real sleepy." More stretching and yawning. "So now that you're so sleepy," Palimak said, "you all decide to go home and take a little nap. And when you wake up you'll feel just great and you won't remember anything."

The young men all nodded, then put the buckets down and wandered back toward the encampment, yawning and mumbling sleepily as they went.

"Don't worry about them, father," Palimak said. "They'll be fine." He gestured at the buckets of clay sitting by the shore. "Besides, we were almost done anyway."

This brought a hot glare from Safar. "Ooops," Palimak said, clapping a hand to his mouth.

Leiria groaned. "I wish you hadn't said that."

"We have a awfully good reason, father," Palimak said. "Honest."

"He's right," Leiria said. "We do."

"Go on," Safar said, climbing off Khysmet. He patted the animal, drawing on its powers of patience. "I'm listening. And it had better be as good as you claim."

Palimak swallowed hard, but Leiria had a completely different reaction. She blew. "Listen here, Safar Timura," she said, standing tall and hooking her thumbs into her sword belt. "In case you haven't noticed, everybody here has gone insane. They are in hap-hap happy land, where the bees don't sting and the wolves graze on grass like the lambs."

"I noticed," Safar said, gritting his teeth. "But that doesn't give—"

Leiria stomped a boot. "That doesn't give you the right," she said, "to come storming in here to dump a camel load of grief on us, after being gone for the gods know how long, and not a word from you, by the way, and we're here with all these crazy people not knowing what to do."

Safar was rattled by this verbal assault. "Still," he said, "you have to admit—"

"Admit nothing!" Leiria stormed on. "What if something happened? What if Iraj attacked right now? Everyone would just stare and giggle while his army cut them down!"

Now it was Safar's turn to be stung by guilt. "You have a stronger point than you realize about Iraj," he said. "But, honest to the gods, couldn't you have waited?"

"I repeat my last question, Safar Timura," Leiria ground in. "What if something happened?"

"It really is a good plan, father," Palimak made bold to say. "I got the idea when I found the clay."

He pointed at the gray, dug up pits at the river's edge. "Leiria and I went fishing right over there. Which is how I found all that fantastic clay."

Palimak glanced at his father and decided a self-serving aside might be called for here. So he made his eyes rounder and more innocent as he said: "Grandfather has been teaching me ever so

much about clay, father. And I've been doing my very best to learn
all I can. And so that's why I noticed the clay right off. All because
of my wonderful, wonderful grandfather, who I love more than
anything anyone can mention at all. So you can imagine, father,
how bad I felt when I put a spell on him. Again! I mean, that's
twice, now. And I knew you'd be mad, because I was mad at
myself, but like Leiria said, what were we going to do?

"Nobody would listen to me. They wouldn't even have listened
to Leiria. They're all crazy, father! Just like Leiria said. So we had
do something! And I figured out what to do soon as I saw that
clay. I was looking at how the water comes out of the turtle. You
really ought to take a close look at that turtle, father, because it is
really, really strange.

"Anyway, I saw right off the clay was not only the kind of stuff
grandfather thinks is the absolute, absolute, best, but it also had a
little bit of magic in it. And I that's when I got the idea!"

"You should have waited," Safar said again, but rather glumly,
with little force to it. "I could have talked to my father. And those
lads. I could have spoken to them and convinced them with little
trouble to help us make those amulets."

He shook his head. "I know what you're up to. You were going
to supply everyone with an amulet of the jester—and that was
clever, Palimak. But perhaps a little too mature." He looked
pointedly at Leiria.

She blushed. "Guilty," she said. "I'm an outsider. Outsiders
noticed things. And one of the first things I noticed about Kyrania
is that the tots are crazy about anything to do with Harle, the
Jester God."

Leiria gave him a defiant look, tilting up her chin. "Since
adults are only children in not so pretty skin," she said, "it only
seemed logical that it would be a figure loved by everyone. From
children to the gray hairs."

"And at the proper moment, I presume," Safar said, "Palimak
was going to cast a spell to wake everyone up to a most unpleasant
reality."

Leiria nodded. "It was acting for the greater good," she said.
"We were thinking about saving lives."

"That's right, father," Palimak piled on. "For the . . . what did

Leiria call it . . . oh, yeah—'The Greater Good.' Sure! That's what we were doing." He threw his shoulders back, intoning, "Acting for the greater good."

"Oh, bullocks' dung!" Safar snorted. "You've both gone as mad as the others!"

He dropped Khysmet's reins, wheeled about and stalked away, muttering, "I'm raising a despot! Befriended another as well! And I'm responsible! By the gods above, if they are awake and listening, please strike me dead on the spot!"

Leiria and Palimak trailed along, shrinking at his mutters. Although they knew they were right, so was he—perhaps even more so.

As Safar stalked up the hill he thought, what a ridiculous, quite human situation this was. It was certainly worthy of Harle, who had a darker sense of humor than most realized. What a joke we all are, he thought. Struggling with silly moral points while the whole world melts about our ears. I'm Palimak's moral mentor, hammering away at rights and wrongs as if they were real. As if they meant a damn. As if the gods were suddenly going to stir in the heavens and take notice that one small person, on one small world, was sticking to his moral principles. Principles supposedly handed down from on high and thereford objects of much heavenly interest.

He recalled a fragment from Asper:

"Why do I weep?" he'd asked.

And Asper's answer, after a few other rhymed musings was:

"I weep because Harle laughs!
So why not laugh instead, my friends . . .
And make the Jester's tears our revenge?"

So Safar laughed. Laughter poured from him, bursting like a pent-up flood suddenly released after much hammering on humor's gate.

He doubled up, holding his sides, wracked with laugh after laugh. What was he worried about? What did it matter if his son, aided by his best friend and former lover, cast spell nets of enslavement over his father and mother and innocent Kyranian lads? It was well meant, that was all that mattered. We're only trying to save the world, here. So we bend things a bit for the "greater good." What's the harm in that?

And wasn't he doing worse?

And wasn't he going to ask even more?

Palimak and Leiria caught up to him. They watched in silent amazement as he choked and gasped laughter.

Then he stood up straight, wiped his eyes and chin, and said, "I love you both, anyway."

He continued up the hill, taking the last few steps to the summit with his arms draped over both of them. He was still laughing, although not so uncontrollably. Just little outbursts, with chuckles building and falling in between. They grinned crazily, not knowing what he was laughing at and if they had they wouldn't have understood. But they grinned anyway. Grinned in empathy, strangely sorry that whatever they had done had made him laugh like this.

When they came to the top of the hill Safar paused to catch his breath. Below them was a broad field decked with many festive banners. And in the center of that field was a huge tent shot with bright, dazzling colors.

A familiar voice thundered from that tent, chanting a joyous, heart-wrenching refrain:

"Come one, come all! Lads and maids of Alllll ag-es! I now present to you—Methydia's Circus of Miracles!

"The Greatest Show In Esmir!"

22

THE GIFT FROM BEYOND

Palimak was circus struck. All his cares, all his troubles, all his toils smashed away by a lightning storm of the senses—color and music and smell and thrilling action crashing here and there and everywhere, all seeming chaos.

His attention, no, his whole being was snatched from one amazement to another, each sight a new experience exploding all that had come before.

But it couldn't be chaos because everything seemed to have a direction, a goal, a point, a moral, a story with heroes and villains and a beginning and middle and end. It was madness—delicious, soul-satisfying madness—but most of all it was orchestrated madness.

Commanding it all was the circus ringmaster, a fantastic, muscular dwarf with a lion's skin tossed over his magnificent torso like an ancient hero.

He had an incredible voice that reached everywhere and everyone, booming and intimate at the same time.

At the moment he was lit by a brilliant pool of light. And he was shouting:

"And now, without further ado, we present our star attraction. A wonder of all wonders.

"A gift from the heavens!"

Music blared and the dwarf gestured—hand coming up slowly, dramatically, commanding complete attention. A slowly opening fist, reaching for the heavens, promising entire volumes of mysteries that were about to be revealed. Music somehow sliding under all that anticipation, lifting it higher and higher on a rhythmic out-rushing tide of drums and pipes and strings all running toward the Mother Moon of imagination . . . and beyond.

And all the while the dwarf was saying, "Only the gods themselves could have created the wonder you are about to see, my friends. A marvel, a mystery, unveiled before your very eyes.

"Look, my friends. Look high above! Look to the heavens themselves!"

As he spoke the music and the gesturing hand crept up to the penultimate point and all eyes were fixed on the dwarf's fist as it came fully open.

Palimak jumped as cymbals crashed and a shower of sparkling bits burst from the dwarf's mighty hand, shooting up and up, carrying Palimak and the whole audience with it to the very top of the tent. It hung there for an agonizing moment, swirling and boiling like a troubled, many colored cloud, slowly forming a glittering curtain of suspense. Seemingly held up only up by the building music.

And the dwarf said, "Ladies and gentlemen, lads and lasses, beings of all ages, I present to you the one, the only . . ."

A skillful pause as the music reached its climax . . .

And then, in an enormous voice that filled the tented arena:

"Arlain!"

Cymbals crashed and the curtain burst, shattering in every direction.

Palimak, along with the entire audience, gasped as all was revealed and they saw a glorious figure dancing high above them on a wire so thin it was nearly invisible.

And the dwarf roared:

"Arlain!

"She's half dragon, half woman, my friends! And oh, what a woman she is! A great beauty, a wonder, known in every nook and cranny of Esmir. Thousands, tens of thousands, have been thrilled and fulfilled by her wondrous feats."

As he spoke fiery bits rained down on the performer and Palimak oohed and ahhed at the sight—a blazing shimmer settling on Arlain like a cloak, setting off her startling body. She was a heady, enthralling sight for everyone, but especially a small boy. For beside the scraps of see-through gossamer Arlain was clothed only in the tiniest of breast coverings, plus the merest scrap of a modesty patch about her loins. The covered part was all too human. The rest of her was just as striking and oddly seductive— an elegant white dragon who breathed fire through pearly fangs and lips, exploding all the particles drifting about her.

Palimak was instantly in love. He could see nothing, feel nothing but the presence of the strangely beautiful Arlain. And amidst all his mental bewilderment one thought leaped out from the rest: She's just like me! Except she's half dragon and I'm half demon. Other then the Favorites, Gundara and Gundaree, Palimak had never seen a being quite like himself.

The boy sat between his father and Leiria, hypnotized by Arlain, the audience's wild applause flowing over him.

He'd never attended a circus before, although he'd often tried
to imagine one. The moment he entered the tent—before he'd
even seen Arlain—Palimak's wildest circus imaginings became
pale things. Not worth ever thinking about again.

It was a place of giddy lights and wonderful music, a place of
mystery where performers did impossible things—flinging themselves across amazing heights, disappearing and appearing in
clouds of fantastic smoke, hilariously costumed clowns—six of
them—clambering out of a box too small for even one.

There was a turbaned snake charmer whose horn seemed to
contain the sounds of all instruments, from strings to drums and
pipes. But his snake was even more incredible. It rose six feet
above the basket, weaving in time to the music, and it when it
turned its head in Palimak's direction he gasped when he saw a
man's face. Then there was the acrobat clown—a husky, seemingly normal person, except that he had a very small head, which
he would continually lose—literally! The head tumbled off his
shoulders and into his hands. Then you could see it still attached
by a long rubbery neck and the acrobat would pretend to fumble
to get it back on, his eyes and mouth contorting into a series of
faces, each more comical than the other. Best of all was the
master of ceremonies, the dwarf with the muscles of a giant, who
spun the tales, leading the audience from one breath-taking
act to the next, plus performing in half-a-dozen roles at the
same time.

Palimak was stunned by all these amazements. They seemed
magical, but yet there was not one bit of real magic being used.
Otherwise he would sense it. The whole idea of this illusion
without sorcery swept him away to the Land of the Circus!

The relief of being freed from his normal cares made him feel as
light as a balloon rising in clear Kyranian skies. Although he was
small, the weight of the world had been heavy on his slender
shoulders. He was only trying to do his best but there were so
many newly discovered shouldn'ts and oughto's—with many
moral gradients of dark to light in between—that sometimes he
thought it was a conspiracy concocted by adults to keep children
in their place—whatever that might be.

Here in the circus, however, everyone was equal. On either side of him his father and Leiria were reacting like children, laughing and clapping in glee.

For a moment he became more aware of the audience, looking around and seeing they were all Caluzians, both human and demon, from infant to granny, completely fixed on the performance. This led to him to the realization that there was some other strange kind of magic in the air. The members of the audience all fed on one another's excitement and joy, becoming a warm, quivering whole reacting as one to the events in the big center ring. It was also the first time he'd seen honest emotion from the Caluzians. What he noticed most, however, was their laughter. He strained hard to think what was different about it. As close as he could get was that it seemed to come from someplace real—a sort of a home for laughter. And this gave shape and form to their laughter instead of the hazy, spell-induced giggles he normally heard.

Thinking this made him suddenly feel very alone, apart from everyone else, examining them, looking at them through the pale, cold glow of his demon side. It was unsettling and his belly lurched. He wanted badly to rejoin them, to be once again part of that warm, quivering mass that made the audience.

Then he saw Arlain and got his wish.

Safar watched the emotions play across Palimak's face, grinning in memory of his own first introduction to the art of entertainment. It was long ago and far away, but it was this very same circus. Methydia's Flying Circus, except they no longer flew and Methydia, alas, was dead.

Even without the wondrous Methydia—who had been not only a great diva, but a powerful witch—the performance was every bit as marvelous as Safar remembered. Arlain was dazzling, witness Palimak's enchantment. And there was his old mentor, Biner, the massive dwarf, who had taught him everything he knew about showmanship and illusion. And he was pleased to see Elgy and Rabix—the snake charming/music act—were just as skilled as ever. No one would ever guess that it was the snake who was the "brains" behind the act. Poor Rabix had the mind of a mouse, playing his instrument wonderfully, but following Elgy's commands. Finally, there was Kairo, he of the small detachable head and almost superhuman acrobatic talents.

Safar didn't know how his friends came to be here, although somehow he wasn't that surprised. Circus people had a way of showing up in the most amazing places and at the most interesting times.

Leiria was as entranced as anyone, but she couldn't help looking over at Safar, trying to imagine him as one of the performers.

It was surprisingly easy. His face was alight, shedding years of care and she could suddenly seem him as a dashing young showman, dressed in tights and a swirling cloak, stealing the hearts of all the women with his magical feats and athletic derring-do.

In the center ring there was a romantic aerial ballet going on, with moody lights and contemplative music.

Music that allowed uneasy memories rise to be examined in a less hurtful light. Bursting pin bubbles of a regret you could savor and enjoy like a rare and effervescent wine. The kind of wine once tasted with a lover. And you remembered its flavor like you remembered the touch of his body.

She imagined Safar, innocent and free. A handsome young performer whose eyes were only on her as he moved from one seductive act to the next.

And she had the dreamy thought: I'd have liked to have known him then. Who knows? Perhaps things would have worked out differently.

Then the music made a sharp change and two clowns rushed out into the center ring.

And Leiria snorted, thinking, Will you be serious, woman! When Safar came into your arms it was to mourn Methydia.

Methydia!

Your first dead rival.

And the damned owner of this circus!

Methydia had not only been Safar's lover but his teacher as well—as only a skilled older woman can teach a young man.

For a fleeting moment Leiria imagined she was a wise, gray-haired beauty, coiling around a youthful Safar.

Then she laughed aloud at herself. No one noticed. They were too busy howling at the clowns—Arlain chasing Biner about the ring, shooting sheets of fire at the seat of his pants.

Leiria joined in, laughing at Biner's comic yelps and leaps, letting the circus take her away.

Palimak stood before his new goddess, blushing and gulping and wishing mightily that he knew a spell to untie his tongue so he could speak.

Arlain looked down at him, a delighted smile lighting her dragon's face. "My goodneth," she lisped. "You're tho handthome! Jutht like Thafar!"

Palimak's tongue came unstuck. "I'm not really his son," he said to his instant humiliation and regret. He thought, what a stupid, stupid, thing to say! Not his son! What must she think of me?

They were in the wardrobe tent, a warren of trunks and costumes and circus props, with a long bank of mirrored makeup tables on one side cluttered with cosmetics and paints and colorful masks. Safar and Leiria were at the far end of the tent, surrounded by Biner and the other members of the circus. It was a glad reunion and there was much laughter and drinking and shouted remembrances of shared adventures on the road.

A moment before Palimak had been safely buried in the middle of that chaos, much fussed over by one and all, but it was so noisy and everyone was so excited at seeing his father, he only had to smile and nod in return. If he said something stupid it didn't matter, because no one could hear him anyway. But then Arlain, who had cooed and gushed over him even more than the others, had drawn him aside "tho we can talk." He was thrilled, then he was chilled, and when he stood before her—alone with this perfumed goddess at last—and opened his mouth he'd made a complete ass of himself.

Palimak struggled for words to set his mistake right. He said, "I mean, I am his son. But, uh, not his son. I'm kind of like . . . you know . . . adopted. I don't know who my real father is. Or my mother, either."

As soon as he was done he gave himself a mental kick. Arrgh! That was just as stupid, he thought. If not stupider!

He hung his head and kicked at the tent floor, not having the slightest idea what to do or say next. He just wanted to escape before she started laughing at him.

Arlain saw his distress and sank gracefully down on a wardrobe truck, lovely white tail tucking around her legs as she sat, her eyes now closer to Palimak's level.

"Tho I gueth we have thomething in common," she said.

Palimak's head jolted up. "What?" he asked.

Arlain sighed. "I don't know who my parenth are either," she said. "I'm an orphan. Jutht like you." She shrugged. "I think my father dropped me when he wath changing the netht."

Palimak forgot his embarrassment. "Were you adopted too?" he asked, feeling very sorry and very protective of her.

"Yeth. But not by very nithe people," she said. She glanced over at Safar, who was engrossed in a story Elgy, the human-charming snake, was telling. "You're really lucky to have a father like Thafar."

Palimak threw his shoulders back, smiling and proud. "He's the best father any boy could have," he said. "The best in the whole world!"

"That'th what I always imagined," Arlain said. "From the firtht time I met him." She leaned closer, a fellow conspirator. "I had a thecret cruth on him, you know," she said. "But don't tell anybody I thaid that. They'll teathe me. And I don't like to be teathed."

Palimak promised he wouldn't. "I don't like to be teased, either," he added with such solemnity that Arlain couldn't help but giggle again.

This time, however, a bit of smoke puffed from between her lips along with a few flames.

"Oopth!" she said, covering her mouth with a dainty paw. "I'm thorry! Thometimeth I get all exthited and forget I'm a dragon. And I accithidentaly thet thingth on fire! I'm tho clumthy, you wouldn't believe it! People get tho mad at me!"

Palimak was absolutely charmed by this confession. Arlain suddenly seemed less intimidating. More like an older sister with ordinary foibles, instead of a gorgeous, distant idol.

"I accidentally set my grandmother's wagon on fire once," he said, trying to make her feel more comfortable. "You can't believe how mad she got!" He sighed. "I guess it's hard for people to understand that you can't always help it."

"I uthed to worry about it all the time," Arlain said. "But now I don't worry tho much. I wath born thith way! Half one being, half another. Nothing I can do about it. I mean, nobody athked me if I wanted to be born."

She looked at him, smiling a smile that melted his heart. And then she said, "I thuppoth it'th the thame with you."

Palimak's eyes widened in astonishment. "How did you know?" he asked.

Arlain pretended confusion. "Know what, my thweet?"

Palimak ducked his head, suddenly embarrassed, although he didn't know why. He wanted to speak, but there was a knot in his throat that wouldn't allow it. He coughed, trying to clear a suddenly constricted throat.

Arlain said, "I'm thorry, I couldn't hear you," as if the cough was a statement.

Her voice was so kind Palimak chanced an answer. Head still down, wanting to get it over with in a quick mumble, but forcing himself to make his words clear.

He said, "How did you know that I'm . . . well . . . uh . . . what do you call it . . . special, I guess . . . Yeah. Special. Like you."

He wanted to say more, but his throat constricted. He coughed again, trying to fight past it, but what came out was still badly crippled.

"Except I'm half demon, instead of dragon. How could you tell? I try to be really careful because people get all upset when they find out. And not just human type people. Demons act the same way."

"You didn't do anything wrong," Arlain said. "I jutht thort of guethed. Maybe beingth like uth recognize each other right away."

She giggled, purposely letting a little smoke and fire leak out. But this time she didn't say, "oops," or apologize.

Instead, she said, "Not that you can't tell thoon ath you meet me," she said, hand moving gracefully through the air, going from dragon face to lush woman's body. "I can't hide who I am," she said. "It wath written all over me by my mother and father."

He nodded, but it wasn't a nod of understanding. It was an abrupt nod, a nod urging her to go on. To explain more. Mind full to bursting with questions, questions, questions. Questions he couldn't put a name to. Questions he didn't know he wanted to ask. A whole tangled fishing net of questions suddenly dragged from the depths and needing an answer. All boiling and roiling about, tantalizing silver flashes of questions, but nothing that could be picked out in all that frantic wriggling.

As his mind raced through all these things Arlain was observing him closely with her dragon eyes—wonderful eyes, eyes like an eagle, eyes that could see far and near and everything in between, eyes that could look into your heart.

Palimak desperately wanted to make some meaningful gesture—something that would show Arlain how close in nature and kind he felt to her. But he was only a boy and he hadn't the words, so in the end he blurted:

"Look at this!" Grinning and holding out a hand, eyes suddenly flaring yellow as claws needled out from his fingers. Then he leaned forward, blew on the claws and his breath became a swirl of colors—a magical imitation of Arlain's dragonfire—playing it across the claws, turning them this way and that as if in forge. Then there was a slap! as the colors burst and Palimak held up a hand that was quite ordinarily human again.

"See?" he said, a whole flood of meanings intended in that single word.

Arlain blinked—and to Palimak she caught all his meaning in that blink—then she clapped her hands in delight, making his heart leap.

"Oh, my goodneth grathiouth," she said. "That'th marveloth! You thould be in the circuth!"

Palimak goggled. "Really?" he said. Then, doubtful. "You're not just saying that to be nice, are you?"

Arlain drew herself up, dignified. "Thirtainly not! I know a born thowman when I see one!"

Then she leaned close and asked, "Would you like me to teach you?"

Palimak's eyes became very wide and very round. "Sure," he

said, heart drumming, thinking of all the things he had seen at the performance, flipping through the thrilling feats and excitement, picking what he like best.

And he said, shy, "Could I learn how to be a clown?"

Safar glanced across the tent, smiling, a little drunk at the sight of Arlain and Palimak together. Biner, sloshing drink into their cups, followed his gaze, then back again, understanding and enjoying Safar's smile.

"Damnedest' thing 'bout the circus," Biner said, "is she always finds her own." He examined his cup, grinning at memories of old times. "Look at how it was with you," he said. "Layin' out in the middle of the desert, mostly dead, then the circus comes along, sees its kindred, and swoops you up. Next thing you know you're earnin' your keep wowin' them at the fairs."

"It seemed like a miracle at the time," Safar said, remembering Methydia's great airship sweeping across the desert toward him. Then he thought of what happened later—all the glorious circus adventures, the applause, the camaraderie, the long nights of loving and learning with Methydia.

And he said, low, "I guess it really was a miracle."

Across from them Leiria peeled laughter at some jest told by Elgy. The other performers joined in, waving their arms, spilling their wine, completely wrapped up in the party.

Safar looked at Biner. "Speaking of miracles," he said, "maybe you'd better tell me about this new one before we get too drunk."

"You mean how we come to be in Caluz?" Biner said.

"Exactly."

Biner eyed him, owlish, amusement in his eyes. "Some might call it a miracle," he said, "some might call it a coincidence." He tapped his head. "Some who thinks they know it all, call it smoke and mirrors." He made a grand gesture— "Illusion! But no matter how smart they think they are, how sharp-eyed, knowin' all the tricks, the circus always gets 'em. Pulls them in. Makes them want to believe so much they ignore the wires even when the lightman's drunk and you can see the glint plain as day."

Safar shook his head, amused. He said, "Either I'm really,

really, drunk," he said, "or I'm not drunk enough. But somehow that makes sense."

Biner sloshed more wine into their cups. "In questions of drunkenness, lad," he said, "it's best to figure you ain't had enough."

They drank as Biner gathered his thoughts, then he said, "I'll give you the poster line first."

He grinned at Safar and said, "Methydia sent us!"

Safar nearly spewed out his drink.

Biner chortled. "Got your attention?"

Safar swallowed hard, wiping the spillover from his chin. And he choked, "Go ahead."

Ever the showman, Biner said not another word but climbed to his feet, hooking up the wine skin as he rose. He stumped away on his thick, short legs, leading Safar to a room off the main tent. Biner turned up an oil lamp and Safar saw the room was crowded with trunks. They were huge things, heavy with all sorts of circus gear, but Biner pushed them about as if they weighed nothing at all.

When there was enough room he perched on the lid of a vaguely familiar black trunk, covered with leather and bound by thick iron straps. He gestured at a place across from him for Safar to sit, took a slug of wine right out of the skin and passed it to Safar.

"Sad times," he sighed, "when last we met."

The sigh stirred bitter memories, carrying Safar back to another tented room where Methydia was laid out on a rough cot dying; Safar and others gathered about her. Outside a whole city was in flames, people weeping and wailing as Iraj's soldiers led them to their doom. Through the canvas doorway they could see the smoking ruins of the wondrous flying ship that was the heart, body and soul of her circus. All dead and dying now. Methydia clutching his hand and begging him to forgive Iraj, to go with him, saying it was his destiny. That it was for the good of all.

Safar was young, easily moved by death bed appeals, and he'd agreed. There were rare days that he didn't think that he'd made a grave mistake.

Then he heard Biner speak and he blinked back to the present to hear the dwarf say, "We wasn't much of a circus after that. Methydia gone. Airship burnt. No spirit in us. So we couldn't put any into the crowds. Our acts felt flat. No spark, no suspense. All of us just going through the motions.

"Not that we didn't care, we just couldn't do anythin' about it. Worse it got, the harder it got. And pretty soon we were hardly sellin' any tickets, cause the word had gone out of ahead of us that we weren't worth seein'.

"We wandered around like that, hittin' whatever fairs we could. Sometimes workin' for not much more'n our suppers."

Biner smiled at Safar, "Not that we were in danger of starvin', thanks to you. We had that fat purse of gold you gave us. Which is how we got through those times. Hells, maybe we would've woke up sooner if we didn't have that cushion. Maybe it made it easier to mope and moan and feel miserable. So instead of the best circus in all Esmir, we were the saddest.

"After awhile maybe you even start liking being miserable, although you don't know it."

Safar nodded. "I've felt that way myself," he said. "It becomes an odd sort of addiction. The emotional version of an opium merchant who loves his wares too well."

"Ain't that so?" Biner said. Then, "But one day we woke up. Threw away the pipe and opened our eyes to what was goin' on around us.

"It was at a performance, last show of the last night at a weevily little fair. You know the kind. Where the folks don't have much more'n corn dust in their pockets—and that's wormy."

Safar smiled. He remembered towns like that when he was in the circus.

"Anyway," Biner continued, "there wasn't but maybe twenty people in the house. And they were so bored even some of them were leakin' away. Then it happened. Right in the middle of the big clown act. Where Arlain's chasin' me around the ring, settin' my britches on fire?

"All of a sudden a kid start's cryin'. And I mean, really, cryin'! It was the most mournful cryin' you ever heard in your life. Like the world was endin' and the kid's scared and wants its momma but then he suddenly knows, way down deep, that when the world ends so does his momma and that is more than he can bear.

"It stopped me right in my tracks. I'm standin' there, ass on fire, but all I can see and hear is that kid, clutchin' at a raggedy woman beside him, bawlin', 'Momma! Momma!' My heart breakin' with every cry. And I'm not the only one. The whole audience is lookin' at him and pretty soon they're leakin' tears and behind me I hear Arlain say, 'Poor thing,' and I know she's cryin' too. And so were the others, Elgy and everybody. Like it was a funeral instead of a show.

"Then it hit me."

"Wait a minute," Safar said, "last I heard your ass was still on fire."

Biner laughed. "It sure was," he said. "And maybe that's what got me unstuck, because the first thing that hits me is that my behind feels like it's being grilled for supper. So I put it out. Stuck my butt in a bucket of water like I always do. And there's a hiss and the steam's risin' up around me and I start laughin' at myself. For the first time in ages I could see myself as a clown again, see in my head what a silly figure I was, squattin' in the bucket. Which, when you think about, is what most of us are doin' in real life— squattin' over our troubles without much of a clue that anythin' else is happenin' 'cause our attention is fixed on our sore asses.

"Then I think, well, we're all fools goin' to a fools' hell, so godsdamn it all!

"Damn everything but the circus!

"So I come up out of my bucket and I see that I'm no lonesome genius, because Arlain and the boys are thinkin' the same thing. We all smile at each other and I give the high sign and boom! Elgy and Rabix strike up the band and boom! we start all over again. Right from the top. The whole show. But this time we're playin' right to the kid.

"Every trick, every laugh-getter aimed for the kid, who's still cryin', still callin' for his momma, but after awhile his cries get quieter, tears goin' from a river to a trickle, until just when me and Arlain did the pants on fire number again the kid gets to laughin.' Startin' with a giggle, then a snicker, then an all out belly laugh that wouldn't quit.

"The whole audience is with us now, laughin' along with the

kid. Havin' the time of their lives. Don't matter what waits for them outside, how bad it might be, how bad it might get, this is the circus. And when you are at the circus you are free and nothin' can get to you long as the music's playin' and the clown's are clownin' and Arlain is flyin' high over your heads, beautiful and makin' dreams come true in the air."

Biner's eyes misted over at the memory. Then he coughed, coming back. "Jump to the chase. We put on one hells of a show. Sent the folks home happy, especially that kid. Just like the old days. Afterwards, we sat up all night and gave each other hells for forgettin' we were circus people. It's not a trade, it's a callin'. Like a holy mission. And the harder the times the more folks need us.

"But most of all we talked about how ashamed Methyida would of been for forgettin' all that. So the next day we packed up the tents and hit the road again. Playin' the fairs and festivals like before. But this time we had purpose. This time we had heart. We were a real circus and it made all the difference in the world."

There was a respectful silence as both men contemplated circus mystique, passing the wineskin back and forth.

Then Biner winked, humor a bright splinter in his eye. "Guess I've given you enough of a buildup," he said. "Maybe I ought to get on to the feature act."

"I wish you would," Safar said, dry. "I bought the ticket for the big tease. Which was that Methydia sent you. If that's not the case, I want my money back."

"Never fear, my lad," Biner said. "This is an honest circus. The sucker—I mean, the honored customer—always gets what he pays for."

He lumbered to his feet, saying in his ringmaster's voice, "Ladies and Gentleman, lads and lasses of all ages . . ." hauling the trunk around until it stood out clear in the light, ". . . I now present to you—"

He stopped in mid cry, hand flourish indicating the trunk. Then he winked again and said, abruptly normal voiced, "Recognize it, lad?"

Light dawned and Safar nodded, excited, "It's Methydia's," he   said.
"That's right, lad," Biner said, throwing back the top, revealing a

bright jumble of costumes and small boxes and jars and packets
and glittering bits of this and that. "It's Methydia's Amazing
Trunk of Tricks."

"That's what she called it," Safar said, smiling at the memory.
"Her Trunk of Tricks. If you needed to fix your costume, or your
act, or even if you were sick, she could always find something in
the trunk that did the job."

Biner started rummaging, tossing things aside, "Arlain came
on this about a year or so ago," he said, talking as he worked.
"We'd forgotten all about the thing and it got lost in all our gear.
But then one day Arlain had a new idea for her act and she was
lookin' for somethin' to help her out and while she was diggin'
around she found Methydia's trunk.

"Well, she figured she was saved, because whatever it was she
needed just had to be in this trunk. So she started going through
it, just like I'm doing now."

Biner was near the bottom, sweeping out the last things. Then
he turned, gesturing for Safar to come closer, saying, "And then
she saw this . . ."

Safar looked inside. At first he was puzzled: the trunk was
empty. Then in the center he saw a scrap of white lace, no bigger
than a thumbnail and he automatically reached to brush it
aside, but it stuck there, stubborn. He plucked at it, but it
remained fast.

"Just give it a bit of a tug, lad," Biner advised.

So he did, pulling gently, feeling some resistance, then it started
to give and he was lifting up a rectangular lid! He goggled at it,
realizing it was dangling from the lace, then, wide-eyed, he looked
down and saw the hidden compartment he'd revealed. It was about
six inches wide and a foot long and lined with thick black velvet.
Sitting inside, cushioned by the velvet, was a glass case.

Safar looked up at Biner, hesitant. "Go ahead, lad," the dwarf
said. "Take her out."

Gently, Safar lifted out the case. As it emerged into the light it
glittered and shimmered with color. Begging the eye to look
closer and be amazed, so Safar did, heart tap-tapping like a cob-
bler's hammers, palms moist with excitement.

When he saw it he gasped like a boy.

"It's the Airship!" he cried, holding the case out to Biner as if he didn't know already. "Methydia's Airship!"

"Sure it is, lad," Biner said, a big grin lighting his ugly face. "A perfect replica from stem to stern."

And indeed it was, a wondrous ship with graceful decks dangling beneath two marvelous balloons that made it a creature of the air, rather than the sea. All in perfect scale down to the copper burners that in real life provided the lifting power.

The lead balloon bore Methydia's beauteous face, with huge exotic eyes and sensuous lips. Beneath it was the legend: "Methydia's Flying Circus of Miracles!"

"It's so real," Safar breathed, "I feel as if I'm on it."

"There's more, lad," Biner said. "You still ain't seen the whole show. Not by half!"

He pointed at the chest. "There's somethin' else in that compartment. Somethin' you missed."

Safar glanced where he was pointing and saw a small roll of white parchment with a blue ribbon tied around the middle and creased where the edge of the case had rested. He handed Biner the glass case and lifted out the scroll.

He slid the ribbon off and as he unrolled the message he could smell Methydia's perfume floating up from the parchment. It made it seem as if she had suddenly entered the room and all he had to do was turn around and see her warm smile.

Then the scroll was fully open, revealing a simple message written in Methydia's elegant, flowing hand:

"To Safar
My heart, my love
My life
Methydia"

"When we saw that," Biner said, "we knew the ship wasn't just a pretty model."

Safar raised his head, dazed. "What?"

"The airship, lad," Biner said. "It's not a toy! It's real, lad! It's real!"

23

THE JESTER'S LAUGH

Safar goggled at the model of the airship, then at Biner, saying, "What do you mean, it's real?"

The dwarf shook his big head, laughing. "You're lookin' at me," he said, "like you think I just cut the last sandbag loose and now there's no tellin' when I'll ever come to ground again."

He put the glass case on the trunk between them. "Maybe you're right," he said. "Maybe old Biner has finally lost his way. Or maybe I was always lost, which is more likely the case. Point is, crazy or not, Arlain, Elgy . . . all of us . . . were so certain what Methydia's gift meant that we've scoured heaven and Esmir to find you.

"We almost gave up a couple of times, because with you on the run from Iraj—duckin' and dodgin' and keepin' out of sight—it seemed like we'd never track you down. Then a couple of months ago we ran into a party of those Asper heads."

"Asper heads?"

Biner grinned. "That's what we call Queen Hantilia and her crew. Not that they're not all nice beings and such. Hospitable as can be. And you couldn't ask for a better audience. Still you have to admit they're damned strange. Happy all the time, but there's something sad and maybe even a little desperate about them."

"So I've noticed," Safar said, dry.

"Anyway," Biner went on, "as luck would have it the group we met up with was late to the party. Or whatever it is they're throwin' here in Caluz. They were broken down on the road and we helped them out. Naturally, we noticed the robes they were wearin', with the Asper symbols on 'em. And just as naturally we knew you were real interested in anythin' to do with the old boy. So we asked and they babbled their heads off about the Oracle orderin' them all to Caluz. Not only that, they said the same Oracle predicted you would be there. That the stars and planets were all linin' up for a big show and you'd be the main attraction. A command performance, so to speak.

"Well, we all figured there were too many coincidences to sail over. And that crazy as those Asper heads might seem, we'd be damned fools if we didn't see what was what. Make a long story short, we went along with them."

He eyed Safar, chuckling. "So here we are . . . and here you are . . . so I guess those Asper heads aren't so crazy after all."

"Apparently not," Safar said, smiling. "And they're aren't enough words to thank you for what you've done. You risked your lives for me."

"Some of it was for you," Biner said. "But mostly it was for Methydia. It's what she would have wanted us to do." He hooked up the wineskin and drank. Then, "Now maybe I'd better explain about the airship bein' real and stuff."

Safar took the wineskin from him. "Wait'll I catch up to you," he said. "I think I'm going to need it." He drank deeply, wiped his chin, then said, "All right. I'm ready."

"Actually, it's pretty simple," Biner said. "But I won't begrudge a man a good drink whether he's goin' to need it or not.

"See, it's like this. Methydia always told us the airship was made by two old lovers each tryin' to get the better of the other. She had different versions of the story, dependin' on her moods, but they all pretty much worked out the same. Which was that the airship was built of a rare wood that was extra light, but still real strong, plus it was powered by special spells to help the burners lift the balloons."

"She also said it was one of a kind," Safar pointed out.

"You're as right as you can be, lad," Biner said. "But you weren't with us much more'n a year. So you couldn't of heard all the things she said on the subject. Like the real particulars on how the ship was made.

"The main thing was, she said it was cast from a model. In other words, a small version was made first. And the airship proper was made from that. We got the idea it was a big damn spell, somethin' that took days to cast. But we always thought she meant the big ship was copied from the model. Measurements taken, or whatever, and copied with saws and hammers and big planks of that rare wood.

"But soon as we found the model and saw that note we started thinkin' differently. She was obviously thinkin' of givin' this to you before she died. Waitin' for the right time, like maybe when you left the circus to go do what you had to do. And believe me, if Methydia thought this was important enough for a farewell gift, it wouldn't be any damned toy. She didn't hold with that kind of silliness and there was no way she'd picture you wanderin' around with a pretty glass case under your arm all the time just so you could remember her."

Safar touched the delicate crystal housing the model. "I see what you mean," he said, running his fingers along the edge. "I wonder how it works."

"She probably intended to tell you in person," Biner said. "Which is why there's no directions along with the note. Hells, we couldn't even get the case open. It appears like all one solid piece with no seams, much less a lid."

Biner sighed, eyes becoming moist. "I guess she wasn't figurin' on dyin' when she did."

Safar only shook his head. What could he say?

Then his fingers bumped against a small gold stud. There was a hot snap! of static and snatched them away. "Ouch!" he said, sucking on his fingers. Then he looked closer and saw a little red needle point sticking up from the stud.

"Hold on!" he said, excitement overriding the sad memories. "I think I see it!"

There were seven other studs arranged in a pattern. Gingerly, Safar pressed them one by one, but with the surprise gone the sensation was nothing more than a barely painful pinprick. As he touched each stud a red needle point popped up, just like the first.

Biner leaned closer to look. He scratched his head, puzzled. Then he brightened. "Maybe we have to link 'em, somehow," he said. "You know, like a wire or a thread, goin' from point to point?"

Safar nodded. "Let's try it."

He found a rough spot on his sleeve, picked a piece of thread free and pulled it out, snipping it off with his teeth when he thought he had enough. Then he wove the thread around each needlepoint until they were all joined together in a web of thread. He stepped back, waiting. Nothing happened.

Biner shook his head. "Maybe it's some kind of special pattern," he said. "Trouble is, unless you got lucky it could take years before you hit on the right one."

Safar smiled. "Fortunately," he said, "I know a quicker way to find out."

He slipped the little silver dagger from his sleeve and laid it across the web, chanting an old, reliable unlocking spell:

"Conjure the key
That fits the lock.
Untangle the traces,
And cut the knot."

Suddenly there was a hiss and the case filled with smoke. The top of the case snapped open and the sides fell away and the room was filled with the smell of a heavy incense.

The airship bloomed into life, tiny burners blazing, bellows pumping, twin balloons swelling, bigger and bigger until the ship lifted off the trunk.

"By the gods," Biner breathed, "it really does work! We weren't crazy, after all!"

Safar caught the model before it could float to the ceiling. Instantly it became lifeless again. He gazed at it, thinking this might just be the edge he needed against Iraj.

He cradled the airship in his arms as if it were the woman who'd loved him enough to make him such a gift.

And he whispered, "Thank you, Methydia. Thank you."

Queen Hantilia smiled down at the scene—Safar cradling the model, Biner grinning at his friend, trunks stacked along the canvas walls of the storage room.

"It's going exactly as we wished," she said to someone behind her. A red-robed assistant moved closer, peering over Hantilia's shoulder at a hand mirror lying on the Queen's makeup table. It was a magical stage, lit by five red candles, where Safar and Biner played out their drama in miniature.

Safar's voice floated up, "Thank you, Methydia. Thank you."

The assistant giggled. "How sweet," she said. "And right on schedule, too, Your Majesty."

Hantilia waved a claw and the scene disappeared. "I'd rather allow things to boil a bit more," she said. "So let's give it another day. Make some excuse for the delay that won't arouse suspicion."

"Yes, Majesty," the assistant said.

"It shouldn't be difficult," Hantilia said. "Even though we've forbidden it, I know Lord Timura will be simply bursting with spells he needs to cast." She chuckled. "This will make it easier for him to hide his work."

"Indeed, Majesty," the assistant said.

"And that will give us time," the Queen said, "to be absolutely certain everything is ready for The Great Sacrifice."

"All will be done as you command, Majesty," the assistant said.

Hantilia sighed. "What a pity," she said, wiping an eye. "He's such a handsome young man."

As Hantilia predicted, Safar was vastly relieved when news was delivered that the date with the Oracle had been delayed one more day.

Leiria, on the other hand, was suspicious. "If it were a bargain sword in a smithy's shop," she said, "I'd pass it by, thinking the price was so cheap it'd be certain to shatter at the worst possible moment."

The two of them were strolling along the riverbank, discussing Hantilia's message.

"I don't know," Safar said, "it seemed reasonable enough. Something went wrong during the purification ceremonies. So certain steps had to be repeated. That sort of thing happened all the time to the priests in Walaria."

"It still doesn't smell right to me," Leiria said. Then she eyed Safar. "And what about you?" she asked. "Why the big change? A couple of days ago you were worrying the bit to get on with it before Iraj showed up."

Safar shook his head. "I'm still worried," he said. "But as things stand now, if he did show up we'd be chin deep in a temple privy on feast day. To start with, all our people are wandering around in a Caluzian pink cloud and it'll be at least two days before Palimak's spell is ready. Then they'll have to be organized. Soldiers whipped into shape as fast as we damn well can. Some kind of rear guard action devised so we can escape. The wagons packed and ready, animals fed and watered and everyone set to go at an instant's notice.

"As it is now, most of the work is going to be on your shoulders, Leiria. I don't know what's going to happen when Palimak and I finally get to meet with the Oracle. Or how long we'll be away. Or, hells—let's face it—even if we'll make it back. So, it's going to be up to you, Leiria. Up to you—my dearest friend—and by the gods sometimes I think you must be crazy to put up with us all."

Leiria laughed. "I'm here for the flattery," she said. "What else?"

Then, more seriously, "Let's go back a bit on your list of to do's," she said. "I'm stuck fast on the part about escaping. And I have not one, but three questions. First, what escape? Second, how escape? Third, and most important of all, where escape?"

She looked around her—the gurgling river, the idealized blue mountains beyond, the exotic city gleaming on the hillside overlooking the great stone turtle.

"Hells," she said, "I don't even know where we really are!"

"Think of it as a big bowl turned upside down in the Black Lands," Safar said. "Everything under the bowl is happy and safe—for the time being. Everything on the outside is just like it was before."

"Except, maybe worse," Leiria said.

Safar nodded. "Except, maybe worse."

Leiria chuckled. "What kind of leader are you?" she said. "Where's the cheery words? Where's the lies that things will surely be better?"

Safar pretended to be hurt. "You should have more faith in me," he said. "Next you'll be doubting that I have a plan."

"Do you?"

Safar grinned. "Actually, no," he said. "But I'm working on it. Which is the main reason why I'm glad Hantilia gave us another day. Intended or otherwise."

"Oh, my!" Leiria said. "Coming around full circle and attacking my flanks, are we? Cutting off my argument with sneaky logic. Now, is that fair?"

"I never promised fair," Safar said. "I only promised a plan."

"Seriously," Leiria said. "Do you even have an inkling?"

"A few glimmers," Safar said. "To begin with Iraj will most certainly come through the same gate we used." He pointed east to the high shale cliffs that divided Caluz from the pass. "So we can't run in that direction."

"We could delay him at the gate," Leiria pointed out. "A small force could hold him there while the rest escaped."

"I like that," Safar said. "The first thing we should do then, is to take the airship as high we can and get a peek on the other side of the cliffs. That will give us an idea of how close Iraj is getting and how much time we have."

"But how do we get out of here?" Leiria said. "Which way do we run?"

Safar pointed north, toward a low range of mountains marked by two high peaks. "Through those peaks," he said. "Somewhere beyond those mountains is the Great Sea. If we bear a little west we ought to hit Caspan, where we can hire some ships to take us to Syrapis."

Leiria grimaced, saying, "Yes, but how far away is it? A week's journey? A month? And another thing, what's between us and the sea? More of the Black Lands? Rough trails or a broad caravan track? Coralean's maps aren't any help. The ones for this area are too old to trust."

"If we have time," Safar said, "we can use the airship to find out.

"Assuming you can figure out how to turn that model into a real airship, that is," Leiria pointed out.

"Exactly," Safar said. "Which is another reason we need time. With luck I'll have it worked out before I go. But chances are, once again, it'll be you—with the help of Biner and Arlain—who will be doing the looking. And mapping the escape route."

Leiria nodded. She was quiet for a moment, then she said, "I have to ask this. What if you don't return? What if you and Palimak don't make it?"

"Then you make it, Leiria," he said, giving her shoulder a squeeze. "And, please, get as many of my people as you can out of harm's way."

"Should I go on to Syrapis?" Leiria asked.

"It's the only place I know of," Safar said, "that will be safe for awhile."

"And after that?"

Safar face darkened momentarily, then he suddenly brightened. "What the hells' the difference?" he laughed. "To misquote a good friend of mine, the 'journey will probably kill you anyway.'"

Palimak eyed the cable doubtfully. It stretched from the platform he was standing on to another platform about ten feet away.

"Go ahead, my thweet," Arlain said, "We won't let you hurt yourthelf."

The cable was only about six feet off the ground, but to the boy it seemed much higher. Arlain was posted on one side of him, Kairo on the other.

"I don't know," Palimak said, "it looks kind of scary."

"Yez done jus' fine when she were lower, me boy," Kairo said. "Matter of fact, old Kairo's never seen anyone take to the wire so quick like."

"Letthon number one in wire walking," Arlain said, "ith that height doethn't matter. Anything you can do at ground level ith no harder than when you're all the way to the top of the tent."

Palimak giggled nervously. "Are you sure?"

"Thure, I'm thure," Arlain said. "I thtarted out the thame way you did. And tho did Kairo. Firtht you put the wire on the ground and thee that it really ithn't that thmall. It only lookth that way to the audienthe when it'th high up. Then you raith it off the ground a little wayth tho you can get uthed to the way it thwayth back and forth when you move."

"We gots yez up to six feet already," Kairo said. "After this— why, the sky's the limit! And that's a fact, me boy, not smoke blowin'."

Arlain glared at Kairo. "Pleathe!" she said. "Thome of uth are thenthitive about that word."

Kairo winced. "Sorry!" Then to Palimak. "But yer gets me point, right?"

Palimak eyed the distance again, gathering courage. Licked his lips. Nodded. "Right."

"Lovely!" Arlain said, waving her tail in excitement. "Let'th go, then. Thout out when you're ready!"

Palimak gulped. "Rea-dy!" he said, voice quavering.

He took his first step. The cable gave slightly under his weight, but remained steady.

"Keep yer toes pointed out," Kairo reminded him.

"Got it!" Palimak took another step. "Toes out and eyes aimed at where I'm going."

He took several more steps, gingerly at first, keeping his outstretched arms steady, resisting the natural but wrong-headed temptation to wave them about and overbalance himself. Arlain and Kairo paced with him, ready in case he should fall.

"Very good, my thweet!" Arlain said.

Taking heart, Palimak picked up the pace and to his immense surprise it suddenly became much easier to keep his balance.

"That's it, me boy," Kairo said. "When it comes to wire walkin' the sayin' is—'briskly does it . . . and slowly goes the fool.'"

Palimak had no wish to be a fool—or a "rube" in his growing vocabulary of circus words. A "rube," he gathered was lower than low. An ignorant, "cud chewing civilian"—another circus disparagement.

He blanked the surroundings from his mind and instead imagined himself strolling along a garden path. Before he knew it he found himself stepping onto the opposite platform. Palimak spun about, gaping at what he'd done. Then the gape became a bright beam of pride.

"Ta-da!" he shouted, raising his arms high in victory.

Arlain applauded, shooting a sheet of smoky flame into the air, while Kairo lifted his head high above his shoulders and cheered.

"Ithn't that wonderful?" Arlain crowed. "Lookth like we have a new member of the thircuth!"

Palimak goggled at her. "Really?"

"Abtholutely," she said. "And it couldn't come at a better time, ithn't that tho, Kairo?"

Kairo let his head fall into hands and pumped it up and down in an exaggerated nod. "That's the truth, me boy," he said.

Palimak giggled at the strange sight—the face grinning at him from its nest between Kairo's palms—long tubular neck snaking up to his shoulders. His body jerked and the head snapped back into its proper place.

"We've been short an act for months, now," he said, looking quite normal again.

Palimak clapped his hands in glee. "Wait'll my father hears the news," he said. "I'll be a circus man, just like him."

Then he looked at them, suddenly shy. "But maybe I'd better practice some more," he said. "If it's all right."

"Sure, yer can, me boy," Kairo said.

"Great," Palimak said. "But let me announce it first."

"Announthe away," Arlain said.

Palimak threw his hands wide, in imitation of Biner's ringmaster pose. "Ladies and gentleman!" he shouted. "Lads and lasses! Beings of all ages! Methydia's Flying Circus now proudly presents . . .

"Half boy, half demon, half fly and that's three half's rolled into one. Brought to you at . . . Enormous Expense!

"Palimak The Magnificent! Ta-Da!"

Then without warning he bolted out on the wire.

"Wait!" Arlain shouted, but it was too late.

In a blink of the eye Palimak was already at the midpoint of the wire while she and Kairo raced on either side of the cable trying to keep up. The boy nearly overbalanced in the center, swaying for a moment, almost looking down and losing it, but then he remembered to fix his eyes and mind on his distant goal and he kept moving, pushing through the momentary clumsiness, until he regained his balance, practically sprinting along the wire until he reached the other side.

Once again he shouted, "Ta-Da!" and made a flourishing bow to even greater cheers from his new friends.

"What'd I say?" Kairo cried. "The boy's a natural!"

"Let's go higher!" Palimak crowed, jabbing a finger at the dim heights of the circus tents. "All the way the way to the very, tip, tip top!"

"Thlow down, thweetneth," Arlain laughed. "You're going too fatht for uth."

"She's right, me boy," Kairo chuckled. "Besides, before we go any higher yer gots to learn the next most important thing about wire walkin'."

"What's that?" the boy asked.

"Yer gotta knows how to fall," Kairo said. "Because if there's one thing that's certain in this life, me boy, it's that someday, somehow, a body's gotta fall."

"The trick," Arlain added, "ith to not get killed when you do."

Gundaree bounced up and down on his chest, chanting, "Palimak's in luu-uve. Palimak's in luu-uve!"

"Shut up!" the boy snarled, pulling the pillow around his ears.

"Don't say shut up, Little Master," Gundara admonished. Then, to his twin, "Stop teasing him! It isn't nice!"

Gundaree giggled. "But it's the truth!" He wrapped his arms about himself. "Ooh! Arlain," he mocked. "I luu-uve you so much!"

At that, Palimak lost his temper. His eyes suddenly glowed demon yellow. He pointing a finger at the Favorite, who gleeped as a sharp claw emerged.

"I don't like that!" he said.

Gundaree's little demon face drooped into infinite sorrow. Even his horn seemed to sag. Big tears welled into his eyes. "I'm sorry, Little Master," he sobbed.

For a change Gundara didn't gloat over his brother's misery. From the look in the boy's eyes he thought it best not to draw attention to himself.

Gundaree sniffed, wiping his nose, and Palimak's anger dissolved. He felt ashamed of himself for frightening the Favorite.

"I'm sorry first," he said. "You were just playing. You didn't mean it and I shouldn't have gotten so mad."

The small crisis past, both Favorites brightened considerably. "Who cares?" Gundaree said. "We're back in the circus again, that's the point."

"The point indeed, lesser brother," Gundara sneered as only he could sneer—little human features elevating into high snobbery. "Instead of teasing our poor master, we should be instructing him." He turned to Palimak, face rearranging itself into something more respectful. "We learned some excellent circus tricks when we toured with your father. If I do say so myself."

"You always say so yourself, Gundara," his sibling mocked, hands on narrow hips. "And that's because you're only talking to yourself because you're so stupid no one is listening."

Gundara sighed. "I'm only glad our poor mother isn't alive to see what her son has come to."

"Don't talk about our mother!" Gundaree shouted. "You know I hatefttuh . . ." The rest was lost as Palimak clamped his pillow over both Favorites, shutting off the quarrel.

Palimak laughed at the muffled sounds of protest. "I should have thought of this before," he said. Then, "You have to promise to quit arguing, or I won't let you out."

He bent an ear close and heard mumbles of what sounded like surrender. "Good," he said, lifting the pillow away to reveal two very rumpled Favorites. "Now it's my turn to talk."

Gundaree, a stickler for tidiness, brushed himself off. "That wasn't nice," he said. "Pillows have feathers. And I hate feathers. They give me a rash."

Gundara plucked here and there, restoring a semblance of dignity. "If you wanted to speak, Little Master," he complained, "all you had to do is ask!"

"Then I'm asking," Palimak said. "You were talking about teaching me some circus tricks. And I wanted to ask, were they magical circus tricks? But you kept arguing and arguing until I thought I was going to go crazy because you wouldn't let me talk."

Gundaree shrugged. "Of course, they're magic. That's what we do, right? Magic. We're not sweaty acrobats, or jugglers, for goodness sakes."

"We do not like to perspire," Gundara sniffed. "Call it a fault, if you like, but we were made for royalty and perspiration and royalty don't go together at all."

"But you like to eat, right?" Palimak asked, rummaging around in his blankets.

Both Favorites eyed his fumbling, then licked their lips as the boy drew out a greasy sack of treats, saying they certainly did like to eat.

"Here's the deal," Palimak said, shaking the sack. Both Favorites slavered at the smell of good things wafting out. "I'll trade you a treat for every trick you teach me. All right?"

Gundaree and Gundara made enthusiastic noises of agreement and before very long they were stuffing their mouths, while stuffing Palimak's brains.

He worked them hard and he worked them late and before they were done both Favorites were fat, full and happily perspiring.

Palimak was so absorbed he didn't sense the dark figure that crept close to his tent to listen. Gundara and Gundaree noticed, but there was no danger so they didn't mention it. Especially since the figure was Safar. He stood there for nearly an hour, face a portrait of fatherly pride at the boy's newly discovered circus talents. Arlain and Kairo were right. He was a natural.

Then a light dawned in his eyes and his smile widened. The boy had just given him an idea. An idea that might solve two problems with one blow.

"Step right up, my friends," Safar shouted. "Don't be shy. Admission is free today, ladies and gentlemen. That's right. Free!"

Dressed in the red silk shirt and white pantaloons of a circus barker, Safar was manning the ticket counter, calling out to a crowd of bemused Kyranians. Behind him the circus had been set up in the open, complete with stands surrounding a wide ring, colorful banners blowing in the breeze, and trapeze and wire walking equipment slung from high poles. Half the stands were already full of Safar's fellow villagers, who were being entertained by the clowns. The rest of the Kyranians were either filing through makeshift gates to join the others or crowding around Safar's booth. He was thoroughly enjoying himself in his old role as a ticket seller, delighting at the looks of amazement he was getting from his kinsmen. None of them, even his own family, had ever seen this side of him.

He kept up the patter. "You heard right, my friends. I said free."

Safar slapped five coins on the counter. "Not five coppers, which is our usual price."

He made a motion and the crowd gasped as one of the coins vanished. "Not four." Another motion, another disappearing coin. "Not three . . . not two . . . not even—" He held up the remaining coin— "one clipped copper." Safar flipped it into the air and to the crowd's amazement it hung there, turning over and over.

Safar gestured and there was a bang! and the coin burst into colorful bits of paper. Everyone jumped at the noise, then applauded as the paper rained down on them.

When the applause faded, Safar jumped back into verbal action. "In just one hour, friends," he shouted, "you will see sights that have dazzled the greatest courts in Esmir. Thrills, chills, and sometimes even spills. A special performance. For Kyranians only. And all for free."

Safar held up one of Palimak's clay amulets—the Jester hanging from a leather thong. Next to him were several boxes filled with similar amulets.

"And that's not all you get, my friends," he cried. "Besides the most exciting performance you have ever witnessed, we have a special gift for each and every one of you."

He waved the amulet. "It's the Jester, ladies and gentlemen, lads and lasses. The Laughing God! The slayer of ill humored devils. The Lord of Luck! Prince of Good Fortune! All wrapped up in this lovely, magical amulet, guaranteed to ward off evil spells."

The Kyranians oohed and aahed at the gift. Scores of people pushed forward, waving their hands, begging Safar to give them an amulet and let them enter.

"No need to crowd, my friends," Safar shouted as he handed amulets out by the fistful, "there's plenty for all."

He stopped a blushing young mother, babe in arms, who was too shy to take more than one. "Don't rush away, my pretty. You're forgetting the baby. He gets one too." She gratefully accepted it and sped away to see the show.

Safar kept handing out the amulets, reminding people to put them on so "the Jester can get to work for you right away. Wasted luck is lost luck, my friends. Remember that!" The Kyranians streamed through the gates, amulets dangling from their necks and found seats in the stands. Soon the whole village was accounted for and Safar rushed away to change costumes.

The first act was about to begin. And he was the star.

Meanwhile—far away, but too close, too close . . .

Iraj raged against the Black Lands, driving his troops mile after mile until they dropped, exhausted; lifting them again by his will alone to go onward, onward to Caluz, pummeled by nature and magic gone wild.

As they marched the earth heaved under them, splitting and groaning open, eager to swallow whole regiments if they were fool enough to come near. Volcanoes shuddered and burst, tornadoes and sand storms lashed out with no warning. Vicious spells, insane spells, rained from the bleak sky like ash, burning spirit and skin until they thought they could bear no more.

But then Iraj would turn his wrath on Fari and his wizards, demanding countering spells, healing spells, spells that would put heart into his troops again. He worked Fari and the wizards even harder than the soldiers. A warrior by birth and inclination, he empathized with the demons and men who made up his army. Even through the cold view of a shape changer he still bled when they bled, hungered when they hungered. If he'd had any love in him left he would have lavished it on them—human or demon, all brother warriors together.

Wizards were a different matter. A creature of magic, Iraj distrusted all sorcery. A soldier at heart, he thought wizards and war magic were only necessary evils and he was disdainful of the soft-fingered spell makers, be they demon or wizard, who made up Fari's private corps. And that's what it was, a private army within an army, a very dangerous situation for Protarus if he let it go on.

For now he was letting it be, even going so far as to let Fari think he was in supreme favor with the king. Just as he allowed Kalasariz to believe what he wanted—and Luka the same.

Poor Luka. He thought he was out of favor now, the fool in

Iraj's eyes. This was true as only a monarch can make things true, especially king to lesser king where every frown or sneer is an iron bolt to the heart. Soon, however, he would make the prince glad. Lift him high up in the royal favor of King Protarus. But at the moment he needed Fari and his miserable wizards, so it was Fari's turn to smile now, no matter how weary that smile.

Iraj took joy in demanding more from Fari and his sorcerers than he did from his troops. He ground it in, commanding more than they could give, then pushing harder and getting it after all. Spell by strength-draining spell from the wizards, blister by bloody blister from his soldiers, every moan subtracting another inch from his goal.

Even so, Iraj was a commander who led from the front, demanding as much from himself as the others, so no one had reason to complain they were being asked too much.

That night, while Safar was rejoined with his old circus mates, Fari and his sorcerers had cast yet one more spell to shield the army from the ravages of the Black Lands. It was only good for three hours at the most and now Iraj—in full wolf form—was charging across the fiery landscape, leading his army as far as he could before time ran out and they had to regroup to cast another protective spell.

A poisonous yellow fog was clamped upon the land and Iraj could barely see the cratered road before him as he bounded along on all fours. Behind him he could hear the tramp of his army and over that the howls of Fari, Luka and Kalasariz, urging the soldiers to hurry, hurry, hurry!

For Iraj the most agonizing part of the ordeal was knowing that Safar and the Kyranians had passed this way before with seeming ease. Only one of his wagons had been found abandoned on the caravan track, while Iraj's army was losing several a day. Many of the king's animals had also died, or were too sick or injured to go on. Yet not once had they found even a lost goat from the Kyranian caravan.

He couldn't understand how it was possible for Safar to accomplish so much single-handedly and with no losses to speak of. Where did he find the will, much less the power?

His spell brothers—Fari, Luka and Kalasariz—had promised

their king once Safar and the demon child were captured all their powers would be his. Then he would be not only king of kings, but the most powerful sorcerer in Esmir.

Once, that promise had been what drove him. Capturing Safar and taking his powers had been Iraj's obsession, his burning goal. But not any longer. Not since Sheesan. Now he had an even greater reason to bring Safar to ground. He had the witch's spell that would free him from his spell brothers forever. Then he could be a true King of Kings. A great emperor unchained from those foul creatures who had tricked him into spell bondage.

It was this new goal—a shining promise—that kept Iraj from falling into despair. But sometimes he couldn't help but wonder—what was it that kept Safar going? What did he see that Iraj didn't see?

And most of all, what did Safar want?

To Iraj, that had always been Safar's greatest mystery. Even when they were boys and fast friends he'd never been able to get Safar to admit his deepest desires. He kept saying he only wanted to remain in Kyrania and be a potter like his father and grandfather. Which had to be a lie, for how could someone as powerful as Safar be satisfied with so little?

Iraj's spell brothers said Safar wanted Iraj's throne. This made a great deal of sense—for what could be a greater goal for one such as Safar Timura?

Yet sometimes Iraj wondered. When his moods were the darkest and most foul he thought, what if they are wrong? What if that's not what Safar wants at all?

And if that were true—what in the hells could he want?

A hot blast of wind swept the yellow fog away. The Demon Moon was at its brightest and the barren landscape leaped up under its harsh red glow. Many miles distant Iraj could see the huge black range where the road ended. Just beyond, his officers and aides all agreed, was Caluz.

Blood suddenly boiling with eagerness to get at his prey, Iraj lifted his wolf's snout to howl. Just then the shield dissolved and the howl was strangled off by the thick yellow fog rushing in again.

Iraj gasped for breath, shifting into human form and rising on two legs. Then the wind shifted and it was easier to draw breath—

big, gulping lungsful of the hot, foul substance they called air in the Black Lands.

He heard Fari roaring orders to his mages and turned to see twenty demons in wizard's robes lofting five spell kites into the sky, each so large that it took four strong demons to control them. The wind whipped the kites high into the air, lighting crashing all around them. Electrical fire ran down wires to the ground, where they were attached to large jars with magical symbols painted on them. The jars glowed with every lightning strike, slowly building up the spell charge. When they were "filled up," Fari and his wizards would create yet another shield to protect the army for a few more hours.

Iraj tugged at his beard, growing angry at the delay.

Then one of the kites broke free, wrenching groans from the wizards who knew they'd suffer Fari's wrath for the delay the accident would cause.

Iraj watched the kite fly free across the boiling night sky and he had a sudden yearning to fly with it, to sail away to a place where he could shed crown and scepter and become an ordinary man, with ordinary cares and ordinary dreams.

And then the thought struck him—isn't that what Safar had said he'd wanted all along?

Just then a bolt of lightning struck the kite and Iraj was suddenly, unreasonably, gripped in the jaws of despair. He groaned as the kite burst into flames and plummeted toward the earth, coming apart as it fell, shattering into thousands of fiery bits. Before the burning mass hit the ground a blast of wind swept it up again, carrying it high into the sky—like a meteor shower in reverse.

Iraj's hopes soared with it, climbing higher and higher, then pausing to hang just beneath the blood-stained heavens.

There it took on a strange form—a human-like figure with a familiar cap and beaked nose. All sputtering with multi-colored fire.

Then it dawned on him—It was the Jester. The playful god. And the Crown Prince of Luck.

Iraj smiled at the omen, confidence flooding back, making him feel stronger than ever before.

It was a promise, he thought, of things to come.

24

ASPER'S SONG

Biner stood in the center ring, resplendent in his dashing ring-master's costume. "Ladies and gentlemen," he cried. "Lads and lasses of all ages. Welcome to the circus!"

The Kyranians were rapt, all wearing huge smiles, clutching their jester amulets and listening closely to Biner's every word.

"This is a special program today," Biner continued, "for all our Kyranian friends. So we won't begin the usual way. First off, I want to tell you that our little company has always held Kyrania dear to our hearts. We had the rare good fortune of meeting one of your sons long ago and heard all about you." He grinned. "That young man, by the way, is known to you as Safar Timura. Some might even call him Lord Timura. But when he performed with us he was known far and wide as 'Safar The Magnificent!'"

He chortled and the crowd laughed with him, especially Khadji and Myrna and the other members of Safar's family who had front row seats of honor.

"Can you imagine, Myrna," Khadji whispered. "Our Safar who was always so clumsy when he was little?"

"That was from your side of the family," Myrna teased. "From my side he got 'Magnificent!'"

Khadji pretended he didn't hear. "Quiet, please, Myrna," he whispered. "I'm trying to listen."

He pointed at Biner, who was saying, "It was a name well deserved, my good people. For as we all know our friend Safar is remarkable in many ways."

Led by Myrna and Khadji, the crowd made loud noises of agreement. Biner used the diversion to palm a handful of explosive pellets.

"So put your hands together, ladies and gentlemen, lads and lasses, and give warm welcome to the one, the only . . ." Biner made a dramatic gesture, at the same time flinging the pellets to the ground, shouting, " . . . Safar The Magnificent!"

There was a heart-stopping blast of fire and a cloud of smoke, red and green and white, burst up. The crowd gasped and all eyes were fixed on the thick, swirling mass. The smoke cleared and there were more gasps as three figures emerged, posing nobly on a small platform decorated with magical symbols. In the center was Safar, wearing ceremonial wizard's robes. On his right was Palimak, decked out in his miniature soldier's outfit. To his left was Leiria, proud and tall in her glittering armor. In her hands was the black box containing the model of the airship.

The stands exploded as all the Kyranians came to their feet, clapping and cheering their village heroes. Safar motioned to his companions and they all bowed together, boosting the applause to even greater heights. He'd lost none of his skills with an audience, knowing how to take people to the edge, then bring them back again just before exhaustion crept in, making them dull and less receptive for a performance. But this time he had to press them past that point—treating the opening of the show as if it were the last encore after a long evening's entertainment. He wanted them limp and receptive to all his suggestions, so when the cheering started to fade he turned, sweeping a hand out to indicate Palimak.

The boy had been well-rehearsed and he drew himself up and gave them all a snappy salute. It had its desired effect—another long round of thunderous applause. And when that began to diminish Safar immediately turned to Leiria. She held the black box over her head as if it were a trophy and although no one in the audience had the faintest idea what was inside, this triggered a new burst of cheering.

His eyes swept the crowd and he felt an all-too familiar pang of guilt when he saw all the happy grins pasted on their faces. Safar's first job was the complete opposite of what any circus performer desired. He had to turn those smiles into grimaces of misery. Then his gaze fell on his father and mother and he saw the merry insanity in their eyes. The machine's spell made them look foolish

and his parents would rather be dead—much less miserable—
than not to have all their considerable wits about them.

So he steeled himself and when he felt the audience reach its
last dregs of energy he threw up his arms and shook his head,
urging them to stop, saying, "Thank you, thank you, my friends.
But, please. Please." His voice was magically amplified and had
the ring of command, not pleading.

Then he brought his hands down and although there was no
magic involved, it seemed like sorcery when the crowd noise sank
along with his hands. And the people dropped into their seats
with happy obedience. Their spirits were like soft clay waiting to
be molded by him.

He whispered to Palimak, "Are you ready?"

Palimak glanced down, checking the two black dots on his
sleeve. They weren't dirt specks, but Gundara and Gundaree
shrunk to the size of fleas. "Ready, father," he whispered back.

Safar nodded and turned back to the crowd. "I hope you'll all
forgive me," he said conversationally, "if I seem a little clumsy up
here. It's been more years than I like to admit since my circus
days." There were chuckles of understanding from the audience.
"And if you can't find any forgiveness to spare," he added, "please
don't blame my assistants." He smiled at Palimak and Leiria.
"Anything that goes wrong will be my fault, not theirs." More
chuckles.

Somewhere close by, Elgy and Rabix started a drum roll—low,
but building quickly.

"And so," Safar said, "without further ado . . ." and his voice
rose to a shout:

"Let the show begin!"

Drums crashed like thunder and Safar stabbed at the sky with
his silver dagger. All eyes jerked up, like puppet heads responding
to a string. A single cloud, golden in the sun and ridged like a
broken cliff face, floated overhead. A red beam of light leaped
from the dagger point, lancing the cloud. Harp music swelled and
the audience sucked in air as one, then let it out in a long sigh of
wonder as a slender stream of golden light spilled from the cloud,
arcing down like a waterfall. It fell on the platform and for a
moment all was obliterated by brilliant light. People threw up

their hands to shield their eyes. The harp music shifted to teasing pipes that made everyone smile.

Hands came down and wonder of all wonders the light was only a faint shimmer, like curtains of the sheerest yellow silk. Palimak stood alone on the platform, bathed by the golden light. The crowd gaped at him, because instead of a small boy, they were presented with a towering, but childishly slender figure, nearly twelve feet tall.

Palimak giggled nervously, which made the crowd laugh. Big as he was, the giggles made him seem like a harmless boy again.

Cymbals crashed and he shouted: "Is everybody happy!"

"YES!" the crowd roared back.

"How happy are you?" he cried.

"VERY HAPPY!" came the reply.

"That's good," Palimak said. "Because I'm going to need your help with this spell. All right?" There was an enthusiastic chorus of agreement.

"Great! Now, do you all have those amulets we gave you?" Everyone shouted that they did.

"Are you all wearing them? I mean everybody—especially the little kids like me, and the babies, too." There was much rustling and adjustment as the people all checked to see.

When he was sure they were ready, Palimak said, "Now I want you all to concentrate real hard while I say this spell."

He stopped. Shook his head. "Oh, wait a minute. I almost forgot. First you have to hold on to the amulets. Then concentrate. Got it?"

Nods all around. "Good. Now, listen real close while I say the spell."

He drew his toy sword and raised it high, chanting in his high, child's voice:

> *"Jester, Jester,*
> *What's the riddle?*
> *Up, or down, or in the middle?*
> *Jester, Jester,*
> *Tell us quick.*
> *Happy, to sad, what's the trick?"*

He waved his stubby sword and his eyes turned huge and demon yellow. A cold shudder rolled through the audience and Palimak no longer looked like such a comic figure. He seemed huge and forbidding—a giant child with a frightening grin and alien powers. The clay amulets suddenly turned uncomfortably warm and people tried to let them drop, but their hands had become unwilling fists, gripping the jester talismans tightly.

No one cried out, but there were low moans of fear that tore at Palimak, almost making him lose concentration. He saw his grandfather and grandmother and they were staring at him in terror. He nearly stopped right then, nearly turned to find his father and go running into his arms, begging him not to make him do this. It was awful. Everybody would hate him.

Gundara's voice shrilled in his ear. "Go on, Little Master! You can't stop now!"

And Gundaree added, "This was your idea, remember?"

Palimak bore down and got his focus back. Now, for the last part of the spell:

> *"I'm so sorry,*
> *I'm so blue.*
> *But a bad spell's got you,*
> *So what else can I do?*
> *Happy to sad,*
> *You're no longer glad,*
> *And I have to make you mad*
> *Because it's good for you!"*

He paused, gathering power from the Favorites, then he lashed out with his sword, shouting:

"Begone!"

He cast the spell and the sky immediately dimmed as a huge cloud moved over the arena. It was accompanied by a chill wind that rolled over the Kyranians, wet and clammy and tasting like salty tears. The villagers groaned as the machine's spell of gladness was swept away and cruel sanity returned.

There was a funeral-like wail as everyone realized they had been living an illusion. Dwelling for awhile in a mirage of happiness, while outside Iraj Protarus and his demon wolves waited, prowling and anxious to feed.

On the platform the golden light had vanished and Palimak was small again, a forlorn little boy, head hanging in shame because he had made his grandparents cry. Then Leiria and his father were embracing him and whispering words of comfort, which made him feel better—but only a little. Then they all took their places again, Safar in the center, raising his hands to address a much different crowd than he had faced only a few moments before.

"There's a lot of things I could say right now," he told them. "Beginning with how sorry I am I was forced to trick you. Such words, however, would be empty of meaning to you now."

His eyes moved from familiar face to familiar face, many of which were flushed and swollen with growing rage.

"Instead I want to caution you," he said. "I can see that many of you are angry with me and I don't blame you. Just be careful you don't turn it on yourselves. Soon you will all feel like fools for allowing yourself to become victims of the machine's spell. For that's all it was—a spell you had no control over. And that spell was caused by the turtle idol you all saw when you entered Caluz. It was the idol—a magical machine—that dulled your wits and feelings and made you insane."

This won some grudging nods from some people and a snort of understanding from his father, who had been glaring at him along with the rest. Of all the Kyranians, Khadji was perhaps the proudest of his ability to reason. To see things as they really are. Only Myrna was his match.

"What I want you to fix on instead," Safar said, "is who you are. Kyranians! The greatest and rarest of people in all the world. Many miles and months ago we set off from our homeland—not in flight. Not in fear. But on a holy mission to save all beingkind."

There were heartening murmurs of approval. Safar pressed on.

"But to accomplish this great deed," he said, "we must first guard our own lives. For if we perish, who will take up our banner? Who will shoulder our cause?"

The murmurs grew louder, especially from the young soldiers like Renor and Seth, who were spurred on by growls of approval from the grizzled Sergeant Dario.

"My dear friends," Safar said, building on that changing mood. "That is why I had to awaken you. We are faced with both the gravest of dangers and the grandest of opportunities."

Safar knew that when good and evil are placed side by side, human nature would instantly grab for the good and give less weight to the evil. So he wasn't surprised when he saw all the faces brighten as hope was suddenly raised from the dead at the news of "the grandest of opportunities."

"In a short while," Safar said, "I will be called to consult with the Oracle of Hadin. This meeting has been our purpose all along. This is why we had to face the terrors of the Black Lands to come here. For we have good reason to believe that many of the answers we seek will be revealed to us by the Oracle."

He saw frowns and knew his people were growing vaguely disappointed. They were expecting an instant pot of gold, instead of a possibly long wait for what might or might not be good news from some mysterious Oracle who might decide to have a cranky day.

Safar smoothly dealt up what they really wanted, saying, "But before that hour comes, my friends, I have a great miracle to show you."

He pointed at Leiria, who held up the long black box. "In there," he said, "is a great gift. A magical gift that will give us the edge we need against Iraj Protarus!"

Prickling with excitement, everyone craned their heads to look as Leiria ceremoniously presented the box to Safar. He opened the lid slowly, heightening the suspense.

Safar stomped his foot and there was a crack! as he set off a smoke pellet with his heel. Purple smoke obscured the platform for a moment, then it dissolved and the crowd gasped when they saw the miniature airship hovering just above his head. Safar gestured and the little furnaces sparked into life and the airship sailed about in ever widening circles, until it came to the edge of the grassy ring where it took up position and skimmed around the edges.

Everyone applauded. Khadji even cried out in recognition. The airship was vaguely similar to magical devices he had helped Safar with many years ago during the demon wars.

"That is only the beginning of the miracle, my friends," Safar said. "In exactly one hour we will cast a spell that will reveal an even greater wonder. To weave that spell I have asked all our circus friends to assist us. When you entered this arena you were promised a show—and a show you shall get!"

Safar raised his arms and shouted, "Let the circus begin!"

And crack! came another explosion of smoke. And boom! went the drums. Music blared and the airship swung about in a long arc. Then the ship plunged through the smoke, lifting it away as it emerged from the other side—as if drawing a curtain.

People rubbed their eyes in amazement. The platform was gone. In its place was a gigantic, blue-speckled egg. There was a low drum roll and the egg began to shake, harder and harder until cracks zigzagged through the shell. Then it burst open and a score of clowns rushed out, colliding and chasing and prat-falling about until the audience was roaring with laughter.

From high above came a wild cry and everyone looked up as Arlain, wearing the filmiest of silk costumes and little under that, swung out of the sky on her trapeze. She breathed long plumes of fire as she plummeted down. Then she was going up, and up, letting go of at the apex of her swing. Then somersaulting, once, twice, three times—shooting flames as she twirled. And at the last moment, hanging there, a breath from a fall to her certain death.

Then the trapeze bar came back and Arlain grabbed it and swung away to safety and thunderous applause.

"Quite spectacular," the Queen said as she viewed the scene through her mirror. "And I must say, the more I learn about our handsome young Safar Timura, the more impressed I become."

She waved at the scene in the mirror—Biner, bared torso rippling, performed an incredible feat of strength. "This is sheer genius!"

"How so, Majesty?" murmured her assistant. "Other than the obvious artistry of entertainment, I mean?"

Hantilia waved a dismissive claw at the mirror. "Oh, that's just a device," she said. "But our Safar is making that device do double duty. Possibly even triple duty, now that I think of it."

Her assistant frowned. "Your Majesty is obviously much wiser than one such as I," she said. "But I would hope my wits weren't so dull that I couldn't see at least one of the three."

Hantilia exposed her fangs in a smile and primped at her hair. "It's a good thing you don't, my dear," she said. "Or I would have to worry about you."

"I don't understand, Majesty."

"The genius I am speaking of," she said, "involves the art of manipulation. Which is what this circus is. Mass manipulation by a very powerful wizard. It's a good thing for his people that he has their best interests at heart. If he were a despot they would be his slaves."

Light dawned in the assistant's eyes. "I think I see the first, Majesty," she said. "He's using the circus to rebuild their spirits. Their morale, as they say."

"Very good, my sweet," the queen replied. "But there's more to it then mere morale. If you had looked closely at the Kyranians—after he took away their false happiness—you would have seen that many of them were on the verge of rebellion. Of outright mutiny.

"They felt, possibly even justifiably, that much of what they have endured is Safar Timura's fault. And they were ready to turn against the only one who can save them. But by the time this circus is over, they will be ready to charge through the gates of the Hells for him.

"Which is a good thing, considering what we have planned for them in the very near future."

"I can see that, Majesty," the assistant said, "but what else is Lord Timura accomplishing?"

Another gesture at the mirror—Kairo, balanced on a pole, juggling three clubs and his head. "All the acts you see are part of the spell he's building. From the silly to the sublime, he is the weaver, they are his strings.

"The egg was the first part of the spell. Followed by the clown acts to call on the Jester. Rebirth from the egg. Strength from the mighty dwarf. Fire from that marvelous dragon woman. And so forth. As the entertainment goes on you'll see what I mean—if you watch closely, that is, and use your imagination.

"He's also mixing the Kyranians—his audience—into his

magical tapestry. So when he casts the spell, they will be wedded to it. Co-creators, if you will, of the final result."

"Which will be?"

Hantilia laughed. "Oh, wait and see," she said. "I don't want to spoil it for you."

Hantilia was only wrong about one thing. She'd imagined the spell as a weaving, but in fact there was no object of any kind in Safar's mind. He was concentrating solely on the image of a person—Methydia.

As the circus continued—one act of amazement followed by another—Safar watched and worked from the sidelines. He was disguised as one of the roustabouts hauling equipment and cables around during scene changes. As each performance reached its climax he lofted a spell on the applause that followed. In a way they were love missives to Methydia. Safar imagined her in the Afterlife—still the great diva—smiling through tears at all the adulation.

The idea for the spell was drawn from Asper. Long ago the demon sage had written:

> *"My love, Remember!*
> *If ever I am exiled from your sight,*
> *Know that with my dying breath*
> *I blew one last kiss and set*
> *It free on love's sighing winds . . ."*
> *To the place where Life and Death*
> *And things that never meet*
> *Are destined to unite."*

Safar had often wondered what had caused Asper to write such a song. Who was the object of this great love affair? What was the tragedy that had ended it? Had Asper ever cast the spell buried in the verse? It seemed to Safar there wasn't enough strength in the spell to achieve Asper's goal. Had the old master wizard used some sort of mass gathering to cast it like Safar was doing with the circus? If so, what had been the result?

He saw Leiria waiting in the wings. She was mounted on a fine horse, every inch the warrior ready to do battle—except for her face which was flushed with excitement. And possibly just a little fear. Safar thought, now, isn't it strange? If Leiria were risking her own life, instead of just an audience's scorn, there would not be one mark of emotion upon her face.

Safar conjured a spell of confidence and whispered it in her direction. Then he hurled a light bomb signaling the grand finale and rushed away under cover of its crowd—dazzling glare to join his friends.

Trumpets blared and Leiria charged into the ring, smoke and light bombs bursting all around. The audience cheered wildly when they saw the standard she was bearing—a blue lake framed by cloud-capped mountains. It was the flag of Kyrania, streaming bravely as she raced about the ring.

She was enjoying herself thoroughly, now that the stage fright was gone. The change had occurred so quickly she was sure Safar had something to do with it. One moment she'd been ready to humiliate herself by spewing her guts, then the sick feeling was gone and she was burning with eagerness to show off to the crowd. Except when she'd dressed up as a clown, Leiria had been miserable, fearing at any minute she'd make a fool of herself, ruining the performance and therefore the spell. For some reason, when she was disguised as a clown it didn't seem to matter. Any clumsiness only added to the fun. Soon, even that respite faded, as the moment approached when she would take center ring and lead off the grand finale. The closer it came, the more terrified she became. When she spoke her voice came in a croak and she had to keep a firm grip on her horse's reins to keep her hands from shaking.

Now her nerves were running with a joyful fire and she laughed, sweeping off her helmet and letting her long hair stream out behind her like the flag itself. The Kyranians cheered and stomped their approval—chopped off by the crack of magical lightning. Leiria, playing her part, suddenly reined in her horse. It reared back on its hind legs and another magical lighting bolt blasted into the ground just before it. The horse trumpeted, pawing madly, nearly throwing Leiria from its back.

Caught up in the drama, the crowd shouted a warning, pointing into the sky where thick black clouds had gathered just above the arena. But it was too late, as six figures with faces like snarling beasts swept out of the clouds, swinging down on trapeze bars to within a few feet from her, then letting go—turning once in the air—and landing like cats, instantly crouching, ready to pounce with their gleaming scimitars.

They charged and the crowd groaned as Leiria was forced to drop the banner to draw her sword and defend herself. Steel clashed in time to wild music as Leiria battled the beastmen. One of the black cloaked figures—short, but massive in girth—grabbed up the banner, roaring through his bear's mask. He displayed the flag to the audience, who hissed and booed and shouted threats as he waved the banner back and forth in victory. And, indeed, for a long, agonizing moment all seemed lost as the beastmen encircled Leiria, coming at her from every side. Magical lightning blasting in front of her each time she threatened to break free.

High above, obscured by the black cloud, Palimak peered anxiously through the gaps at the action going on below. Dressed in his soldier's costume, he was standing on a platform, anxiously awaiting his turn. Safar was beside him, snapping a safety wire to his belt.

"I wish I didn't have to wear that, father," Palimak said. "It doesn't look right!"

Safar chuckled. "You're sounding like a star already," he said. "Don't worry. No one will see it. They'll be too busy following the action."

Palimak giggled. "More smoke and mirrors, father?"

"That's right, son. More smoke and mirrors. With a hefty dose of magic—applied frequently and liberally."

Safar rubbed the boy's shoulders. "Relax. You still have a little time before you get your cue."

Palimak licked his lips and nodded. Then, "Do you think she'll come, father?"

"I don't know. I hope so."

The boy became suddenly shy, ducking his head and mumbling. "Did you . . . you know . . . love her very much?"

"Yes, I did."

His voice dropped lower. "More than . . . well . . . you know . . . my mother."

"Nerisa?"

"Yes."

Safar shook his head. "I can't say," he replied. "I don't know any way to measure such a thing. I hope to never find one."

Palimak relaxed, smiling. "That's good," he said. "Thanks, father." Vague as Safar's answer was, it satisfied him. Now he could turn his full attention on the job ahead.

He patted the stone turtle in his pocket, alerting the Favorites. His father gave him a hug, saying, "It's time, son. Break a leg!"

Palimak laughed, feeling warm all over—because he was now part of the family of entertainers who knew this really meant extra special good luck. You weren't actually supposed to get your leg broken, which the boy thought was a wonderful joke.

Then Safar jerked a chain that shut off the flue of the smoke generator bolted to the top of the pole some seven feet above them. He jerked another chain, which operated a spark machine bolted just below the generator. Sparks showered through the widening gap in the cloud.

"Go!" Safar shouted, casting a spell that formed the sparks into a lighting bolt that crashed into the ground below.

Heart hammering, Palimak stepped out on the cable, which sloped to a lower platform some fifty feet away. He whispered to the Favorites, "Better get to work!"

Then he let go and slid down the wire, shouting a shrill war cry.

Safar was right, no one noticed the wires when he made his entrance. All they saw was a brave little figure in golden armor—a bow clutched in one hand—flying out of the clouds—shouting defiance at the beastmen, who had all but toppled Leiria from her horse.

When he reached the platform, he quickly drew a golden arrow from the quiver on his back, fixed it into his bow and posed his best and boldest pose—which he'd rehearsed for hours.

Palimak fired and the arrow sped toward the beastmen. It struck near the massive leader, who was still displaying the standard of Kyrania. Smoke exploded and the beastmen shrieked in anger, whirling to face Palimak. The boy fired again and this time the chieftain dropped the banner in his scramble to get away from the exploding smoke.

The tide was turned and the crowd roared in delight as Leiria recovered and attacked from the rear, knocking beastmen aside, then leaning down in an amazing feat of horsemanship and scooping up the fallen banner.

The crowd went insane, cheering their heroes on. But Safar wasn't done with them yet. Another lightning blast rocked the arena and a frightening figure dropped out of the sky. It was Arlain, dressed like an assassin in form-fitting black with a gold sash about her waist, breathing long tongues of fire at the scene below.

The Kyranians screamed warnings to their heroes but the assassin was too quick, snatching Palimak from the platform and swinging away with the boy clutched in her arms.

She dropped to the ground and held the boy high for all to see.

"Help!" Palimak shrieked. "Help me!"

Leiria saw his plight and spurred her horse forward, but Arlain froze her with a shout:

"Surrender! Or the boy dies!"

Leiria sagged, sword dropping, bowing to the inevitable.

And that's when Safar struck! A huge blast shook the arena, raising a huge bank of smoke swirling with every color. Khysmet came charging out of the smoke, horse armor picking up the colors and shattering them toward the beastmen. Another blast rocked the heavens and a great black hole opened like a gate in the cloud above. Safar, dressed in gleaming white armor and carrying a white shield emblazoned with the snake-headed sign of Asper, soared out of the cloud, roaring:

"FOR KYRANIA!"

A wire so slender it was invisible to the audience carried him down to meet Khysmet, who was circling the arena, taking his measure of the beastmen. Sparks showered out and at the same time Safar punched the release lever on his belt and dropped into Khysmet's saddle as smoothly as if he had vaulted from a sturdy fence.

And then came the organized chaos of what Biner called "The Big TBF, my lad!" Meaning, The Big Finish. It was fast, it was furious, but also quite stylized and elegant. There was none of the fake gore favored by other circus troupes. Methydia would have never permitted such a thing. "People have troubles enough," she always said, "without being reminded of the terrible things that are done. Give it art. Give it drama. Give them a little sex, a little comedy, a clown chase. And then a nice bit of action, with a happy ending that will send them all home to sweeter dreams than they had before the circus came."

So that's what Safar did. He gave the Kyranians lots of action, but with no hidden pig's bladder of blood bursting when a sword stroke was made. The battle was one of daring acrobatics and high drama, with many illusions—some circus trickery, some magical spells cast by Safar—to tell the tale. In the end, Palimak was rescued. The three heroes regrouped. The villains were driven off. And the standard retrieved.

On horseback now, Safar, Palimak and Leiria turned to the crowd and in a flourish of trumpets announced victory over the forces of evil. Leiria waving the flag of Kyrania as fireworks shattered the black clouds away and the bright sun and sweet breezes swept through the arena again.

Any cheering that had gone before was nothing to what happened now. There were whistles and screams and shouts, hands imploding, feet stomping so hard the stands swayed and creaked. Then they all poured out of their seats and into the arena, surrounding the whole circus troupe which had come out to take its bows.

Someone shouted, "For Kyrania!"

And they all took it up as a chant—all thousand of them. Refugees, torn from a sweet land, standing in the center of the Hells, shouting:

"KYRANIA! KYRANIA! KYRANIA!"

Safar let the emotion carry him until it reached its highest point. The others must have felt it too. Leiria gave his hand a squeeze and Palimak whispered, "I'm ready, father."

A gesture from Safar brought the little airship sailing out of nothingness to soar above the arena. The crowd, as if sensing something, was suddenly silent, staring up at the magical airship. Safar cast the final spell, letting it ride up and up, like a trapeze racing to its apex.

He imagined Methydia. Her smoky almond eyes. Long black

tresses streaked with silver. Cheeks bones dramatically high. Fruited lips parted in a smile. First he chanted the Balloonist's Prayer. The one Methydia had chanted every eve and every dawn:

> *"Come to us Mother Wind.*
> *Lift us in hands blessed*
> *By the warm sun.*
> *We have flown high.*
> *We have flown well.*
> *Take us in your arms, Mother Wind.*
> *And when you are done,*
> *Set us gently on the ground."*

Then he sang the words to Asper's poem:

> *"My love, Remember!*
> *If ever I am exiled from your sight,*
> *Know that with my dying breath*
> *I blew one last kiss and set*
> *It free on love's sighing winds . . ."*

He heard Palimak whisper/singing with him and smiled. Then the circus troupe and the crowd joined in, singing:

> *" . . . free on love's sighing winds*
> *To the place where Life and Death*
> *And things that never meet*
> *Are destined to unite."*

She came in a gentle wind off the river, at first nothing more than a gray wisp of fog. But it was a fog heavy with the scent of violets and soon it grew and took form. A face gradually emerging.

Safar sucked in his breath.

It was Methydia.

And she called, "Sa-fahrr."

The voice came from everywhere, but at the same time it seemed right next to his ear, saying, "Sa-fahrr . . . Sa-fahrr." Each like a long sigh.

And Safar said to the ghost, "I'm here, Methydia."

She saw him and smiled, nodding, "Safar. I see you, Safar."

He was nearly overwhelmed by the ghostly presence, her perfume and haunting voice unhinging him from his moorings. Then he saw the ghost frown—sad . . . disappointed.

Safar remembered. "Thank you for the gift, Methydia," he said. Then he held out empty hands, saying, "But I have nothing so grand for you, my love. I have only this . . ."

And he blew her the promised kiss.

He heard Methydia's deep-throated laugh of pleasure. Saw her ghost reach up with a wispy hand to mock catch his kiss. She held the closed fist to her lips—kissed it. Then opened her hand and blew . . .

Her ghostly kiss came on a heady breeze and Safar drank it in, sighing, nearly drunk with the wine sweetness of it.

Then the ghost said, "Farewell, Safar. Farewell."

And Methydia was gone.

Instead, yawning over their heads as large as any galley that sailed the Great Sea, was the airship. Transformed to full size by Methydia's ghostly kiss. The breeze singing in its lines, magical bellows pumping, fire gouting, twin balloons swollen and straining to sail away.

The Kyranians were overawed by the miracle. First there was a murmur. Then a low mutter of amazement. Then the mutter became a shouted chorus of:

"Kyrania! Kyrania!"

Biner pushed through the crowd to Safar. "By the gods," he cried, slapping him on the back so hard he was nearly bowled over. "We're ridin' the winds again, lad," he cried. "Ridin' the winds."

Queen Hantilia smiled through tears. "That was quite touching," she said, wiping her eyes.

She looked away from the scene in her mirror where the Kyranians, led by Safar, rejoiced. "I'm such an emotional creature," she said to her assistant. "My heart strings have always been plucked too easily."

"I must say, Majesty," the assistant said, "that the airship was quite a surprise. I never expected Lord Timura to do such a thing."

"He does have an amazing way of working his magic," the Queen replied. "Most of us mages just want to get the spell over with—and do the minimum required. In this case, the minimum would never have worked. Ghosts aren't easy to summon. And this Methydia was apparently a great witch—and those kinds of ghosts are hardest of all to deal with. Actually, I'm not sure anyone has ever managed what he just accomplished."

"Surely, the great Lord Asper, Majesty?" the assistant protested.

Hantilia rubbed her brow, thinking. Then she murmured, "Possibly. Just possibly." She looked at her puzzled assistant. "I'm only guessing," she said, "but part of that spell did have the ring of Asper to it."

"Pardon, Majesty," the assistant said, "but a little while ago you said that Lord Timura was attempting to accomplish three things. But you only named two. What, pray, was the third?"

The Queen gestured at the mirror, where Palimak was sitting astride Safar's shoulders, waving to the cheering crowd.

"The boy," she said. "The spell you just witnessed was a dress rehearsal for something much, much bigger. And the only way he can do it is with the boy."

The Queen sighed. "Another sad little tale in the making," she said.

She waved a claw at the mirror and the scene disappeared. "Send for Lord Timura," she commanded.

"It's time for the Great Sacrifice to begin!"

The Queen's messenger came and went and Safar retired to his tent with Palimak to get ready. They dressed in comfortable clothes—trousers, tunics, cloaks and boots—as if they faced a long journey, instead of just a short stroll to the Queen's palace.

They both carried small packs filled with magical devices and potions, as well several purses of various things hanging from their belts. Besides this, Safar had his silver dagger tucked into his sleeve and Palimak had the stone turtle containing Gundara and Gundaree tucked safely away in a large pocket inside his tunic. For weapons, Safar made sure they both had bows and a quiver of arrows. Palimak's bow was the one he'd used in the circus act, which Safar deemed more than sufficient to do the job.

As for swords, however, Safar made a little ceremony out of

giving Palimak a steel blade that been especially cut down for him, as well as a knife to balance out his belt.

Palimak straightened, a few more years of added maturity furrowing his youthful brow.

Safar stood back to admire the figure he cut. "With you at my side, son," he said, "they don't stand a chance."

Palimak chortled with delight, eyes turning demon yellow with excitement. "Let's go get them!" he said.

With that they exited the tent to say their farewells.

The Timura family waited outside. Leiria stood a little away from them, holding Khysmet's reins, saddle bags packed and ready.

Safar's mother and sisters and female cousins fussed over them, weeping all the while, while his sisters' husbands slapped them both on their backs and wished them "gods speed."

When they came to his father, Khadji knelt and embraced the boy, saying, "I'll show you some new pottery tricks when you get back." As always, Safar's father had difficulty saying what he really meant.

Palimak patted him and said, "I can hardly wait, grandfather." Trying to sound really excited about the promise and that the shining adventures he believed awaited him would be boring delays for when that moment came.

Khadji nodded, then rose to face his son. He was frowning, a little ashamed. "I guess I haven't been much help to you these last few days, son," he said.

"It was a spell, father," Safar assured him. "Nothing to do with you. There's no fault."

"Still," his father said, "I'm not happy with myself." He straightened, looking at Safar squarely. "It won't happen again."

Safar covered a confusion of emotions by giving his father a bear hug, slapping his back and telling him everything was going to be "fine, just fine."

Then they pulled apart. Safar's father seemed about to say something—lips opening, a clot of words gathering to be blurted. The moment passed and he shook his head.

"Tell the Oracle she'd better treat you right, son," he said. "Or she'll have another Timura to deal with!"

"I will, father," he said.

Safar took Palimak's hand and they turned and walked to where Leiria waited with Khysmet.

"Biner and Arlain send their apologies," she said. "They're busy rigging out the airship and loading up the gear."

"Make sure they take those packs I set aside for them," Safar said.

"They were loaded first," Leiria replied. "I watched them do it myself."

In the distance they heard Sergeant Dario curse the laziness of an errant soldier. Safar smiled.

"Sounds like you have everything else in order, too," he said.

"Dario and I are being extra hard on everyone," she laughed. "We both figure they had their fun in Happy Land. Now it's time to whip out the rest of the softness in them."

"After all these months," Safar said, "I can't think of anyone who's still soft."

"Neither can I," Leiria grinned, "but you tell that to Dario! He thinks everybody's too soft. I swear, when he dies they'll make a special rank for him in the Hells. Tormentor in chief, or something."

The two of them laughed. Palimak joined in, although a little weakly since he wasn't quite sure what they were laughing at. From what he'd seen of Dario he deserved the title, so where was the joke? There were some drawbacks to getting older and Dario, he'd decided, was definitely one of them. He shuddered when he thought of the day he'd join the older lads in training under Dario's baleful eyes and snarled insults and orders.

He snapped his fingers, saying, "I'm not worried about this Oracle at all!"

Safar and Leiria stared down at him. "What did you say?"

Palimak blushed, realizing he'd spoken aloud. He shrugged and gave the child's universal answer: "Nothing."

Leiria gave him a hug. "No matter what happens," she said, "I want you to remember Auntie Leiria's First Rule of Soldiering— When In Doubt, Find A Big Rock To Hide Under."

More laughter, final good-byes, and Safar swung into

Khysmet's saddle. He hoisted Palimak up behind him, blew Leiria
a kiss and wheeled the horse to trot away.

Leiria stared after them, wondering if she'd ever see them
again.

25

COVENANT OF DEATH

There was not a soul to be seen as Safar and Palimak rode toward
the city. The fields were empty, the farm house chimneys cold.

When they came to the gates there was no one to greet them,
much less challenge them, and when they entered the city it
seemed more like a great mausoleum, with only ghosts to watch as
they passed by shuttered windows and closed doors.

"Where is everybody, father?" Palimak asked, unconsciously
whispering.

"I don't know," Safar said.

Then they heard faint music and even fainter voices lifted in
song. The sound was coming from Hantilia's silver palace.

Safar nodded toward the sound. "I expect we'll have our answer
soon enough."

He tapped Khysmet's reins and the horse turned toward the
palace, hooves clip--clopping in eerie time with the song.

They paused at the open palace gates. Inside were hundreds
upon hundreds of red-robed Caluzians—so many the Queen's
grand courtyard was filled to the overflowing. Her acolytes made a
great circle many beings deep and in the center was Hantilia—
most regal in her Asper robes and golden crown perched above her
demon's horn. She was sitting upon a glorious throne made of
ivory studded with many colorful gems. It had a sweeping back
rising to form the symbol of Asper—the two-headed snake, wings
spread wide as if ready to strike.

Hantilia sat calmly, a beatific smile on her face, as her subjects sang:

"It is our fault, it is our fault,
Sweet Lady, Lady, Lady.
We take the sin, we take the sin,
Holy One.
On our souls, on our souls,
Sweet Lady, Lady, Lady.
No one else, no one else,
Holy One.
It is our fault, it is our fault,
Sweet Lady, Lady, Lady . . ."

It was a haunting chant that stirred deep emotions in Safar, although at first he didn't know why it should hold any meaning for him. Then he remembered the vision in Asper's tomb where Queen Charize had reigned over a nest of blind monsters. Charize had claimed to be the protector of the master wizard's bones.

Harsh-voiced memory recalled the monster queen's song:

"We are the sisters of Asper,
Sweet Lady, Lady, Lady.
We guard his tomb, we guard his tomb,
Holy One . . ."

Safar stared hard at Queen Hantilia, all his magical senses alert for the lie behind her subject's song. But there was none to be found.

Gripping the saddle, Palimak leaned back as far as he could to see around his father's bulk. The sweet voices of the great choir made him feel sorry for Hantilia's people. He didn't know why the chant should make him feel that way. It just did.

He listened as the chant continued its circuitous quest:

"It is our fault, it is our fault,
Sweet Lady, Lady, Lady.
We take the sin, we take the sin,
Holy One.
On our souls, on our souls,

Sweet Lady, Lady, Lady.
No one else, no one else,
Holy One.
It is our fault, it is our fault,
Sweet Lady, Lady, Lady . . ."

Then Queen Hantilia saw them and her smile broadened. She gestured with a crystal-topped scepter and the acolytes' voices faded to a whispered, "It is our fault, it is our fault . . ." on and on without stop.

Hantilia gestured again and the crowd parted to make a long avenue leading to her throne. Safar noticed there were crushed flower petals strewn over the path, scenting the air with their sunny corpses. He slipped off Khysmet and hitched Palimak forward into the saddle, then he took up the reins and led horse and boy down the flower-strewn avenue to meet the Queen,

When he reached the steps leading up to the throne he stopped and bowed low, tugging at Khysmet's reins, who dipped like a veteran parade horse. Palimak surprised himself by instinctively going with the current and he made his own pretty bow from the saddle.

Hantilia applauded, saying, "My! What manners! You must have been an elegant sight at Iraj Protarus' court, Safar Timura!"

She nodded at her whisper/singing acolytes. "I wish you had time to teach them what real manners are," she said. "Unfortunately, my court has always been so small and unimportant that my subjects never received much practice."

Safar made a small bow, but said nothing. It was the sort of royal statement wanting no comment. Hantilia was merely setting him at ease and it would be the height of rudeness—an implied insult to her people—to agree.

The Queen turned to Palimak who was not used to royalty at all and was a little frightened by this imperious being. Moreover, with Khysmet between him and the ground he was nearly at eye level with Hantilia and he had shyness to add to his fears for being such an obvious target of scrutiny.

The Queen said, "You must be Palimak. I've been looking forward to this meeting for quite some time." Her smile broadened.

"For one so young," she said, "you cut quite a dashing figure on that horse."

Palimak just stared at her, blushing and feeling like a goggle-eyed, frozen-tongued babe. Her voice was warm and friendly, her manner seemed genuine. But the atmosphere had unnerved him—all those beings whisper/chanting, " . . . We take the sin, we take the sin,/Holy One." Except they stretched out the "Holy One" so it was "Hoo-llyy Won-ahh." With a long hum stretching the "ahh" even more so it all sounded like a funeral.

He felt a stir in his tunic pocket and Gundara piped up, using his magical voice that could be heard by no other. "Don't be stupid, Little Master. She's only a queen. And not a very important queen at that!"

"Our queen was much grander," Gundaree added. "Much, much grander."

"Even she had to get someone to wash her dirty underwear," Gundara said. "Just like any normal being."

"No one is so royal," Gundaree put in, "they don't need to change their underwear."

Palimak started to giggle, then came unstuck. He dipped his head, and in the manner of a courtier he touched fingertips to his brow, then his breast, saying, "Your Majesty is too kind!"

Delivered in his high boy's voice, feet dangling many inches from Khysmet's stirrups, his little speech stirred laughter in the Queen. She covered with a cough, so as not to embarrass the child.

"Fine manners seem to run in the family, My Lord," she said to Safar. "You raised him well."

"Thank you, Majesty," Safar murmured.

The Queen's attention was still fixed on Palimak so Safar said nothing more. The exchange between them gave him time to cast a few sniffing spells to see what Hantilia was up to. So far he'd had little success.

"It's a pity your mother couldn't see you now," she said to the boy. "She'd be very proud."

Once again Palimak's tongue froze. He gaped at her a moment, then managed to stammer, "Y-y-you kn-kn-knew my mother?"

"I believe so, my dear," Hantilia said, demon eyes glowing softly. "Although I can't be certain, the resemblance is amazing."

Safar forgot about his spells. He was as riveted as the child. Neither one noticed that the voices of the chanters had risen slightly. Singing, "On our souls, on our souls/Sweet Lady, Lady, Lady."

And Palimak blurted—"My mother was human?" For some reason he'd always imagined his real mother was a demon.

The queen shook her head. "No, but even so, my dear, you are quite like her. Your eyes . . . the shape of your face . . . all very much the same. The more I look at you—even though she was pure demon—the more certain I become."

Hantilia leaned forward, examining him closer. She settled back in her throne. "Yes, I'm quite sure of it," she said. Then: "We called her Baalina."

"Baalina," Palimak said, rolling the name around, fixing it in his mind. "Baalina," he said again—but firmer. Then he looked at the Queen, expectant.

"She was the daughter of one of my royal attendants," Hantilia continued. "Everyone knew and admired Baalina. She was not only a great beauty, with many suitors for her hand, but she was also a very powerful and promising young sorceress."

She turned to Safar. "She was with us when the Oracle appeared and bade us to begin this journey." She sighed. "We had no experience with the road, you understand. Many of my people were lost during those early days. Including the Princess Baalina."

"Then you don't know what happened to her," Safar said. Although he was intensely curious—Baalina's talent for sorcery explained much about Palimak's extraordinary abilities—Safar asked the question more for his adopted son than for himself. The boy clearly wanted to know, but was afraid to ask.

"I can't say," Hantilia replied. "Although we heard several rumors. The most reliable was that she had been rescued by a young soldier. A human soldier. The story was that they fell in love. A child was conceived and born." She nodded at Palimak. "You, my dear." She frowned, trying to remember if there were any other details. Finally, she shook her head. "That's all I know."

"You mean, they could still be alive?" Palimak asked, voice trembling.

"No, my dear," Hantilia said, kindly as she could. "I don't

mean that. All the tales I heard agreed on at least one thing—they died in some tragic incident. That, and the fact that the child was somehow rescued."

She smiled at Palimak, saying, "And now we know that's true, don't we, my dear?" Palimak nodded. To say more would have burst a dam of tears.

Safar eyed Hantilia. Why was she bringing this up now? Why hadn't she told him this tale before so he could break the news to Palimak gently, instead of possibly unnerving the boy on the very day when he needed all of his strength and concentration.

"We'll never be able to repay Your Majesty for this kindness," he said to the Queen. "My son has long wondered about the mystery of his birth. Now he knows for certain what all of the people who love him have guessed for many years. That his mother was the kindest and sweetest of beings. A princess admired by all."

Then, to Palimak, "Maybe when we get back from seeing the Oracle you can have a longer visit with the Queen and she can tell you more."

Hantilia gazed at the two. It was a touching scene—father comforting son as best he could under the most trying of circumstances. She sensed Safar was suspicious of her motives. She was sorry for that. She wished she could tell him that all she'd done and said had been either ordained or commanded. But she couldn't.

Meanwhile, the boy was looking at her expectantly. And so the Queen said, "Your father's right, my dear. We can have a nice long chat when you return. And that's a promise."

At that moment the first of Iraj's scouts reached the entrance to the Caluzian Pass. There were six of them, all demons, and all hand-picked for their magical skills as well as for their tracking abilities.

Like Dario and Leiria they instantly saw the danger of ambush. They could also sense the strong magic emanating from somewhere deep within the bowels of the passage. This time, however, instead of the spell of humor and giddy well-being that had greeted the Kyranians, a tremendous sense of dread and certain doom radiated out at them. The spell was so strong it leaked through the shields Fari and his wizards had cast to protect them.

Shivering and gnashing their fangs in fear, the scouts drew back until they were out of range. They regrouped, repaired their shields and considered. Courage regained, several of the younger scouts wanted to continue on. Huge rewards had been offered to the first scouts who picked up the trail of Safar and the Kyranians.

Their leader, however, was a scarred veteran of similar encounters when golden bounties had outweighed common sense.

"All the gold in Esmir," he said, "won't buy us a drink in the taverns of the Hells. Let some other fiend get rich, if he dares."

With that, he unsaddled his mount and settled down to wait for the rest of the army to catch up. He broke out a package of rations and started to eat, calmly ignoring the others who were heatedly debating the pros and cons.

In the end, rare common sense prevailed over greed. Grumbling about missed opportunities, they followed his example.

Deep within the passage hollow eyes peered out at the scouts. Pale lips parted in a ghastly smile of anticipation at all the blood that would soon flow.

Then the Guardian warrior lifted his spectral horn and blew.

Hantilia shivered. The warning was for her ears only and so no one else heard the Guardian trumpeting news of Iraj Protarus' approach. The Queen signaled her assistant, who was posted at the far end of the courtyard. Then she turned to Safar and Palimak, hiding her concern with a broad smile.

"It is time, my dear ones," she said "for us to bid you farewell."

Despite her efforts to hide it, Palimak caught the eddy of magic emanating from the Queen as she gathered her powers.

At the same moment Gundara whispered a warning, "Watch out, Little Master. Something's going to happen!"

Khysmet shifted under him, snorting and swishing his tail. Alarmed, Palimak glanced at his father, who gave him a slight nod—he'd noticed too. The boy felt something soft fall over him as Safar cast a shielding spell to protect them from betrayal. Nerves tingling, the boy glanced over at the Queen. The flame in her eyes burned brighter. Whether there was good or evil there, he couldn't say.

Then the acolytes lifted their voices higher, singing, " . . .It is our fault, it is our fault,/Sweet Lady, Lady, Lady . . ."

And Hantilia intoned, "In the name of the Mother of us all, I command the Way be opened!"

She gestured and the far wall of the courtyard dissolved before their eyes. Beyond was a flower-lined pathway leading down a graceful hill to where the two rivers met. And where the Temple of Hadin waited.

The Queen pointed a long claw at the temple. "Go!" she commanded. "The Oracle awaits!"

Safar didn't hesitate. It was too late in the game for doubts, or for second-guessing Hantilia's motives. He grabbed the reins and swung into the saddle behind Palimak.

He saluted the Queen. "Until we meet again, Majesty," he said.

Hantilia smiled at him and he saw tears gathering in her eyes. "Yes, Safar Timura," she said, forcing one last lie. "Until we meet again."

Safar flipped the reins and Khysmet started forward—the chanting crowd parting to let them through. He felt Palimak shudder.

"Are you sure you want to do this, son?" He whispered. "Say the word and we'll turn back now."

Palimak shook his head. "I'm not afraid for us, father," he said. "Just for them."

From her throne Queen Hantilia watched Safar and Palimak ride toward the gateway—and the flowered path beyond. Unlike Leiria, she didn't have to stop and wonder if she'd ever see them again. She knew better. The Oracle had been quite clear on this subject from the very beginning.

They reached the gate and Khysmet hesitated a moment, then pressed forward. The air shimmered and there was a faint pop! like a bubble bursting, and then the horse and its riders were gone. But she could still hear the clip, clop of Khysmet's hooves on the seemingly empty pathway.

The Queen gestured and the gateway closed. She turned to her red-robed acolytes.

"Let the Great Sacrifice begin," she commanded.

Their voices rose in a loud chorus and she joined them in song:

"It is our fault, it is our fault,
Sweet Lady, Lady, Lady.
We take the sin, we take the sin,
Holy One.
On our souls, on our souls,
Sweet Lady, Lady, Lady.
No one else, no one else,
Holy One.
It is our fault, it is our fault,
Sweet Lady, Lady, Lady . . ."

Behind her the snake of Asper stirred into life, two pairs of eyes glowing blood red. Tongues flickering out to taste the air.

In the Kyranian encampment everyone heard the singing and stopped what they were doing, turning toward the city to listen.

"What in the Hells are they up to?" Leiria said to the group gathered about the airship.

The ship, which was straining against the strong cables that kept it earthbound, was crowded with crates of equipment that Leiria, Biner and the others had already loaded.

The muscular dwarf scratched his head. "Singing, I guess," he said.

Arlain, who was passing up a crate to Kairo, snorted. "Of courth, they're thinging!" she said. "Anyone with ear'th on hith head can tell that! The quethtion ith, why are they thinging?"

"I hope Safar and Palimak are all right," Khadji said. "I still think we should have sent a good strong force along with them . . . just in case."

Leiria sighed. "Once Safar gets a plan set in mind," she said, "there's no moving him from his course."

"Maybe it still isn't too late," Khadji said. "I could get Dario to gather up a few soldiers and go investigate."

"You won't hear me arguin'," Biner said. "For all we know those Asper heads have finally dropped their sand bags and gone starkers. He could be surrounded by a whole slaverin' bunch of them for all we know."

Leiria shook her head. "Much as I'd like to," she said, "we'd best stick to what we all agreed on. Which is to get everybody ready to run like the winds when Safar gets back." She pointed at the airship. "Plus, get that thing off the ground and do a little snooping to see what Iraj is up to."

"I thuppoth you're right," Arlain said, starting to hand up another crate to Kairo. "If we thray from the plan now, we might all be real thorry later."

"I still don't like it," Khadji said. He looked around at the others, but they'd all returned to work, lifting and stacking and stowing the gear.

"I wish I could say something to make you feel better," Leiria told him. "But anything I said would be a damned lie."

Safar heard the gates crash shut and suddenly he was enveloped in darkness. There was a blast of heat, the choking smell of sulfur and long tongues of flame snaked out to devour them. Khysmet whinnied in pain and alarm, but Safar tightened his grip on the reins to steady him, at the same time throwing his cloak over Palimak.

He dug in his knees and the great horse charged forward. There was a feeling of resistance, a thick, oily stickiness dragging at them—then they burst through and found themselves charging down a rocky path, the Demon Moon gibbering overhead. Wild spells rushing in from every side with hungry mouths to devour them.

They were in a nightmare reversal of Caluz—a barren valley with black rocks ripping through hard, blood-red dirt where gentle fields filled with fat grains and fruited orchards had once reigned. The flower-bordered pathway was now a ruined roadway filled with razor sharp pebbles and limb-threatening potholes.

Ahead loomed the huge stone turtle that was the Temple of Hadin, straddling two roiling streams of inky water—a veritable sewer of greasy liquid spouting from its beaked mouth.

Drawing on Palimak's powers, as well as his own, Safar hurled up a shield to protect them from the insane magic of the Black

Lands. Then he chanced a quick look behind and saw a blasted ruin where the Queen's palace had once stood—columns of foul-smelling smoke rising from the rubble.

The ground heaved under them and Khysmet nearly lost his footing, hooves scrabbling on loosened rock. Safar threw his weight forward and the stallion broke through, hurling himself down the steep roadway toward the temple.

Palimak peered through the folds of Safar's cloak and saw the temple growing larger as they raced toward it.

Then from somewhere a great horn trumpeted and suddenly the temple seemed to retreat.

He heard his father urge Khysmet on and he felt the stallion strain with effort for still more speed. But the faster he ran, the farther away the temple seemed to be. Retreating across the valley—rivers and all—until it was a mere pinpoint lying against the black mountains forming the most distant wall of the valley.

"It's a trick, Little Master!" Gundara squeaked from his pocket.

"To the right! Go to the right!" Gundaree urged.

Palimak nudged his father. "That way, father!" he shouted, pointing to the right of the distant temple.

Instantly, Safar veered Khysmet off the path and down a boulder-strewn slope. Now they were heading across the valley floor—appearing to angle away from the temple. They had gone no more than a few yards when the landscape shifted and once again they were closing on the huge stone turtle.

On either side of them the ground erupted like boils bursting and hot, oily liquid spewed out, flowing across their path.

Safar pressed his knees into Khysmet's sides and the stallion gathered himself like a giant spring, then leaped across the smoking streams. He landed with barely a jolt and sped onward.

Huge gray boulders hunched up in their path. Khysmet gathered himself to leap, then reared back as the boulders came alive. Rising up on saw-toothed insect legs—vicious heads beetling out from under the gray shells, pincer jaws scissoring wide.

Safar drew his sword, hacking at the nearest. There was a terrible shriek as he cut into the creature, splitting its shell. Khysmet trumpeted defiance, striking out with his front legs, crushing the attacking insect with his hard hooves.

Palimak struggled to free his own small weapon, but as it came out of its sheath a nightmare face reared up and mighty jaws snatched the sword from his hand. Safar slashed and Palimak heard another shriek, then the creature was gone.

He had time to see several other giant insects fall on their wounded brothers, tearing hungrily at the shells to get at the flesh beneath.

Khysmet carried them out of the bloody chaos and they were free, racing toward the temple—now only a few hundred yards away.

Just then the ground opened up under them and they were falling, Khysmet shrilling in fear and flailing his legs.

Below a huge mouth yawned wide and a long tongue lined with fangs shot out to take them.

In Hantilia's courtyard, the Queen came to her feet, throwing her hands high to beseech the heavens.

"Dear Mother!" she cried over the chanting acolytes. "Two innocents seek your counsel. Two innocents whose presence you commanded."

Behind her, the twin-headed snake of Asper reared up from her throne, wings spreading like a cobra's hood, venom dripping from its fangs.

And the Queen intoned, "Know them, Mother! Spare them! Keep them safe! Remember our bargain, dear lady.

"Take us in their stead!"

Hantilia stared up at the heavens, waiting. Arms spread wide to embrace her fate—and the fate of her followers. For the first time in many years she felt at peace. Her mission was done. What would be, would be.

Then lightning blasted from the skies. She felt a terrible, searing pain.

And all was darkness.

And all was peace.

Leiria was thrown from her feet by the force of the blast. She hit the ground hard, breath knocked out of her. She heard people cry out—some in fear, some calling to others to ask if they were all right.

Then she could breathe again, gulping in all the air her lungs would hold. Awareness returned and the first she noticed was that the air tasted like blood—as if she were suddenly transported to a gigantic meat market, with aisle upon aisle of freshly skinned animal corpses hanging from hooks.

She groaned to her feet, ears ringing from the blast, looking around the encampment with dazed eyes, expecting the worst. To her amazement no one appeared hurt. Like her, people were climbing to their feet, patting themselves for signs of injury, or soothing crying children.

"By the gods who hate us," she heard Biner exclaim, "would you look at that!"

She turned to find him pointing at the city—or at the place where the city had once stood. Now it was nothing but a smoking ruin perched on a blasted hilltop. Only the Queen's palace still stood—towers oddly twisted and sagging.

Leiria heard someone moan and saw Khadji, who was staring at the ruins, tears streaming from his eyes.

"Safar!" he groaned. "Safar!"

Leiria felt as if her heart had been torn from her chest. She raced for a panicked horse, grabbed its loose reins and vaulted into the saddle—wrenching the poor beast's head around until it faced Caluz, then digging in her heels, spurring it forward. She was halfway up the hillside before anyone else had wits enough to follow.

Leiria was a soldier who had seen many horrors, but there was nothing in her experience to brace her for the devastation she witnessed in Caluz. Other than the palace, not one building was standing. Everything, including the strong walls encircling the city, had been reduced to waist-high piles of rubble as if a gigantic hand had flattened them. The streets were buckled, pavement hurled up in every direction, making it difficult for the horse to walk, much less gallop at the pace she'd originally demanded.

By the time she reached the palace several others, including Khadji, Biner and Sergeant Dario, had caught up with her. They all paused at the open gates, fearful to look inside. Leiria spurred her horse forward. It whinnied in fear, eyes rolling wildly, mouth frothing, fighting her so hard that she finally gave up and dismounted. The horse bolted away as soon as she dropped the reins. Leiria braced herself and walked through the gates.

At first it seemed a peaceful scene. Hundreds upon hundreds of red-robed figures were lying on the ground—limbs and clothing all neatly arranged as if they had fallen asleep. Raised on a platform in the center of the courtyard was the Queen's ornate throne, presided over by the carved Asper snake. Slumped at the foot of the throne was the still body of Hantilia.

"Dead!" she heard Dario growl. "Ever' blessed one of 'em."

Numb, Leiria stalked forward, stepping over the robed figures, until she came to the throne and mounted the steps. She looked down at Hantilia's corpse, feeling oddly removed, as if looking down from a great distance. The Queen's features were peaceful. Smiling.

"Where's Safar?" she heard Khadji demand. "And Palimak! Where's little Palimak?"

Leiria glanced around the courtyard, picking over body after body, heart hammering at her ribs, expecting at any moment to discover Safar lying among them.

"I don't see him," she mumbled. "Or Palimak, either." She kept looking, wits dull as old brass. "And the horse," she said. "Khysmet. There's no way you could miss him!"

Someone caught her arm and she looked around and found Khadji staring at her, eyes desperate.

"Where are they?" he demanded, acting as if she were cruelly withholding information.

"I don't know," she said.

Khadji gripped her arm harder. "Do you think they're dead?"

"I don't know that either," Leiria said.

One moment Safar and Palimak were falling toward a ghastly death and then there was a great clap of thunder and suddenly they were trotting along the rocky floor of a huge cave, dazzled by the sunlight streaming through the entrance. There was the sound of bursting waves and a shallow river of foamy water rushed into the cave, hissing around Khysmet's legs as he splashed toward the light.

The light broke across them as they exited the cave and they found themselves traversing a peaceful beach—a cool, salty breeze blowing, while overhead gulls wheeled in clear blue skies, crying for their supper.

Khysmet was the first to recover. He snorted in surprise, then shook his head in delight at still being alive and trotted through the foamy surf toward a distant spit of land jutting out into a rolling ocean.

Palimak came out of his shock, peering out at ocean. "Is this real, father?" he said, voice croaking in wonder. "Or are we still in the Black Lands?"

Safar laughed and gave him a hug. "What a son you are!" he exclaimed. "One minute we're facing certain death. The next, we appear to be safe. And the first words out of your mouth are—'is it real?'"

Palimak flushed happily at the compliment. But his eyes were drinking in the vision of the rolling seas and gently crashing waves. A child of the mountains, he'd never experienced the ocean before.

He shook himself—not unlike Khysmet. Still the vision of an endless rolling horizon persisted, beckoning to him, calling with the voice of the gulls.

Again he asked, "Is it real, father?"

Safar threw back his cloak to catch the fresh breezes. "Real as can be, son," he said.

Palimak sighed relief. Then he frowned. "But where are we, exactly?"

Safar studied their surroundings—the ocean was to their left and to the right was a vast range of green mountains hugging the coastline. He mentally correlated what he could see with his memory of the maps Coralean had given them.

He pointed south at the mountains. Two peaks commanded the center of the range. "As near as I can tell," he said, "Caluz—and the Black Lands—are beyond those peaks." He nodded at the vast ocean to their left. "And that's the Great Sea," he added. "It could be nothing else. Near as I can tell, some magical way has been opened between Caluz and the sea."

The boy was only mildly surprised. He was still young enough so it didn't seem so strange that they'd been transported hundreds of miles.

He studied the vast oceanic distances for a moment, then said, "And Syrapis is somewhere out there?"

"Yes. I believe so."

"But it must be very far. How do we get there?"

"The same way we got here, son," Safar answered. "Magic."

Although his manner was sanguine, Safar was just as surprised as the boy. From the very beginning, he hadn't been sure what to expect. Even if he had let his imagination run free, he would never have dreamed such a thing could happen. He peered ahead, studying the small peninsula they were heading toward. A powerful wave of sorcery was emanating from that direction, pulling at them—urging them onward.

Safar was certain that the Oracle was waiting for them there.

Then Khysmet perked up his ears. He whinnied and quickened his pace. Up ahead, riding off the land spit, was a sight that made Safar's heart jump—a glorious woman with long ebony limbs and flowing hair trotted toward them on a spirited black mare.

The woman waved at them. Her laughter was sweet music floating on the ocean breezes and Safar forgot all caution.

"Do you know her, father?" Palimak asked.

"Yes," he answered, voice husky. "I know her."

Khysmet broke into a gallop and they skimmed across the sandy beach toward the woman.

Palimak felt a scratching in his pocket. Then Gundara spoke up: "Little Master! There's something you should know. I hate to contradict Lord Timura, but everything he's said about this place is wrong!"

"None of this is real, Little Master." Gundaree added. "Can't you feel it? We're inside the machine! And Lord Timura doesn't know it!"

At that moment the light suddenly dimmed and a freezing wind blasted off the seas.

And it began to snow.

Part Four

Spellbound

26

IRAJ AND THE UNHOLY THREE

The first attempts on Caluz were a disaster.

Iraj sent one hundred hand-picked men and demons into the pass and not one returned. He sent a hundred more, setting up a throne post at the entrance—guarded by his toughest and most loyal troops—so he could closely observe everything that happened.

He saw nothing, but he heard more than enough to ice even his shape-changer's veins. There were trumpets and challenging shouts, the clash of weapons, screams from the wounded and a chorus of ghostly groans as his fighters breathed their last and shed their souls. Then all was silence.

There was movement at the mouth of the pass. Through narrowed eyes Iraj saw a lone figure stagger out. It was a man, bearing his weight on his spear, dragging the remains of a shattered shield behind him. It made Iraj glad the sole survivor was human. One of his own, as a matter of fact, from the make of his costume—spurred boots and baggy breeches, short bow over his shoulders, scimitar at his waist. An old soldier from Iraj's homeland on the Plains of Jaspar.

Iraj was deeply affected by the sight of the battered soldier. Old emotions, human emotions, emotions that had been long absent in his heart, surged into the light. First pity welled up, then homesickness, then guilt for allowing one of his own to be so mistreated. Iraj bolted from his throne and went to his kinsman, guards and servants scampering to keep up.

When he reached the soldier the man stopped, wavering, confused at having his way blocked. His eyes were wild, his face a

bloody mask and when he finally noticed Iraj he shrieked and
threw up his ruined shield to protect himself, spear point rising to
counterstrike. Iraj jerked back, easily avoiding the spear. But then
all his speed was called for as his guards leaped in to kill the man
for daring to threaten the king. Iraj sent two big demons
sprawling from the force of his blow.

"Hold!" he shouted, freezing the others in place. His retinue
goggled at him, desperately trying to decipher the king's intent.
He ignored them, turning back to the old plainsman.

"Pardon, Cousin," he said gently as he could, "but you seem to
be without horse." Meaning, in the argot of Jaspar, that the man
was in great difficulty.

"Monster!" the man shouted, stabbing at the air with his spear.
"You took my horse but you won't take me!"

Iraj brushed the spear aside and grabbed the man by the shoulders. "What's wrong with you?" he barked. "Have you gone
mad?"

Then he saw his own reflection in the man's eyes—a great gray
wolf rearing up—and he knew the reason for the man's fear—why,
he'd called his own kinsman "Monster!"

Iraj concentrated, making his form as human as possible, and
the old soldier suddenly recognized him.

The man fell to his knees, babbling. "So sorry, Majesty! Didn't
mean to . . . I must've been mad to think . . . But it was awful,
Sire! Bloody, awful! Nothin' but ghosts in there, I tell you!
Nothin' but ghosts. You can't get a hand on 'em, much less a good
poke with your spear . . ."

The man broke down, tears making a bloody track on his face.
He shook his head. "I'm . . . I'm . . . I'm sorry, Majesty. I have
failed you!"

Iraj was powerfully moved by the sight of one his most faithful
and long-serving kinsmen brought so low. Then the man drew
himself up—turning from shambling wreck to a proud old
soldier.

"Give me the knife, Cousin," he demanded, plucking at Iraj's
belt for the curved knife hanging there, "so I can end my shame!"

Iraj let him take it, but as the soldier shifted his grip to plunge
the knife into his heart he stayed his hand.

"This isn't necessary, my friend," he said. "You are not at fault this day! No failure can be laid at your feet." Iraj thumped his chest. "It is your king's doing, Cousin," he said. "Blame no other."

The man sagged in relief and Iraj caught him, slipping the knife from his hands and returning it to its sheath. He steadied the soldier, turning him toward the great pavilion that housed his traveling court.

"Come," he said. "Let us eat and drink and boast of the deeds of our youth. And when you recover your horse, your strength, we can talk about what went on this day."

The two of them—Iraj nearly carrying his charge—moved toward the pavilion. Without being ordered, servants ran ahead to prepare an impromptu banquet for the king and his new companion.

Iraj paused at the entrance to speak with his aides. "Send for the Lords Fari and Luka," he ordered. "And that bastard Kalasariz, if you see him about. Probably hiding under some rock is my guess. Tell them their king wishes to speak to them immediately!"

The aides rushed off to do his bidding. Iraj looked down at the old soldier, who seemed to be recovering somewhat.

"What is your name, my friend?" he inquired. "What do the other men of Jaspar call you?"

"Vister, Majesty," the man replied. "Sergeant Vister at yer service!" He tried to draw himself up in salute and nearly toppled over.

Iraj steadied him. "Let's get a few drinks in you, Cousin Vister," he said, "before you try that again."

As they strode into the pavilion the first few flakes of snow began to fall. Then the flakes became a flurry and the skies turned pewter gray. The snow fell harder—flakes the size of small pillows drawing a blanket of white across the stark terrain. Even the Demon Moon became diminished—an orange grin peering through the gray. Soon the entire encampment was buried in snow and the soldiers were turned out to dig paths to the tented barracks and clear the main road.

Fari and Luka arrived at Protarus' headquarters but were denied entrance while the King supped with Vister. Finally

Kalasariz arrived, shivering in the cold despite the thick fur cloak he wore. He was surprised when he saw the two demons cursing and stomping about in the snow.

"What's the difficulty?" he asked. "Is the King in one of his foul moods again?"

"Who can tell?" Luka grumbled, horned brow made pale green by frost. He snorted twin columns of steam in the frigid air. "Foul or fair, all his moods seem for the worst these days."

Fari gestured at the Caluzian Pass, where several of his demon wizards were huddled miserably by the entrance tending smoking pots of magical incense.

"From what I can gather," the old demon said, "all our efforts have been brought to a massive halt so our master could talk over old times with some lowly sergeant." He shrugged, miniature avalanches of snow cascading from his shoulders. "It's a pity, really. All this snow is a great help to us."

Kalasariz frowned, then realized how much better he'd felt since the snow started. No more constant battering of wild Black Lands spells.

"I thought perhaps you had come up with some new shield," he said to Fari.

The old demon snorted. "Who has had the time for such experiments?" he said. "No, it's the storm that's doing it. As near as I can tell the snow blocks—or possibly even blinds—the machine at Caluz."

"Which means the devils inside that pass," Luka broke in, "ought to be ripe for the plucking. It's my guess that one more attack ought to knock them loose."

Kalasariz cocked an eyebrow, amused. "I assume you've told the King this," he said.

Luka barked laughter. "No, my Lord," he said, making a mock bow. "We were waiting for you to bless us with your esteemed presence. You seem to be in the greatest favor with our Lord and Master these days. We thought you could tell him for us."

Kalasariz grinned. "And wouldn't that make me the prince of fools," he said. "Especially when I know for a fact that neither of you are sure who exactly is opposing us in that pass."

"I really must speak to you at length someday," Fari said, "on your spying methods. Not even the flies in the latrines escape your notice."

"That's true," Luka said. "Sometimes I think you can see up our arses."

"Now you've guessed my secret," Kalasariz joked. "The flies are in my employ."

All three of them laughed—forming a temporary bond in this rare moment of shared humor.

Fari was old enough and wise enough to recognize opportunity first. "Let's speak honestly for a change, my brothers," he said. "Or should I call us the Unholy Three." He chuckled. "I've heard that name for us bandied about in the ranks. Rumor has it that the King himself calls us that behind our backs. However, no matter the intent of the fellow who originally coined the term, I think it fits us all quite well."

"The Unholy Three," Kalasariz murmured. Then he smiled. "I like that. I think we should keep it."

Luka snorted. "Forget the game playing, my Lord," he said. "Call us what you will. But please . . . get to the point."

Fari was careful not to take offense. "Very well," he said. "I'll dispense with pleasantries and reach down for the final sum of our woes. In a few minutes the King will call us before him. How shall we advise him?"

"How can we advise him," Kalasariz said, "when we don't know what's happening in that pass?"

"We do know it isn't Safar Timura or his Kyranians who are killing our soldiers," Fari said. "All my castings at least show that."

"Then Timura must have an ally," Luka said. The careful tone of the others had made him feel awkward. Unpolished. Definitely not royal. So he tried to be as smooth and diplomatic as he could when he said—"I know that's so obvious it may make me seem foolish to say it. However, knowing such a thing and understanding what it means are not the same. For instance, the King believes Lord Timura chose Caluz for his destination because he wants to form an alliance with the Oracle of Hadin." He shrugged. "This could be true. However, I've never heard of an Oracle with an entire army at its disposal."

"All excellent points," Kalasariz said.

"Yes, yes, I agree," Fari said, impatient. "But we're all forgetting we have an actual eyewitness to what occurred in that pass." He pointed at the king's pavilion. "And right now he's in there with Protarus telling him the gods know what! So how can we, uh . . . guide our master—if you understand what I mean—if we don't know what is being said? Much less his reaction to it."

There was an uncomfortable silence as each being considered. Finally Kalasariz said, "Let me start. To begin with . . . might I be so bold as to propose a truce?"

The others considered. Brows furrowing. Weighing what this might entail. The first— and by far the largest—was trust, which slowed down the thinking considerably.

Kalasariz hastened to fill the gap. "Only a temporary truce, of course."

Fari's brows climbed in approval. "Ah!" he said. "That might work."

"Yes, yes, it might," Luka agreed. "Go on, please."

"Well, as Lord Fari so wisely pointed out a moment ago," Kalasariz said, "King Protarus will summon us soon. None of us can predict how he will behave. What he will do or say. Except we do know this—no matter what passes, he will demand an immediate response."

He paused, looking each demon in the eyes by turn. "True?"

Luka nodded. "True."

"I most fervently agree," Fari said.

"So, to protect ourselves," Kalasariz said, "wouldn't it be prudent to see what transpires before we act? Then instead of each fighting the other . . . we can examine the situation calmly . . . rationally . . . without fear of attack from our own ranks. Finally, when we speak we should speak with one voice. None of us trying to win the advantage as long as the truce lasts."

"I can see much value in that line of reasoning," Fari said.

"As long as we remember the truce is temporary," Luka added. "There's no sense pretending it could be anything but that."

"No, there isn't," Kalasariz said, "In fact, why don't we make the truce for the duration of our visit? In other words, when we leave the king's company the peace will end."

A harried aide rushed out of the pavilion. "King Protarus calls, my Lords," he said. "Hurry, if you please! He's in no mood to be kept waiting."

To the amazement of the aide the three burst into laughter as one.

Then Kalasariz said, "Well, my Lords. What is your thinking? Are we in agreement?"

Luka eyed the aide, who was shuffling about, wondering what was being said. "What about him?" Luka said, jabbing a talon at the aide.

Kalasariz smiled. "Don't worry," he said. "He's one of my flies."

More laughter.

Then Luka stretched out his right claw. "To the Unholy Three," he mock intoned.

Kalasariz and Fari caught the spirit. "To the Unholy Three," they chorused, layering hand and talon with his.

Then, chuckling and shaking their heads, they stomped the snow off their boots and went inside to see what was in store for them.

Iraj was waiting—lolling in his throne, booted legs supported on the naked back of a comely slave. He was completely at ease— frighteningly so for the Unholy Three. He was in his human form and they'd rarely seen him in such control. Only the red glow of his eyes gave him away.

Sitting to his right—on a smaller throne—was the soldier, Vister. He was wearing only a clean white loin cloth and was being tended by several pretty human and demon maids, who had just finished washing him and were now rubbing scented oil into his limbs. In one hand he had a silver flask of wine, from which he took frequent pulls. In the other, he clutched a thick sandwich of roasted lamb with several large ragged wounds in it.

Heaters had been brought in when the storm began and the throne room was uncomfortably hot. Sweat poured from the sol- dier's body, mixing with the oils and coating his heavily muscled torso with an heroic sheen. Vister's age and experience were apparent in the thatch of gray hair on his battle-scarred breast.

When the Unholy Three were announced, Vister's head wobbled up to blear at them through half-closed eyes. He was drunk, he was exhausted, he was wounded in body and soul. The maids had to keep at him constantly, bathing away blood and sweat, changing the bowls of scented water frequently as they became discolored and fouled.

At first he didn't recognize them and waved a drunken hand. "Come and join us, friends," he shouted. "Me and my cousin, the King here, are havin' a party!"

Under Protarus' glare, the Unholy Three chuckled kindly, covering their reaction at being addressed so rudely. In normal circumstances Vister would have been beheaded before he finished the first sentence of his greeting.

Then the old plainsman's eyes cleared and he realized who they all truly were. He choked on a mouthful of meat, the wine he'd just taken to wash it down dribbling from the corners of his mouth.

He pushed weakly at the maids and tried to come to his feet, sputtering apologies.

"Please, my dear fellow," Kalasariz said smoothly. "Don't trouble yourself." As much as this foul peasant's manners turned his stomach, under the circumstances he had to be treated with the utmost respect.

"Yes, yes," Fari came in. "Don't interrupt your meal, my friend. You must replenish your strength after such a trying day."

"We salute you, brother," was Luka's skillful addition, touching ringed talons to royal brow, "for all you have suffered in our service."

Still, Vister was clearly overcome. He fell to his knees, babbling, "Please, Masters. I am not worthy!"

His words snapped Iraj's crossbow trigger. The King leaped from his throne, roaring, "Never say master to ones such as these! You are a soldier from the Plains of Jaspar! Worthy of any company!"

He helped Vister back into his seat, casting foul looks at the Unholy Three as if they had tried to humiliate the old soldier. Making much of the gesture, Iraj personally fetched up the flask that had fallen from Vister's hands, feeding the wine to him as if he were a child.

"There, there," he said. "Rest easy, Cousin. Your brave toil is done. Only honors await you."

Vister gurgled down the wine, eyes glazing over. Finally he pushed the flask away, wiping his lips and belching. A bold, drunken grin spreading over his features. Iraj patted him and sat back, coldly observing the Unholy Three.

"Speak to them, kinsman mine," he said to Vister. "Tell them everything you told me. Explain to them in the simple, common logic of a plainsman what they have been doing wrong."

Vister belched loudly. Then he said, "They're killin' too many of us, that's what!"

Iraj sneered at Fari and the others. "Do you hear, my brothers?" he growled. "The answer is as plain as the frowns on your ugly faces—which I have grown to despise more with each passing day. By the gods, you're killing too many of my soldiers! And I won't stand for it. Everyone knows how much I love my soldiers. Demons as well as humans, they are more brother to me than any of you. And be damned to your Spell of Four!"

He gestured at Vister, whose attention was now totally fixed on human needs. He was staring at either hand, trying to decide what to do next—bite another hunk off the sandwich or slobber down more wine. In the end he did both, biting and drinking, biting and drinking. Crumbs and dribbles of wine splattered his lap—the maids giggling and fussing over the mess as if it were all a marvelous jest.

Iraj turned his full attention on the Unholy Three. "I told Sergeant Vister that I—Iraj Protarus, his kinsman, his king, was to blame," he said. "And this is true. I am not only king, but king of all kings in Esmir, so it is only right that final responsibility must rest on my shoulders."

He paused dramatically, throwing an arm around Vister's shoulder. "However . . . This . . ." Aand he dabbed at one of Vister's wounds with a napkin. ". . . This was never my intent! I have made it plain from the very beginning that I dislike having the lives of my soldiers shed needlessly."

"I assume you are speaking of the pass currently in dispute, Majesty?" Luka said.

"Of course I'm speaking of the pass!" Iraj roared, eyes turning to red coals. "What else what would I be talking about? We've lost two hundred of our best so far. And not an inch of gained ground to show for it!"

He patted Vister. "Instead we have won only pain and torment for those I value most."

Luka wanted to laugh. Protarus thought nothing of hurling a thousand demons and men to their doom—if it won him what he wanted. But now he was presenting the face of an innocent. Posing as a king who wished only the best for his subjects and required little for himself—except for their kind opinion of him.

Fari rapped his cane and Kalasariz coughed, bringing Luka back to reality. Just in time he realized his wolf's snout was about to break through.

To cover, Luka bowed low and thumped his breast abjectly, murmuring, " . . . a misunderstanding, Majesty. The fault is entirely my own."

When he'd regained control over his shape-changer's body, he straightened, saying, "Your words have given expression to the confusion of all our most worthy ideas, Majesty." He gestured at Fari and Kalasariz. "The three of us were only just discussing this most terrible of affairs. And we all agreed that we have failed you, Sire."

Fari broke in. "Except, perhaps I am more to blame then the others, Highness," he said. "After all, this is sorcery we are fighting in that pass. And things involving sorcery are my responsibility and no other."

"I beg to differ, my great and good king," Kalasariz said. "Lord Fari and his wizards have done their utmost. It is I who is most at fault for not discovering what we were up against before we sent men such as this . . ." he nodded respectfully at Vister, who grinned like a baby and burped— ". . . correction, heroes such as this . . . into battle."

"Some of what you say is true, my brothers," Luka said to Kalasariz and Fari. "But in the end, it is I who direct all special missions. I should have been at the forefront . . . leading both attacks. But I listened to my cowardly aides who claimed the King would be badly served if I were killed." The Prince shook his head. "I'll dismiss them from my service the moment I return to my headquarters."

Vister croaked laughter and everyone swiveled to see him hoist himself upright on his elbow. "Sounds like we're gonna have a nice day o' executions tomorrow, lads," he said. "There's nothin' like a couple of whacked necks to fix a soldier's mind on his job, I always say." He leaned closer, elbow nearly slipping out from under him. Grinning at Luka. "Course, you'd be talkin' about officers and such, wouldn't you, Sire? Maybe that's not such a good idea. Neck whackin' don't come so easy with the officer class. Might not have the same affect it does down in the ranks. Maybe it wouldn't be so good for morale."

Then he lifted his haunches and farted.

Iraj slapped his thigh, howling laughter. "That's telling them, Cousin!" he said. "The truth—and from deep, deep within you, by the gods!"

Vister chuckled drunkenly, lifting the flask to his lips. Then he frowned, turning the flask upside down. Nothing came out. He shook it, frown growing deeper.

"It's empty," he said in a voice so mournful you'd have thought he was announcing the death of his dear mother. One of the maids traded it for a full one and he was happy again.

He drank, then thumped his chest. "I was the only one!" he said. "Me! Vister! The rest are dead and rottin' in that pass. We all went in. Like so." He wriggled his fingers, making walking motions. "Then along comes the ghosts and whack!" He chopped at the air. "Ever'body's dead . . . 'cept Sergeant Vister." He settled back in his chair, chuckling and drawing a maid onto his lap. "Now I'm guest o' the King! Ain't that a tale to tell!" He tapped just beneath his right eye. "And these are the eyes what seen it!"

"A marvelous tale indeed," Kalasariz murmured. He turned to Fari. "Pardon, my good Lord Fari," he said, "but it seems the good sergeant is too modest to tell his story more fully."

Fari nodded. "He's too tense, poor fellow," he said. "That's his trouble."

Luka took the cue. "Wouldn't it be prudent, Majesty," he said to Iraj, "to see if we could learn more?" He laid a ringed claw of sincerity across his breast. "Let the good sergeant be our teacher, Majesty. And we his humble students."

Kalasariz muttered from the side of his mouth. "A little thick, don't you think?"

"What was that?" Iraj demanded.

"I was only agreeing with Prince Luka, Highness," Kalasariz replied.

Now Fari was up to speed. "Yes, let this humble hero instruct us, Majesty," he said. "As all know, I have always been particularly sensitive to the lower classes. Like Your Majesty, I pride myself on listening most intently to their crude words of wisdom." He shrugged. "Of course, sometimes we need a little assistance to understand their meaning."

Iraj raised an eyebrow. "What's to understand?" he said. He turned to Vister. "Tell them what you told me, my friend. And leave nothing out."

Vister struggled upright and the maid slipped off his lap and resumed her place with the others. "Sure," he said. He snapped his fingers. "Nothin' to it! Simple as all the Hells! The problem is this, see. There's ghosts in that pass. Hundreds, maybe thousands of 'em. And they can kill you, but you can't kill them. And that's all there is to it!"

He gave Luka an owlish look. "So all's you officer sorts gotta figure out is how to turn the whole thing around. Like we get to kill them, but they don't get to kill us." He tapped his nose. "Simple as the nose on your face." He gave Luka another look and giggled. "Oops!" he said. "Didn't mean to speak outta turn there, Sire. You bein' a demon and all, I'm not so sure that's a nose you got stickin' out there. Could be another horn, for all's I know. No offense intended, Sire."

Luka dipped his head. "None taken," he murmured, thinking he'd like to rip this filthy human's heart out. Fari's cough and Kalasariz' sudden grip on his elbow helped steady him. He turned to Iraj. "As first field reports go, Majesty," he said, "that was most enlightening. But I, for one, would certainly want to know more."

"That's why I called you here," Protarus said. "To listen and learn." He turned back to Vister. "Tell it again," he said, "but in more—" a loud snore cut him off. Vister was sprawled his seat, head lolling on his chest, sound asleep.

Iraj chuckled kindly. "Let him rest," he said. "He deserves it. We'll question him later."

"Pardon, Highness," Fari said. "But what I had in mind will be much easier while he sleeps. What I propose is that we witness his travails first hand. I don't need much in the way of preparations." He indicated an ornate charcoal brazier that had been brought in to warm up the throne room during the snow storm. "In fact," he said, "I can use that for our stage." He pulled a pouch from his wizard's belt, opening it to sniff at the contents. He nodded in satisfaction. "I have everything we require, Majesty," he continued, "for all to be revealed."

Iraj studied the Unholy Three from beneath lowered eyelids. He appeared bored, but he was observing them closely—growing warier by the minute. At first he couldn't put his finger on what was bothering him. Then it came to him that the three were displaying remarkable unanimity. He certainly didn't feel violent waves of tension between them—which was by far the more normal state of affairs within his inner court.

For a panicked moment he wondered if they had uncovered his secret—the spell the witch, Sheesan, had given him that would not only destroy Safar, but free him from the Unholy Three. Were they were conspiring to foil him?

Then he relaxed. How could they know? Say what he might about his brothers of the Spell of Four, they had worked hard to bring him this close to his goal—the capture and ritual slaying of Safar and Palimak. If the Unholy Three knew about his plans, they certainly wouldn't have pressed so hard to bring them to fruition.

So—what were they up to? Were they seeking a means to break the bonds with him? That would certainly be the worst case conclusion he could make. But the more he thought on it, the more unlikely such a scenario seemed.

Very well. The best way to find out what was going on, he thought, was to give way to their suggestions and see where that carried him.

"Proceed, my lord," he said to Lord Fari. "Enlighten us all with your magic."

Fari bowed low, then quickly assumed command of the shapely maids tending Vister. Naked, except for modesty patches at their loins, gleaming with a faint film of perspiration from the over-heated room, giving off the scent of the most remarkable perfumes, the female humans and demons made exotic magical assistants for the old master wizard.

Taking a lesson in magic as entertainment from Timura, the Lord Fari made the most of the maids' presence—drawing out and changing his spell so that it showed off their jiggling forms to the best advantage.

When he reached the penultimate moment he glanced at Protarus and was sorely disappointed when he saw how unaffected the king was. Instead of being flushed with excitement from all this mystery and magical erotica, Protarus sat boredly in his throne, fingernails tapping impatiently.

Fari hurled a handful of votive powders into the brazier and there was a flash of smoke, a swirl of colors. Despite himself, Iraj's pose of unconcern dissolved and he bent closer to see. Timura was right, Fari thought. The King can't resist magic, especially when accompanied by a little showmanship.

As Iraj stared into the brazier the smoke began to shape itself into a deep canyon with high walls. He heard Vister groan in his sleep and suddenly the throne room vanished and Iraj found himself sitting on a nervous warhorse, those steep walls now towering over him on either side. He was in the lead group of a tightly-packed force of men and demons moving cautiously through the Caluzian Pass.

Iraj felt somehow diminished. Weaker—not just in muscle and bone, but weaker of spirit, of self, of . . . he fumbled for the word, then it came in a flash—Authority!

He glanced down and found filthy leather breeches covering his legs. He raised a hand and saw something strange and gnarled and quite unfamiliar rise up—the hand of another man! And then it came to him that he was in Vister's body, reliving the moments leading to the second battle in the pass.

"Easy, Majesty," he heard Fari murmur. Voice close, but distant at the same time. "We are with you!"

"Yes, Highness," came another voice—Kalasariz'. "I am here."

"As am I, Majesty, as am I," he heard Luka say.

He looked at the mounted soldiers on either side of him. All were grizzled and filthy. Of the lowest of the low-ranking, be they demon or human. Fari and the others were among them, but he couldn't tell which was which.

He heard a clatter of falling stone and Vister's body jerked in alarm. Eyes probing here and there, every nerve screaming ambush, but nothing real to place the feeling on no matter how hard he strained his senses.

Then he heard a steady, tromp, tromp of many marching men and he twisted in his saddle, steadying his skittish horse, looking for the source of the sound. All around him the other soldiers were doing the same and the air was filled with whispered curses and clanking armor.

A great trumpet sounded—blasting through the narrow canyon and resounding off the walls.

Iraj/Vister whirled to the front, shouting and clawing for his sword when he saw the ghastly army march into view.

They were huge men, so heavily mailed they turned the pass into a solid wall of armor. Their flesh was pale, corpselike, their lips the color of blood. They had huge hollow eyes that seemed like the darkest and deepest of caverns.

He heard his companions cry out and draw their weapons. Attack orders were shouted and Iraj/Vister raked his horse's flanks with his spurs and charged straight ahead. All his sensibilities were hurled aside. His own life became insignificant as he joined the thundering cavalcade intent on slaughtering the enemy marching towards them.

He heard a hoarse voice shout: "For the King!"

And the others took up the cry—"FOR THE KING!"

Iraj/Vister found himself shouting along with his brother warriors and for a few seconds he thought the greatest thing he could ever accomplish would be to die for his king.

And then he thought, But, I'm the King!

At that moment he smashed into the armored ranks of the enemy.

The expected shock of collision never came. To his amazement his horse swept through the densely packed enemy ranks as if they didn't exist. Helmed faces rose up to confront him. His horse, a veteran of many such attacks, lashed out with iron hooves, screaming in panic when it encountered nothing except insubstantial smoke and air.

A huge enemy warrior lunged at him with a spear. Iraj/Vister tried to knock it aside with his sword, but like the horse, his weapon encountered nothingness and he was nearly toppled from the saddle from the force of his own blow.

They're ghosts! his mind screamed as he clawed himself upright, losing his sword in the process. Ghosts!

He righted himself just as the ghost warrior's spear caught the edge of his chain vest. The spear skittered across the links and he felt the all too familiar white hot sear as a sharp point needled through the links and cut into flesh. Experience as much as fear dulled the pain and Iraj/Vister kicked through, mercilessly raking his horse's flanks.

His body was violated many times during the charge through that ghostly mass. By the time his horse was cut down he had suffered many small wounds and lacerations. He'd fought hard, yet not one of his enemies had been harmed. Every blow he struck met no resistance. The enemy soldiers seemed to dissolve as he thrust and slashed at them.

In the end he relied on his professional skill as a horseman, dodging this way and that, avoiding many of the blows aimed at him. All around him his companions were being slaughtered by the score.

Then a javelin took his horse and the poor beast squealed and folded under him. Iraj/Vister tried to roll free, but his wounds made him weak and the horse rolled on top of him. Amazingly, he found himself lying under the animal not only alive, but still mobile. Several corpses propped the dead horse up just enough so that Iraj/Vister was sheltered from the one-sided battle raging in the pass.

All desire to fight was gone. Now it was all he could do to keep from gibbering with fear and giving himself away to the enemy.

He peered through a small opening and saw the last of his mates dragged from his horse by the ghost warriors. They forced him to kneel and one giant grabbed the soldier by the hair, while another sliced off his head. The execution was so close that blood sprayed Iraj/Vister's face.

Then all became blackness.

Iraj's eyes blinked open. He felt strength flood back into his limbs and he realized he'd been returned to his own body.

He was back in the throne room, the Unholy Three standing before him, studying his reactions through conspiratorial eyes.

Iraj coughed and sat upright, squaring his shoulders. "Very informative, my Lord," he said to Fari, making his voice casual.

Fari bowed. "Yes, Majesty," he said. "Quite informative indeed."

Luka said, "Give me the right spells to fight them, my Lord Fari, and I will clear the pass by tomorrow night." Then, to Iraj, "And it is my solemn vow, Highness, that not one drop of the blood of our soldiers will be shed without just cause."

Kalasariz suddenly felt left out—vulnerable. He was a spy master, not a warrior or a wizard. He had nothing of value to offer at this most crucial moment. Then he glanced over at Vister and saw that the old soldier was no longer snoring in his chair. Instead he was quite still, his face yellow and waxen.

Just then one of the maids noticed something was amiss and placed a hand on Vister's chest. She was too well trained to cry out—possibly drawing the wrath of the moody King Protarus. Nevertheless, big tears welled up in her eyes and she began to weep.

Kalasariz saw his opportunity and took it. "I fear, my Lord," he said to Luka, "that your promise to our king came too late for at least one of our most noble heroes."

He gestured and everyone turned to see Vister slumped in his chair, the maid weeping over his body.

"Unless I am mistaken," Kalasariz continued, "the good Sergeant Vister is quite dead." He looked pointedly at Fari, who was fuming at this early betrayal of the truce. "Apparently your spell was too much for the poor fellow," he said. "Although you assured us otherwise."

"Look here, Kalasariz!" Luka snapped, "it's easy enough to criticize when one—"

Iraj cut him off. "It so happens, my Lord," he rasped, "that our brother, Kalasariz, happens to be echoing the criticisms of your king!"

He rose from the throne and went to Vister, pushing the maids away and hoisting the body up in his arms, cradling the big soldier as if he were a babe.

"This is your fault, Fari," he said to the old demon. "And yours as well, Luka," he said to the prince, "for the reasons I gave before."

Fari and Luka, reduced to the Unholy Two, bowed, spewing many fervent apologies.

"Know this," King Protarus said. "The man you see in my arms was my kinsman, my cousin. He had followed me faithfully for many years over many miles and suffered much in my service. I do not take his death lightly. Do you understand me?"

Fari and Luka assured the king they understood quite well. Kalasariz said nothing, edging to the side to separate himself from the others.

"Go then," the King ordered. "Win me my victory, but remember this man. Remember him well!"

Kalasariz added his own voice with others, saying, "Yes, Majesty! All will be as you command."

All three bowed, then crept away.

Iraj watched them go, relieved. First, that their unity had once again been shattered. Second, that for the moment his secret still seemed safe.

He looked down at Vister's dead face. "They don't know a blessed thing, do they cousin?" he said.

Then he dropped the body into the chair. "See to it that he has a proper burial," he said to his servants, then strode away.

27

SPIES ON THE WIND

"Steady!" Biner shouted. Then: "Launch!"

The ground crew let go the cables and the airship shot into the sky—furnaces roaring, the twin balloons taut till near bursting.

Leiria's stomach lurched at the unaccustomed feeling of weightlessness. She leaned over the side, fearing she was about to get sick, then saw the rapidly diminishing figures on the ground and felt sicker still. She closed her eyes, willing the sickness to be gone. She kept them closed for a long time, concentrating on the sounds around her—Biner's shouted orders, the aircrew's reply, the pumping bellows and roaring furnaces. And finally, the oddly melodic song of the wind strumming the great cables that held the ship to the balloons.

The sudden snowstorm had delayed the launch well past the chosen hour. Biner had held everyone at ready, ground crew poised at the cables, aircrew scrambling about knocking off ice. Meanwhile, teams of Kyranian volunteers shivered in the cold as they kept the area swept free of snow.

Then there'd been a brief respite as the sun broke through, revealing a small patch of blue sky and Biner had launched the ship.

Now Leiria was crouched on the steering deck, wishing for all the world that she could be somewhere else. Anything, even a charging horde of demon cavalry, would be better than this. At least she'd be on nice safe ground.

"I know what yer thinkin', lass," she heard Biner say. "That if the gods meant yer to fly, they'd a provided yer with the belly for it."

Leiria opened her eyes to find the dwarf standing next to her. She nodded weakly. "I would have thought wings," she said, "or at least a few pin feathers. But you're right. Whatever god made birds must've started with the belly."

She groaned to her feet, forcing herself not to look over the edge. "I think I'm going to live," she said. "Although I'm still not sure if I care."

Arlain came up, carrying a steaming mug. "Thith'll do the trick," she said. "Ith an old balloonitht cure for air thickneth."

Gratefully, Leiria drank. It was delicious—a thick, forthy elixir heavily laced with brandy. Her queasy inner world suddenly settled.

"Oh, that's much better!" she said. "My stomach's practically cheering."

"It's usually much smoother than this, lass," Biner said, taking her elbow and leading her over to the big ship's wheel.

"Here," he said, putting her hands on the wheel. "This'll give you somethin' to hold onto." He pointed to a mountain ridge off in the distance. "Keep her headed that way," he said.

Then to her great surprise and alarm, he bounded down the gangway to berate a lazy crewman.

"Wait," she cried, "I don't know how to—"

She bit off the rest as the dwarf vanished below. And she thought, if Biner wasn't worried, steering the airship couldn't be that difficult.

Leiria concentrated on the ridge, moving the wheel whenever the nose of the ship veered away from it. At first she tended to oversteer and the ship yawed widely from side to side. She kept expecting someone to come running to push her aside and take the wheel. When no one came she soon forgot about everything else but steering the ship and quickly saw the way of it.

The combination of Arlain's elixir plus having something useful to do gradually did its work, and before she knew it, Leiria was actually enjoying herself. The air was clean and bracing and there was an incredible sense of freedom that came from floating so high above the earth. They were sailing just above a thick cloud cover, blue skies and a bright sun, mountains stretching away in every direction as far as she could see. At least that's how it appeared for a time. About a half mile from the ridge Biner had aimed her toward, it began to dawn on her that something was wrong.

Instead of fleeing as the airship approached, the horizon grew closer. The sky in that direction was still blue, but the blue seemed more . . . solid was the only description she could think of. But not hard, like metal, but soft, like . . . like . . . some kind of cloth. And now that she thought of it, the cloth was moving . . . billowing . . . as if an immense window had been left open and the wind was pushing through the curtains.

Biner and Arlain must have sensed something was up, because they both came running up on the deck. As Biner took over the wheel, Leiria pointed.

"Look," she said. "Through there . . ."

She was pointing through the gap of what she thought of as "curtains." Biner cursed and Arlain covered her mouth in alarm. Glaring through the opening was the familiar, evil face of the Demon Moon.

The sight of their old celestial enemy was driven home by the heavy throbbing of a huge machine and the whiff of the foul air of the Black Lands.

"No use cryin' over spilt air," Biner said grimly. "Besides, we were half expectin' it ever since we started on this little spyin' trip."

"I thirtainly wath never exthpecting that again!" Arlain said, jabbing a claw at the leering moon. "Thomebody thould of warned me!"

"And then what would yer have done?" Biner said. "If we'd of spelled it out real plain—so we could be sure yer were scared sand-less. I mean, Safar told us we were livin' in a false Caluz. That outside that little valley was the real world. Which is where we gotta go if we're gonna do any worthwhile eagleyein'."

"I know that," Arlain sniffed.

"So, if we'd a painted a picture for yer," Biner went on, "and made sure yer knew we'd be in the Black Lands again, complete with Demon Moon and crazy sorcery, what would yer have done, lass. Decided not to go?"

"Don't be thilly," Arlain said. "Of courth, I'd thtill go! I haven't been flying in yearth! You couldn't have kept me off thith airthip with a whole army of Demon Moonth!"

She sniffed. "But it thirtainly wouldn't have been impolite to warn me!"

"Listen," Leiria broke in. "I don't know you all very well. Maybe this little bantering between you is just your normal way of facing a dangerous situation."

She indicated the flowing curtain, which they were moments away from sailing through. "But while you've been talking, we've been getting closer to that!"

Biner frowned at her. "So? That was the plan, wasn't it, lass?"

"Yes," Leiria said. "But we weren't supposed to do it naked!"

Biner slapped his forehead. "Damn! I fergot!"

He shouted orders and several big crewmen raced to break out several large kegs. It was a little too late, however, because they were just knocking the tops off the kegs when the airship sailed through the curtains and suddenly they were sweeping over a bleak landscape—a frozen plain pierced by huge, tortured black rock formations.

As they entered the Black Lands Leiria was wracked with sudden pain. Every joint and muscle ached and her head throbbed as if she'd been stricken by some dreaded plague. She heard Biner and Arlain moan and the harsh wrenching sound of a crewman coughing up his breakfast.

Safar had warned them about entering the Black Lands without a shield to protect them from the wild spells. He'd even provided them with the means to make one—the contents of the casks the crewmen had been opening.

Leiria forced herself off the steering deck, going down the gangway step by agonizing step, feeling as if she were carrying a heavy load of hot bricks on her shoulders.

She stumbled over the crewmen, who were writhing about the main deck, clutching their heads and calling for their mothers. When she came to the first cask she almost broke down, falling to her knees and cracking her head on the rim. Somehow she found strength and pulled herself up, blood streaming down her face from a cut. She dug out her tinder box, feeling like an old arthritic woman as she tried to light it.

Finally it caught, and she threw the entire tinder box into the cask, hurling herself backward just in time as flames and smoke exploded up and out.

Leiria stayed flat on her back, watching the smoke curl under the air bags, then flow around the sides until both balloons looked like immense white clouds. Gradually, as Safar's shield took affect, she felt better. For the second time in less than two hours, she thought she felt well enough to care if she lived.

She clambered to her feet, muttering, "Damned flyers! Not a brain in their heads!"

The crewmen were also recovering and she set them to work tending the casks. They were to wait until the first barrel burned out, then light the next, and so on until someone told them to stop.

She returned to the steering deck, expecting to find Biner and Arlain waiting with shamed expressions and many apologies.

Instead she found them intent on the scene below.

Leiria's eyes widened when she saw what they were looking at. Beneath them was an immense army, drawn up under a thick steaming blanket of snow.

She heard camels bawling and the racket of armorers pounding out dents in shields.

Rising out of the center of the encampment was a snow-covered pavilion topped by a waving banner—the Demon Moon with the Comet rising.

Iraj had finally caught them!

28

THE ORACLE SPEAKS

"We're inside the machine, father!" Palimak shouted. But Safar had sensed the wrongness a moment before the boy's warning.

The air became very cold and gulls shrilled warnings overhead. The breeze coming off the sea carried the sudden stink of sorcery. Ahead of him the Spirit Rider wheeled her horse and charged away. Instinctively he knew this was no tease, no game of seduction in a dark wood.

He dug his knees into Khysmet and the horse leaped after the black mare. Both of them knew the threat came from behind— not ahead. Snow started to fall, then Palimak cried out his warning—"We're inside the machine, father!" Putting words to the half-formed thoughts in his mind.

There was a loud crash! behind them—so heavy it shook the ground.

Safar glanced around and saw huge white jaws reaching for them. Khysmet surged forward just in time, the jaws clashing together on emptiness. Safar turned his head away, but the creature's huge eyes—burning with the blue fires of some icy hell—caught his. He felt numb, his strength drained away by sudden cold. It took all his will to force his eyes away from the creature's and his strength flooded back the moment he was facing forward again.

The creature roared. Palimak tried to turn and see, but Safar leaned forward, blocking him, telling him, "Whatever you do—Don't look back!"

There was another crash—this one much closer. Khysmet stretched to his fullest, straining to gain more speed.

The snowstorm intensified and Safar lost sight of the Spirit Rider. All he could see was a snatch of the shoreline to the side and just ahead of him—chunks of ice hissing in and out of the mist on steely waves.

Again there was the sound of something heavy slamming down behind them. The ground quaked, but this time the beast didn't seem quite as close. At least he hoped so.

A large wave boomed in from the side and Khysmet veered from the shoreline to escape it. The mistake was evident within a few seconds. Without the shoreline to guide them visually, and the sound of the sea lost beneath Khysmet's pounding hooves, they quickly became lost in the blizzard.

Their enemy, however, had no such trouble. The crashing sound suddenly gained on them—coming closer than ever before.

Then a beacon flared well off to the left and Safar turned Khysmet toward the light.

He heard a marrow-freezing roar and a cold foul breath blasted across his back. Safar fumbled a small pouch from his belt, bit the drawstrings apart and hurled the pouch and its contents behind him—his shouted spell ripped from his lips by the storm:

"Fire to cold,
Cold to fire.
All hearts burn
On Winter's pyre!"

As he hurled the last words into the winds one of the beast's claws caught his cloak, pulling him back. He jerked forward against Palimak, feeling cloth and flesh tear.

There was a spellblast behind him, followed by the howl of some great beast in pain, and the claw was snatched away.

The beacon grew larger in his view and then he gradually began to make out the shadowy figure of the horsewoman racing ahead of him through the storm—a bright magical brand held aloft in one hand.

There was a violent crash behind him and he realized the ice creature had only been slowed momentarily by his attack spell and was pursuing him again. From the sound of its roaring—hate mingled with pain—it was back to full strength, more determined than ever to bring them down.

He heard waves crashing on both sides of them and realized they were now out on the narrow peninsula. Now there was no way open but straight ahead. And when they reached the end they'd be trapped against the raging open seas.

To gain time he repeated his previous attack, hurling the spell blindly over his shoulder. The action had even less effect than before—the creature had evidently learned from the first experience. Safar groaned in disappointment when the spellblast went off and all he heard was a sharp yelp of pain as their pursuer dodged most of the impact.

"Let me help you, father!" Palimak cried and Safar plucked the last pouch from his belt—reaching for the boy's strength to add to his. But there wasn't much there—he could feel Palimak's weariness, sense his struggle to add to Safar's powers.

Still, it was just enough, and when he cast the spell he heard a satisfying shriek from the beast.

He saw the Spirit Rider reach land's end, but to his surprise, instead of turning about she kept going, riding straight out onto the water's surface.

Safar put all his trust in the woman, riding after her without hesitation. Even so, as Khysmet plunged ahead, he braced to be swallowed by icy waters. The expected shock never came and a moment later they were racing across the boiling sea as if it were the firmest ground.

Behind them he heard the beast roar in frustrated fury and with every stride Khysmet took the roars became fainter and fainter, until they faded altogether.

The snow fell harder until everything above and below was obscured from view. He felt as if he were riding through a strange world where only the color of white existed—except for the beacon of light bobbing ahead of them as the horsewoman led them onward.

They rode like that for a long time. How long Safar couldn't say, except to note that Palimak had fallen into an exhausted sleep. Safar might have slept himself—he'd find himself dozing off, eyes closing involuntarily, then being jogged awake and seeing the ever-present beacon still moving ahead of them. Even Khysmet seemed to tire, his pace growing gradually slower as they went on.

Safar was shocked from his stupor by a loud rumbling sound. The sea heaved under them and Palimak snapped awake, crying out in fear—"Father! Father!" Safar was too busy holding on to answer as Khysmet shrilled surprise, leaping high into the air. Safar and Palimak were nearly hurled off when he landed—hooves skittering on what seemed to be a reef rising from the ocean floor. They were rocked from side to side, but still Khysmet managed to keep his footing.

For a moment all was still. Then a blast of wind sheered in from the side, sweeping the snow away.

They were presented with an incredible sight. Looming over the tiny, barren island they now found themselves on was the immense stone image of a demon. It had a long narrow face topped by heavy brows that arched over deep-set eyes. Whoever had designed the statue had given it a sad smile, which added to the effect of the deep-set eyes, making the demon seem incredibly wise.

Safar remembered the face very well. It had been carved on the coffin lid he'd seen in his vision long ago. It was the face of the great Lord Asper.

As they rode toward the statue Safar saw the Spirit Rider had stopped. She was waiting in front of a wide stairway that led up to the statue's open mouth—beacon still held high.

Khysmet perked up, whinnying at the black mare, who whinnied greetings in return. Safar's pulse quickened as they drew near.

The woman was just as beautiful as he remembered back in that moonlit clearing so many miles and months ago. Her face and form were so perfect she looked as if she'd been carved by a master artist from some rare ebony wood and her bright smile of greeting warmed the frozen lump deep in his heart.

She called out to him, "Only a little farther, my friend. Only a little farther."

Then she whirled the mare about, shouting, "This way to Syrapis!" And plunged up the broken staircase to disappear into the mouth of the statue.

Safar didn't have to urge Khysmet to follow. The big stallion lunged up the staircase after the mare and a moment later they were leaping through the opening.

There was a flash of white light. Then darkness—marked only by the distant beacon carried by the Spirit Rider. The beacon light steadied, then stopped.

Palimak whispered, "There's no danger, father. Everything's fine, now."

The light grew stronger then wider, until Safar realized it was no longer a beacon, but natural light shining through a cave opening.

A moment later they cantered out into soft sunlight. Safar blinked. The woman was gone! His heart wrenched in dismay. Under him he could feel Khysmet's sides heaving and knew the animal was just as deeply affected by the disappearance of the mare.

"We're not in the machine anymore, father," Palimak announced.

"What?" Safar was so dazed he barely heard.

"Gundara and Gundaree say we're out of the machine," Palimak said.

Safar glanced about. Gradually his surroundings sunk in. There was no island. No raging seas. No blinding snowstorm. All had vanished.

Instead, they were riding along a narrow mountain ridge, breathtaking vistas stretching out in every direction. To the south was a snow-dappled range of low mountains, marked by two familiar peaks. Caluz was beyond those mountains—and not so very distant. Safar could see a yellow tinge lying low on the horizon and knew it was from the poisonous atmosphere of the

Black Lands. Further evidence were puffs of smoke from all the active volcanoes. He looked closely at the mountains the Kyranians needed to cross when he went back to fetch them. To his joy he saw the faint scar of a caravan track running between the peaks.

Even brighter news beckoned from the north. Not many miles beyond the ridge they were riding along was a shining sea. He could even make out a few dots of white that were sailing craft skimming across the peaceful waters. There was no sign of the snow storm he'd just experienced. The fields were green and summery. Far off he saw the curving slash of a road running along the shoreline. Beyond that was a dazzling city of the purest white.

Hovering over the city was a vast field of golden clouds—flattened so they looked like fabulous islands in the sky.

Caspan!

The last jumping off point to Syrapis.

Palimak's voice jolted him out his reverie. "There's someone waiting for us, father," he said, pointing to a little deer trail leading off the ridge and down to a little grove of trees. "Down there."

Safar tensed. "Is it dangerous?" he asked.

Palimak hesitated while he conferred in whispers with the Favorites. Then, "They're not sure," he said, scratching his head. "They go back and forth. It's all pretty confusing. The only thing they agree on is that we have to go there—no matter what."

Safar loosened his sword. "Let's assume the worst, son," he said. "Then we won't have any reason to be sorry later."

Palimak nodded, arranging his cloak and belt so he could reach anything that might be needed. Young as he was, the boy was now quite trail wise—speaking only when necessary. He quietly got himself a drink of water and a handful of dried dates to munch on.

Safar was pleased the boy seemed so alert, all signs of exhaustion gone. As for himself—well, he felt as if he'd been through the hells and back. Which, now that he thought of it, he had. Pity he didn't possess the restorative powers of the very young. He was only in his third decade of life. Right now he it seemed like five more had been added to that span by the ordeal.

He glanced up at the sun to mark the time. To his surprise he saw it was barely mid-afternoon. Which meant only a few hours had passed since they'd left Hantilia's palace. If he had been asked, Safar would have sworn at least a week had gone by. This was very powerful magic, indeed.

There was no time to ponder such mysteries. He needed a clear mind for whatever faced them down that trail. Taking a lesson from Palimak, he got himself a drink and something to eat. Except he chose a palmful of jerky and a hefty slug of wine from the flask at his hip. Refreshed, he turned Khysmet down the narrow deer trail.

The path was steep and deeply curved so it was impossible for the riders to see very far ahead. Also, the grove of trees below them was too dense for them to make out what it hid. Skin prickling, eyes shifting back and forth, Safar guided Khysmet down the trail.

There was no warning. They came around a bend, the path dipped, and suddenly they were trotting into the grove. A gentle sun streamed down through the tree, giving the light a holy cast. A musical fountain played in the center of the grove, mist rising from the playing waters to glow in the sunlight. The fountain itself was a scene out of the Book of Felakia—the goddess revealed in all her beauty as she bathed in a stream, dipping up a cup of water to pour over her marble tresses.

Other than the life-sized statue of the goddess there were no structures in the grove, only a few stone benches set about the fountain. It was the sort of place one might expect to find in a temple garden—certainly never in the middle of a forbidding wilderness.

Just then Safar spotted someone waiting for them by the fountain. His heart jumped in amazement.

"It's the Queen, father!" Palimak blurted. "Queen Hantilia!"

The Demon Queen, graceful and royal as ever in her flowing red Asper robes, raised a claw of welcome.

"Greetings, Safar Timura," she said. "I have waited long for this meeting."

Safar goggled at her. What in the hells was she talking about? Where was the Oracle? Most important of all—how did she get here? Meanwhile, the Queen was eyeing him, looking him over as if she'd never seen him before.

"I didn't know you'd be so handsome," she said. "For a human, that is." She turned to Palimak. "And you, young Palimak Timura," she said in her musical voice, "I mustn't neglect you. You are quite handsome as well. Handsomer than your father, if I may be so bold. It's the demon in you that makes the difference."

Safar slid out of the saddle. "Pardon me for sounding rude, Majesty," he said. "But you're talking nonsense. And before anything else is said, I'd appreciate it greatly if you answered a few questions. To start with, could you please explain how in the hells you got here!"

Hantilia laughed. "Be patient, my lord," she said. "And all will be revealed to the best of my ability."

She waved at a bench across from hers. "Come sit and rest," she said. "And take a little refreshment, please. You must be hungry and tired after your long journey." Another wave and the small table in front of the bench was suddenly filled with plates of delicacies and mugs of drink.

Safar started to object. He was tired of the Queen's constant evasions and pleas for patience. He wanted answers, by the gods! Safar took half step forward, then paused. For the first time he noticed how insubstantial Hantilia seemed to be. In fact, if he turned his head slightly he could see right through her to the other side of the grotto where the trees moved gently in the breeze in a shadow play scene tinted red by her robes.

"She's not a ghost, father," Palimak said. "Gundara says she isn't real. But Gundaree says she's sort of real." He shook his head. "They're not being very helpful today."

"What do you say, Safar Timura?" Hantilia said, again indicating the bench and the table of food. "Will you take a chance with me? You've taken so many just to get here, what could be the harm?"

Safar sighed, accepting whatever fate had in store for them. Palimak took the sigh as a signal and scrambled off Khysmet. They quickly unsaddled the horse and set him free to graze on the tender grasses fed by the playing fountain.

As soon as they sat down in front the table of food they became famished and fell to. Hantilia sat quietly while they ate and drank. To Safar's surprise the magical food was delicious—in his experience such things always tasted like paper forgotten in some musty nook of a old library. There was never any substance or nourishment to that kind of food—when you finished eating you realized there had been no meal at all and you were left feeling just as empty as before. The drink she provided was equally as marvelous. Safar's cup proved to contain a never-ending supply of a rich, earthy wine, while Palimak's was an ever flowing container of what he said was a delicious fruit punch.

When they were done and the world seemed much brighter than before, Hantilia said, "Ask your questions, Safar Timura. I've been waiting for many a day to answer them."

Safar eyed her. Things were beginning to make a glimmer of sense.

"You're the Oracle of Hadin," he said—a statement, not a question.

Hantilia chuckled. "What did you expect? Some sort of great, goddess-like figure descending from the heavens? If so, I fear you must be very much disappointed. To begin with, if you are a student of Asper, you'll realize there are no gods or goddesses about. They're all asleep, you know. Slumbering away in their celestial beds while the world is turned to ashes."

"I'll try again," Safar said. "Are you the Oracle I seek?"

Hantilia shrugged. "I'll have to do," she said. "The original Oracle is . . . dead, isn't quite the word for such a being. Dissolved, I suppose, is more descriptive. However you put it, she was destroyed when the Caluzians failed to halt the machine." She touched claw to breast. "I am her replacement, so to speak."

Palimak snorted. "Why didn't you just say so right away?" he piped up.

"Good question, son," Safar said. Then to Hantilia, "Do you have an answer?"

"A simple one, actually," she replied. "If I'd have spoken then it would have ruined the spell."

"What spell?" Palimak broke in. "I didn't sense any spell. Neither did Gundara or Gundaree."

"That, my dearest, is because the spell was cast after you left the palace," Hantilia said.

Her form suddenly wavered, weakening, until she seemed

about to vanish. Then it firmed. Safar saw moistness in her deep-set demon eyes.

"Forgive me," she said, wiping away an escaped tear. "But I was thinking of what must have happened after you departed."

She paused to compose herself, then said, "The Hantilia you see before you, as you've no doubt guessed, is not a living creature. I suppose you couldn't call me a creature of any kind, living or otherwise. I am merely part of the overall spell—the Great Sacrifice, is what we named it. In reality—if there is such a thing—I and all my followers are dead."

Safar and Palimak were rocked by this statement. They also had no doubt but that it was true. Safar remembered when they left the courtyard Palimak said he felt sorry for Hantilia and the others. The boy must have sensed the tragedy about to unfold.

"It was necessary for us to sacrifice ourselves," Hantilia said, "for the final part of the spell to be cast. Otherwise there wouldn't have been enough power."

Safar reflected on their perilous journey and realized they never would have made it this far without some outside help. An enormous amount of help, at that, considering the magical snowstorm—which he now realized had been for their benefit.

"To be frank," the Queen continued, "I'm a little surprised my people and I had the will to act when the moment came." She sighed. "At times I wondered if we had all become insanely religious, like those strange cults you hear about in the wilder areas of Esmir."

"You said before that it began with a vision," Safar said. "Of the Lady Felakia appearing before you."

"I lied," Hantilia said. "Or at least my other self lied. I suppose there's not much difference. I'm truly sorry, but it was the easiest way to avoid uncomfortable questions I was forbidden to answer."

"Then what is the truth, Majesty?" Safar asked.

Hantilia indicated a large stone at Safar's feet. "Lift up the rock," she said.

He did as she directed and the stone came up like a lid. Beneath the stone, in a brick-lined hollow, was a packet wrapped in oil cloth.

Safar fumbled the package open, gasping when saw what it

contained—an old, leather bound book emblazoned with the sign of Asper.

He leafed through the book with numb fingers. It was a much larger and fuller version of the battered little volume he'd carried with him for so many years. Like the other, it was annotated in the master wizard's hand.

An even greater surprise awaited him in what Hantilia said next.

"I am kin to Lord Asper," she announced. "A direct descendant, to be exact. His great, great—oh, I can't count how many greats you'd put before it—granddaughter. That book has been in my family for many centuries. It was handed down with specific instructions for its use when a certain day came—the doom Lord Asper predicted for the world. It was my misfortune to be the one chosen by the Fates to carry those instructions out."

Safar frowned—he believed her, but some of what she said didn't quite make sense. "How could Asper know of me?" he asked. "I'm more than aware that he was wise and far seeing—but what you are speaking of would require so much specific knowledge of the future it defies imagination."

"Oh, your name isn't in the book, my dear Safar," Hantilia said. "Although if you read deeply you'll see he predicted someone very much like you."

She chuckled. "However, I think he believed you would be a demon like him. Regardless, you're getting the wrong idea. There are no details in the book on exactly what to do when doomsday comes. As you said, how could he predict all the events that have occurred? However, there is a spell in the book we were instructed to perform when trouble began.

"When I cast the spell, I was immediately stricken with a terrible malady." She shuddered at the memory. "I was unable to move from my bed for many weeks and the whole time I suffered the most horrible visions. It's a wonder I wasn't driven insane. In fact, until you rode into the grotto just now I wasn't certain if perhaps I was insane. Anyway, when I recovered I knew exactly what to do—up to and including the Spell of the Great Sacrifice, which was the most important and frightening requirement. I don't know how this knowledge was passed on to me. The point is, the knowledge was there and I felt obliged to act on the plan."

She hesitated, then said, "Strange as it may seem, as time went by and different things happened, I suddenly knew what I had to do next."

Hantilia smiled wryly. "The appearance of the Lady Felakia was my own idea. Actually, when I was ill I did see her in my dreams. She was one of the nicer visionary beings to visit me. I built on that dream to convince my followers of the rightness of the cause. A lie, to be sure. One I'm quite ashamed of and my real self is probably suffering in the hells right now for that sin. And rightly so. But I had to turn my followers into zealots. For who else but a zealot would agree to shoulder the blame for the sins of all human and demonkind—and then commit mass suicide as penance?"

Safar thought of how he'd manipulated his own people to what he believed was for the overall good. He hadn't asked them to commit suicide . . . although perhaps he had. Look at the situation they were all in—trapped in the Black Lands with Iraj ready to pounce at any moment. The odds were so short it was a grim joke to call it anything else but suicide. Even worse, he wasn't done with his kinsmen yet. If they survived this test he'd have to ask even more from them.

"I see from the look on your face, Safar Timura," Hantilia said, "that you have some . . . experience, shall I say . . . in matters of manipulation to achieve your own ends."

"That I do, Majesty," Safar said fervently. "That I do." He collected himself, then said, "I assume you were . . . uh . . . created by your . . . uh . . . living self, correct?"

"There's no need to spare my feelings, Safar," Hantilia said. "The real me no longer exists. And this image you see before you will vanish in a short while. But, to answer your question—Yes. She created me. I was placed here to await your arrival. The Great Sacrifice, you see, could only be performed in Caluz. Away from the machine and the Black Lands. Part of the spell's intent was to open a portal between the Black Lands to the shores of Caspan, where I was to greet you and instruct you further."

"When I first met your creator," Safar said, "she told me it was vital that I destroy the machine somehow. Was that true, or only a necessary lie?"

"It was partly true," Hantilia said. "I don't know what was going through my real self's mind, since I wasn't there. But I suspect I told you that was my desire so you would think I had a selfish, and therefore believable, motive for my actions. After all, if I had told you I planned a mass suicide to assist you I doubt if you would have listened much further."

Safar grimaced. That was certainly the truth!

"However, it is no prevarication that the machine presents a dire threat," Hantilia continued. "Regionally speaking, of course, since what happens to Esmir is happening everywhere else. From what I've been able to determine the machine is an open wound between Hadin and Esmir. If it isn't stopped, Esmir will cease to exist in not many years."

"And if it is stopped?"

"Another decade or so will be added to Esmir's span." The Queen frowned. "But it won't do more than delay the inevitable. Unless you can find a solution to the disaster destroying this world, that is. Frankly, I have grave doubts you can succeed. When you study the book I gave you, you'll see that my ancestor, Lord Asper, had the same doubts.

"There's a chance to save the world. But a very slim one, indeed."

She gave another of her elegant shrugs. "Destroy the machine, or don't destroy it. That's up to you. You will most certainly have the power to attempt it, thanks to the Spell of The Great Sacrifice."

Palimak fidgeted on the bench. He was getting restless and a bit bored with all this talk of things that happened in the past. He was here for the future!

"When do we get to the Oracle part?" he asked. "You know, when you tell us what to do to get to Syrapis?"

Hantilia smiled. "Would now be soon enough?" she asked.

Palimak nodded. "Maybe we'd better," he said. "Gundara and Gundaree say we don't have much time. I'm sorry everybody is dead and everything. Especially you. But we're not dead and I get the idea that any minute now you're going to go—poof! And disappear. Forever, probably."

Safar frowned. Although his opinions were bluntly put, Palimak was right. Safar could sense the magical creation that was Hantilia fading in and out—growing a bit weaker with each cycle.

"How do we start?" he asked the Queen.

She nodded at the book he held in his hands. "Give it to the boy and let him open it," she said.

Safar did as she asked. Palimak held the book gingerly, a little nervous.

"Go ahead," Hantilia gently urged. "Open it, my dear."

"Which page?"

"Let the book decide," was Hantilia's only reply.

Palimak's brow wrinkled in puzzlement. "I'm not sure I understand," he said.

"Just open the book, dear one, and you'll see."

Palimak took a deep breath and squared his shoulders. But being a child he went at the task perversely, carefully choosing a point about a third of the way through the book. He tried to pull it apart, but the pages stuck together and the book insisted on parting in the center.

The boy peered closely at the pages, expecting a miracle, but seeing nothing but a few poems.

"What do I do now?" he asked.

"Read one of the poems," Hantilia answered.

He looked back down at the book, trying to choose, but the words seem to skitter across the pages.

Hantilia sensed his difficulty. "Don't try to pick one," she advised. "Just open your mind to all possibilities."

Palimak squirmed, impatient, wanting to tell her this was stupid. For not the first time, he wondered why witches and wizards didn't speak plainly. They always used such funny words that didn't really mean anything when he thought about them later. Like Hantilia saying he should "open his mind to all possibilities." How do you open a mind? It's closed up in your head, for goodness sakes. And as for "all possibilities," that was just plain silly. It didn't describe anything. Or maybe it was the other way around. Maybe it described Everything. Was that what she meant?

Suddenly, to his amazement, words took form and a poem practically leapt from the page.

"This is great!" he exclaimed. "What do I do next?"

"Read to us," the Queen said. And so he did, chanting:

"The Gods are uneasy in their sleep.
They dream of wolves among the sheep.
Brothers in greed, kin to hate,
Wolves bar the path to Hadin's gates."

As Palimak spoke the last words, red smoke whooshed up and he reflexively jerked his head back in alarm.

"It's all right, Little Master," Gundara whispered. "It won't hurt you."

Palimak nodded and sat quite still, watching the smoke curling up like a snake. Then lips formed in the smoke—full lips parting in a woman's seductive smile.

Safar instantly recognized that smile. He'd first seen it as a boy, except Iraj had been with him then. He leaned closer as the lips opened to speak. Safar heard a woman's voice say:

"There is a veil through which no sage can see. For there is no lamp to light the fates. Yet know that in the place where the heavens meet the hells—good and evil, foul and fair, life and death, are all coins of the same value. Spend them wisely, seekers, or spend them foolishly, it makes no difference to the sleeping gods. But do not hesitate, do not stray from your path. And remember above all things—what two began, three must complete."

The smoke vanished and the book snapped shut.

Safar looked up at Palimak, expecting to see wonderment on his face. Instead, the boy was sneering.

"If I ever make one of those things," he announced, "I'm going to figure out how to make it talk so people can understand what it means."

Serious as the moment was, Safar couldn't help but laugh. "If you ever do, son," he said, "you'll have witches and wizards with fists full of gold lined up for miles to buy one minute of your oracle's time."

"Maybe," Palimak said absently. Then his eyes brightened. He started to say more, but Safar made a signal and he stopped, looking over at Hantilia.

To the boy's surprise her form had faded so much that she was nearly a shadow. In a few moments she would be gone.

"I have one other thing to tell you before I go, Safar Timura," she said.

"Go on, please, dear lady," Safar said.

"You will need ships to sail to Syrapis," she said. "So you must travel to Caspan next. There is a friend waiting for you there who can help.

"But do it immediately. Haste is of prime importance. I can't stress that too much.

"You have three days at the most to make your arrangements and return to Caluz for your people. The portal will be closed after that."

"Who is this man?" Safar asked.

"He's called Coralean," she said.

Safar reacted, surprised. But before he could ask more, the Queen turned to Palimak.

"Answer me quickly, dear one," she said. "I have little time left. Back at the palace . . . Did my temporal presence tell you about your mother?"

"Yes," Palimak said, trembling.

Hantilia smiled. "Good," she said. "Good."

She raised a hand of farewell, barely visible now.

"Wait!" Safar shouted. Hantilia's form steadied. "What about the lady? The Spirit Rider who led us here? Who is she?"

"Lady?" Hantilia said, eyes widening in surprise. "I know of no lady."

And then she was gone.

29

CORALEAN'S BARGAIN

As beautiful as Caspan had seemed from a distance, up close it was a horror. It was late afternoon when they reached the city. Plague bells were tolling and there was an awful stench of death rising from the great ditch encircling the city's walls—a sure sign even routine burials had been abandoned. The gates were wide open and people with the wild looks of refugees were streaming out, their belongings piled onto carts or on their backs. The walls, which had appeared so pristine white from the hills, were a filthy gray, marked further by crumbling stone and breaks in the wall due to civic neglect.

Palimak shuddered. "Do we have to go in there, father?" he asked.

"No, thank the gods," Safar said. "Coralean never liked city life. Too many people spying on you from alleys, is how he puts it."

They traveled a few miles more until they came upon a magnificent villa built on a hill that overlooked a graceful bay. In the dying sunlight Safar could see scores of white sails sitting off the coast and he idly wondered why so many ships were anchored in the same place.

As they approached the villa's gates—closed and barred against the coming night— Palimak suddenly said, "Look out, father!"

Before he could react a hard voice rang out from behind them. "Hold, stranger!"

Startled as he was, Safar knew better than to whirl around to see who was challenging them. He reined Khysmet in and sat quite still, whispering to Palimak that he shouldn't move a muscle. He heard heavy boots moving toward them, estimating by the sound that he was being confronted by at least half-a-dozen men.

Then three heavily armed thugs came into view, sidling up on either side. A crop-eared man grabbed Khysmet's reins while the others spread out, crossbows cocked and ready. Behind them, Safar could hear the other men cock their bows.

The scar-faced thug spoke to the others. "If the bastard moves, kill him! Don't wait for orders."

"What about the boy?" one of the men asked.

Crop Ear shrugged. "Kill him too."

Then he turned to Safar. "Talk," he commanded. "And you'd better make it good. We've got some graves down the bottom of the hill dug specially for liars."

Safar grinned down at the man. "It sure is good to see your ugly face again, Gitter," he said. "And I notice you still have one ear left. You're either a better thief than you used to be, or you've made good your promise to end your evil ways."

Gitter jerked back. Then he peered closer at Safar, an ugly smile slowly spreading across his face as recognition dawned.

"Ease off, lads," he ordered the men. "And, you, Hasin, run and tell the master Lord Timura's come for a visit."

"I once believed that Coralean was the luckiest man in the whole history of Esmir," the caravan master rumbled. "I thought that when the gods coined luck they must have kept back the fattest purse for Coralean's glorious arrival to this world."

He raised a crystal goblet in toast. "But now I know that I, Coralean, who has prided himself these many years for not only being lucky, but also on being rarely wrong in his judgment, was most grievously in error. You, my friend—not Coralean—won the fattest purse of all."

Safar clinked goblets with him. "Thank you for the words of hope," he said, "but I fear that when it comes to luck . . . I'm down to my last few coppers of the stuff."

They were taking their ease in Coralean's spacious study, which sat atop a specially built garden tower looking down on the bay. It was night. From the huge window Safar could see a forest of ships' lights playing on the waters. It was a peaceful scene, an idyllic scene, marred only by the face of the Demon Moon peering through a high cloud cover.

Both he and Palimak were bruised from the big man's hearty embraces of welcome. Coralean had then ordered his wives to see his visitors were fed, bathed and massaged with soothing oils. Palimak had fallen asleep during his massage. Now he was peacefully slumbering in a soft bed with silken sheets and perfumed pillows—the finest bed he'd known since he was a babe in Nerisa's luxurious care.

Coralean refilled Safar's goblet, then topped off his own. "I must confess I had grave doubts this meeting would ever occur. In fact, if I had any worthy competitors left, I would have suspected them of concocting a wild plot to diminish Coralean's hard-earned fortunes. Consider, my friend. A fellow in red robes and fiendish eyes shows up at my gates with news of your imminent arrival. It had been so long since I had heard anything of you, I thought you dead."

"We've been stranded in the Black Lands for quite awhile," Safar said.

"So you've told me. That also explains why I've heard nothing about Iraj Protarus' progress. It was as if his whole army had disappeared from the face of Esmir while hunting you. An impossibility, of course. Which gave Coralean hope that Safar Timura still survived. Otherwise our good king would be marching through these streets at this very minute, proclaiming victory over the evil Lord Timura."

"Which is why you listened to Hantilia's courier," Safar said. "Otherwise, Gitter would have planted him in your little garden of liars at the bottom of the hill."

Coralean grimaced. "What a world we live in, my friend, where a gentle man—a man who is loathe to kill a flea, who is, after all, only going about his honest purpose—could be forced to condone such deeds."

Safar buried a smile. Coralean was not a casually brutal man, but he had not made his great fortune by avoiding bloodshed. Many a new caravan track had been opened by Coralean over the

years—all well-marked by the heads of bandits—and other enemies—stuck up on posts.

"But to return to our wild-eyed stranger in red," Coralean said.
"He was not a man I would normally take seriously. I would have
given him a few coins and sent him on his madman way. However,
when he presented me with a bag of gold—a gift from his queen,
he said—well, I felt obliged to listen. I'd never heard of this
Queen Hantilia, but the payment was so unnecessarily large I
thought only royalty could be that foolish. I think the crowns they
wear are to blame. They squeeze their heads so tightly there's no
room for common business sense."

Safar chuckled. Then, "I still find it amazing you believed him.
If someone—even if it were the royal personage herself—told me
that a fellow hunted in every corner of Esmir would show up at my
door, dragging a thousand people behind him, I'd have declared
them insane to their face and called in a guard to escort them from
my presence."

Coralean stroked his beard. "Is it really a thousand, Safar?" he
asked. "You really did manage to carry away your entire village?
All of Kyrania? Without fatalities?"

Safar's face darkened. "I wish I could say no one died," he
replied. "I'm to blame for many deaths in this mad contest I've
been caught up in with Iraj. Besides war dead, many old people,
who should have been sitting at home spoiling their grandchil-
dren, have given up the ghost before their time." Then he smiled.
"But there's still at least a thousand of us," he said. "More, I suspect, than when we started because so many of our women have
given birth on the trail."

The old caravan master eyed him, considering. Then he
nodded. "Now I understand why you never claimed credit for
saving my life," he said. "You let Iraj take the greatest share of the
glory. This puzzled me at the time, because I suspected what you
had done but was loathe to embarrass you by asking for an
explanation."

Safar blinked, seeing the mental image of a young Iraj leaping
on the demon's back to rescue Coralean from certain death.

"It was Iraj who saved you," he objected. "Not me. No matter
what has happened since you can't deny that he was once a hero."

"This is true, my friend," Coralean said. "Iraj was . . . and is . . . a brave man. And I think that once he had good in his heart. Coralean is the most ambitious of men and he truly understands how ambition, however well meant in the beginning, can turn the most charitable men into devils. So understand, I was not slighting that particular deed. However, we still would all have fallen to those demon bandits if an avalanche had not suddenly, miraculously, swept that band of fiends back into the hells they came from."

He oiled his throat with a sip from his goblet. "Coralean is a believer in many things. In repose, with his wives begging his favors, he is quite a romantic fellow." He snorted, sounding like a bull. "But I am always suspicious of coincidence. You must admit, Safar, that the avalanche was too convenient to be marked up to coincidence. Then I didn't know, although I suspected, that you were a wizard. Now you are alternately cursed and hailed as the greatest wizard in all Esmir. So confess, my friend. It was you who caused the avalanche, was it not? It was you who ultimately spared my wives the awful grief of losing their dear, sweet Coralean."

Safar grinned, mischievous. "I'll never tell," he said. "Was it chance, or was it purpose? Come now, Coralean. You'd never expect a wizard to reveal something like that!"

Coralean slapped his thigh. "Well said," he rumbled. "You should have been king instead of Iraj. With me to advise you, we would have built the grandest fortune the world has ever seen."

Safar turned serious. "Thrones or fortunes," he said, "mean nothing in these times. Perhaps they never did. Perhaps they never will. It's useless to speculate."

Coralean shrugged. "Speculation is my nature," he said. "Speculation is the sole reason I not only listened to the red robed one, but waited many days after my planned departure from Caspan to see if what he said was true."

He pointed to the bobbing ship lights. "I even hired ships on the doubtful word of an insane messenger, who claimed to speak for an unseen queen whose name had somehow escaped Coralean's notice."

Coralean paused to empty his goblet. "I told you I thought you lucky. Luckier even than Coralean. You are also wise. Not as wise as I am, to be sure, but that would be an impossibility." He tapped his head. "No, in wisdom I am your superior. Just as I am every man's superior when it comes to the art of pleasing women. Strong brain, strong loins, those are things that make Coralean, Coralean."

"I'll grant you both with no argument," Safar said. "Especially wisdom. Who else but Coralean would be calculating enough to remain Iraj's confident, but still place a wager on his worst enemy?"

Coralean grinned. "Only a portion of it was due to calculation," he said. "The rest was because of my deep feelings of friendship towards you."

"And my luck."

Coralean's grin widened. "And your luck. Especially your luck."

Safar nodded at the ships sitting offshore. "What happens when Iraj finds out what you've done?" he asked.

The caravan master grimaced. "Coralean has no intention of lingering in Caspan long enough to realize the depths of Iraj Protarus' wrath. My original intention was to seek retirement as far away as my gold would take me. My thinking was, once Iraj caught you he would start looking at men like me with suspicious eyes. And that would be my end. Once that decision was made, I didn't know where to run. Either Iraj would eventually find me, or I would die a trivial but agonizing death in the chaos that has afflicted Esmir."

Safar laughed. "Now I understand," he said. "You couldn't flee Esmir, because no one really knows what lies beyond the Great Sea."

"Except for you," Coralean said. "One of the things that madman told me was that you had a goal. A peaceful island you knew of far across the sea."

"Syrapis," Safar said.

"Yes," Coralean said. "Syrapis. I like the sound of it. A good place for business."

"You really are casting the dice, my friend," Safar said. "Things must be desperate for you."

"Desperate enough," Coralean replied, "to consider things that go against my generous nature. A lesser man than I might threaten to deny you passage on those ships if you did not agree to carry him away from this cursed place."

"I have no objection to your company," Safar said. "In fact, I welcome it."

Coralean refilled both their goblets. "Good, it's settled then. A nice bargain for both of us, with each thinking he got the better of the other, but not too much to injure friendship."

Safar started to speak, then hesitated, thinking. Finally he shrugged and dug an old map from his pocket.

"You gave me maps once," he said. "They saved my life and the lives of my people. Now, let me return the favor."

He unrolled the map, copied in his flowing hand from the Book of Asper. It showed the Great Sea from Caspan, to a large island many miles away.

Coralean studied it with an expert eye. "Yes," he said. "I see how to go."

Safar rolled the map up and handed it to him. "Here," he said. "Take it."

The caravan master was so surprised by this gesture that his mouth fell open and for a moment he looked like a huge, bearded fish.

His jaws snapped shut. "Surely you have another."

"No, that's the only copy," Safar said. "I have three days to accomplish what I have to do. If you don't see me by then, sail without us."

Coralean grinned. "How do you know I'll wait?" he asked. "Coralean is a man of his word, but sometimes urgent business forces a man of industry and ambition to make regretful decisions."

Safar looked at him, measuring. Then he nodded. "You'll wait," he said, flat.

"I suppose if I don't," Coralean pressed, "you will cast some wizardly spell of misfortune upon me, correct?"

Safar chuckled. "Another sort of question no wizard will ever answer, my friend," he said. "But let me tell you this. If I do, your wives will be the first to notice!"

The caravan master roared laughter, leaping to his feet to drag

Safar from his chair for another tortuous embrace of Coralean friendship.

"What a man you are, Safar Timura!" he cried. "What a man!"

Then he broke away to refill their goblets.

"More drink, Safar," he said. "More drink. It's the only honorable way to seal a bargain between such like-minded brothers.

"To Syrapis!" he shouted, raising his glass.

"To Syrapis!" Safar replied. "And may we live long enough to see it!"

30

THE FACE OF MURDER

Luka was a fighting prince. Born of rape and murder, teethed on steel, he had carried his father's royal banner into scores of crucial encounters. Under Iraj, he had seen warfare on an even greater scale. When it came to the shedding of blood and the taking of life, Luka firmly believed he had seen it all. But when he led his shock troops into the Caluzian Pass all his previous experiences seemed like nothing.

The road through the pass was treacherous. The storm had left a thick blanket of snow in its wake, hiding the pits and broken rubble, turning them into traps for the unwary. Overhead, a threatening sky boiled with clouds that cast everything into intermittent shadows, making travel harder still. Even the demon steeds with their fierce natures and huge cat claws were sorely tested. Several suffered broken limbs and had to be destroyed before they'd progressed beyond the second bend.

Luka thought he knew what to expect. Fari's vision had given him a good look at the enemy he would face. Powerful spells had been cast to sheath their weapons so they would cut through ghostly flesh and parry ghostly thrusts. Even so, he was not prepared when the horde of warriors rose up to confront him.

The battle for the Caluzian Pass was to consist of three waves, of which Luka's was easily the most dangerous. He was to lead a shock force composed of his best cavalryfiends. His mission was to charge through and break the enemy formation. Under no circumstances was he to engage in fixed fighting or worry about what was happening behind his back. He was to charge and keep charging, leaving the next two waves of troops to deal with whatever was happening behind him. Not only that, but he must maintain his demon form to inspire his soldiers, thereby abandoning the extra magical powers and strength of a shape changer. In short, if the slightest thing went wrong he would be the first to fall.

Skilled as he was, brave as he was, Luka had no love of battle. As a prince his death was always ardently sought—on both sides. The enemy wanted his head as a trophy of their prowess. And in his own court so many would gain from his assassination that he had to be constantly on lookout for a knife in his back from one of his own soldiers. So he despised battles. Distrusted the motives of those who sent him to fight.

Killing, he firmly believed, was a dish to be enjoyed in private. It was like torturing an animal bound for the table—the greater the entree's agony, the tastier the dish. In other words, the fear and pain should be confined to the victim with no danger to the chef.

Luka was thinking of such things when he entered the pass and so he shouldn't have been surprised when he was stricken by a sudden feeling that he'd entered a kitchen where he was set to be the main course. Never mind that Fari had warned him—and armed him—against the spells of fear and hopelessness the enemy was sure to employ against him. A vision leaped into his mind's eye of a demon bound to a spit slowly rotating over a slow fire—twisting and screaming and begging his tormentors to end the agony with a swift and merciful death. The demon was Luka.

The prince might have been overcome there, the battle lost before it had even begun. But the moans and wails of his brother warriors jolted him to his senses. Cursing himself as a fool and a coward, he cast Fari's spell. There was nothing to mark one moment from the next. No fiery blast, no sorcerous smoke, only an immediate feeling of heavy shackles falling away—and then he was free.

His demon brothers shouted gleefully, as if they'd already won a great victory. Jokes and laughter ran through the ranks, punctuated by loud boasts from young warriors about what they'd do to the enemy when they found him. Luka was too experienced to be drawn in. He had no doubt this would be only the first of many spells hurled against them. And if his opponent was wily he would be saving the worst for last.

A dedicated survivor, Luka granted extreme cunning to his enemy. But he couldn't pause or turn back to study the extent of his enemy's perfidy. In such circumstances a prudent soldier, a soldier loath to have his fangs plucked from his lifeless jaws to make a necklace for some tavern wench, knows he has only one recourse—madness.

Luka signaled his buglers to sound the attack, unsheathed his sword, and raised it high—desperately driving away the memory of the human, Vister, in identical circumstances. Digging deep for all the courage, all the blind battle lust he could muster.

"For the King!" he shouted over the blare of the horns.

"For the King!" his brothers roared in return.

And with no enemy in sight they charged.

In the end, it was this act of madness that saved him.

As Luka came around the bend, honor guard lagging several paces behind him, his mount's claws broke through the snow's crust into a hidden pit. The beast stumbled, nearly foundering, Luka sawing on its reins and raking its sides with his spurs to bring it up. Hissing in catlike fury, the animal's head snaked around, long fangs bared to punish him. He leaned forward, whacking its sensitive nose with the flat of his blade to remind it who was master and who was slave.

At that moment the air was suddenly filled with the deadly song of the arrow and something passed over his head. He heard meaty thunks of arrows striking their targets, cries of the wounded, surprised coughs of those who would never breathe again.

He came up, raising his shield in time to deflect a second swarm, cursing Iraj for putting him in such a place. Shouting orders to rally his warriors out of the shock of ambush.

It was then that he saw the enemy. Time was knocked from its course and Luka's whole world became a long and frozen moment. Hundreds upon hundreds of ghostly warriors were marching toward him. There were no challenging roars, no shouted insults, no loud chorus of what would be done to them. He heard none of the words that give a normal army its voice. Curses that warriors are encouraged to shout when they advance on their foes. Shouts of bloody purpose crafted by bullying sergeants long ago and passed down from one generation of soldiers to the next. All calculated to shrink the enemy's courage and enlarge the imagined prowess of the aggressor.

Luka, who would have ignored such things like a fishing hawk ignores water when it dives for its prey, was unnerved by their absence. His entire existence was suddenly filled with the image of silent men, deadly men, marching in measured steps to crush his life away. The thud of their boots, the clank of their armor, hammering their purpose against his.

Fari's final words of warning crawled to the fore. "There is no single heart to this enemy," he'd said. "No single head we can lop off to defeat them. Each one will fight until the end. The only way to defeat them is to kill them all."

Luka forced himself to ignore the mass of advancing warriors. He fixed on one man—a huge ghost with hollow eyes and bloody lips—one step ahead of the others.

The demon prince spurred his mount forward, shouting for his soldiers to follow.

He had time for one long breath, then he was on them. The large ghost he'd aimed for hurled his spear with such force that it broke Luka's shield in two. He threw the shield away, slashing with his spell-charged sword. He had a moment's satisfaction of feeling his blade bite through ghostly flesh, seeing the man fall, mouth coming open to spew blood-red smoke, then he felt the shock of collision as his mount crashed into the advancing soldiers. That shock followed another and then another as his fiends waded into battle, cutting and jabbing, forcing their way through by the sheer weight of their massed charge.

Made vulnerable by Fari's spells, the ghosts no longer had the protection of shadowy afterlife. When they were struck they died, bloody smoke spurting from their mouths. Even so, they did not die easily. They fought with wild but still silent purpose. Luka killed many of them, but he saw just as many of his own soldiers die as well.

For what seemed like an eternity the struggle was stalled at the point of first collision. It seemed that every ghost who died was immediately replaced by another. Luka felt as if he were pressing against a huge wall. And no matter how hard he fought, the wall would not give.

Just when he thought all was hopeless, he sensed a sudden weakening. He pressed harder, driving his mount against the armored mass, crying out for others to join him.

Then the line broke and Luka burst through the first formation. A moment later he was surrounded by his own soldiers who were streaming through the gap.

Luka had enough time to see a second force—mighty as the first—coming toward him.

He charged, once again bracing for the shock of collision.

Then blood lust overcame him and he knew no more.

Biner turned away from the scene below, sickened by the slaughter.

"I can't watch anymore," he said to Arlain. "Got nothin' left in me guts to heave."

Hidden by the magical cloud cover, the balloon was hovering over the Caluzian Pass spying on Iraj's fight to take it.

"Poor devils," Biner said. "Dyin' once seems hard enough. But twice!" He shuddered. "Makes me skin crawl even thinkin' about it, much less havin' to watch! It's more'n a sensitive showman like meself can take."

Arlain stood well away from the railing, trembling, tears streaming down her face. She hadn't been able to watch at all.

"Ith it over yet?" she asked.

Biner nodded. "Almost," he said. "For awhile I was hopin' them Guardians wouldn't break. But they did. And then old Protarus hit 'em twice more. Mos' awful thing I ever did see—or ever hope to see. Protarus' fiends are down there now finishin' off what's left."

"Pleath!" Arlain protested. "Don't tell me anymore. All I think of ith what'th going to happen if thoth awful tholdierth catch uth."

Biner squared his massive shoulders. "They won't!" he vowed. "Not if old Biner can help it."

"If only Thafar would get back," Arlain said.

"Never mind Safar," Biner said. "He's either gonna make it or he ain't. We have to be ready either way."

"Maybe they won't find the gate into the valley," Arlain said hopefully. "Maybe they'll mith it and jutht keep on going."

Biner snorted. "Sure," he said. "And smoke don't rise, the wind don't change, and if you dump the balloons the airship'll just keep on flyin'!"

King Protarus was agitated as he approached the group gathered around Lord Fari. From the angry tone of the voices he heard echoing across the gory snow, the king was riding into the middle of a debate. It was an argument so heated the participants didn't notice the imminent arrival of the royal party.

Iraj pulled up his horse, raising a hand to bring his aides and guards to a halt. Pushing aside the reason for his agitation, he leaned forward, listening.

"This is insanity, Fari!" Luka was raging. "You're holding up the entire godsdamned army with all your second-guessing."

"I must agree with Prince Luka," Kalasariz said. "There's a time for caution and a time to strike onward."

Then their voices dropped to more normal levels and Iraj couldn't hear what was said. He let the shape-changer's side of him come to the fore, snout erupting, bones cracking and shifting horribly, forming the head of a giant wolf sitting on a human body. There were involuntary gasps of terror from his men and he snarled for silence.

With his heightened senses he could hear their words with startling clarity.

"How many times must I repeat myself," Fari was raging, "before you two fools understand what I am trying to tell you. Lord Timura's trail ends here. It does not continue on through the pass."

"Something must be wrong with your sniffers, Fari," Luka said. "And as always you are too stuffed with pride to admit it when your magic fails you. I'm the one who is most at risk here. I'm the one who nearly died I don't know how many times today. I am the one most likely to die as a result of your pride. But never mind that. The point is, this halt you ordered is not only likely to result in many unnecessary casualties, but also endangers the entire expedition. The longer we wait to clear the rest of the pass, the more time we give the enemy to regroup."

"And for Safar Timura to escape," Kalasariz put in. "Which is far more important. I guarantee you that if we bring him to ground, Protarus won't care how many of our soldiers' lives were wasted."

"I warn you both," Fari said. "If you prevail over me with the king Lord Timura has an extremely good chance of prevailing over us."

Kalasariz sneered. "You've underestimated this man all along, Fari. As have you, Luka. I have more experience with him than either of you. I first tried to kill him when he was nothing more than a ragged-cloaked student in Walaria with barely enough funds to pay for the crusts he ate. I even had him on the executioner's block. On his knees, mind you. His neck bent for the sword. He escaped despite what any rational fellow would judge as impossible odds against him. Just as he has escaped us countless times ever since."

Fari rasped laughter. "What's this?" he mocked. "You tried to kill Timura before? During a time when it was known to all he was the king's dearest friend. Why, it was my impression that you told the king you were Timura's secret ally in Walaria. You repeated that tale when we went to the king with charges that Timura was conspiring against him. A tale you told in the manner of a man who was shocked to learn of Timura's perfidy."

Kalasariz started to answer, but just then the three sensed Iraj's presence. They turned, gaping when they saw him, burying their reactions as quickly as they could.

Iraj kept his wolf's head intact for a long moment, making sure they'd worry about how much he'd overhead. The spy master, whose remarks gave him reason to have the most to fear, was the first to recover.

"Hail, O King!" Kalasariz cried. "Once again you have inspired us to win a great victory!"

Fari and Luka shouted similar bold words of praise.

Iraj resumed his human shape, flicking the reins for his horse to amble forward. He sat easily in the saddle as if he hadn't a care in the world, letting a sarcastic smile play across his face to heighten their tension. Inside, his emotions were boiling to a froth. There were two more battles he had to win before the day was done. First, Safar. Next, his spell brothers. To build confidence and bring his emotions under control he imagined Safar's corpse under his boot while he confronted these three—his final enemies. From this moment on he had to view everything as a sport. A sport in which Iraj Protarus, king of kings, had no master. With one hand he would display a whip of fear, with the other, a broad palm heaped with the gift of the king's favor.

As Iraj closed the distance between them Fari caught a whiff of the king's intent—plus . . . something else. Something he couldn't quite put a talon on, except that it did not bode well for him or his companions in conspiracy. In his long life Lord Fari had advised and survived many kings. It was his ambition that Iraj Protarus would be the last royal fool he had to suffer. A master wizard, a demon of incredible cunning, Fari knew every mask a king could present to his royal advisers. And in Iraj's face he read his demise. His old heart bumped over the rocky road of logic. It was the Spell of Four that chained Protarus to them. A spell that he had created and cast. A bond that could be rearranged—with Fari as the ultimate mechanic—but not broken. Then suspicion, his most faithful friend, crept into his bosom. The king has a secret, he thought. A secret that did not bode well for any of them.

Before Iraj came within hearing distance, Fari whispered, "Beware, brothers! If you want to live, be with me!"

"Bugger you!" Luka whispered. "We're in the right. You are most grievously wrong."

"Who cares?" Kalasariz hissed. The spy master didn't have to reflect on Fari's warning. He too, sensed danger. "New truce. Quick!"

"And let you be the first to stab me in the back?" Luka replied. "Bugger you as well!"

"Trust me!" Fari urged. "Or all is lost!"

"Truce, dammit! Truce!" Kalasariz said.

Iraj rode up before Luka had a chance to answer. On horseback Iraj towered over them, his crown sparkling with jewels and rare metals. Shoulders squared, head uplifted, that knowing, scar-twisted smile playing across his lips, making his face unreadable.

The king raised his sword to Luka in salute. "It is you who should be congratulated for this victory, my good and loyal friend," he said. "Your bravery is an example to us all."

As the demon prince bowed in humble thanks the sense of peril became so strong his skin pebbled and began to itch as if he were about to molt.

"I am not worthy, Your Majesty," he murmured.

"Don't be so modest," Iraj said. "It is you and you alone who deserves full credit. And to reward your great deeds I will give you the honor of leading my army onward to even greater glories."

Not far away Kalasariz' assassins were roaming the battlefield cutting the throats of the enemy fallen with magical knives. Making certain no Guardian would never rise again. Luka heard the tell-tale hiss of ghostly life fleeing the temporal world and reconsidered.

"Modesty has nothing to do with it, Your Majesty," he said. "The fact is, at this time it would be imprudent of me to assume such an honor."

Iraj let his eyebrows rise as if he were surprised at this statement. "Is there some problem?"

"Only one of indecision, Your Majesty," Luka said. He gestured at his companions. "At this moment we were debating the merits of what to do next."

Out of the corner of his eye Luka saw Fari and Kalasariz visibly relax. The truce was on.

"What's this?" Iraj said. "A disagreement? At such a crucial moment for us all?"

"Only a small one, Majesty," Fari said, wringing claws of humility. "My brothers think we should continue on until we reach the end of this pass. And, presumably, come upon Lord Timura waiting for us in Caluz. I, on the other hand, believe that some sort of trick has been played on us."

Further down the pass they heard a chorus of frustrated howls from a pack of sniffers. Fari nodded toward the sound. "Safar Timura doesn't wait for us there, Majesty," he said. "At least that is my opinion. I think we will only find the machine that has been bedeviling us since we entered the Black Lands. If I am right, many of us will die before we have time to turn back. And once again Lord Timura will most certainly be laughing up his sleeve at us as he makes his escape."

Iraj peered down at Kalasariz. Although he was smiling, his eyes were deadly. "And you, my lord?" he asked. "Where do you stand?"

"With Prince Luka, Majesty," Kalasariz said. He nodded at Fari. "No disrespect intended, of course. Only an honest disagreement among brothers who wish to serve you well."

Iraj already knew the substance of their disagreement. But he didn't know the reason. He brought himself up short. There were many perils in the double-think necessary to this game he played. Above all things, Iraj reminded himself, you have to remember that Safar must come first. Once that game was won, the end of these traitorous bastards would quickly follow. Before he shifted his attention, however, he made special note that once again his three opponents had overcome their personal animosities to oppose him as one.

Then he had another thought and his belly crawled. But what of his dream? The one that had been bedeviling him when he came upon these deadly conspirators. He gritted his teeth, remembering his terror. Yes, the dream. A dream within a dream so complicated it defied rational interpretation. And yet it was the sort of dream a man could relive in its entirety in the blink of an eye.

Iraj blinked.

And relived the dream . . .

He was only a boy, too young to be alone in the mountains. His name was Tio and he had spent a sleepless night guarding the goat herd against imagined horrors. Now he slept the sleep of the exhausted, the gentle dawn rising over the peaceful Kyranian mountains.

Iraj was a wolf, a great gray wolf, slipping across the meadow, leading his ravenous spell brothers to the kill. His plan was to slay the boy but leave the herd untouched. A coldly calculated murder intended to strike terror in the hearts of the Kyranians and undermine their faith in their vaunted hero, Safar Timura.

During Iraj's time with these people, who in his youth had shielded him against his enemies, he'd learned that wolves killed goats, not people. So poor little Tio, defenseless Tio, a child who whose death would wring pity from the hardest of hearts, would be his meat that day. He and his spell brothers would gut him, ravage him, and when the villagers came to investigate they'd find the goats bleating over the child's remains.

Then Kalasariz howled a warning, "Interlopers!" and Iraj spotted Graymuzzle and her starving pack descending on the goats. His rage was immediate and uncontrollable. How dare these wizened creatures plot to spoil his carefully wrought plan? His pent up shape changer's fury exploded and he charged into the pack, scattering them. All he could think of was "kill, kill," and so he killed and kept killing until there was nothing left alive on the meadow except Graymuzzle, trapped against a rock outcropping.

But as he went for her, instead of cowering and meekly accepting death, she suddenly roared in a fury as wild as his own. She leaped at him, slavering jaws snapping to do whatever damage she could before she died. Iraj caught an image of pups whining in a cave and knew the reason for her blind, suicidal attack. It made her death all the more delicious and his spell brothers crowded in close beside him to lap up her torment.

Ordering the others back, Iraj went to the little stone shelter alone, eager to feed on the child who waited there asleep. He rushed into the shelter, every nerve firing in delightful anticipation. Tio bolted up, screaming in terror, raising his puny goatherder's staff to protect himself.

Iraj bit the staff in two, then killed the boy.

Suddenly the child was sitting up again, but this time instead of screaming, he was smiling, and it wasn't Tio's face he was looking at. It was Safar's! A young Safar, the Safar he'd known long ago with those gentle blue eyes that could see the good in him.

Shocked and frightened to his core, Iraj reeled back.

Safar said, "So tell me, brother. How do you like being king?" And then he laughed.

Iraj recovered, more furious than ever, hysterically so, thinking how can this be, how can this be? Safar smiled the whole time he was killing him.

But he wouldn't stay dead. He kept rising, calling Iraj brother, his laughter becoming more mocking each time he died.

Finally, it was over and the corpse lay still under his paws and Iraj knew it would rise no more.

Exhausted, emptied of all emotion, Iraj stared down at the body.

But when he saw the youthful face staring up at him the horror came full circle.

For the face was his own!

"Majesty?" Fari was murmuring. "Is something wrong?"

Iraj blinked and he was back in the Caluzian Pass, his spell brothers looking at him anxiously.

"No," he said, shaking off the dream. "There's nothing wrong. I was only considering our problem." He turned to Fari. "I've heard all sides of the dispute," he said. "Save one thing."

"Yes, Majesty?" Fari asked.

Iraj said, "What do you propose we do? Luka and Kalasariz say we should continue on through the pass. You say we shouldn't. But you haven't said what we ought to do instead. We can't just sit here scratching our heads forever in dumb amazement at Safar's latest trick. If, as you say, it is a trick."

Fari drew himself up, confidence restored. He said, "Majesty, if you we allow me two hours—three at the most—I think I can solve the riddle of the vanished Lord Timura." He pointed at a rock outcropping bulging from a nearby canyon wall. "His trail ends there. Our sniffers have searched and double-searched the area in all directions. But they keep coming back to this point."

"Go on," Iraj said.

"I suggest," Fari said, "that I be allowed to gather my wizards together and make a casting to find out exactly what happened."

Iraj looked at Luka and Kalasariz, then back at Fari, thinking.

There was good logic on both sides. It was Iraj's nature to favor quick action. But on the other hand—Iraj chopped off further speculation and made his decision. And he said to Fari:

"Call your wizards!"

31

THE FIGHT FOR CALUZ

Leiria thought the valley was particularly beautiful that day. Blue skies, sweet breezes, joyous birds swooping over fruited fields and babbling rivers. Looking down on them from the hilltops the city of Caluz shone under the gentle sun, seemingly full of promise and hope and welcome.

Leiria thought of the palace courtyard heaped with all the Caluzian dead and turned away, choking on bile.

The business awaiting her didn't make her feel any better. At the moment she was sitting at a small camp table going over last minute arrangements with Khadji Timura and Sergeant Dario.

"No one is very happy about this latest plan of yours, Leiria," Khadji said. "They want you to reconsider. Some of them are even demanding it."

Leiria sighed, shaking her head. Civilians! What could you do with them? They kept imagining orders were open to debate.

"Tell them no," she said.

Khadji frowned. "You really ought to at least hear them out," he protested. "Frankly, I'm in agreement with many of their complaints."

Leiria's eyes hardened. It was all she could do to keep from snapping his head off. Sometimes Safar's father could be a most difficult man. Then her lips twitched with a sudden urge to smile. And so is Safar, she thought. And his mother. And his sisters. Hells, all the Timuras were absolute mules. Even Palimak seemed to have caught the disease.

Calmed, she did her best to temper her words. "I don't know how many times we've been over this, Khadji," she said. "I thought we were in agreement. It might not be the best plan, but it's the only one that might, just might mind you, give us a chance."

"I'm with the Captain, here," Dario broke in. He nodded at the nearby field where young Kyranian soldiers were pawing through their gear, keeping some things, but throwing most of it away. "And you can tell the knotwits on the Council of Elders that so are my lads."

"You don't understand," Khadji said. "We've already lost our homes and almost all of our possessions. All we have left of our old lives are the few things we've managed to carry along in our wagons. Now you want us not only to abandon them, but to leave the wagons as well. Plus most of the animals. You're even begrudging us a few extra clothes."

"You can't eat clothes," Leiria said. "You can't fight with clothes. That's a lesson everyone should have learned by now."

Dario glowered at Khadji. "And you can't eat clay pots, either," he said, "in case that's what's really stuck in your craw."

Khadji blushed. "I'll admit that was on my mind," he said. "If only I could—"

Leiria put a hand on his. "Listen to me, Khadji," she said. "I promised Safar that if Iraj found us before he got back I'd do everything I could to see that as many of you as possible escape. I'm not trying to be cruel or unfeeling, but the way I've outlined is the best I can manage."

Drawing on her last reserves of patience, she went over the plan one more time. She'd divided the Kyranians into two groups—those who would fight and those who would run. The latter was by far the largest group, women and children and those too old or infirm to fight. When and if they got the signal all of those people, led by Khadji who had the maps, were to head for the mountains.

"Aim for those peaks," Leiria said, pointing at the twin pillars that towered over the range. "With luck, you'll find a track there to make things easier. Just make sure the track heads north to the Great Sea."

Khadji nodded. "There's a port at Caspan," he said. "I saw it on the map."

"Yes, Caspan," Leiria said. "Safar said we might be able to get some ships there. And I've given you the gold he left to hire them to take us to Syrapis."

"What about Safar?" Khadji said mournfully. "What about my son? And little Palimak! What about him?"

"I think it would be best if you put them out of your mind," Leiria said. "Concentrate on getting to those peaks. Then set your sights on Caspan. Let the rest of us, including Safar and Palimak, worry about how we're going to catch up to you."

Then she carefully explained the rest of the plan. As Khadji and the villagers fled, Sergeant Dario and the bulk of the soldiers would follow in their footsteps as shields.

Meanwhile, Leiria and a small force of their best soldiers would attempt to hold Iraj at the breakthrough point for as long as they could. When the inevitable rout came the survivors would fall back to join Dario. The strategy from there would be to fight a rear guard action—using every trick Dario and Leiria had drummed into the young men to keep Iraj from overtaking the refugees.

"Speed is our only real defense," Leiria said. "Iraj taught me the value of speed long ago. That, and surprise, win more battles than not. When Iraj breaks through he'll think his job is nearly done. In his mind all he'll have to do is overtake a caravan moving at the speed of the slowest group. Ox-drawn wagons and heavily laden people on foot. Which is why I want to leave all that behind and fool him at the start. We won't fool him long, but gods willing it will be just long enough."

To accomplish this, Leiria had ordered that everything be abandoned but the barest necessities. Anything the Kyranians took with them would be loaded on the goats and llamas and horses, with experienced mountain lads to drive them along. The old and the sick and the very young would ferried to safety on horses and camels.

Dario gave a sharp nod of agreement when she was done. "A fine plan," he said. "One of the best these old ears have ever heard."

Khadji wavered. "Maybe," he said. "Maybe."

Dario snorted. "No maybe to it," he said. "Quit chewin' on it, man, and swallow."

"I'll do my best to make them listen," Khadji said. "But I can't promise what their reaction will be."

Leiria's patience collapsed. "I'll make it easy for you," she said. "From this moment on army rules will apply to all situations."

Ignoring Khadji's puzzled look, she turned to Dario.

"Sergeant!" she snapped.

Dario stiffened. "Yes, Captain."

"You will tell your men that once the enemy is engaged anyone who disobeys my commands is to be killed on the spot. No questions. No excuses. No arguments. And no hesitation. Do you understand?"

Dario buried a grin and snapped a salute. "Yes, Captain," he growled. "And I'll make it my personal business they start with the Council of Elders."

Khadji goggled at her. "You wouldn't really do that!" he said.

She gave him the hardest look she could. "I swear on my friendship and love of Safar, your son, that I will do everything I say."

Before he could respond there was a loud explosion from overhead. Their heads jerked up and all eyes were immediately fixed on the airship sailing over the mountains into the valley. A bright green flare guttered in its wake. Immediately there was a second explosion as Biner fired off another of Safar's magical flares.

"Iraj has found us," Leiria said, flat. "Now we'll see who wants to live and who wants to die."

An hour later she was standing next to the outcropping that marked the magic gate into Caluz. A few feet away Renor and Seth were inspecting the weapons of the brave few who would make this last stand. Off in the distance she could see the Kyranians streaming out of the valley as fast as they could. It was the oddest caravan she'd ever seen. Bleating goats and llamas, light packs tied to their backs, were leaping ahead of the refugees, scrambling over the rocky path that led into the mountains. Old men and women swayed back and forth on bawling camels, infants clutched in their arms. Just behind them came the main group led by Khadji, followed by Dario and his soldiers, who were cracking whips and roaring for everyone to "hurry, hurry, hurry!"

And not once did she see anyone stop to argue. Leiria had only a moment's satisfaction. Safar would be pleased. Then she suddenly felt very cold and very alone. Was this how she would end? In this bedamned valley with no one to care and no one to mourn her passing? A knot rose in her throat and she suddenly felt very sorry for herself. If only she could see Safar once more. If only they could kiss one final time, she thought, it might all seem worthwhile. Then she became angry with herself for allowing such weakness. She swiped at a leaky eye, muttering all the curses at her command, lashing confidence and resolve back into life. It was difficult. Surprisingly so. Fear scuttled into her belly when she realized just how far and how deep her morale had plummeted.

Then she heard a shout from overhead. Leiria look up and saw the airship settling closer to the ground, Biner and Arlain and the other circus performers gathered at the rail to look down at her.

"We're with you, Leiria!" Biner roared in his loud, pure, ring-master's voice.

Arlain waved to her, shooting a long, gaily colored stream of dragon flames from her mouth. Kairo tipped his head in salute, making funny faces. Elgy and Rabix played a stirring tune, filling the air and her heart with glad music.

Then they all leaned far out over the railing to chorus, "Damn everything but the circus!"

And she was no longer alone.

Laughing and weeping tears of relief, Leiria waved at them.

At that moment the ground lurched under her feet and the outcropping bulged outward as if under extreme pressure. Shale broke and Leiria ducked as debris showered down on the path.

Then all was still and all was silent.

Her temples pulsed in slow time with the beat of her heart. Once . . . Twice . . . Thrice . . .

Wolves bayed and she drew her sword, boots spreading apart into fighting stance. Renor and the other young soldiers gathered around her, their weapons at the ready, cursing loudly to control their chattering teeth.

Then the outcropping swung away on magical hinges and Leiria peered into the revealed darkness.

Nothing.

She looked deeper.

Still nothing.

And deeper still, nerves winding tighter, neck muscles cabling with tension, each second a water drop trembling to fall.

It was almost a relief when nothingness ended and the yellow-eyed demons scrambled out of the darkness to get her.

She shouted a challenge and braced herself to meet them.

This time Biner couldn't turn away. This time Arlain made herself watch. They saw the earth shudder, saw the gate swing open and then Leiria's shout reached out to chill them. To fix them on the scene below. They saw Leiria brace, saw her soldiers flow in to form a line—Leiria at its center. Suddenly a demon horde burst out of the gateway, ululating war cries shattering the air.

Then the two lines converged and Leiria was swallowed up in the chaos of battle.

"Now! Now!" Arlain cried. "Do it now!"

She lunged toward a pile of crates heaped near the railing. Biner stopped her, gently pulling her back.

"We have to wait," he said. "It's not time for our entrance."

Arlain heard cries of pain from below and trembled. "We have to help her," she pleaded.

"Not yet," Biner said. Then, to cut through—"Remember how we rehearsed it."

Arlain sagged, overcome by performer's logic, and turned back to the railing. Whispering the actor's mantra for strength: "Character, timing, plot, character, timing plot . . ." and so on as the tale unfolded beneath her.

She made herself think of it that way. A tale to be told in two acts. Act One: The villains attack. Heroes fight bravely, but are overwhelmed. Act Two: Heroes retreat, villains in pursuit, all seems lost. Cue The Forces of Good. Which was Arlain's cue, the circus' cue—the big It Was All A Clever Trick Surprise. Villains routed, heroes rewarded, cue the music— Happy Ending, ta da!

Arlain watched the horror below, doing a very bad job at keeping her actor's pose, visibly shrinking as the sights and sounds of battle increased. Awaiting her cue.

Leiria was a calm center to the storm raging about her. It was place where there was no fear or anger. No shrill relief when she parried a well-struck blow, no fierce animal enjoyment at slipping a guard and killing her opponent. She was a cold, calculating killing machine, ripping through every weak point her enemy revealed. And there were many. So many weaknesses she could end the fight now with a rallying cry for her men to charge the demons and seal the gap.

She and Safar had planned for this moment. The doorway between the pass and the valley was no more than two wagons wide. No matter how large the force Iraj hurled at them only so many could come through the gap at a time. A handful of determined soldiers would be enough to stop them. The problem was, this handful could only kill a finite number and with the enormous force opposing them it was only a matter of time before they were overwhelmed. To give the fleeing villagers any chance at all more time and more enemy casualties were needed.

Leiria kept her mind fixed on the plan, an impersonal observer of very personal events.

A demon towered over her, roaring in her face. Slicing at her with a huge battle ax and at the same time lashing out with a demon spell of hopelessness—the image of a cowering rabbit about to be carried away by an owl.

In theory it was an unequal contest. Demons had size, speed, and magic over humans. But Leiria was a former captain of Iraj's personal body guard, trained and blooded in all varieties of encounters—be they human or be they demon—and so these things meant nothing to her. She was doubly armed that day, as were all the Kyranians, with Palimak's necklaces. Which made it even easier to turn back the demon's spell so that He was the bleating rabbit, and She was the owl.

Whoosh! as the ax swung down.

Shriek! as Leiria's owl froze the demon.

Snack! Snack! and Leiria's sword parried the faltering blow.

Then another Whoosh! for her final stroke and then the sounds became very ugly as the demon fell, farting and shitting his last dinner, crying for his mother as Leiria stepped over him to meet the next ax.

On either side of her she heard Renor and Seth hoot with owl-like glee as they similarly dealt with their opponents. The hoot was taken up by the other young men, and they pressed forward, shrilling "hoot, hoot, hoot," killing and killing until the demon line began to waver.

Leiria was nearly overtaken by their blood lust. She saw hundreds of yellow eyes swirling in the darkness, howling for blood, hurling curses to diminish her.

Do it now! she thought. Do it now!

And she signaled the retreat.

Biner saw the Kyranian line waver, then break. He immediately shouted orders to dump the ballast and all hands rushed to the side to drop the sandbags.

The airship, suddenly relieved of weight, shot upward, climbing high above the battle scene. Clouds passed under the ship and the figures below became very small. Even so, they still kept their significance and Biner felt a mailed fist clutch his guts as Leiria made her dangerous maneuver.

To his amazement, it seemed to be working. When the Kyranians fell back it was as if a pent-up flood had been released and hundreds of demon warriors burst through the gate, swarming down the hillside after Leiria and her retreating soldiers. From his vantage point Biner could immediately see the grave error the demons had made. The error Leiria had been counting on.

As the enemy warriors rolled down the hill they suddenly found themselves milling about in a small valley—a dip in the terrain their officers had no way of knowing about. It looked like a bowl from the airship, a bowl quickly filling up with confused enemy soldiers who had only one way to go and that was straight up the hill to where Leiria stood her ground.

Leiria reformed her line and began firing arrows into their ranks to block the advance.

Biner waited until the valley was nearly brimming over with soldiers, then turned to Arlain and the others.

"Showtime folks!" he said. "Showtime!"

Leiria and her men were down to their last few arrows when the flaming crates and barrels came tumbling out of the sky.

"Get down!" she shouted, and everyone leaped for cover.

Just then the first crates struck and the ground was rocked by explosions. More immediately followed, a fast series of whump! whump! whumps! Leiria's whole world suddenly became very small as stones and clods of earth rained over her. Waves of heat followed each blast, searing her back. She hugged the ground, trying not to listen to the screams of the demons.

Iraj watched his panicked soldiers pour back through the gateway, crushing fallen comrades beneath their feet in their desperation to escape. His spell brothers were knotted around his traveling throne, stunned by the rout.

"I wouldn't call that a glorious first effort," he said dryly.

"It was merely a probe, Your Majesty," Prince Luka said, quickly trying to diminish the size of the defeat. "To feel out the enemy's defenses."

Iraj sneered at him. "Now we know," he said. "And the answer does not inspire my confidence in you."

"Pardon, Majesty," Kalasariz said, "but I don't think we should be too hard on our brave prince. Or make too much of what just happened. After all, how many times can Lord Timura withstand our assaults?"

"Kalasariz makes an excellent point, Majesty," Fari said. "Even now our wizards are preparing a spell that nothing can withstand. Not even Lord Timura."

Their gradually hardening unity disturbed Iraj. He had to get this over with before they discovered what he was up to. He had to get into that valley immediately. He had to defeat Safar. But he had to do it quickly so he could cast the spell that would free him from his spell brothers forever.

"Do it now," he said to Fari. "Get your wizards into that tunnel and do it now."

"But, Majesty," Fari protested. "We won't be ready for at least another—"

"Do it, Fari!" Iraj thundered. "Do it!"

Leiria surveyed the results of her victory. It was not a moment to savor—the valley had been turned into a enormous blackened grave, heaped with smoking bodies.

Behind her, she heard Seth and some of the other young men choking on the horror. She glanced up and saw the airship floating closer to the ground, the circus performers crowded along the rail looking down on the scene with haunted eyes.

Renor pushed up to her, his face pale and many years older than before.

"I hope I never have to see such a thing again," he said.

Leiria got herself under control. "You won't," she said. "Because next time it won't work."

She regretted the remark when she saw Renor's shock. He really hadn't had time to consider what they still faced.

"We'd better get ready," Leiria said. "I don't know how much time we have."

Just then she heard a familiar shout. She turned, heart leaping with joy when she saw who was riding to meet her.

It was Safar!

32

SPELLBOUND

The moment their eyes met Leiria thought something was wrong. Safar was smiling, laughing, genuinely glad to see her, but he seemed withdrawn—as if he were hiding something. Even Palimak was strangely subdued, hesitating when she embraced him, then suddenly hugging her tightly as if he were afraid.

Then the soldiers and circus performers were crowding around shouting and babbling nonsense and the sense of wrongness was swept away in the happy reunion that followed. But the pall of death from the nearby battleground soon penetrated their happiness—a grim reminder that there was little time for such things.

Safar pulled everyone away, quickly explaining what had to be done next while he led them down to the field where the airship waited, straining at its cables.

"We have to move fast," he said, "before Iraj sticks his ugly head through that hole again."

Biner forced a grin. "And won't he be surprised when there's not a blessed soul waitin' for him."

Arlain shivered. "Thurprith?" she said. "What could thurprith a . . . a . . . thing like him?"

"It's Dario's surprise I'm thinking about," Renor said with a small laugh. "Imagine his face when he sees we're still alive. He probably thinks we're dead by now."

There was weak laughter at this, but there was a hard bite of hysteria to it. Safar put everyone to work stripping the airship of all unnecessary weight so they could board the ship and flee.

The sense of wrongness returned when Safar pulled Leiria aside.

"Walk with me," he said, taking her elbow and guiding her to a path that twisted down to the river.

Palimak walked next to her, still silent and oddly subdued. Khysmet plodded patiently behind, reins looped over the saddle horn.

Safar told her what had happened—about the distance-collapsing magical portal that waited on the other side of the mountains to carry them to Caluz, about the ships he'd hired to take them to Syrapis, and the agreement he'd made with Coralean.

Finally they reached the river bank, where Safar stopped. They were just a few hundred yards downstream from the peninsula where the Turtle of Hadin churned out its mechanistic magic.

When he stopped Leiria knew what was wrong. Especially when Palimak clutched her hand.

"You're not coming with us," she said—a statement, not a question.

Safar sighed. "I was getting to that," he said.

"But why, Safar?" Leiria cried. "Why!"

"There's no other way," he said. "I've already discussed this with Palimak. Ask him. He'll tell you—much as he dislikes admitting it."

Palimak's head dropped and he said, low and forlorn, "Father's right. There's no other way."

"But we're finally almost free of Iraj!" Leiria protested. "All the villagers—your family, your friends, everyone—are so far into the mountains now that he'll never catch them. In a few minutes we can join them, thanks to the airship. And then we're off to Syrapis with no reason ever to look back."

Safar shook his head. "I have to stop the machine," he said. "If I don't it will be the end of Esmir."

Leiria felt as if she'd just been clubbed. When she heard Safar's reason she knew there was nothing she could say or do—even if she had a tongue that coined only words of silver and a thousand years to argue in—that would change his mind.

Still, she had to try. "To hells with Esmir!" she said. "We were leaving here anyway."

"You don't understand," Safar said. "Actually, I didn't myself until after I spoke to Hantilia and got Asper's book. Some force—don't ask me what force, I can't yet say—is devouring the world from the inside out. I think of it as a voracious worm, a parasite, tunneling through the earth's belly looking for the weakest place where it can burst through and spread destruction. Hadin was the weakest point, the first place the worm broke through."

"And Esmir is next?" Leiria said.

Safar nodded. "Yes. At Caluz."

Leiria slumped, defeated.

"Don't worry," Safar said, trying to sooth her. "I have every chance of making it."

"Oh, of course you do," Leiria said, angry again. "In a few minutes several thousand blood-thirsty soldiers will be charging into this valley—led by four great wolves from the hells. While you're hammering away at that machine, or whatever you plan to do to disable it. And you'll be there all by yourself with no one to guard your back, or help you."

"Actually," Safar said with a thin smile, "I was planning on asking Iraj for help."

Leiria waved, dismissing the remark. "We don't have time for silly jokes," she said.

"It really isn't a joke, Aunt Leiria," Palimak broke in. "He has to have Iraj there or the spell won't work."

Leiria stared at Safar. The more she heard, the worse it became.

"Listen to me, Leiria," Safar said. "We really don't have as great a lead on Iraj as you think. He'll be in those mountains before the blink of an eye and everything we've done up to this point will be a tragic waste. I can delay him, perhaps even defeat him. Either way it will give my people the chance they need. When you catch up to them, use the airship to speed things up. All you have to do is get them to the top of those mountains. Palimak can show you how to go from there."

"Please, Safar!" Leiria said. "Give me a chance to think. This is moving too fast and I don't know where it's going."

Safar put an arm around her. "The same place we've planned on from the beginning," he said. "Syrapis. But only if you do exactly what I tell you. Hear me out, Leiria. You have less than two days to get them through the portal before it closes. It shouldn't be too difficult—Palimak and I had no trouble getting back here. Even so, that's not much time to get to Caspan and meet Coralean."

"That's right," Leiria said, feeling numb. "Otherwise he'll sail without us."

"And he'd be insane to do otherwise," Safar said.

They heard people shouting and turned to see that everyone had boarded the airship and was ready to go.

"Aren't you even going to say goodbye to them?" Leiria asked.

"I wish I could," Safar said, eyes becoming moist. "But they'd only argue with me and there isn't time."

Leiria started to speak, but Safar stepped in, pulling her close. Crushing her to him, kissing her long and deep. A kiss of farewell. A kiss of regret.

Then he pulled away, saying, "See you in Caspan!"

Leiria nodded. "All right," she said. "Caspan."

She turned and started for the airship, walking slowly so Palimak could catch up after he'd spoken to his father.

Safar knelt beside the boy. "We've already talked about this," he said, "so you know what to do."

Palimak rubbed an eye. "Sure I do, father," he said, voice trembling.

"Do you have the book?"

Palimak patted the package in his tunic and nodded. "Yes, father," he said.

"And when you get to Caspan," Safar pressed, "what then? What did we agree?"

Palimak dodged the question. "I'm supposed to wait for you," he said.

Safar pressed harder. "Yes, but if it comes time to sail and I still haven't shown up—then what?"

Palimak started to cry, but Safar grabbed him by shoulders, stopping him.

"Then what, son?" he insisted. "Then what?"

Palimak sniffed. "We leave without you," he said.

Only then did Safar pull him close, hugging him and whispering that he loved him and calling him a brave boy, a noble boy, who could do all the things his father asked of him.

Finally, Safar stood up. "You'd better go, son," he said.

Palimak straightened his shoulders, trying to look manful. "Goodbye, father," he said.

He started to turn to leave, then stopped. "But what if they don't listen, father?" he asked.

"They'll listen," Safar insisted.

"Sure, but what if they don't?"

And Safar answered, hard—"Then make them!"

When Iraj stepped into the passageway he suddenly became frightened. Attack seemed imminent, danger a densely coiled spring ready to snap. He smelled the fear in his spell brothers and knew they were experiencing the same sudden cold dread. Never mind they were surrounded by a veteran guard of soldiers and wizards prepared to die to protect them. Never mind the passageway into Caluz had been declared safe—the enemy driven back.

The feeling of dread persisted, growing stronger with each step they took down the wide, torch-lit corridor. Where every wavering shadow seemed an assassin gathering to strike.

Moments before they had declared victory. The trouble was the victory had come too easily. True, Fari and his wizards had cast the mightiest of battle spells to clear the passageway—and beyond. They'd reamed it with magical fire, followed up by soul-shriveling spells no mortal could withstand. At the same time, expecting a counter-assault from Safar, they'd thrown up impenetrable shields designed to turn his own attack against him. Luka had quickly followed up, sending his best fighters rushing behind the spells to wipe out any force that remained.

Safar's expected counter never came and when the soldiers burst into the light on the other side, there was no one to meet them, with only the bodies of their own dead for evidence that any fighting had gone on before. Confident, Iraj had brushed aside all doubt and ordered his party forward to finish off Safar.

Now, as he moved toward the light shimmering at the end of the passage, all those doubts returned—and in greater strength. He thought, it's impossible . . . Safar couldn't have been defeated so easily. Then a second fear—what if he were dead? Iraj had to catch Safar alive, then kill him with his own hands or all his plans would be for naught.

Mind in turmoil, belly roiling with conflicting emotions, Iraj burst out of the passageway into dazzling light.

And found—nothing.

Iraj blinked in the strong sunlight, struggling to regain his bearings in the odd beauty of Caluz. All was serene, all was peaceful, but no matter where he looked he saw not one living soul.

He sniffed the air—Safar's spoor was so strong he knew he still must be there. His companions evidently agreed.

"It's only one of Timura's tricks," he heard Fari say.

"Yes, yes, a trick," Kalasariz agreed.

"A pitiful trick at that," Luka added. "There's no place he can hide that we can't find him."

Just then—on the hill directly opposite them—Iraj saw a lone horseman ride into sight. The man waved at him, almost cheerily, as if greeting an old friend.

It was Safar!

And he rose in his stirrups to shout: "This way, Iraj!"

Then Safar swung the horse about and cantered easily back down the hill as if he had nothing to fear in the world.

The airship hovered just above the mountain path, a sentinel for the last group of Kyranians streaming out of the Caluzian Valley to safety.

Palimak crouched in the observer's platform, watching the villagers pass under him. In a few minutes the airship would get the signal from Dario that all had crossed. Then it would be Palimak's duty to lead them through the portal to Caspan. He tried hard not to think about what would happen after that.

As the refugees passed by some of them spotted him on the platform. They cheered and waved and he forced himself to wave back, feeling like the blackest, the cruelest of liars. Because when they saw him they naturally thought Safar Timura was there, falsely raising their hopes that all was well.

He touched the package beneath his tunic—the Book of Asper. Suddenly the entire weight of world crushed down on him. What if his father didn't make it? What if his father were killed?

For a minute he couldn't breathe, then when he could he was overwhelmed by self pity. It wasn't fair! He was just a boy! Too young to be alone with so much sorrow, so much responsibility. How could they expect . . . and so on . . . and then a little voice piped up from his pocket:

"It won't be so hard, Little Master," Gundara said. "You can do it."

"That's a stupid thing is say," Gundaree broke in. "We're talking about saving the world, here!"

"Don't call me stupid!"

"Well, I don't know what else to call it. The whole thing's impossible no matter how you look at it. Saving the world, indeed! If I told Lord Timura once, I told him twice, there's no use. So why bother trying?"

Palimak broke in. "Gundaree?" he said.

"What, Little Master? How may I serve you?"

"Shut up, please!"

For some reason, he suddenly felt a little better.

* * *

Safar guided Khysmet toward the river shallows where he could cross over to the temple. The big stallion kept pulling at the reins, wanting to run, wanting to get the hells out of here before they were surrounded by all the known villains in the world.

Safar soothed him, saying "It's all right . . . it's all right . . ." Knowing all the while that it might very well not be all right! That any number of things might be happening right now, the least of which would be a swarm of arrows winging their way toward his exposed back.

To keep his nerve, Safar reminded himself that only two things could occur and he was prepared for both eventualities. The first—the worst—was that as soon as he had called out to Iraj, he would have four great wolves and an entire army charging down his back. This would be a very foolish thing for Iraj to do because Safar would make him pay with his life and still accomplish his purpose. Iraj was no fool and would know this, which led to the second possibility.

The possibility that allowed for Safar's survival, which made him rather prejudiced in its favor.

When Khysmet splashed through the shallows and still nothing had happened, Safar knew that Iraj had chosen correctly.

He started thinking he might live after all.

The Unholy Three immediately wanted to charge after Safar, but Iraj stopped them in place with a curt, "Hold!"

His command caught them in mid transformation. They were so surprised that they froze there, an ugly mixture of parts. Skin marred by erupting patches of fur, wolf snouts bursting under demon horns, shape-changer eyes burning out of deep pits. What monsters! Iraj thought, disgusted, horrified, at the sight of them. Then he saw himself in their ugliness and hated them even more.

Iraj pointed at Safar, who was riding down the hill toward the river. "Don't you think he knows?" he hissed, finger quivering. "Don't you think he's ready?" He fought for calm. "This is Safar Timura, you fools! If we charge after him we'll all be dead before we reach the top of the rise!"

While he was berating them his spell brothers had come

unstuck and shifted back to their mortal forms. Good, Iraj thought. The weaker the better.

Fari sniffed the air, then shuddered as he caught the scent of all the killing traps Safar had conjured in their path.

"Your Majesty is certainly correct in his caution," he said. "Lord Timura may be trapped, but he can still bite."

Luka wasn't happy with this. He thought, no matter what that bastard Timura has up his wizardly sleeve, he can't stand up to a whole army. But Luka was wise enough to say nothing. He let Kalasariz beg the point and ask the diplomatic question.

The spy master nodded to his king. "We bow to Your Majesty's wisdom," he said. "Tell us what to do."

Iraj shrugged. "Follow him," he said.

When Safar reached the temple grounds he dismounted and sent Khysmet on his way. He fed him a palmful of dates, turning away all the questions trembling on the whiskers of Khysmet's tender mouth as the horse nuzzled him. Whispering assurances all the while.

Then Safar drew away and said, "You know where to meet," and slapped him gently on the rump. Khysmet snorted, reared up, then came down to whirl and gallop away. In no time at all he was across the second river channel and heading for the meeting place they'd imagined together.

Safar glanced up and saw Iraj riding down the hill toward the temple. He started to count how many were with Iraj, then shrugged. At this point it didn't matter.

He swung his pack off his shoulder and dumped it upside down. Then he crouched beside the jumbled heap, sorted a few things out and soon had a little oil fire burning in a bowl. Safar heard the sound of many horses splashing across the shallows, but ignored them. Instead he pulled a small book from his sleeve and drew his little silver dagger to cut it up. He paused, looking fondly on his old friend, the little Book of Asper he'd carried with him since Walaria. He felt guilty about what he had to do with it. He almost wished Hantilia hadn't given him the second book— the one he'd bequeathed to Palimak. Otherwise he never would have thought of the spell.

The sound of horses cantering across the peninsula toward him broke the reverie. He started cutting up the book and feeding the leaves into the fire, chanting:

> *"Hellsfire burns brightest*
> *In Heaven's holy shadow.*
> *What is near*
> *Is soon forgotten;*
> *What is far*
> *Embraced as brother;*
> *Piercing our breast with poison,*
> *Whispering news of our deaths.*
> *For he is the Viper of the Rose*
> *Who dwells in far Hadinland!"*

He burned all the pages save one, which he kept back. Ignoring the sounds of soldiers dismounting and the approaching boots, he carefully twisted the page into a narrow stick, then lit the end. It burned slowly, like incense—smoke curling thinly from the glowing tip.

Finally Safar looked up and saw Iraj standing not ten feet away. Prince Luka was on his left, Fari his right, and Kalasariz leered over his shoulder. Framing them were at least a hundred soldiers, weapons ready, bows tensed for the killing command.

He paid no attention to any of them, fixing only on Iraj. Golden hair and beard blazing in the sun, royal armor gleaming, helmet under one arm, hand resting on the jeweled hilt of his sheathed sword. There was no doubt who was in command here.

Safar came to his feet, lazily twirling the burning stick between two fingers.

He smiled, saying, "So tell me, brother, how do you like being king?"

The words struck Iraj like a fire bolt fresh from the forge. The dream of the boy he'd slain, the boy who became Safar, with the gentle blue eyes that looked into his heart, whispering the question that had no answer. "So, tell me, brother, how do you like being king?"

"Enough of this nonsense!" Fari growled.

"Kill him now!" Luka demanded.

"Beware his cunning, Majesty!" Kalasariz hissed.

Safar twirled the burning stick of paper, still smiling, friendly, open, as if this were the most normal of meetings.

"Tell them, Iraj," he said, quite mild. "Tell them it's not as good for them as they think."

Iraj recovered. He smiled back, just as friendly. Just as open. It surprised him that it took so little effort.

"I already did, Safar," he said, with a small laugh. He tapped his head. "But sometimes they have trouble remembering the things I say."

"Oh, they listen," Safar said, returning Iraj's laugh. "We all listen! When the king speaks whole armies of clerks sift and sort his words so their masters can study them for their true meaning."

Iraj chuckled. "You mean they listen but they hear only what they want to hear."

Safar shrugged. "If had I put it that plainly," he said, "you never would have made me Grand Wazier. More words equals greater wisdom—that's what the priests taught me in Walaria."

Iraj snorted. "Priests! You know what I think of priests!" Another smile—reminiscing. "But there was one priest . . . old Gubadan."

Safar nodded, remembering the kindly schoolmaster who had overseen the unruly young people of Kyrania. Iraj and Safar had been the most mischievous of the lot, combining forces to bedevil him.

"What a windbag!" Iraj laughed. "But I liked him." He shrugged. "He was my friend."

"A commodity of great value," Safar said. "Even for a king." He gestured at Fari and the others. "Especially for a king."

Safar paused, eyes going back to Iraj's spell brothers. "Forgive me for not acknowledging you before, my lords," he said.

Then he addressed each one in turn, saying, "Greetings to you, Prince Luka," bowing slightly, waving the burning stick of paper, " . . . and you, Lord Fari," another bow, another wave of the stick, " . . .and, of course you, my dear, dear, Lord Kalasariz!"

He came up, spell nearly completed, turning to face Iraj.

"It seems that when it comes to friendship, Iraj," he said, "you have more reason than most to consider that homily."

One more bow, one more wave of the smoldering paper stick, and the spell was done. Safar gave himself a mental kick for thinking that. It wasn't done! This was only the end of the first act. He was only in the middle, the great sagging center of the tightrope. Now for the rest. He fixed his mind on his goal and prepared to move on.

Fari spoke up: "That was a very clever little spell, Lord Timura," he said. "It took me more time than my good reputation as a wizard can bear to unravel it. I assure you, however, that in the end, age bested wisdom. Look for yourself and I think you'll agree. Your spell has been effectively terminated."

Safar obediently concentrated, testing the magical atmospheres with his senses, confirming what he already knew, which was that Fari had fallen for Safar's spell-within-a-spell trick.

Calling on his most subtle acting abilities, Safar blinked with dismay—sinking the hook.

Another blink, then he forced a smile, making it overly wide and bold in a pretended attempt at recovery.

Barely controlling a trembling voice, he said, "We shall see, my lord, we shall see," as if he were supporting a bluff doomed at the first call.

Iraj observed all this, confidence growing by the minute. The game was going as he wanted, never mind Safar's spell, which he guessed was still in place regardless of what Fari had said.

He didn't need magic to sniff out his friend. The moment he saw Safar appear on the hill he knew his intention.

And when he heard his voice ring out, "This way, Iraj!" he knew it was more than a challenge. It was an invitation. An invitation that fit perfectly into Iraj's plans.

So he said, "Why don't we end this pretense, Safar? We've been friends—and enemies—much too long to be dishonest with one another. I am here for one reason, there is no other. And that reason is—"

"To ask my help?" Safar said, cutting him off.

He'd meant to be sarcastic, but when he saw Iraj's reaction he was surprised how close he'd come to the mark. He quick-sniffed the magical array against him. Double checked his defenses. Then he sensed it! A threat from Iraj he hadn't noticed before. He glanced at Iraj's spell brothers, noticing their growing awareness that something was amiss. And it wasn't Safar. It was—

"Listen to me, Iraj," he hissed, moving quickly, swiftly rearranging his plans. "You think I'm here to kill you. I won't deny it. But the main reason is to stop that machine!" He jerked his chin, indicating the stone temple. "Help me with it," he said. "Help me if you want to be free! That's what you want, isn't it? To be free?"

Iraj recoiled, shocked that Safar had guessed his secret. Shocked even more at the pitying look on Safar's face and the humiliating offer of rescue. So shocked he didn't notice Fari sniff the air, then stiffen in alarm.

Iraj shouted: "To the Hells with you, Safar Timura. I can free myself!"

All his pent up fury of emotions exploded and Protarus drew back to cast the spell.

But before he could act he heard Fari shout: "Betrayal, brothers!"

Then Luka: "Kill the king!"

And Kalasariz, crying "Kill them both!"

And then three great wolves rose up to ravage Iraj, so furious and strong in their combined wrath they caught him by surprise. His mind had been fixed on Safar, not the others, and now he saw the error.

Iraj had the sudden vision of the child he'd killed, the child in the dream who was only a boy, too young to be in the mountains. The child who was first Tio, then Safar, and he'd killed them over and over again until only one face was left.

His own!

And Iraj suddenly understood. Awareness struck like a thundering dawn over Kyrania. Despair instantly followed and he thought, This is it . . . I'm too late . . . I'm a fool from beginning to end . . .

Then the wolves rushed in and Iraj cast the spell, shouting: "Safar! Safar!"

Safar gathered in Iraj's spell. He was surprised at the strength of it. But he was even more surprised at the spell's suddenly changed intent. Iraj's cry of "Safar! Safar!" echoed in his head, resounding like temple bells. "Safar! Safar!" A shout of contrition.

Safar slammed the door to a torrent of conflicting thoughts and emotions. Working quickly, very quickly, he absorbed the power of the spell. Never mind Iraj. Never mind what was happening to him now. Never mind repentance, never mind forgiveness, never mind, never mind . . .

. . . Safar heard the wolves coming for him, their howls filling his ears, shriveling his heart. Coming so fast he realized he was taking too long and he fumbled at the complexity of the spell. Trying to put it together, knowing he was too late, too late, and he was only a boy, too young to be in the mountains and this was the end of him.

And once more he heard Iraj cry, "Safar!"

Suddenly he knew the answer.

Prayed he knew the answer.

He flung the paper into the air, shouting, "Syrapis!"

And the world became a white hot explosion.

33

THE BECKONING SEAS

Coralean paced the docks, rumbling, "We must go, my friends! Hurry, hurry!"

And Leiria shouted, "By the gods, Coralean, you'll wait! Or I'll cut out your greedy innards to feed the fish."

Palimak listened to them argue, feeling cold and apart from the scene. He already knew the answer, but was too frightened to voice it. He turned away, looking out over the Caspan harbor where the hired ships were sagging under the weight of all the Kyranians and their goods. The airship hovered over the refugee fleet, engines fired up and ready to go.

Only three tarried on the shore, Coralean and Leiria, pacing and arguing and waving their hands, while Palimak listened, gathering his nerve to speak.

"We must wait for Safar!" Leiria said. Then she pleaded. "Just a little bit more, Coralean. Give him a chance."

She pointed at the distant mountains that ringed the port city of Caspan. A thick column of yellow smoke rose up from the lands beyond. "You only have to look at that," she said, "to know that he destroyed the machine."

Coralean nodded. "Granted," he said. "And we also have the word of several wise priests to support what our eyes want to believe."

"Then Safar must live!" Leiria said.

Coralean shook his shaggy head. "Alas, my good Captain Leiria," he said, "that does not necessarily follow. In fact, those same priests said when the machine was destroyed it was impossible for anyone to have survived the holocaust that resulted."

"Safar said he had a way," Leiria insisted. "He was sure he would live."

The caravan master sighed. "This quarrel grieves me deeply, Captain Leiria," he said. "Safar was my friend as well. And he was not so certain of success as he apparently led you to believe. Perhaps he was trying to spare you, which would be so like him. However—and this is a most important however—Safar and I agreed that I would wait for three days. Those three days have now passed. And so, tragic as this realization is to one so tender as I, we must assume that our good friend, our most beloved friend, Safar Timura, is dead. And we must carry on for him."

"To hells with your agreement," Leiria said. "Safar could be riding to us now." She gestured at a hill overlooking the harbor. "Any moment now he could appear over that rise."

Palimak's eyes went to the hill, praying with all his strength that what Leiria had said would suddenly be so. And his father would appear, sitting tall and proud on a prancing Khysmet. Both man and horse eager to face whatever the Fates had in store for them.

Then Gundara said, "He's not coming, Little Master."

"That's definitely true," Gundaree added. "No sign of him at all."

Palimak gulped back tears. Then he hardened himself. Squaring his shoulders and lifting his chin.

"That's enough!" he said to Leiria and Coralean.

The two turned to him, surprised at his sudden interruption.

Palimak said, "My father told us not to wait." He shrugged. "So I guess we'd better not wait."

He turned and started walking toward a skiff tied up at the shore. Leiria caught up to him, grabbing his arm.

"What's wrong with you?" she demanded. "We're speaking of your own father!"

Palimak looked up at her, smiling gently. Demon eyes glowing yellow as he cast the spell.

"I love you, Aunt Leiria," he said. "But we have to go to Syrapis."

And so they flew away on bully winds blowing all the way from far Kyrania.

Where up, up in the mountains the stars are setting and the High Caravans greet the Dawn of Nothing.

Up to where the eagle cries over a ruined land that was once a paradise.

Oh, make haste!